MW00357062

the memory of us

ALSO BY DANI ATKINS

Fractured
The Story of Us
Our Song
This Love
While I Was Sleeping
A Million Dreams
A Sky Full of Stars
The Wedding Dress
Six Days

Then and Always (US title for *Fractured*)
Gone Too Soon (US title for *A Sky Full of Stars*)

Perfect Strangers (A novella)
When I Awake (A novella)

the memory of us

DANI ATKINS

HEAD
of ZEUS

An Aria Book

Head of Zeus
First Floor East
5–8 Hardwick Street
London EC1R 4RG

WWW.HEADOFZEUS.COM

To Dusty
Best Listener.
Best Friend.
Best Dog.

2011–2023

For there is no friend like a sister

Christina Rossetti

PROLOGUE

They could have been anyone.

They could have chosen to come at a different time, on a different day, or even to a different beach. It was chance that made them swing their four-wheel-drive vehicle off the narrow lane and on to the sand dunes at that precise location.

Lashed to the Range Rover's roof rack was a robust orange dinghy and a pair of oars. In the back of the car was a tackle box and two state-of-the-art rods. But the men weren't fishermen. The local newspaper would call them guardian angels, but their real-life occupations were more prosaic: they were doctors.

They'd left their warm beds and sleeping wives in their luxury holiday rental and crept through the darkened house like excited schoolboys, hell-bent on adventure.

Dr Adam Banner, A & E consultant, was behind the wheel. He was grinning as he sipped hot coffee from a Thermos and drove over the rippled sand towards the water's edge.

Beside him, Dr Phillip Digby, consultant anaesthetist and highly competitive angler, was proposing a wager over who was likely to catch the most fish that morning when he caught a glimpse of something in the headlight beams.

'Hang on a sec. What was that?'

With one foot already moving from accelerator to brake, Adam took his eyes from the deserted sand dunes and turned to his passenger and oldest friend beside him.

'What was *what*?'

Phil shook his head, craning forward in his seat to peer through the inky black expanse of sand and sea, broken only by the line of frothy white surf where water and shore collided.

'There was something way over there, to the left. By the mudflats.'

Adam slowed the car and stared into the darkness.

'What kind of a something?' he asked. He shivered involuntarily, remembering the warning a local old-timer had given in the pub just the night before after overhearing their fishing plans. 'You need to mind where you go walking on them mudflats,' the old man had advised, happily accepting the pint Adam had offered him. 'Seen 'em suck a man down right up to his waist.'

Phil was frowning. 'I'm not sure what it was. It looked like a bundle of material or something.'

'It's probably just an old ripped sail, washed up by the tide,' Adam replied. But even so, he was already turning the car in a slow circle, trying to capture whatever it was Phil believed he'd seen in his lights.

'There!' Phil cried triumphantly. On the periphery of the headlights' beam, perilously easy to have missed, something *was* flapping in the wind. It was pale and fluttered like a flag. From this distance, it looked too flimsy to be part of a thick waxy canvas sail. It looked more like a bundled-up dust sheet.

Wordlessly, Adam pointed the car towards it, feeling the consistency of the sand begin to change the closer they got to the mystery object. The car was sitting lower now, sinking into the dunes, which were sucking on the tyres even on a vehicle like theirs, built for off-road terrain.

The wheels were beginning to spin as they sought to find traction and with a helpless shrug Adam brought the car to a stop, with the object they were going to investigate squarely lit by the headlights. With unspoken agreement, the two men got out of the car and reached in unison for the heavy quilted jackets they'd thrown on the back seat. It was five o'clock in the morning in late January and neither needed a thermometer to know the temperature was below zero.

They walked swiftly and with purpose, unconsciously emulating the way they travelled the hospital corridors. 'Real-life doctors don't run the way they do in those TV shows,' Adam had once told his wife, who was addicted to medical dramas. 'And after twenty years as a physician, I've never once said "*stat*",' he added for good measure.

'It's bound to be just a piece of rubbish,' Phil declared, tugging to free one foot from the greedy sand.

'If it is, you owe me a new pair of trainers,' Adam said, releasing his own foot with a noisy squelch. 'In fact—' He never got to finish his sentence. Because that was the moment when he saw the woman's foot.

Neither of them could remember crossing the final twenty metres that separated them from the casualty. But they did so at a run. Phil had reached for his phone and was swearing softly at the absence of signal, while Adam dropped to his knees beside the unconscious woman. She was lying on the mudflats, dressed in a thin cotton nightgown, one naked leg exposed to the elements, the other lost beneath the surface of the mud.

'Fuck! No reception,' Phil said, abandoning his mobile and hurrying to join Adam, who was already shaking his head as he sought for a pulse at the base of the woman's long, slender neck.

With slick choreography, Phil bent his ear to the woman's blue-tinged lips. No breath warmed his cheek, her chest didn't rise or fall. He reached for her hand, slapping the back of it as though searching for a vein.

'Hello? Hello? Can you hear me?' he shouted, but the woman was unresponsive.

'We need firmer ground for CPR,' Adam said, his teeth chattering from the cold.

There was probably an efficient technique to extract someone from the enveloping mud but neither doctor knew it, so they locked their hands beneath the woman's armpits and hauled her out roughly, knowing that ribs could mend, dislocated joints could be fixed, but there was no coming back from lack of oxygen to the brain.

'Here. Check mine,' Adam said, tossing his phone to Phil before bending to the woman. This was what he did. It was his job, and yet in all the years since he'd qualified, this was the first time he'd attempted to resuscitate anyone outside of a hospital ward.

Her ribcage lifted from the strength of his first rescue breaths but failed to take over the task when he'd finished. There was an unfamiliar tremor to his hands as he locked them in position in the middle of the woman's chest and began compressions. As he breathed into her lungs and rhythmically forced her heart to circulate blood around her body, Phil tried their phones one more time.

'I need to get back on the road to call for an ambulance,' he said. Adam looked up from his patient, sweat dripping down his face from his exertions. How could he possibly have felt cold just a few minutes ago?

Phil had turned towards the car when a lightning-bolt memory shocked him into immobility. 'That pub last night. Wasn't there an AED cabinet on the outside wall?'

The moon slid out from behind a cloud, illuminating the look of hope on Adam's face.

'There was! And it's only a couple of miles from here.'

It took fifteen minutes for Phil to reach the pub, call 999, get the code to release the defibrillator from its cabinet and drive back to the beach. The sight of his car's headlights splitting the darkened beach was one of the best things Adam had ever seen. His arms felt like they were on fire, and his own breathing was ragged, but his rhythm hadn't faltered, not for a second.

He'd scarcely looked at the inert figure on the sand whose life he was desperately trying to save, but he did so now as Phil rapidly opened the defibrillator. The device was intended for hands far less skilled than theirs, and yet the men followed the machine's instructions as though they hadn't both done this more times than they cared to remember.

Adam winced as Phil tore open the woman's nightgown to access bare skin and saw the mottled marble hue of her torso. He kept up the compressions until the very last second, stopping only when Phil shouted out the command: 'Clear.'

When the AED informed them that a heartbeat had been found, Adam wasn't ashamed of the tears falling down his cheeks. They were still there as the welcoming sound of a distant siren heralded the arrival of the ambulance.

1

The drone of the plane was soporific. I hadn't expected to find sleep, yet I'd somehow managed to slip several layers beneath its surface when a panicked cry jerked me awake. There are several things in life you never want to hear: a fearful scream on a commercial flight is one of them, and your phone waking you up in the dead of night is another. I'd experienced both in the last four hours.

As I fumbled with the button to return my seat to its upright position, I noticed I wasn't the only passenger to have been disturbed by the cry. Several seats had their overhead lamps switched on, spotlighting their occupants like actors on darkened stages. It took longer than it should for me to realise that while *I* was still looking around to see who had cried out, everyone else was looking at *me*. If further proof was needed, a member of the cabin crew was striding purposefully down the aisle towards me. The 747 was shadowy enough to hide my blush, but I could still feel it scorching my cheeks.

The flight attendant spoke in a hushed voice, not wanting

to disturb my fellow passengers, although her thoughtfulness was probably redundant after my noisy outburst.

'Is everything alright, ma'am?' she asked gently.

I nodded, caught off-guard by the kindness in her voice. At this point, I'd have coped better with anger or irritation. Compassion could very easily unravel me.

'I'm sorry. I must have been having a bad dream. I didn't mean to wake everyone.'

Her smile came readily. 'That's okay. No one sleeps well on a red-eye anyway. You'd be surprised how many passengers have nightmares when they're flying.'

I smiled wanly, because my nightmare was still very much with me, even after screaming myself awake.

'Can I get you something to drink, or eat?' I shook my head, declining the offer of food as I'd done several hours earlier, shortly after take-off. My body clock was still on New York time and unaccustomed to eating a meal with no identity in the middle of the night.

'Maybe I'll go and freshen up,' I said, glancing up and noting with relief that the nearest WC was currently unoccupied.

I mumbled an embarrassed apology to the passengers in the surrounding rows, many of whom were still looking at me curiously, perhaps waiting for my next diverting outburst. There would be none, I was sure of that. Sleep would elude me now for the rest of the night until our plane touched down at Heathrow.

After sliding the lock in place, I leant back heavily on the bifold toilet door. The closet was as small as a sarcophagus and several hours into the flight was now borderline unpleasant. I pulled a handful of paper towels from the dispenser and ran them under the cold water tap before pressing them to my heated face. *No one* looks good under lighting that harsh, but the overhead fluorescent strip was particularly unkind to my pale skin. The freckles that could look like scattered gold dust on a good day now resembled splatters of mud. It was an unfortunate analogy.

She was covered in mud – her feet were thick with it.

My mother's voice had scored into my memory and her words were still with me at 38,000 feet.

I stared back at my reflection as though I'd never seen it before. My cheeks were pinched, and my eyes looked huge – not in a cute, Disney-character way, but round and fearful, the way they'd been for the last four hours. My chestnut hair looked dull and flat and in desperate need of the shampoo it had been promised in the morning. But plans for the relaxed day I'd intended to spend had been erased by my mum's frantic middle-of-the-night phone call.

Jeff heard my phone before I did. His left arm, which was flung wildly across both his pillow and mine, dropped to shake me awake.

'Your cell is going,' he mumbled, the Brooklyn twang of his voice disappearing into the memory foam of my pillows as he burrowed away from the sound.

After four years in the US, I still called it a mobile, but I knew what he meant.

I frowned as I reached for my phone, noting first the hour and then the identity of the caller. Some of my old UK friends still got the time difference wrong, adding when they should subtract, but not Mum. There were clocks set to New York time all over her house.

I swung out of bed, shivering in the cold air of my apartment – that term I *had* adopted. Grabbing a chunky cardigan from the back of a chair, I shrugged into it as I hurried into my narrow hallway, answering the call as I went.

'Mum?' Habit put a question mark after her name, even though my phone had already identified her. I had no idea why she was calling, but there was already a hint of a tremor in my voice.

The peculiar sound at the other end of the line had nothing to do with cell phone reception or distorted sound waves. It took me several seconds to process it, because in all my thirty-one years, I'd only heard it a couple of times before. She was crying.

'Mum, what is it? What's wrong?'

More tears and then a garbled phrase that was impossible to decipher.

I'd gravitated to the ancient radiator in the hallway, the one that held its heat long after the other pipes had cooled, but an icy terror had crept into my veins. It was almost as though I already *knew*.

'Has something happened? Are you sick?'

Built like an emaciated sparrow, my seventy-three-year-old mother actually had the constitution of a fairly robust ox.

'It's not me. It's Amelia,' she said on a wail.

My knees liquefied and I slid slowly down the wall beside the radiator.

'Mimi?' I asked, the childish nickname emerging from the vaults of my memory. I hadn't called her that since I was about six years old, when my tongue had finally mastered its way around my older sister's name.

'She's been taken to hospital. That's where I'm calling you from,' Mum replied, and for the first time I noticed the echoey quality of the call and an unfamiliar soundtrack in the background.

'Is she ill? Has she been in an accident?' I fired off my worst fears, as though they were bullets in a gun.

'Yes... and... well, no, it wasn't an accident, exactly. You see, she got lost, or so they think.'

'While she was driving?' I asked, frantically trying to piece together a story I could make sense of.

'No. While she was walking along the beach. During the night.'

There were too many confusing facts to assimilate in that single sentence. 'I don't understand, Mum. What was she doing wandering on the beach in the middle of the night in January? It must have been freezing. And how on earth did she get lost? She knows the coastline by her cottage like the back of her hand.'

'I don't know, Lexi. None of it makes any sense. *She's* not making any sense. They had to sedate her at the hospital because she was getting so distressed.'

Out of all the terrifying things Mum had said so far during our call, that was the one that scared me the most. Amelia was the sensible one. The 'wise head on young shoulders', that's what everyone had called her when, at just sixteen, she'd become the rock both Mum and I had leant on after losing Dad in that tragic and inexplicable accident. My sister had always been the one I turned to first. It was Amelia who'd taught me how to use tampons, how to solve quadratic equations and even master a three-point turn, which my driving instructor had despaired of me ever grasping. I'd always been the dreamer of the family, the one with her head buried in the pages of a book. But Amelia had practically come out of the womb a fully fledged adult.

The idea of my capable older sister wandering lost on a wintry beach – one she walked on every single day of the year – was nothing short of inconceivable.

'They're worried she might have hypothermia,' Mum continued. 'She was so very cold when they brought her in, you see.'

I looked out through the hallway window where New York was already under six inches of snow. The last time Amelia had visited me in winter, I'd teased her for kitting up like an Arctic explorer whenever she walked even a block from the apartment.

'She was found just before dawn on the mudflats,' Mum said, her voice wobbling as she painted an incomprehensible picture. 'It was minus one outside, but she was wearing nothing except a nightie, and her feet were bare.'

'What the fuck?' Jeff said, blinking dazedly as I snapped on the overhead light. 'What's going on?' he asked, reaching for his phone on the nightstand. 'Jesus, Lexi, it's half past two in the morning.'

'I have to pack,' I said, my voice tight as I hauled my suitcase down from the top of the wardrobe. It bounced on the mattress, connecting with Jeff's foot, which had admittedly encroached on to my half of the bed.

'Is this about that phone call?' Jeff asked. He was still middle-of-the-night slow, whereas I was running on high-octane adrenaline.

'It was my mum on the phone,' I said, pulling a random

handful of clothes from the dresser and throwing them haphazardly into the case. 'Amelia's been taken to hospital. They think she's got hypothermia.'

Jeff ran a hand through his thick sandy hair, which was already awry from the pillows. 'Shit. That's rough. I thought England was more wet than cold?'

I pulled an armful of jumpers from a drawer and lobbed them in the direction of the case. Most of them found their target. Sensing this wasn't the moment to discuss the climate of my homeland, Jeff grappled for his discarded boxers and swung out of my bed.

'Can I do something? he asked, reaching once again for his phone. 'Do you want me to check for available flights?'

My grateful smile wobbled and was gone before he even saw it. I was already pulling on clothes for my long journey home as he headed to the kitchen to make coffee that I doubted there'd be time to drink.

Fifteen minutes later I was standing beside a bulging suitcase that was probably over the weight limit *and* filled with all the wrong clothes. It didn't matter. Amelia and I were the same size. I could borrow anything I needed from her.

'Passport? Charge cards? Cell phone?' Jeff asked, eyeing the tote bag slung over my shoulder.

I nodded. We'd not spoken much as I'd raced through the apartment, binning the perishables in my fridge and scribbling a note to slip beneath the super's door on my way out. I had no idea how long I'd be away and when Jeff asked what I was going to do about work, I'd looked at him as though he was speaking a foreign language. Work hadn't even crossed my mind, not the way it would certainly do his if our situation was reversed. 'I'll call them and explain when I land,' I said, reaching for my laptop almost as an afterthought and shoving it into my hand luggage.

'Shit timing, what with the job offer and everything,' he said.

The look I threw him spoke volumes. Family was everything to me, something Jeff had never really understood.

'I'm sure it'll be fine,' I said, with a confidence that could well be misplaced. Working as an editor in the US was very different from working as one in the UK, and opportunities like the one I'd just been offered at work were rare.

My building's rickety elevator, which took perverse pleasure in terrorising the residents, juddered alarmingly as it took us down to street level. I kept my eyes riveted on the gauge throughout the descent. *Do not break down. Not tonight. Not now.* It was good advice for both the temperamental lift and me. It delivered us to the foyer with a bone-jarring shudder.

I scarcely noticed the cold night air biting my cheeks as we hurried down the steep steps to the street. 'The intersection's probably your best bet for getting a cab,' Jeff announced, lifting my suitcase free of the frozen snow coating the pavement.

I peered through the falling flurries for a canary-yellow taxi, the kind that had so delighted me when I'd first moved to New York, as though I hadn't really expected them to exist outside of films and TV shows.

'There's one!' I cried, breaking into an unnecessary run that the smooth soles of my boots couldn't cope with.

'Mind the sidewalk!'

Jeff's warning cry came too late to stop my feet from pinwheeling like a cartoon character before flying out from beneath me. I landed on the icy surface with the kind of force that was going to have left a bruise. But it wasn't pain that brought the tears to my eyes. It was the unrelenting anxiety, and a feeling of foreboding so thick it was practically suffocating. I scrabbled back to my feet with the speed of a fallen figure skater.

'You okay?' Jeff asked, a hand already raised to hail one of the many cabs passing through the intersection. Just as he'd predicted. I'd lived here for four years but I'd never felt less like a New Yorker than I did tonight.

I gave the driver my destination and watched as he hefted my weighty case into the boot of the taxi.

'Do you want me to come with you?' Jeff asked, and I spun so fast to face him I almost landed on the ground again.

'Really?' I asked, the tears I was fighting to keep at bay already blurring my vision at the generosity of his offer. 'You'd do that?' There was an awkward silence followed by a race to see which one of us would realise my mistake first. 'Oh, I see. You mean to the airport.'

Stupid, stupid, stupid. I berated myself, knowing I'd not been quick enough to wipe the disappointment from my face. *Of course* Jeff wasn't offering to get on a plane and travel three and a half thousand miles across the Atlantic with me. Our relationship was too on-again/off-again for that kind of commitment.

'Or I could just catch a cab from here back to mine,' he completed lamely.

The driver, who'd finished stowing my case, flashed me a look of sympathy. Even total strangers could see that Jeff and

I were not going to go the distance. Why was it taking us so long to see that too?

'Thank you. It'd be nice to have some company on the ride.'

'No problem,' Jeff said, holding my elbow as I climbed into the back of the cab. 'We can go through the flight options I found.'

I didn't pay as much attention as I should have during the forty-minute drive to the airport. I *yep*-ed and *uh-huh*-ed a lot as Jeff listed the various routes he'd found online, but my eyes kept sliding to the cab windows where New York was currently disappearing under a blanket of snow. Had it been this cold on the beach where my sister had been found? Can a healthy, otherwise strong, thirty-nine-year-old woman bounce back from hypothermia? And what had driven her out into the night in the first place?

Those unanswerable questions were still running through my head as we pulled up outside the Departures terminal. Before I could reach for my purse, Jeff was already settling the fare. It was a nice gesture and I refused to think he was doing so out of guilt.

'Good luck,' said the driver, lifting my case from his cab and setting it on the pavement beside me. I chose to believe he meant for my journey home rather than in my relationship.

The city that never sleeps had lived up to its reputation on the roads, and things were just as busy in the bustling airport terminal. I already knew from Jeff's search that I was five hours too early for a direct flight, but I was happy to take anything that would shave even minutes off my arrival time in London.

Jeff was tall and broad, a college football player who used

his former skills to carve a swathe through the crowds to the airline desk. We got there without colliding with a single wheeled case or piled-high trolley. The good news was that there wasn't a queue ahead of me; the bad, this was because there were hardly any flight options left for me to take.

'Maybe you *should* wait for a direct flight?' Jeff suggested, his handsome brow creased in a frown after listening to the zigzag route through the skies that the airline rep had just proposed. 'You might even snag a seat in Business if you hang on.'

Was that the moment when I realised that a shared love of Chinese food, art-house films and pretty amazing sex wasn't going to be enough to keep us together for the rest of our lives? Jeff was an only child, and not particularly close to his parents, either geographically or emotionally, while I was at the exact opposite end of the spectrum. I might live thousands of miles from Amelia and Mum, but the ties that bound me to them had never felt stronger than they did right now.

Ignoring him, I turned to the woman behind the plexiglass screen. 'I really don't care where I'm seated. Put me in the hold with the luggage if that's the only choice. Just help me get home as fast as I can. Please.'

I slid my passport and credit card across the counter and didn't even wince at the eye-watering price of my last-minute ticket.

'One way?' the airline rep asked, her fingers already flying over the keyboard at an impressive speed.

'Yes. I think so.' I heard Jeff's indrawn breath but didn't turn around; I was too busy swapping my suitcase for a boarding pass and following the woman's instructions to 'run like crazy' to the gate.

I was too winded from the sprint to Security to say half the things I should probably have said to Jeff. They'd all have to wait. But perhaps he sensed them, for there was something hurried and detached in the kiss he pressed on my lips.

'Thank you for coming with me,' I said, already moving towards the automatic barrier.

'Let me know when you land,' he called as the gate spat me out on to airside.

It already felt as though there was a continent between us.

2

London was cold, foggy and wet and felt immediately like home in a way New York, for all its efforts and allure, never could. It seemed like the kind of day when the airline would surely lose my suitcase, or we'd be diverted to some airport in the Midlands because of bad weather. But miraculously, everything went smoothly. For the first time *ever*, my bag was the first on the carousel, and even the snaking queues at passport control moved with surprising speed.

Admittedly, the family ahead of me at the car hire desk seemed to be taking an excruciatingly long time to choose the model of car they wanted to rent, and just as long picking out the type of child seat they needed. My foot was doing an involuntary tap dance of frustration, but I stifled my impatience and used the time to rattle off messages to both Mum and Jeff, letting them know I'd landed safely. Mum's relieved reply pinged back almost instantly, but from Jeff there was only silence. We'd had plans for brunch with friends and then tickets for the ice hockey at Madison Square Garden. Jeff was a big fan of the New York Rangers.

Me? Not so much. There was obviously no reason for him to have cancelled his plans, but I couldn't help wondering who was sitting beside him in the seat that should have been mine.

The indecisive family in front of me finally settled on a vehicle and I stepped up to the counter. I took whatever they had to offer, which turned out to be bigger and more powerful than anything I'd driven before. I passed the Avis rep my UK driver's licence, grateful that the form I'd completed hadn't asked: *And exactly how long is it since you last drove?*

I pulled out of the airport car park with all the confidence of an eighty-year-old learner on their driving test. It was years since I'd been behind the wheel of a car, and I'd have preferred not to be doing so now, in the dark, on a wet, foggy evening. But somewhere in Somerset, my older sister was lying in a hospital bed, seriously ill, and I'd have crawled the three hundred miles to reach her on my hands and knees if that was the only way to get there.

My lips twitched at the notion. It was the sort of over-the-top comment I'd probably suggest deleting in a manuscript. But this wasn't a story I could edit to my liking. I shivered and turned the car heater up to maximum, but I still couldn't seem to get warm.

I stopped just once on the three-hour drive. I'd had less than four hours' sleep in the last thirty-six hours and knew it was madness and dangerous to keep going when I was this tired. I pulled off the motorway, in need of industrial strength caffeine.

The motorway services was too everything. Too bright, too loud, too full of people who had no idea this was one of the most terrifying days of my life. My memory kept spinning me back in time to another contender for that title. And suddenly I was eight years old again, watching the blood drain from my mother's face and the phone fall from her hand as she took the call that had destroyed our happy little family. Why did it seem as though every piece of devastating news begins with that one dreadful phone call?

I practically inhaled two flat whites in the cafeteria, drinking them back to back as though it was a contest, and then got up and ordered a third to take away. I took one last look at the sandwich I'd bought, with its single, mouse-sized nibbled corner. It was wasteful, but I scrunched it up inside its cellophane package and dropped it into the nearest bin.

The fog was even thicker when I emerged from the services and I wasted precious minutes searching for the hire car, which blipped plaintively back at me in the mist before I eventually managed to track down where I'd parked it. There would be no more stopping until I got to the hospital, I resolved, which was probably a foolish plan given the amount of liquid I'd just consumed.

The only good thing about the atrocious driving conditions was that they forced me to concentrate on nothing but the road. But as soon as I reached the hospital site, it was as though a catch had been sprung on my emotions. I'd been focusing only on how to get there as quickly as I could, but now I could feel the panic starting to stream through my veins like a virus.

The hospital multistorey car park had hundreds of vacant spaces and yet I still managed to park badly, straddling two bays in my eagerness to reach my family. I sent Mum a one-word message – 'Here' – and then walked briskly to the stairwell, following signs to the main entrance.

The hospital foyer probably looked very different during the day. There would be patients, visitors and hospital staff milling around. The shops would be brightly lit and open for business, not shadowy and deserted, shuttered behind metal grilles. And there would definitely have been someone sitting behind the Enquiries desk who could have directed me to Amelia's ward.

There was an unsettling eeriness that made it feel like an empty soundstage waiting for someone to yell 'Action'. I don't spook easily, but I jumped when the silence was broken by a loud ping behind me. I spun around just as the metal doors of the lift slid open, for a moment failing to realise the small, weary-looking woman inside the carriage was my own mother. Until she called my name.

I fell into her arms, or she fell into mine, I couldn't tell which. She'd always been slighter than both her daughters, petite and delicately framed in a way that we weren't. And yet as children we'd clung to her when knees were scraped or dreams were scary, as though she was an Amazonian. I did so again now, inhaling all the things about her I never realised I missed until the moment I found them again. The tang of her hairspray that always caught the back of my throat, the sweetness of her perfume and her own unique scent. Her arms were warm as she folded them around me. It was strange, I hadn't realised how cold I was until her hug began to thaw me.

'How is she?' I asked, skipping straight past 'hello', even though we hadn't seen each other for over eight months.

'She's been given something to help her sleep,' Mum

replied. For a retired primary school teacher, it was an evasive politician's answer.

'But is she okay? I've been googling hypothermia. It can be really dangerous.'

Something shifted in my mother's eyes. It alerted me, even before she reached for my hand.

'Why don't we go and sit down over there, where it's quiet,' she suggested, nodding towards a horseshoe of vacant seats in the far corner of the room. I glanced around the foyer. It was quiet *everywhere*.

'What is it, Mum? What's wrong?'

'Let's just go over there, out of the way,' Mum insisted.

Apart from a solitary cleaner who was leaning idly on his cart while checking his phone, we had the entire place to ourselves.

'Please, Lexi,' she said, and that was when I heard the tremor in her voice.

I dropped on to the hard plastic chair so fast it jarred my spine. Mum lowered herself on to the one beside me, with an elderly person's caution. It was a troubling observation that I stored away for another time.

She reached again for my hand. Hers were hot and dry, while mine felt cold and clammy with fear.

'Things... things are a little more serious than I told you on the phone.'

My heart dropped as though every anchoring artery had been severed. My sister had been found on a beach in the middle of the night, lost, confused and hypothermic. How much more serious could it get? I had no idea.

'Amelia wasn't awake when they found her.'

'What do you mean? She was asleep?'

Mum shook her head as though frustrated. I wasn't sure if it was with me or herself.

'I mean, she wasn't conscious.'

The words hit me like a slap. 'She'd passed out? Was it from the cold?'

Mum sighed and the words she'd been trying so hard not to say were finally set free.

'She wasn't breathing, Lexi. When the people found her on the beach, she'd stopped breathing. They don't know how long for.'

I blinked, like an animal caught in headlights. I kept trying to think of something more articulate to say than 'Oh my God', but in the end that was all I could manage.

'Technically she was... she was...' Mum couldn't finish that sentence. What parent could? I did it for her.

'Dead?'

Mum gave a single nod.

'Why didn't I know this?' Our eyes met. Hers light grey, mine – like Amelia's – a deep cerulean blue.

'I didn't want to tell you any of this before you got on a plane. I didn't want you to have that thought in your mind for all those hours in the air.'

I shook my head, because that hadn't been my question. I repeated it with more emphasis.

'Why didn't I *know* this? I should have known it... here.' I brought my fist up to my heart. Beneath my curled fingers, I could feel it racing alarmingly.

Mum's eyes fell to her lap. She had no answer. But then no one had ever been able to explain the curious connection Amelia and I shared. It was something we all took for granted.

'The men who found her were doctors. It's a miracle really,' she said, her voice barely more than a whisper as she fumbled for the tissue tucked into her sleeve. 'They gave her mouth-to-mouth and then shocked her with one of those machine things. They got her heart beating again.'

'Do you know how long she was like that?'

Mum shook her head. 'It could have just happened before they found her, or it might have been much longer.'

My thoughts were spinning as I tried to formulate a sentence that didn't include the words 'brain damage'. I'm not sure if it was Mum I was trying to protect, or me. I might edit romantic fiction for a living, but I was a big fan of thrillers. And somewhere in the vaults of my subconscious I probably knew exactly how long before irreparable damage was sustained when a heart stopped beating. I stopped searching for the answer because I really didn't want to know.

'Can I see her?'

'Of course. The nurses have been so kind, explaining everything they're doing. But you need to prepare yourself, Lexi. She's hooked up to machines and monitors and has wires and tubes going everywhere—' She broke off with a cry and I drew her against me. Wordlessly, we rocked back and forth on the hard plastic chairs while a tsunami of fear crashed down upon us.

We rode the lift back up to the ICU floor in silence. Our footsteps echoed hollowly on the linoleum corridor, and unconsciously our voices dropped to church-like whispers.

'Have you been able to speak to her at all?' I asked, my feet faltering as I spotted the double doors to the ward.

'No. They said she was very disorientated and distressed, so they gave her something to calm her down before I got here. She wasn't really herself. She kept calling out for someone.'

I turned to Mum, my eyes bright with tears. 'Me? Was it me?'

I don't know what was more heartbreaking, the truth or the lie my mother quickly substituted it with. 'I think it probably was.'

3

I opened the ward doors and slipped into the unit on a wedge of light from the corridor. Mum had already told me which bed Amelia was in and I hurriedly tiptoed towards it. My mother, never a rule breaker, had pointed to the sign beside the door that stated only one visitor to a bed was permitted.

'I've been with her for hours,' she said, and I thought I could see the strain of every last minute of that time in the droop of her shoulders. 'You go and sit with her for a while. I'll wait out here.'

Amelia was one of only four patients in the ICU. The main ward lights were turned off, but each bed was illuminated in the soft yellow glow of a night light. Every patient had their own dedicated nurse, standing like a guard beside each bed. The level of care couldn't be faulted, but I hated that Amelia needed it.

'I'm her sister,' I whispered, swaying a little as I finally stood beside the bed, where Amelia looked lost and vulnerable beneath a tangle of medical paraphernalia. Mum had done her best to warn me and yet I still wasn't prepared for this level of equipment.

'How is she doing?' I asked, tearing my eyes away from Amelia to face her nurse.

'Oh.' He sounded shocked as the light above the bed illuminated my face. His head whipped from me to his patient and then back again, as though he couldn't quite believe his eyes. It was such a familiar reaction, I scarcely even noticed it anymore.

I reached for Amelia's hand, careful to avoid the cannula embedded in her smooth white skin.

'She's comfortable,' the nurse replied, having finally regained his composure.

My smile was watery as I looked down at my sister, who had intravenous tubes in both her arms and a bag hanging by the bed, which I assumed was fed by a catheter somewhere. I doubted 'comfortable' meant the same thing to him as it did to me.

'Mimi,' I said, my voice cracking. 'It's me. Lexi. I'm here now.' I focused on her blue-veined eyelids, willing them to open, but they didn't so much as flutter at the sound of my voice.

'She's heavily sedated right now,' her nurse explained. 'We needed to keep her calm and she was very distraught when they brought her in.'

I shook my head, trying and failing to process what he was telling me. Amelia was the epitome of calm. Look up the word tranquil in a dictionary and you'll probably see my sister's face beside it.

'That's not my sister.'

This time the nurse did a genuine double take, as though the evidence of his own eyes was irrefutable.

I reached down and gently brushed the hair off the same face I saw in the mirror every morning. 'I mean, that behaviour isn't my sister. She's not like that.'

The nurse gave an understanding nod. 'You have to remember she's been through an enormous ordeal. Her body needs time to rest and recover.'

'And what about her mind?' I asked, lacing my fingers through Amelia's the way we'd done a thousand times before. Our hands, like everything else about us, looked practically identical – if you ignored the huge needle embedded into the back of hers, that is.

'The doctors will be able to tell you more about that tomorrow,' the nurse replied diplomatically.

I stayed for only half an hour. I would happily have sat there for the rest of the night, and I really don't think they'd have asked me to leave. But I was painfully aware that on the other side of the ward doors sat a seventy-three-year-old woman who'd lived through her own trauma today. I was fairly certain there was only one way to persuade her to leave the hospital, and that was to tell her I needed to get some rest.

It was odd having to be directed to Mum's new house. As we drove past the entrance to our old road, I felt a sharp pang of longing for the family home I'd grown up in. I knew it had been far too big for her and the garden had become too much to cope with, but suddenly all I wanted was to pull into the familiar drive and climb the creaky stairs to my old box room tucked away beneath the eaves.

'You can park in one of the visitor bays,' Mum directed as we pulled up in front of the neat one-bedroom property. They were called starter homes, although in Mum's case it was probably the last place she would ever call home. The thought was so sad it made me want to cry, so I spent longer than necessary hauling my suitcase out of the car's boot, until I was certain my eyes were dry.

She'll be happy there once she's properly settled in, I could remember Amelia saying. When did we have that conversation? A month ago? Longer? Had I even spoken to her since Christmas, I wondered with a jolt of shame. She'd been vocal in encouraging me to focus more on my life in New York, and I'd stupidly let our weekly phone calls slide. How could I have prioritised anything over my sister? My own flesh and blood. Quite *literally* my own flesh and blood. The thought weighed even more than the case I was struggling to lift over the threshold. How had Jeff made it look so light? I batted the thought away like an annoying wasp. The last time I'd checked, Jeff still hadn't replied to my message. The fact that I never referred to him as 'my boyfriend' seemed suddenly to make an awful lot more sense from a distance of three thousand miles. But still, how long does it take to rattle off an *I hope everything is okay* text?

'You must be hungry,' Mum said, steering me gently from the narrow hallway into the lounge.

My reply was a non-committal grunt because food was the *last* thing I wanted, and looking after me was the *only* thing she wanted to do.

'I am dying for a cup of tea,' I said, realising too late that I couldn't have picked a worse figure of speech if I'd spent all night looking for one. We both pretended not to have noticed my gaffe.

'Then you sit down and get comfy and I'll make you one.'

'Why don't we switch that around, Mum, and I'll make *you* a cuppa,' I suggested, my hand already on the door handle to the kitchen.

'Because you don't know where anything is kept,' she said firmly, and then, with a hint of her old spark, added, 'And that's a storage cupboard you're about to walk into.'

I smiled, and it felt like a huge relief that I could still remember how to do so.

'Okay. But just tea, Mum. No food.'

A few moments later I heard the rush of water filling the kettle, and cocked my head in anticipation as I waited for the sound of plates and cutlery. They followed right on cue. It looked as though I would be eating something after all.

As I waited for her to come back, I looked around her new lounge. It was strange seeing so many things I remembered in an unfamiliar location. It was as though pieces of my past had been slotted into a new jigsaw. They didn't quite fit, but you had to be part of the family to fully understand why not. Almost as though I'd been drawn there magnetically, I found myself walking towards the fireplace. It wasn't a brick inglenook like we'd had before, but a neatly tiled aperture with a gas flame-effect fire. But it wasn't the heating source that had caught my eye from across the room. It was the collection of newly framed family photographs that stood proudly above it. My eyes smarted as I picked up the last photograph of the four of us, taken just weeks before the day when Dad, an experienced angler who'd fished in the same cove for decades, had somehow got cut off by the tide and drowned. In the photo, Mum was beaming at the camera, her arm around Dad's waist as she cuddled up close to her husband, her head a couple of inches below his shoulder. On his other side was Amelia, at sixteen already a whole head taller than Mum. I completed the line-up, skinny-limbed and freckle-faced, with a gap in my grin where an incisor tooth should have been. I reached out, tracing each face with my finger. I lingered longest on Amelia's and then my father's. 'Look after her, Dad,' I whispered.

I managed three buttered crumpets, which tasted about as appetising as the packaging they'd come in. But at least they seemed to satisfy Mum that I wasn't about to keel over from starvation.

'They always were your favourite,' she said, gathering up the butter-smeared plates.

They weren't, actually. They were Amelia's preferred teatime treat, and it was unusual for Mum to make that kind of mistake. But given the day we'd lived through, it was hardly surprising. It must be hard separating childhood histories when your younger child looks exactly like your elder, who'd been born eight years earlier. There were times when even *I* struggled to know which one of us I was looking at in old snaps in the family album.

It had been easier in my teens, when I went through a period of rebellion that featured outrageous hairstyles in a shade of red never found in nature. I ran my fingers now through my shoulder-length hair, long since restored to its natural colour. I couldn't even remember why I'd tried so hard to push every boundary or break every curfew back then. Amelia once said she thought I'd been trying to create a big enough chasm between us to assert my individuality. With the benefit of hindsight, and having now read quite a bit on the subject, she was probably right. Apparently, it's a fairly common phenomenon with twins – even ones as startlingly unique as us.

Eventually, the need to look different, *be* different, was nowhere near as strong as the ties that bound us as sisters. I still felt the tug of those strands, perhaps more strongly than Amelia ever had. Despite our outward similarity, our personalities remained totally different. Amelia had a way with numbers, more of a gift really – think Rain Man on an off day and you wouldn't be far off. But for me, maths remained a conundrum I had no interest in solving. I used to wonder if, during the IVF, when the cells divided in the Petri dish, she'd somehow ended up with all the mathematical genes, leaving me to scoop up the ones for language.

It felt like a forgone conclusion that Amelia would study mathematics at university, get a first and end up working in finance. Almost as inevitable as that the girl who'd always had a book in her hand would wind up working in publishing, with opportunities she'd never dared to dream of finally being within her grasp.

The tea had cooled in the pot and our conversation was going round in circles, all of them careful to avoid the uncertainty of Amelia's medical prognosis.

'What I don't understand,' I said, looking at a recent photograph of my sister as though asking her to help me out, 'is what the hell made her leave her cottage in the middle of the night?' I blamed my job and lack of sleep for my very dramatic shortlist of possibilities. 'Could she have been trying to escape from someone? A home invasion, maybe? Or perhaps her cottage was on fire? Or she could have heard someone calling for help and gone outside to investigate?'

Mum loved me too much to call my suggestions ridiculous. 'I was thinking more along the lines that she'd been putting something in the outside bin and had accidentally locked herself out and had wandered off to get help.'

'Hmm, yeah, okay. That *does* make more sense,' I conceded.

'Except that it doesn't,' Mum said, with a worried sigh. 'You see, after they'd confirmed her identity, the police went to Amelia's cottage to check it out.'

I sat up straighter in my seat, back in darkest thriller territory once more.

'What did they find?'

'Nothing,' said Mum. 'Absolutely nothing. They said everything appeared to be in order, except for the fact that her front door was wide open. She wasn't locked out at all, Lexi; she could have gone back inside whenever she wanted.'

We fell into a troubled silence, punctuated only by the persistent ticking of the carriage clock on the mantelpiece. I was so busy running impossible scenarios through my head, I failed to notice Mum's responses were getting slower and slower until eventually they stopped altogether. It was only when a soft delicate snore came from her direction that I realised she'd fallen asleep right there in her armchair, her tea still held in cupped hands.

I got to my feet and gently eased the mug from her grasp. It was an old favourite from the past and I was surprised to see it had survived the years and a house move. The ceramic paint was no longer brilliant red, and the words *I love you,*

Mum had all but faded away from a thousand cycles in the dishwasher, but tonight, of all nights, she must have pulled it out from the back of the cupboard. I thought I knew why.

'Come on, Mum,' I said, gently rousing her. 'Let's get you to bed.'

She climbed the stairs weirdly, one step at a time, like a toddler who'd recently mastered the art. Was that something new, I wondered? It was the second time that day that her age had given me cause for concern. My knee-jerk reaction was to remind myself to ask Amelia about it, and the idea that she might not be able to tell me, not tomorrow, nor the next day, or maybe even ever, was a dreadful thought to hold in my head for the rest of the night.

My heart felt heavy with nostalgia as I made my way back downstairs with a bundle of bed linen in my arms that I'd found in the hall cupboard. I made up a bed on the couch, knowing if Mum had been in charge there would have been perfectly neat hospital corners on the folds. It made me think of Amelia, lying alone and scared in a hospital bed. I was projecting, of course. I had no idea if that was how my sister was feeling. The drugs they had her on were probably strong enough to knock out a shire horse, so she was probably feeling nothing at all.

But I couldn't claim that luxury when I switched off the low-wattage table lamp and lay down on the makeshift bed. Every time I closed my eyes, I saw only the beach where Amelia had mysteriously got lost. I knew the mudflats where she'd been found. They were less than a fifteen-minute walk from Amelia's cottage door. How had she not been able to find her way back there? It felt as though I was stepping into her thoughts as I visualised a moonlit sky, the sting of salt and spray on my face and the harsh gritty feel of sand and stones beneath my bare feet. I opened my eyes. Was I actually seeing what Amelia had seen? Was she reaching out through the abyss of time and space between us and telling me how it had been, or was it simply the result of the overactive imagination of someone who's read too many suspenseful stories?

It used to make people uncomfortable when we spoke about those snatched shared emotions and sensations. So, over the years we'd learnt it was best to keep such stories to ourselves. But there was no logical explanation for how Amelia had felt mysteriously queasy for twenty-four hours before learning I'd been suffering from food poisoning in New York. Or how I'd been doubled over in pain, far worse than hers, when *she'd* been the sister with appendicitis.

More shaken than I wanted to admit, I wriggled upright and reached for my phone to check the time. As weary as I felt, my body clock was still firmly set on New York time, where it was – I did a quick calculation – still only nine o'clock at night. The realisation caused a frisson of irritation as I noted that Jeff still hadn't messaged me back.

Amelia would not be impressed, I thought with a sad smile. I'd sensed a decided coolness between her and Jeff when she'd last visited me. Not that we had ever had the same taste in men, and however much we looked alike, we certainly seemed to attract totally different types. Amelia had always gone for serious partners, with strongly held political views. She'd even dated an MP for about six months before realising he was far more invested in his career than he was in her. She went out with people only when it suited her and seemed perfectly happy with a series of impermanent relationships.

And then, not long after her last birthday, she'd made a crazy statement about being too old for the nonsense of adapting her life to suit a man. She liked things the way they were and enjoyed the freedom of sleeping diagonally across her double bed, having sole control of the TV remote, or eating cold baked beans from a can for dinner if that was what she felt like doing. Being single suited her.

But that hadn't stopped her from criticising my own love life. 'You pick men who come with an expiry date,' she said, with the lack of filter only a sibling can get away with. 'It's almost like you choose them deliberately because you know they're not right for you.'

'That's not fair,' I argued.

She'd stopped me in my tracks then by suddenly looking sad. 'No, it's not, Lexi.'

I remember the lump in my throat that had made it almost impossible to swallow when she'd gripped my hand to ask, 'Don't you want to share your life with someone?'

'I've shared my entire life with *you*,' I replied, not sure why my voice was suddenly wobbly.

'That's not the same and you know it,' she countered. 'And besides, I live on the other side of the Atlantic, so I hardly qualify as a suitable companion.'

'Miles don't count with you and me. You know that,' I said.

The memory of those words came back now, strong and potent. I reached out to her with my thoughts, hoping that somehow she'd feel them, hear them, and use them to find her way back to us.

★

Sleep hit me like a freight train I hadn't seen coming. I came out of it about five hours later to the sound of drumming water from the shower. I slowly unfurled my stiff limbs, acknowledging that at five foot ten I was several inches too tall to have slept on the couch.

I reached for my phone and anxiously punched in the hospital's number. I was still on hold, waiting for an update and imagining all kinds of medical complications, when I heard Mum's footsteps on the stairs. She headed straight to the kitchen, where I joined her a few minutes later. She saw the phone in my hand and her eyes flickered nervously. I shook my head and smiled.

'I just phoned the hospital and spoke to the senior staff nurse on the ward.'

Mum was holding a tea towel, twisting it in her hands as though wringing it dry. I reached over and took it from her.

'They're pleased with how she's doing and much happier with her body temperature now. In fact, they hope to move her out of Intensive Care later this morning and start easing her off the sedation.'

And suddenly we were both crying again, the way I'd known we always would after receiving news – either good or bad. We hugged each other and silently thanked the doctors, fate, and maybe even my dad that the tears we were shedding were the happy kind.

4

Everything about the hospital felt different this time. It was crowded, for a start. There were other visitors riding the lifts to the wards, easy to identify by their flowers and grapes. I gave Mum a rueful smile across the width of the carriage. We'd come empty-handed, but hopefully Amelia wouldn't mind.

We followed a different set of signs when we got to the eighth floor. HDU. A new acronym that was about to become part of our everyday vocabulary. High Dependency Unit. Hopefully Amelia wouldn't be there for long. The signage was confusing, and I was about to ask a passing nurse for directions when a voice I knew rang out in a tone I really didn't know at all. I threw a worried glance Mum's way as unconsciously we both quickened our pace.

'Well, *someone* must know where they are.'

The voice was coming from a room at the end of the corridor but was loud enough to be heard some distance away. It didn't sound like Amelia's usual cadence at all; it jarred, like music played in the wrong key.

'Has anyone even looked for them?'

There was no mistaking the anxiety in my sister's voice, and I could only assume she was asking about us.

'I'm not sure. I'll ask again. Please don't worry, Miss Edwards. We'll find them.'

A junior nurse with brightly flushed cheeks was backing out of the room, looking decidedly uncomfortable and awkward.

'Please stop calling me that. My name is—'

'Amelia!' I cried, squeezing past the embarrassed young nurse like a bomb disposal expert on their way to defuse something that was about to explode.

My sister looked simultaneously dreadful and wonderful. Her face was pasty, except for two bright-red splodges of colour on her cheeks, put there, I imagine, by the feisty exchange with the nurse who'd now disappeared into the corridor. There were panda-like circles beneath Amelia's eyes and her lips were dry and cracked. I was so pleased to see her awake, I happily ignored her unhealthy pallor.

'Lexi?' she said, blinking at me as though I was a mirage. 'What the fuck are you doing here?'

It was hard to formulate a reply above the alarm bells clanging in my head. Amelia never swore. She was a *Fudge it* or *Oh sugar* kind of person, which I used to tease her about mercilessly.

'I'm here for you. Obviously,' I said, hurrying towards the bed. There were trailing tubes attached to drips and wires hooked up to monitors to negotiate, but it would have taken more than that to stop me from enfolding her in my arms. She felt the same, she hugged the same, but beneath the antiseptic smell of the hospital I thought I could detect the briny smell of seawater on her skin.

'Darling, it's so good to see you awake. How are you?' cried Mum, her voice wobbling. 'We've been so worried.'

I stepped back and could feel a lump forming in my throat as I watched Mum almost sag with relief as she gathered her daughter into her arms. When released, Amelia flopped back on the mountain of pillows piled up behind her as though her energy was suddenly depleted. Her eyes darted from Mum to me and then – curiously – to the doorway.

'Is it just the two of you?'

I followed her gaze to the empty door frame, which she was looking towards with a sense of urgency.

'Yes. It's just us.'

Something was off here. Mum was settling herself on the visitor's chair beside Amelia's bed and didn't seem to notice that anything was wrong. But to me it felt as though every ion in the air was suddenly charged the wrong way. And Amelia's next question did little to dispel my concern.

'What am I doing here? I can't get anyone to tell me why I'm in hospital.'

'You don't know? You don't remember?' I asked, feeling as though I was tiptoeing through a minefield. There had to be a reason why the doctors hadn't said anything to her yet about what had happened.

'You collapsed,' I said carefully, pulling out a chair on the opposite side of the bed to Mum and sitting down.

'I did?' Amelia's question sounded incredulous, as though I might possibly be making it up. 'When? Where?'

'Yesterday. At home,' Mum said quickly, shaking her head slightly when my eyes flew to hers at the lie.

Amelia's face crumpled, and I could see tears begin to fill her eyes.

'I don't remember anything. Why can't I remember it?'

'It'll come back,' I said, taking her hand and squeezing it gently. I had no idea if I was right, but she was getting stressed and you didn't need a medical degree to know that couldn't be good for her.

Amelia looked down at our hands and something I didn't understand flared in her eyes. 'And where are my rings? What have they done with my rings?'

Her voice was climbing, getting louder again. I released my hand from hers and bent down to open the small bedside cabinet. On the lower shelf was a clear plastic bag, inside which I could see Amelia's sodden nightdress. I thought about withdrawing it, and then changed my mind. The garment was ripped and covered in mud and sand and if she really didn't remember being on the beach in the middle of the night, this wasn't the way she should find out.

'There's nothing in here,' I said, slamming the door shut on the lie. 'Your rings, are they valuable?'

I don't think I've ever been on the receiving end of a look so withering in my entire life.

'*Of course* they are.'

'Then let me go and ask someone about them,' I said, getting to my feet. 'Perhaps they lock precious items like that away in a safe.'

I squeezed Mum's shoulder as I walked past and felt the thrum of tension running through her slight frame. She might be smiling down at her elder daughter, but she was just as aware as I was that something was very amiss here.

I headed towards the nurses' station, looking around for the young woman who'd fled Amelia's room when we arrived. It now seemed likely that it was my sister's rings rather than her family that she'd been dispatched to find. When there were so many other things to worry about right now, I simply couldn't understand why Amelia was so concerned about a couple of pieces of jewellery.

I couldn't find the nurse, but someone who I suspected was far more senior emerged from a small office behind the desk.

'You must be Miss Edwards' sister,' she said with a kindly smile. 'I'm very sorry I wasn't here when you first arrived. I wanted to have a quick word with you before you went in.'

My stomach took an unpleasant flip. 'About Amelia?' I shook my head at the ridiculous question. *Of course* about Amelia.

The senior charge nurse gave a nod and there was a degree of concern in her eyes that troubled me. 'The consultant overseeing your sister's care was hoping to have a word with you and your mother today, but unfortunately he's been called away on another emergency.'

I tried to hide my disappointment. I was desperate for answers, but it looked as though we were going to have to wait a little longer to get them. 'We're really anxious to discuss what happened to my sister... and what it means.'

'I'm sure he'll be able to answer all of your questions,' the nurse said, picking up a folder with my sister's name on it.

'She seems extremely distressed and anxious.' I knew I was going to feel foolish for asking my next question, but I'd made Amelia a promise. 'And she's rather worried about some missing jewellery. Do you happen to know if it's been put away for her somewhere?'

There was something in the older woman's eyes that told me this wasn't the first she'd heard about the alleged missing items.

'Your sister wasn't wearing any jewellery when they brought her in. I personally checked with the other ward.'

I opened my mouth to speak but was distracted when I noticed my mother appear in the doorway of Amelia's room. Her eyes were urgently searching for someone. Me.

I was already hurrying towards her, with a hasty 'Excuse me' thrown over my shoulder. It had been a long time since I'd seen my mother look that scared. She grasped me by the elbow and steered me back into my sister's room.

There was an entirely fake smile on Mum's face as she turned towards her older child. 'Amelia, can you describe the rings to Lexi, like you just did to me.'

Amelia shook her head as though she'd only just realised she'd been born into a family of simpletons.

'You both know what they look like. You've seen them a thousand times. A plain white gold band and a diamond solitaire. How can you not remember what my wedding rings look like?'

'Here you go,' I said, setting down two vending machine cups of dark-brown liquid.

'Is that tea or coffee?' Mum asked, reaching for the closest cup. Her hand was still trembling.

'Possibly a hybrid of the two,' I said, grimacing as I took a sip. 'But it's hot and sweet.' I wasn't lying. There were enough sugar sachets in Mum's cup to cause spontaneous tooth decay, but I was fairly sure that's what you were supposed to give to someone in shock. Mum definitely ticked that box – her face was a sickly grey colour and her cheeks had taken on a dough-like appearance that really worried me. She looked almost as unwell as Amelia.

The hospital cafeteria had been a good shout. It was far emptier than the cheery coffee shop down in the foyer. Here, the lunch rush was long over and the early evening one had yet to begin. It gave us the privacy we needed to talk.

'I didn't know what to say to her,' Mum said, dabbing an already damp tissue to her eyes. 'My own daughter, and I had no idea what to say for the best.'

'Whatever we said was always going to be wrong,' I said, biting my lower lip as the scene that had shaken our world replayed once again in my head.

'What do you mean, Mimi, your *wedding* rings?' I asked.

'The rings that Sam gave me two years ago, on the day we got married,' Amelia said with a long-suffering sigh, as though my idiocy had just plumbed new depths.

My hand was shaking as I reached for hers.

'Amelia, honey. You're not married,' I said gently.

She snatched her hand free of my grasp as though I'd scalded her.

'*Of course* I'm married. Why would you say that I'm not? You were our bridesmaid, for God's sake. How can you have forgotten that?'

'Because it never happened,' I said, turning to Mum, whose hand had gone to her throat as though witnessing an accident taking place in front of her.

Amelia also turned to Mum. 'Why's Lexi saying these things? Tell her she's wrong, Mum.'

'I... I...' Mum broke off helplessly, her eyes going from one distraught daughter to the other.

'Fuck this,' muttered Amelia, reaching up and grabbing the handful of wires that connected her to the monitors. She ripped them free of the electrodes. 'I have to get out of here.'

Everything seemed to happen at once after that. There were alarms sounding, and I was shouting at Amelia, trying to stop her from pulling the intravenous needles from her arms.

Strong hands settled on my shoulders, moving me away from the bed. A burly, no-nonsense-looking male nurse was talking gently to Amelia. She stopped struggling and began to cry. I think that was the most heartbreaking moment, when she looked over at Mum and me with reproachful tear-filled eyes. 'Where's Sam? Why isn't he here?'

Brisk footsteps sounded in the corridor and the senior charge nurse strode in, her gaze sweeping the room in a swift assessment.

'I think Miss Edwards needs a little time for us to get her settled again,' the older woman said.

Amelia was shaking her head from side to side, as she protested with a plaintive cry: 'It's *Mrs Wilson*. My name is Amelia Wilson.'

'Does Amelia even *know* anyone called Sam Wilson?' I asked Mum now.

'I don't know, Lexi. I've never heard the name before today.' Mum reached for another tissue and quietly blew her nose. 'She certainly isn't married to him, I can tell you that.'

My laugh was brittle, like glass shattering, for there was nothing even remotely funny about this situation.

'This is just going to be a reaction to the drugs she's on,' I assured my mother, crossing my fingers beneath the table, because I had no idea if that was actually the case. 'Once she's off the medication, everything will be fine.'

'What if it isn't the medication? What if this is a result of what happened when her heart stopped?'

I shuddered, realising I wasn't the only family member to have searched the internet about the devastating effects of lack of oxygen to the brain.

'Let's cross that bridge when we come to it,' I said, knowing the phrase was one of the few things that could put a watery smile on Mum's lips right now.

'That was one of your dad's favourite sayings.'

I squeezed her hand warmly. 'I know.'

This time, the senior charge nurse was waiting to waylay us before we reached Amelia's room. She motioned us into her office. It felt like being summoned to the headteacher's study.

'I won't keep you long,' she assured, sensing our hesitation.

We declined her offer to 'take a seat', which she seemed to have been expecting. She nodded and then took a deep breath.

'Amelia is much calmer now. We've given her a light sedative, so you might find her a little sleepy when you go back in.'

'But is she still... deluded?' I didn't like the word, but I could think of no other to substitute it.

'*Confused* is perhaps a better way of looking at it.' Involuntarily, her eyes went to a family portrait on her paper-strewn desk. Inside the wooden frame was a photograph of a man and two young children under sunny skies. 'Amelia is adamant that she is a married woman. She believes it as strongly as I believe the people in that photograph to be my own family.'

It was incomprehensible and overwhelming, but more than anything it was impossible to fix, and I was a born fixer. 'But Amelia's never even *wanted* to be married. She's so fiercely independent. Out of all the things to fantasise, why this?'

The charge nurse looked at us with kindly eyes. 'I have no idea. Hopefully, Dr Vaughan will be able to tell you more about it than I can when you meet with him. He'll certainly want to outline the clinical and neurological investigations he feels would benefit your sister.'

The future suddenly looked very dark and scary and unconsciously I reached for my mother's hand and squeezed it tightly.

'As difficult as it is for family members in this kind of situation, unless your sister's care team advise you differently, I think the best thing right now would be to go along with whatever Amelia believes to be true.'

'You want us to pretend that we can see someone who isn't actually there?' Mum asked incredulously.

The charge nurse shook her head. 'Amelia isn't hallucinating. She isn't seeing invisible people, she's just remembering a different past from the one that actually took place. For the time being, I think it's more important to avoid distressing her than it is to convince her that she's wrong.'

Amelia's eyes flashed to the doorway when she heard the sound of our footsteps. It was hard not to feel crushed by the disappointment in her eyes. We were her family, the people who loved her most, but we weren't who she was hoping to see.

The beeping of one of her monitors rose in a worrying crescendo, and guilt as thick as bile threatened to choke me. But I would do or say whatever I had to, to help my sister get well. If she wanted to claim black was white, she'd get no argument from me.

'How are you feeling?' I asked, bending to kiss her cheek. A nasal tube delivering oxygen had been fitted during our absence, and I gently freed a strand of her hair that was trapped beneath it.

'Drowsy,' she mumbled.

Mum moved to reclaim the visitor's chair, but I perched on the side of the bed and lifted Amelia's hand to slot my fingers through hers.

'Is there any word yet from Sam?' she asked. Her eyes – identical to mine in every way – held my gaze prisoner. It was a test. But it was one I had no intention of failing.

'Not yet. Hopefully soon.'

She nodded and something passed between us. I wouldn't let her down again.

'It'll be the time difference, I suppose,' she said sleepily.

'Huh?'

'He's working in New York right now, remember?'

Mum's head immediately shot up, while I tried very hard to appear nonchalant, which isn't easy when your heart is pounding as loud as a drum in your chest. It's just as well *I* wasn't the one attached to the monitors, or there'd be a crash team heading towards us right now.

'New York? Well, that's quite a coincidence.'

Amelia shrugged, as though it hadn't even occurred to her

until this very moment that I too worked in New York. It felt as though I was playing a very dangerous game and I had absolutely no idea what the rules were. This whole thing was seriously screwed up.

'I think maybe you two could go home now. I'm feeling really tired and I just want to go to sleep,' Amelia said, yawning hugely, like a cat.

'That's a good idea, sweetheart,' Mum said, getting to her feet to kiss her elder child goodbye. 'You get some rest now. We'll be back to see you again tomorrow.'

'I was thinking I might stay at your cottage, if that's okay with you?' I asked as I got to my feet. 'Mum's sofa isn't the comfiest bed in the world.'

Amelia nodded, her eyes already drooping to a close.

I pulled out my phone and clicked on the Notes app. 'Is there anything from home you'd like me to bring in tomorrow?'

'Nightclothes, hairbrush, toiletries,' Mum suggested.

I rapidly typed up a list. 'Is there anything else you want?' I asked Amelia.

With a real effort, she forced her eyes back open. 'My locket. The big silver one I got from Gran,' she said. 'It has my favourite photo of Sam inside it.'

'Great. Locket,' I said, keeping my eyes on my phone screen as I added the item to the list. Fortunately, Amelia couldn't see the row of exclamation and question marks I put beside it.

5

Amelia's cottage was either someone's dream home or their worst nightmare. If you liked isolation, the constant cawing of seagulls, and a lane so narrow there was no option but to back up if something was coming the other way, then the two-hundred-year-old former fisherman's cottage, set directly on the beach, would be your idea of heaven. But if you'd spent the last four years in the hustle and bustle of a city that proudly advertises its own insomnia, it might not have the same appeal.

Mum had insisted on filling two large carrier bags with food from her own cupboards when I'd dropped her home from the hospital.

'I'm fairly sure Amelia will have some stuff in her fridge or freezer. And if she doesn't, I'll probably drive past a dozen supermarkets on my way there.'

Mum tsked in a way she had perfected to an art form over the years. 'You're not in the Big Apple now, remember. Shops don't stay open twenty-four hours a day around here.

And you certainly won't be able to phone for a pizza to be delivered at two o'clock in the morning.'

I pulled her into a hug and kissed her cheek warmly. 'I think someone may have been watching too much American TV,' I teased. 'I've lived over there for four years and I've never once ordered takeout in the middle of the night.'

Mum looked down at the bulging carrier bags, clearly itching to add more provisions. 'I just want to take care of you.' There was so much maternal guilt tied up in that statement that it sliced straight into my heart. 'This isn't your fault, Mum. Whatever happened to Amelia isn't because of anything you did or didn't do.'

'But there *has* to be a reason for it.'

I sighed heavily. 'I'm sure there is. And eventually we'll get to the bottom of what's happened. For a start, this Dr Vaughan guy should be able to give us some answers.'

'Guy?' scoffed Mum gently. 'And you think New York hasn't rubbed off on you?'

She made a good point, because I certainly felt like a lost tourist some forty-five minutes later when I left the main road and built-up suburbs behind and headed towards the coast. I'd stayed with my sister several times over the years, so the route should have been familiar, but in the dark – without the benefit of streetlamps or landmarks – it all looked different. It was more than a little unsettling. Was this how it had been for Amelia, when she'd got hopelessly lost on the beach in the middle of the night?

The thought was more jarring than the bump of the car's tyres as they left the last section of tarmacked road and moved on to the hard-packed dirt and sand that earmarked the final leg of my journey to my sister's front door.

My headlights picked up the outline of the cottage's roof, and I gave a small sigh of relief. I slowed down to a crawl, pulled on to the hardstanding area beside Amelia's own car and thankfully switched off the engine. As grateful as I was to have reached my destination, I didn't immediately jump out of the car, but instead rolled down the driver's window. The silence and the dark felt as alien as another planet. It was the polar opposite to my home in New York. For the first time, I realised how odd it was that Amelia and I, so alike in many ways, had chosen to live in such contrasting locations. However quietly beautiful Somerset might be, I couldn't imagine trading living in one of the most exciting cities in the world to be here.

Eventually, the need to stretch my legs outweighed my weird hesitancy to step inside my sister's home. 'You're being ridiculous,' I told myself, jumping at the way my words echoed against the soundtrack of waves hitting the shore. I gave my eyes a minute or two to adjust and finally the velvet blackness began to separate out into clumps of rough grass and endless sand dunes. I turned towards Amelia's home and the other three cottages that shared this stretch of beach. They were spread some distance apart on the sand and always reminded me of miniature Monopoly houses that had been randomly dropped somewhere they didn't belong. Three of the cottages were in total darkness. That was hardly surprising as two of them were holiday rentals that were occupied by a constant stream of visitors in the summer months, but at this time of year stood empty, waiting for the seasons to turn. The final cottage in the row was owned by *the last salty sea dog on this stretch of coastline* – or at least that's how Amelia always described her irascible elderly neighbour. She actually knew very little about Tom Butler, the retired fisherman who'd lived there for most of his life, which apparently was just the way he liked to keep things.

I dragged my case to Amelia's front door and dug in my coat pocket for the spare key Mum had slipped off the not inconsiderable bunch she carried around. I've no idea which locks they all opened, but the gleaming bronze key slid smoothly into the one in front of me.

I experienced a peculiar moment of uncertainty as I approached the house, convinced that the entrance would be obscured behind criss-crossed yellow tape, emblazoned with the words *Police. Do Not Enter.* I laughed nervously when I saw no such thing. *Now* who'd been watching (or reading) too many thrillers? Mum had already told me the police had found nothing untoward when they'd visited the cottage, so they'd simply closed Amelia's front door and left. Which meant there was no reason at all for my heart to be pounding in my chest as I pushed open the door.

'Why don't you bring in the heavy stuff; you're much stronger than I am,' I called over my shoulder to an imaginary companion. I paused on the threshold, adrenaline coursing through me in preparation for flight, but the cottage was silent and, more importantly, it was also completely empty.

Even so, I grabbed a meat tenderiser from the jar of kitchen utensils and brandished it like a cudgel as I climbed the rickety staircase to the upper floor. Every single tread creaked while I kept up a one-sided conversation with my non-existent muscular friend on the ground floor. Eventually, I had to concede that the police had done their job properly, or that any intruder in the cottage was so deaf it would be easy to sneak up behind them.

The door to Amelia's bedroom was wide open and my footsteps slowed to a halt as I approached her bed. It was unmade, the pillows still bearing the dent from her head, the duvet thrown back as though she'd left in a hurry. It told its own story. Face down on the bedside table was a current bestseller – it was one I'd recommended to her just before Christmas. I turned it over, my smile sad as I noted she was just about to get to the good bit. 'Always an editor,' I murmured on a laugh that wasn't quite as steady as I would have liked.

The room smelled of Amelia and the urge to fall on to her bed and burrow my face in her pillows was worryingly strong. *Stop this*, I told myself firmly. She'll be back here in no time. She will get better. She *has* to get better.

The bathroom held no clues as to what had happened in the cottage two nights ago. Nor did the second bedroom, although finding the bed already made up and a little stack of clean towels on the room's small armchair shook me somewhat. It was almost as though she'd been expecting me.

I made Amelia's bed before going back downstairs to bring the rest of the things in from the car. I have no idea why it seemed important to do it, I just knew that it did.

I phoned Mum to let her know I'd arrived safely and saw I'd missed two new messages from Jeff. We'd spoken briefly earlier in the day and although he'd asked all the right questions and said all the right things, something about the whole conversation had felt 'off'. It was worrying how little that seemed to matter now there was an ocean between us. Or perhaps there always had been one, and I'd just needed the physical distance to realise it. We'd been on borrowed time for quite a while, I knew that, but it didn't make failing any easier. It never did.

I unpacked Mum's collection of emergency provisions, squeezing them into Amelia's already well-stocked fridge and cupboards. I was shifting things around to make space on the lower shelf of her fridge when I found the pack of beers tucked away behind two cartons of juice. I stared at my discovery for so long the fridge began beeping angrily at me to close the door. Amelia didn't drink much, except for the odd glass of wine now and then. She claimed not to like the taste. It was – undoubtedly – one of the weirdest differences between us. She certainly didn't drink beer. But someone did. I pulled the pack to the front of the shelf. There were two cans missing from the carton. Who'd drunk them? Sam?

I slammed the fridge door shut on the crazy idea, as though to trap it inside. There *was* no Sam, I told myself furiously. I would willingly go along with whatever pretence the doctors suggested, but that's all that it was, a charade. Sam Wilson was a phantom husband and the quicker we managed to exorcise him from Amelia's head, the better.

After spending much of the day in the ridiculously overheated hospital, I was longing for a shower before bed. But fifteen frustrating minutes later, I still hadn't managed to coax Amelia's ancient boiler into life. I glared angrily at the unit; it had failed to respond to a barrage of swear words *and* two resounding thumps, which had hurt me far more than the boiler.

It was out of character, but I could feel tears of despair stinging my eyes at my defeat.

'You're just tired,' I told myself, 'and a little punchy,' I added on a nervous laugh as I realised I was talking to myself again.

I rummaged in my case for my warmest pyjamas and hurriedly pulled them on, while outside the cottage windows the wind continued to pick up. It was hurling grains of sand against the panes, which sounded like the scratch of an intruder's fingernails. Suddenly, Mum's tiny couch didn't sound like such a bad option after all.

I climbed beneath the duvet and pulled it up to my chin. Eventually, the cottage creaked and groaned its way into silence, but the wind and the sea were as loud as ever. Amelia claimed the sound of the waves was soothing and lulled her to sleep. But they were having the opposite effect on me – and I was tired enough to sleep standing up! Finally, I gave up trying and clicked on the bedside lamp.

I'd spoken to my manager in New York earlier in the day and although she had sympathetically agreed to me taking some 'personal time' – albeit out of my vacation allowance – she'd nevertheless managed to squeeze in a reminder that they would need a decision on the job offer very soon. I understood the urgency. The promotion to executive editor with my very own imprint was a huge opportunity, which most editors would kill for. But those editors didn't have to face the dilemma of putting down roots thousands of miles away from their loved ones. The last four years in New York had felt like an extended work adventure, but taking the promotion was a commitment to make America my long-term home, and that was what was stopping me from pulling the trigger.

Although my 'out-of-office' was on, no one had bothered to

inform my body clock, which was still firmly set on American time. So I decided to put my insomnia to good use and read one of the many pending submissions waiting on my Kindle.

Two hours later I was halfway through a novel, but I'd have been hard-pressed to name any of the characters. It might be the next industry bestseller or total rubbish, I had no idea which. My thoughts kept straying away from the plot and circling back to Amelia's inexplicable claim, like a plane with nowhere to land. Why had my sister's subconscious created a fictitious husband? Could this Sam person be someone she actually knew in real life? Someone she hadn't wanted to tell her family about? Could Amelia be having a secret affair?

Out of all the questions carouselling in my head, that one was surely the most ridiculous. Amelia wouldn't do that. But then again, if you'd asked me if she'd ever go walkabout on the beach in the middle of the night, I'd have said 'No' to that one too.

I fell asleep with the beginnings of a headache that was still there four hours later, when a bunch of noisy seagulls decided it was time for me to wake up. Thankfully, the uncooperative boiler had undergone a change of heart and decided to heat a tankful of water. I drained at least half of it beneath the jets of a shower so hot that I emerged from the cubicle in a cloud of steam, like in the movies, with my skin a new and interesting shade of lobster pink.

I'd packed for the trip in such a rush that many of my essential toiletries were still sitting in my New York bathroom. But Amelia had grown up with a younger sister constantly borrowing her things, and it felt rather comforting to be doing so once again. During my search of her bathroom, I unearthed an empty toiletry bag into which I began packing essentials to take to the hospital. There's a thin line between searching and prying, and I could feel myself crossing it as I began to look for items that Amelia would have no use for in hospital, or anywhere else come to that. On my own bathroom shelf were Jeff's spare razor, his shaving gel and deodorant – and he didn't even stay over at mine all that often. But Amelia's cupboard held nothing similar. I closed the cabinet and caught the dual expressions of guilt and relief in the mirrored doors. If Sam *had* been real, then it meant I didn't know my sister nearly as well as I'd thought. But then again, the woman who claimed I'd been her bridesmaid two years ago was just as much of a stranger to me.

There was enough food in the kitchen to feed a small army, so it felt wasteful that all I wanted was a slice of toast. I took it – and the mug of strong coffee I'd made – to Amelia's door. The wind had died down considerably overnight, but it was still cold enough for me to reach for the chunky cardigan my sister had hung on a hook beside the door.

The sky was the dark purple of a bruise, but slowly daubs of deep pink tinged the horizon and began working their way higher and higher. The sea changed from black to violet as dawn pushed the night out of the way. I've seen sunrises on both sides of the world, but none that have taken my breath away in the same way as this one did. It felt primal and elemental and there was a beauty and a wildness to the beach that I'd never really appreciated before. It was as though I was seeing it through Amelia's eyes and not my own.

I felt strangely calmer as I returned to the cottage, as if I was no longer alone. Even though she was miles away from me in a hospital bed, I felt closer to Amelia than I had done in a very long time. It was a sister thing... a twin thing, and I hadn't even realised I'd missed it until unexpectedly I found it again.

Opinion has always been split in our family as to whether there really *was* an inexplicable connection between Amelia and me. *They're sisters, that's all there is to it,* I remember my no-nonsense maternal grandmother saying with an authoritative harrumph. It was the sound she finished practically every sentence with.

'They're more than just sisters – they're twins,' Mum had firmly corrected.

I can't say for sure, but I imagine that was met with another harrumph.

'That's just science mumbo jumbo.'

To this day, I can remember Mum's eyes finding mine across the width of our old kitchen and the warmth of her smile. I was a product of that science 'mumbo jumbo' and so too was Amelia, and both of us had been made aware of just how special that made us from a very young age.

My parents had wanted a house full of children, especially Dad, who'd been an only child, adopted as a baby, and had grown up longing for siblings. But Mum had struggled to get pregnant, and Dad – who would have given her the moon on a string if she'd asked for it – had happily agreed to IVF, a procedure that was still relatively new back then. And it had worked for them. Given Mum's tiny frame, the doctors had decided to implant just a single embryo and freeze the other. It always seemed crazy to me that some unknown embryologist had chosen which sister would come first and which would be frozen in liquid nitrogen and stored away until the time was right for them to be born.

'You were like Sleeping Beauty,' my big sister told me when I was old enough to question why my 'twin' was actually eight years older than me.

'So did a handsome prince come along to wake me up?' I asked.

Amelia had snorted that notion away. Even as a young teenager, she was all about the logic and not the magic. 'You didn't need any dumb old hero to save you,' she said derisively.

Which made it even more confusing that for some reason, from the depths of her subconscious, she'd apparently created one now for herself.

6

I stared into the weekend bag on Amelia's bed. Should I add one more nightdress to the three I'd already packed? The sides of the holdall were already bulging, largely due to the number of *Oh, I've just thought of...* messages Mum had sent throughout the morning.

'Toiletries, undies, slippers, dressing gown,' I murmured, checking the items off the list on my phone. I scanned Amelia's bedroom one last time and picked up the book from her bedside table and placed it on top of the clothes. Beside it was a dangling charger wire, still plugged into the wall socket. But there was no mobile phone. I'd looked for it everywhere and even tried calling it, only to get an annoying message telling me *This person's phone is currently unavailable.*

'Oh, I do hope she hasn't lost it again,' Mum said, when I called to ask for suggestions of where else to look. 'She got really upset a couple of weeks ago when she mislaid it.'

Getting upset was the last thing Amelia should be doing in her current condition.

'I'll keep looking for it,' I promised. I was standing beside Amelia's bedroom window, watching a clutch of seagulls swooping down from the sky to the beach. My fingers suddenly tightened around my own mobile. 'Do you think her phone might be on the mudflats somewhere? She might have had it with her the other night and dropped it?'

Mum sighed and her voice sounded worryingly old. 'I don't know, Lexi. I'm beginning to wonder if we'll *ever* find out what happened that night.'

Amelia's phone wasn't the only troublesome item on my list. Even though I hadn't seen it in years, I wasn't worried about recognising the locket, with its elaborate silver scrollwork. Ten-year-old me had coveted it from the moment our grandmother – the harrumphing one – had given it to Amelia for her eighteenth birthday. I assumed I would find it in the jewellery box on the bedroom dressing table. But the photograph inside it, of a husband who didn't exist, would be somewhat trickier to locate.

Various faces had graced the inside of the locket over the years: our parents, me, much loved pets, even the odd boyfriend or two. But who would I find inside it now? I was surprised to see my hand was trembling as I lifted the lid of the jewellery box. The locket was right there on the top tray, nestled in a red-velvet-lined compartment. The silver glinted in a watery ray of winter sunlight as I plucked the necklace from the box. It was heavier than I remembered, and my fingers fumbled awkwardly with the clasp before it finally sprang open. I didn't realise I'd been holding my breath until I let it out now on a long, expelled sigh. There were no photographs in the locket. It was empty.

I'm not sure how long I stood there with the irrefutable

proof in my hands that Sam Wilson did not exist. I was usually good at making decisions, but I couldn't make up my mind which was worse: to present Amelia with the empty locket or lie and say I couldn't find it.

'What do you mean, you couldn't find it? Did you look in my jewellery box?'

I shifted uncomfortably beside Amelia's hospital bed, busying myself with repositioning the jug of water to make room for the belongings I *had* brought with me.

'I did,' I said, unable to meet the disappointment in her eyes. The locket was the first thing she'd asked for as soon as I arrived. I thought the missing phone would bother her far more – it certainly would me – but she was fixated on the locket.

'I just want to see his face,' she said, sounding so forlorn that her pain made my own eyes tingle. She brought her hand up to the place where the electrodes were fixed to her chest. 'I wanted to wear it so I could keep him right here.'

'Perhaps it's fallen into a drawer or something. I'm sorry, Amelia. I just ran out of time to search, and I didn't want to be late for visiting.'

'Your sister has had a bit of a rough morning,' the charge nurse had informed me on my way to Amelia's room. 'I just wanted to warn you that you might find her a little out of sorts.' That had to be the understatement of the century. 'She became quite distressed during her MRI this morning, so much so that they had to abandon it for today. Were you aware that she suffers from claustrophobia?'

I wasn't. But suddenly the weird feeling I'd experienced

a few hours earlier made much more sense. One minute I'd been perfectly fine, working on my laptop, and the next my heart had begun inexplicably to race, and I'd broken out in a cold sweat. It had felt as though the walls of the cottage were closing in on me and I'd thrown open the front door and stood on the beach, gulping in huge lungfuls of salt-tinged air. And then, just as suddenly as it started, the sensation had passed. I'd never had a panic attack in my life, and that *could* have been what I'd experienced today. But memories of getting menstrual cramps when I wasn't the one having a period, or an aching jaw when Amelia visited the dentist with a particularly nasty abscess, made me think there might be another explanation.

The day had clearly left its mark on Amelia. She was still horribly pale, and although I tried very hard not to stare at the monitors she was attached to, it was impossible not to be aware that her heart rate was all over the place – one minute terrifyingly fast and the next desperately low. I'd watched enough episodes of *Grey's Anatomy* to know that couldn't be good.

'She didn't bring the locket in,' Amelia said disappointedly to a nurse who'd come in to take her blood pressure.

'Oh, never mind. I'm sure I'll see that handsome hubby of yours soon,' she said consolingly, throwing a friendly smile in my direction.

You do know there is no husband, don't you? my eyes silently quizzed the nurse. *We're just humouring her until she can separate reality from fantasy.*

The nurse was either an Oscar-worthy actress or had yet to be briefed about Amelia's condition.

'I am sorry, hon,' I apologised again. 'I promise I'll search for it when I go back later. I'll turn the place upside down until I find it.'

My sister's eyes met mine, and there was a look in them I'd never seen before. 'You won't have to. It's in the jewellery box, like I told you.'

It felt like a gauntlet being thrown down and I swallowed nervously, afraid to pick it up.

'I've been telling everyone all morning about how Sam and I first met.'

The nurse's smile looked totally natural, while my own felt like a frozen mask.

'That's nice,' I said, trying not to let my eyes stray to the door of the room. Mum was making her own way to the hospital by taxi; it had been a long time since I'd felt this desperate waiting for a parent to arrive.

'Yes,' Amelia said on a sigh that straddled a line between nostalgia and exhaustion. 'It was so romantic, wasn't it?'

She shifted in the bed, looking uncomfortable. That made two of us.

'How would *you* describe Sam, Lexi?' Amelia asked. She was testing me. The monitors behind her showed her elevated heart rate. But if they attached a set to me, mine could have overtaken her easily.

'He's… he's like someone out of a romantic novel… a real hero,' I settled on, pulling the neck of my jumper away from my throat. It was starting to feel incredibly hot in there.

'Well, I'm sure I'll see him soon,' the nurse repeated.

'Actually, you *could* see him today,' Amelia declared. My stomach took a lurch, the kind that normally only happens in rapidly descending lifts. 'Is there a shop that sells stationery in the hospital?' she asked bizarrely, turning to me.

I nodded, beyond confused now.

'Could you buy me a sketch pad and some pencils, so I can draw him?'

There was probably a goldfish-like quality to my open-mouthed amazement. 'You're going to draw him... Sam?' I asked. His name felt weird in my mouth.

She flopped back on the pillows. 'It's the next best thing, seeing as you didn't bring in the locket.'

Amelia couldn't draw. I don't say that to be mean. It's just a fact. She can't draw, in the same way that I can't sing or understand a spreadsheet. I'd studied art at A level, but my older sister had opted for all the sciences. *This is going to be interesting*, I thought, as I travelled down in the lift to the foyer.

It took a few moments to find the items I'd been dispatched to buy. While searching, I threw a couple of sudoku magazines into my wire basket, as well as two bars of her favourite chocolate and a packet of paracetamol. The last was for me.

For a hospital gift shop, they had a surprisingly wide range of drawing materials. I picked up an A3 size sketch pad and several boxes of pencils. The carrier bag felt heavy, or maybe that was just the feeling in my heart, as I once again made my way to the lifts. As far as I was aware, Amelia's style of drawing had peaked at stick people, with right-angled hands and feet and big balloon heads. I was already worrying about how to react when the drawing she presented looked more like a game of hangman than an illustration of her husband.

There is *no husband*, a voice in my head pointedly reminded me.

⋆

I greeted Mum like she'd just returned from an Arctic expedition.

'You're here,' I cried delightedly, enveloping her in a huge hug. Amelia was watching us closely, so I had to hope that my extra-hard squeeze alerted her that things with Amelia hadn't *sorted themselves out after a good night's rest* the way she'd hoped.

'The nurse was telling me you went for some tests this morning,' I said hesitantly, turning to my sister.

Amelia's eyes moved reluctantly from the carrier bag in my hand. 'Yes. Although I'm not sure what they're looking for because I can't get a straight answer out of anyone.'

'You still can't remember anything about the night you collapsed?'

She shook her head.

'Or being on the beach?' I added tentatively. The ground I was walking on was suddenly as unstable as the mudflats where Amelia had been found.

'Why on earth was I on the beach?'

That was a very good question and one that none of us could answer.

'I'm sure the doctors will figure it all out very soon.'

Mum's faith in the wisdom of anyone with a medical degree had always been unshakeable, but her daughters were a little more sceptical. Amelia's eye caught mine and in that single moment she was back; she was one hundred per cent my capable older sister, with her quick wit and MENSA-level IQ. She reached out her hand and I stupidly thought it was to grasp mine, only she flapped me away and pointed at the carrier bag. 'Did you get me the drawing stuff? I'm going to do a sketch of Sam,' she explained to Mum.

'From memory?' I couldn't resist asking.

Amelia gave me a glare that should probably be accompanied by a *Duh!* speech bubble.

'Well, obviously, seeing as he's still in New York. There's been no word yet, has there?'

I shook my head sadly, but not for the reasons she might think. It felt like we'd taken one step forward and two back. Amelia's journey to recovery still felt impossibly long.

She upended the contents of the plastic bag on to the bed and was studying the selection of pencils I'd bought, looking for all the world as though she actually knew what she was doing. I drew my chair closer to the bed as she began covering the top sheet of paper in the pad with long sweeping strokes.

It took less than two minutes for me to realise that Amelia wasn't just a competent artist... she was actually very good. Better than me, in fact, although there was a marked similarity in our drawing styles.

Before my eyes, a horizon appeared and then sand dunes and a coastline. She glanced up a couple of times, as though visualising something none of us could see, before returning her attention to the sketch pad balanced on her knees. Mum was keeping up a constant flow of chatter, talking about people I didn't know, but I doubt Amelia even heard her. Her concentration sharpened as she abandoned the beach and slowly the outline of a figure appeared on the sand. The person was crouched down low, his weight on one knee. Amelia took her time with the sketch, filling in hundreds of tiny details before turning her attention to the man's features.

I watched in silence as the face of the brother-in-law I didn't have finally emerged.

Amelia had been right, he *was* handsome. His jaw was strong, and his features were clearly defined – chiselled was probably how they'd be described in the pages of a novel. I'd never used the term before to describe anyone in real life, but it seemed to perfectly fit the image on the page.

Amelia had bent low over the sketch pad to fill in his features with painstaking care. I saw a network of tiny lines that crinkled at the edges of his eyes, the hint of a cleft in his chin and the warmth of his smile. It was a smile that was mirrored on my sister's face as she filled in every detail. With gut-wrenching shock, I saw the love in her eyes for the man her pencil had created. This figment of her subconscious was clearly as real to her as her own family.

'That's how he looked on the day we met,' she said, turning her pencil to the man's thick shock of dark hair that was caught in the breeze. She held the pad at arm's length, turning it towards the light. 'That's pretty much exactly how he looks in the locket photo,' she said with a satisfied nod at her own handiwork. 'You'll see that when you bring it in tomorrow.'

I swallowed nervously and pasted what I hoped was a natural smile on to my lips. Desperately, I sought to change the subject. 'Since when have you been able to draw like this?' I asked, taking the pad from her hands and studying the expertly sketched illustration. Up close, her style looked even more like mine... except I hadn't picked up a sketch book in years.

'I'm not sure, a while I guess,' she said, flopping back against her pillows as though the artwork had drained something out of her. 'I'd always wanted to give it a go, so I found an online course and…' – she gave a small shrug – 'I discovered I had a hidden talent.'

'But you never even mentioned it to me.'

Amelia's head darted towards the doorway, where a nurse had just appeared with a trolley of medication. Did she do that every single time she heard someone approach, I wondered sadly?

'I'm sure I told you,' Amelia said, holding out her hand for the beaker the nurse had prepared. It was filled with an assortment of coloured pills, which she swallowed all together.

'No,' I said, 'I'd have remembered if you'd mentioned it.'

'Would you? What makes you so sure? You managed to forget I had a husband.'

Touché.

The moment the nurse left the room, Amelia reached once again for the sketch pad. Over the next two hours, she filled page after page with sketches. Every drawing was of the man on the beach. Sometimes they were close-up portraits, so detailed I could practically see the sweep of his individual eyelashes. In others he was striding along the wet sand, hands deep in the pockets of his jeans, his thick chunky jumper keeping out the winter chill. The man in the sketch pad was tall and broadly built and seemed to grow in substance in my head with every new drawing and turn of the page. The tide and elongated shadows on the sand seemed to indicate the time was early on a winter's morning.

Strangely, it was Amelia's final drawing that was the most surprising.

'How could I have forgotten to include Barney?' she exclaimed, rapidly pencilling in a new shape beside the man who I now felt certain I could pick out from a line-up.

'Who's Barney?' I asked, trying to peer over the top of the pad, which she'd now angled away from me.

'Barney,' Amelia said, shaking her head at my apparent amnesia. 'Barney is Sam's dog.' I took hold of the edge of the pad and tilted it towards me. Barney was indeed a dog. A very large and shaggy Old English Sheepdog. In the sketch he was standing up on his hind legs, his two enormous front paws placed squarely in the middle of Sam's chest.

'I... I forgot Sam had a dog,' murmured Mum, trying so hard to say the right thing, if only someone could tell her what that might be.

'Well, we could never bring him over to yours. He doesn't travel well in the car.'

'And is Barney in New York with Sam right now?' I asked carefully, hoping out of all the questions I could have posed, I'd chosen one that would cause the least distress. Unfortunately, I hadn't.

'No. You can't take dogs with you on work trips. He's... he's... Is he at the cottage?' she asked uncertainly.

Imaginary husbands I could just about get on board with, but not imaginary dogs.

'No, honey, he's not there.'

Amelia's face crumpled like a child's. 'Then where is he? Did he die? Did Barney die?'

I had no idea how to answer that one and hoped my helpless shrug would suffice.

'Why can't I remember it? I should be able to remember. But my head feels like it's full of holes and all the important things keep disappearing down them every time I try to grab hold of them. Why is this happening to me?'

She was crying now, and it wasn't until I tasted the saltiness on my lips that I realised I was too. I gathered her into my arms and rocked her gently.

'I don't know, hon, but we'll get to the bottom of this.' I reached out my hand and grasped Mum's, which was extended towards us, completing the family circle. 'We'll work it all out, I promise.'

'I'm sure he *is* busy,' I told the ward assistant at the nurse's station. 'But my mother and I really need to speak to Dr Vaughan. Right now. Today.'

'That's not how it works—' the young woman began, before being shut down by a hand placed firmly on her shoulder. I'd been trying to keep my voice down, but clearly the senior charge nurse had heard me even through the thickness of her closed door.

'Let me see if he's still in the hospital and can spare you a moment,' she said with a kind smile at Mum – who *hadn't* been raising her voice – and a nod of acknowledgement at me, who had.

Amelia was visibly exhausted and had made no protest when I told her I was going to take Mum down for something sweet and sticky from the Costa in the hospital foyer. I'd had to almost tug Mum from the room. 'I don't really want any cake, Lexi,' she said when I'd eventually managed to persuade her into the corridor.

'Nor do I. But I do want answers. So, let's see if we can get some.'

★

Dr Vaughan's consulting rooms were two floors below Amelia's ward.

'Come in, come in,' came a voice that sounded much younger than I was expecting, in response to our knock.

It wasn't just Dr Vaughan's voice that was youthful, the rest of him was too. I'd been hoping for a doctor who could hand on heart declare that they'd *been there, done that, got the T-shirt.* I wanted a physician who'd seen it all and knew all the answers. But I was already afraid from the look in his eyes as he shook our hands that the reality might be somewhat different.

'Please, sit down, both of you,' he invited, gesturing towards two chairs on one side of the desk. He waited politely until we were seated before dropping down on to his own chair.

There were piles of patient folders on his desk, which surprised me in this age of computerisation. From one tower, which looked dangerously close to overbalancing, he plucked the topmost file. Even upside down, I could read my sister's name.

He flipped the folder open and then spent several moments flicking through the paperwork within it. His forehead creased a couple of times at whatever he was reading, and his lips pursed and twisted, as though dispatching a persistent toffee, as he ran a finger down a chart that even if it *had* been the right way up, I couldn't have deciphered. Finally, he sighed, leant back in his chair and folded his arms across his abdomen. I deemed him at least a decade too young to pull off that manoeuvre successfully, but I imagined he thought it gave him gravitas.

Somewhere in his room there was a clock with an annoyingly loud tick, and if the doctor hadn't broken the silence himself right then, I would have had to do so myself, just to shut out the noise.

'Amelia is a very, very lucky young woman.' It was a good sentence to lead with. 'In fact, I'd go so far as to say she is quite remarkable.' He'd certainly get no argument from the two women on the other side of his desk about that.

He unclenched his hands and leant closer towards us, resting his elbows on the desk as he turned to Mum. 'You have obviously been told about your daughter's condition when she was found on the beach and then brought in by ambulance?'

'She had hypothermia,' Mum replied hesitantly, as though answering a particularly tricky question on *University Challenge*.

'Indeed. Indeed,' said Dr Vaughan, nodding like a professor in a lecture hall. 'What's important to understand is that in *this* country we see very few cases of accidental hypothermia.'

I was familiar with the term from my Google searches, and it always struck me as slightly ridiculous, as though there might be a companion condition called 'intentional hypothermia' where you did it on purpose.

'What is even more rare – at least in the UK – is for hypothermia to drop the body's core temperature so low that it results in hypothermic cardiac arrest.'

'When the heart stops beating altogether,' I said for Mum's benefit, in case she hadn't been googling the same searches as me. But she was already reaching in her handbag for a tissue, so I guess she had.

'Exactly,' said Dr Vaughan. 'But even rarer still is when

after an indeterminate period, when the patient is technically not breathing, they are then successfully resuscitated.'

'As Amelia was,' I said, pausing to give Mum a quick reassuring smile.

'Exactly. But I don't want to give you the impression that we're completely out of the woods just yet. Amelia's coronary readings are still giving us cause for concern, and it's too early to be able to give you a satisfactory long-term prognosis, which I realise is what you both want to hear. What I *can* assure you is that we're going to be monitoring her very closely in the days and weeks to come.'

'Could there be other organ damage, Dr Vaughan, in addition to the heart?' I hesitated before continuing, as if saying the words out loud would make it real. 'Could she have suffered any brain damage?'

His eyes dropped to a sheet in Amelia's file. 'The head CT taken on the night she was admitted doesn't indicate any abnormalities, but we'll obviously be conducting other examinations. In fact, there are a great many tests we'd like to undertake, but we need to be mindful that your sister has been through an incredibly traumatic experience and her emotional well-being is just as important as her physical state. I understand she became very distressed today during her MRI.'

He paused as though weighing up his next words and wondering just how honest he ought to be. 'I'm going to be completely frank with both of you. Amelia's is the first case of this kind that I have personally encountered. Which is why I have reached out to colleagues at one of the major hospitals in Sweden, who have far more experience dealing with this condition.'

I bit my lip worriedly. 'And have any of the doctors in Sweden had patients with... memory issues?' I asked.

Dr Vaughan nodded slowly. 'Some, yes. A large proportion of patients appear remarkably unscathed by the event – and some have been clinically dead for periods of up to six hours, which we believe was *not* the case with Amelia. But yes, in answer to your question, I understand that some patients have memory loss ranging from quite mild to severe.'

I shook my head. 'Not memory *loss*, doctor. New memories. False memories of things that have never happened.'

He opened his mouth to reply but I silenced him as I reached for the illustration that I'd torn from Amelia's sketch pad. 'My sister drew this a couple of hours ago. It's a picture of a man she is adamant is her husband. A man who I can tell you absolutely and categorically does not exist.'

'Do you think he's right, telling us to keep up the pretence with her?' Mum asked as we stepped into the hospital's revolving door. The contrast from the overheated hospital air to the January chill was enough to take my breath away.

'I don't think he knows *what* to suggest, Mum,' I replied sadly. 'At least he was honest enough to admit he's never known a case like hers. Not that it helps us much. He seems confident that she'll soon let go of the fantasy and realise there are too many things that don't make sense for it to be true.'

I linked my arm through Mum's. 'Finding her phone and showing Amelia it *isn't* filled with photos of her and Sam would be a good place to start.'

'But what do we tell her in the meantime? We have to say

something when she asks why Sam hasn't been in touch,' Mum said, struggling with the clasp of her seat belt. I reached over and clipped it in place for her. This would be the last time I'd drive the rental vehicle, which was going to be collected the next day. From now on I'd be using Amelia's car. It made sense and sadly, from everything Dr Vaughan had said, Amelia wouldn't be needing it herself for the foreseeable future.

I waited until the car park barrier had lifted to release us before I returned to Mum's question.

'We need to find a plausible reason why he can't get in touch with her,' I said.

'Perhaps we could say he's been kidnapped and we're trying to raise the ransom money?'

My lips twitched in the first natural smile I'd given that day.

'Orrrrr,' I said, drawing the word out, 'we could think of something that didn't sound like the plot of a Netflix thriller.'

Mum didn't take offence, but she gave back as good as she got.

'Like what? What do you suggest?'

I worked in the world of fiction. I must have heard a thousand different plots over the years. Surely one of them could provide me with a solution? But when I allowed my thoughts to travel to the place where I worked, the answer came from real life rather than the pages of a book.

'I've got it! Merle, one of the other editors at work, has just come back from a ten-night stay at a silent retreat in upstate New York. It's a place where people go to meditate and recharge in strict silence. And the best thing is, the retreat insists there's absolutely no communication with the outside world. No phones, no technology, nothing.' I turned to grin at

Mum, like a magician who'd found the rabbit and successfully pulled it out of the hat. Disappointingly, Mum didn't look convinced.

'I'm not so sure, Lexi. I don't know if that's the kind of thing Sam is into.'

'Mum,' I said gently, 'there *is* no Sam.'

She laughed nervously, looking so embarrassed that I took one hand off the wheel to squeeze hers gently. 'I know. This is all kinds of fucked up. But at least it gives us something to say to Mimi when she asks.'

It was a measure of how distracted Mum was that she didn't even flinch when I swore; she just nodded slowly in agreement.

7

The pizza hadn't gone down well. I should have known better than to order one with extra jalapeños at the restaurant where Mum and I stopped for dinner. Two hours after switching off the bedside lamp I was still tossing and turning, unable to get comfy in Amelia's extremely comfortable guest bed. Jet lag was bad enough, but when coupled with indigestion, sleep was a virtual impossibility.

Longing for the bottle of Pepto-Bismol I'd left back in New York, I threw back the duvet and scurried across creaky floorboards towards the bathroom. Yesterday I'd spotted an old packet of Rennies in the cabinet and, ignoring the fact they were three years past their use-by date, I perched on the edge of Amelia's bathtub and crunched two of the chalky tablets. Despite an icy chill that made the bathroom as cold as a meat locker, I was in no hurry to return to my bed. Not because I wasn't tired, but because I knew exactly where my eyes would be drawn the moment I returned to the room.

In hindsight, I should probably have slipped the locket back into Amelia's jewellery box where it belonged, rather than leaving it in my room. But I was too afraid I'd 'accidentally' forget to take it with me to the hospital the following day. *As if*, observed a wry voice in my head.

The importance of the necklace and how it would impact on Amelia's state of mind had begun as a small worry and then, in the way trifling fears have a habit of doing, had grown exponentially throughout the sleepless middle-of-the-night hours.

It had become so bad, it almost felt as though the oval locket was watching me from across the room, like an evil eye. It was hardly surprising that I had indigestion, I thought, giving myself a strict mental shake before returning to the guest bedroom.

Of course I went over to the locket. How could I not? I'd played out what would happen the next day when I took it to the hospital so many times, it now felt more like a memory than a prediction.

I could see me reaching into my pocket and extracting the necklace. I could see the glint of the silver under the bright hospital lights as the locket and chain dropped like a tiny anchor into my sister's outstretched hand.

But it was what would happen next that was impossible to predict. When Amelia opened the locket and found it empty, was I really going to lie and say the photograph must have fallen out? Or was that the moment to say, as gently and as kindly as I could, that there'd never been anything in the locket in the first place? Or was option three the way to go? I shivered, wondering if I was a good enough actress to pretend I could actually see a photograph in the empty locket, if Amelia said she could too. *The Emperor's New Clothes* had always been one of my favourite stories as a child, but living through it, pretending to see something that I knew wasn't there, felt disturbingly dark.

I woke up before the sun again. It was a new and unappealing habit that I was looking forward to breaking. Disappointingly, the boiler – which I still hadn't managed to befriend – was two hours away from heating up enough water for my morning shower. Too restless to go back to bed, I decided that exercise was what I needed. Jeff was an ardent Central Park jogger, and occasionally he'd persuade me to join him on an early-morning run. It always put me in a better and more positive frame of mind for the day, and that was something I could definitely do with right now.

I hadn't brought any gym clothes with me, but I found a pair of leggings and a matching hoodie in Amelia's wardrobe. Feeling virtuous, I splashed cold water on my face and tied my hair back in a loose ponytail before pulling on the borrowed sportswear.

It was colder than I expected when I let myself out of Amelia's home. I could see my breath pluming like speech bubbles as I performed a few half-hearted stretches, which I was possibly doing all wrong, but for once Jeff wasn't around to correct me. I paused for a moment, waiting to see if a pang of missing him was about to follow that thought. It didn't, which was something 'future me' should probably think about. But right now, the only thing on my mind was the beach, my run, and the joy of catching another sunrise as the first tentative rays of daylight began to spill on to the sand.

I paused for a moment by the cottage's low wooden gate that led directly on to the beach. Going right would eventually take me to the nearest village, with the promise of a welcoming café with hot coffee and pastries. Turning left would lead nowhere except to the mudflats. I overruled my grumbling stomach and turned left.

As expected, I was the only person on the beach at that hour. But I wasn't looking for company, so that was fine with me. After about two minutes I slowed down to a gentle jog, because running on sand was way harder than doing it on paved pathways. But more importantly, I still hadn't given up the hope of finding Amelia's phone on the beach. Logically, I knew my chances of doing so were probably less than scooping up a lottery win, but I still felt compelled to try. If only she'd installed Find My Phone, or if the device hadn't been switched off, there might have been a glimmer of hope to my search. And bearing in mind that the phone would now have spent several days buried in either sand or mud, it would be nothing short of a miracle if I found it.

But it was a morning for miracles.

It was forty minutes since I'd left the cottage, long enough for the sun to have kicked the moon to the kerb and taken its place in the sky. I stopped to catch my breath and looked around, absently wondering how far I'd run, when I saw I was no longer the only person on the beach. Down near the water's edge, where the tide was gradually receding, a tall figure was jogging on the wet sand.

I couldn't make out much about them, except that they were moving with an easy rhythm that I definitely hadn't mastered. They probably weren't pink-faced and sweaty either, I thought, as I pushed back yet another damp strand of hair that had escaped from the ponytail. I turned away, about to retrace my footsteps in the sand, when a sound brought me to a standstill. It halted the other runner too, for the figure slowed to a stop and then turned to face the sea, as though waiting for something.

The sound came again, easier to identify this time. With a chorus of loud, joyful barks, a shape emerged from the breaking surf. The barking identified the animal as a dog, even though it was practically the size of a small donkey. Transfixed, I watched as the animal stopped at the water's edge and shook itself. Even from this distance I could see the water spraying in every direction, like a fountain. The sound of a man's laughter carried clearly on the wind.

This was the point when I should have turned away, but something was beginning to stir inside me. The man. This beach. The enormous dog.

The man produced a ball and threw it in an impressive overarm bowl along the wet sand, and his dog bounded after it like a rocket. The animal's coat was still wet from its dip in the sea, but not so much that I couldn't make out exactly what kind of dog it was. An Old English Sheepdog.

The dog was hurtling after the ball, the man was jogging after his pet, and suddenly – without any conscious thought or decision – I was running after both of them.

'Hey! Wait!' I gasped out as I ran, but my lungs were too busy coping with the unaccustomed spurt of speed to provide me with sufficient breath to shout. The wheezy words were frustratingly whipped away on the breeze. The man and the dog were still running, faster than I'd ever be able to match, and the distance between us was lengthening.

Every muscle in my legs was on fire and the stitch in my side felt like a genuine stab wound, but I ran on. I was now at the water's edge, my trainers sending up tiny plumes of spray as I splashed through the foam of the outgoing waves. It was easier to run on the compacted wet sand, but I still would never have caught up with the man if he hadn't picked up the bright-yellow tennis ball and lobbed it into the water. His dog delightedly chased after it and finally I was close enough for him to hear my cry.

'Wait. Please, can you wait?'

The man was still about fifty metres away, but my plea brought him to a stop. He turned around and I felt my knees instantly buckle. He immediately began running towards me.

The world was spinning crazily, and it had nothing to do with the way I'd pushed myself beyond my physical limits. Somehow, I managed to scramble back on to my feet. Amelia's fancy sportswear was wet and caked in sand, but that was the furthest thing from my thoughts right then.

'Hey, are you okay?' the man asked with concern.

I stared up at him, the power of speech suddenly lost.

'Are you hurt?' he continued.

I shook my head so violently I felt the slap of my ponytail strike first one cheek and then the other.

'Okay,' said the man, a little uncertainly, taking an almost imperceptible half step backwards. 'Were you calling out to me just now?'

I nodded. It was incredible. Amelia had captured every last detail of this man's face. The sketch, which I'd probably looked at a hundred times since the previous afternoon, had literally come to life and was standing right there before me.

'Was there something you wanted?' the man asked. His voice was deep and pleasant, but there was more confusion than concern in it now.

I'm not sure what he was expecting me to do or say, but

he definitely looked surprised when I held out my hand to shake his.

'Sam,' I said confidently.

There was a very long moment before he lifted his own hand and placed it in mine.

'Hello, Sam. It's nice to meet you.'

I frowned. 'My name isn't Sam, it's Lexi,' I said encouragingly, as though willing him to give the right answer. 'I'm Amelia's sister.'

There was something in the man's eyes and it definitely wasn't the spark of recognition I was hoping for. If I wasn't mistaken, it looked an awful lot like panic.

'I think you may have me mistaken for someone else.'

I shook my head, aware that I was sounding more than a little unhinged. 'No. It's you. It must be you.'

There was no mistaking the backward step now. The dog had retrieved the ball and the man bent down and swiftly clipped him back on his lead. He was obviously in a hurry to leave.

'You must know me. Don't you recognise my face?' I asked, realising that with the sun directly behind me, he might not have been able to make out my features. I stepped to one side and reached up and released my hair from the ponytail that my sister never wore.

'How about now?' I urged. 'Surely you know who I am?'

He shook his head. 'I'm sorry, but I don't. Are you famous?'

His words were like a blow. He didn't know me from Adam. Which meant he didn't know Amelia either.

'Your name isn't Sam, is it?' I asked sadly.

'No, it's Nick,' replied the man who was meant to be married to my sister.

The dog at his side gave an impatient bark. There was clearly too much standing around on this walk for his liking.

'And he isn't called Barney, is he?'

The man continued to look dumbfounded. 'He's a she, actually, and her name is Mabel.'

This time it was my turn to take a step away. This man clearly didn't know nor had ever met Amelia.

'I think my sister may have seen you and Mabel on this beach. She lives not far from here,' I offered by way of an explanation.

He shrugged. 'It's possible, although I don't come this way very often.'

'Do you live around here?'

There was a growing wariness in his eyes, and I could hardly blame him. 'Not too far away,' he said carefully, clearly unwilling to reveal more than that.

'I'm really sorry to have bothered you,' I said, holding up my hands as though in surrender. I already knew I'd be reliving this scene, in all its mortifying glory, for a very long time to come.

Nick smiled politely and I could tell he was waiting for me to go. And I would have done, if at that very moment Mabel hadn't grown too impatient with her owner and jumped up, placing her large front paws squarely on Nick's chest.

I gasped. It was the exact same pose as Amelia's final drawing. The man's dark hair was blowing in the breeze, the sun was right behind him, glinting on the water, exactly as Amelia had captured it. It was so identical to her sketch it was practically a photograph.

My lips parted in shock.

'Look. I know this is going to sound crazy, but are you in a tearing hurry to leave?'

'Why?' he asked, drawing out the word carefully.

'Because I'd really like to take your photograph,' I said. I could feel my cheeks flaming with embarrassment. It sounded like a truly sleazy chat-up line.

'Are you a photographer?' Nick asked. He ran his hand through his hair and there it was again, yet another image straight out of Amelia's sketch pad.

I swallowed nervously. 'No, I work in publishing. I'm an editor.'

Nick was still frowning, trying to put together a puzzle that clearly made no sense.

'And what do you do?' I asked, trying to spin the conversation back into something that would sound a little less bizarre.

'I work with animals,' he said evasively. It was the cue he needed to glance down at his watch. 'And I'm probably going to be late if I don't get going now.'

'Please,' I begged, aware that my voice was suddenly cracking in desperation. 'Please don't go. Can I just take one photograph of you? If I explain why, it'll only sound crazy.'

'Right,' he said, a glimmer of a smile on his lips. 'Because everything so far has been entirely normal.'

I laughed nervously. He hadn't said yes, but at least he wasn't slamming the door shut in my face. 'I know this isn't your problem, or anything to do with you, but if I could take just one photo it would really, really mean a lot to my sister.' I paused, knowing it was probably going to sound like a lie, even though it was the truth. 'She's not very well right now. She's in hospital.'

'I'm sorry to hear that,' he said, and there was enough compassion in his voice to give me hope. 'And this photo you want to take... it would really help? It would mean that much to her?'

'You have no idea,' I said with feeling.

He glanced once more at his watch and then gave an *I-can't-believe-I'm-doing-this* shrug. 'Okay then, let's make this quick.'

The good thing about having studied Amelia's drawing so closely was that I knew exactly the position Nick needed to be in for the photograph.

'Can you just crouch down, with one knee on the sand?' I asked, frantically fiddling with the filter settings on my phone's camera.

'Like this?' Nick asked, laughing as Mabel took advantage of his proximity to sweep a long tongue across his cheek. 'Do you want Mabel in the picture too?' he asked, ruffling the dog's ears.

'No,' I said, checking and double-checking the image on my phone screen. 'Barney wasn't in this one.'

He'd only just started looking at me as though I was relatively sane, and my comment had clearly set things back. Time and his patience were obviously both running out.

'If you could just move a little to your left so that the sun falls—'

He did as I asked and suddenly there on my phone screen was the picture I needed. The money shot, or so a real photographer would call it.

'And if you could turn your head this way and smile as

though you're looking at someone who *doesn't* scare the shit out of you.'

He laughed at that, and that was the moment when I took the photograph.

I knew without even checking that it would be perfect. And it was.

I'd always been good at making tough decisions, but lately I seemed to have lost the knack. It was bad enough being indecisive about the job promotion, but now I had an even more pressing issue to deal with concerning the locket. And somehow it felt harder than deciding to relocate to London for my career, or taking a gamble that the six-month dream job in New York would lead to something permanent. Although my instincts had never let me down in the past, my inner moral compass was spinning wildly on this one.

At least three times during my shower, I made up my mind to give Amelia her locket with the stranger's photograph in it, only to change it back again. My cornflakes grew soggy in their bowl as I sat at the kitchen table, flipping from one course of action to the other like a mental gymnast.

It would have been so much easier to decide if I knew the answer to one crucial question: would this make things better for Amelia, or worse? I could understand why we'd been asked to play along with her delusion, but this was different. This was *enabling*. This was helping to build a foundation for a fantasy.

In tricky situations, my knee-jerk reaction was always to ask my sister for advice. I'd never felt more lost or cast adrift as I realised this time I was truly on my own.

But there was one thing of which I *was* certain. If Amelia was to be in hospital for longer than we'd initially thought, I needed to do more to help Mum. It terrified me that I could practically see her ageing a little more each day, and it was only going to get worse. I'd never stop her from worrying about her elder daughter, but I *could* lift some of the burden from her shoulders. When Amelia was eventually discharged, she'd need someone to look after her until she got back on her feet. And – whether she'd admit it or not – Mum wasn't going to be able to do that on her own. My employers were expecting me to catch a plane back to New York in ten days but, as hard as I tried, I couldn't see that happening.

One thing Mum *had* happily agreed to, however, was splitting the extended hospital visiting hours between us.

'If you take the first shift,' I suggested, 'we can overlap for an hour or so in the middle and then I'll stick around until they chuck me out and turn out the lights.'

'That sounds sensible,' she said, making my stockpile of persuasive counter-arguments totally redundant.

That's where she'd be right now, I thought, as I glanced at the kitchen clock and bent to pull on my boots. There was still an hour or more before I needed to leave, but I was already dressed in my warm coat, with a thick scarf wound around my neck. The biting January wind hit me like a blast wave, trying to wrench the front door from my hand when I opened it. Today, the sea looked more grey than blue and was hitting the shoreline in angry, choppy waves. Grains of sand, whipped up by the wind, stung my cheeks, and yet I still paused on my way to the car to watch the wild but strangely mesmerising weather. Behind me, every windowpane was rattling in its frame, so violently I wondered how the cluster of beachside cottages had withstood the years and the elements for this long.

Safely inside Amelia's car, I checked my bag again to make sure I had everything I needed to carry out my mission. It was all there, just as it had been the last five times I'd checked. If I needed proof that I was nervous about my plan, there it was in my new-found OCD.

As I pulled away from the cottage, I spotted a figure in the distance making their way up the lane. Their progress was slow, and the wind had bowed their body into a crescent shape, yet they continued trudging doggedly up the pathway. I guessed it was Amelia's elderly fisherman neighbour, Tom Butler, who lived in the last cottage in the lane.

I slowed down to a crawl, anxious not to spray him with sand from the tyres. That still didn't stop him from looking up and glaring angrily in my direction. I responded with a cheery wave and a smile that was at odds with the colourful expletive I muttered under my breath. *And they say New Yorkers make bad neighbours.*

I found a town with a Boots self-service photo-station and, as I was running late, I parked Amelia's car on a private forecourt and prayed I wouldn't return to find its tyres clamped. Twenty minutes later, as I hurried back through a sudden downpour, I noticed something pinioned beneath one of the wiper blades. Swearing softly, I pulled the sodden piece of paper from the windscreen, not bothering to examine it until I was back in the car. Thankfully, it wasn't a parking fine, just a very soggy flyer for the business on whose forecourt I was illegally parked. It was an unsubtle reminder that I wasn't meant to be there.

The dashboard clock clicked like a metronome as I slid the photograph I'd just printed from its envelope and stared down for a long moment at Nick Whateverhisnamewas, the handsome stranger on the beach, who just so happened to be a doppelganger for my imaginary brother-in-law, Sam Wilson.

I'd remembered to bring along a pair of nail scissors and began rapidly snipping the photograph to shape. *Are you sure about this?* my inner Jiminy Cricket questioned one last time. I ignored him and carefully inserted the photograph into the locket.

8

My heart appeared to have moved to the back of my throat, where it was pounding uncomfortably, while everything I'd eaten today was suddenly spinning in my stomach on a fast cycle. I did my best to ignore my treacherous internal organs as I exited the lift and pressed the buzzer to gain entry to Amelia's ward. I was starting to recognise the nursing staff, and the one who let me in was one of my favourites.

'Good afternoon, Amelia's sister,' she said with a smile.

Once, long ago, I would have bristled at that. Back then, I hadn't wanted any of my sister's hand-me-downs – and that included her face. It was hard to remember why it had bothered me so much, because now that constant physical reminder of what future me would look like felt like a unique and magical gift.

'How is she doing today?' I asked while slathering liberal amounts of disinfectant on to my hands.

'She had a couple of wobbly moments earlier,' the nurse said, picking her words with deliberate care. 'I think she's feeling frustrated and beginning to suspect that no one really believes her.'

I pulled my tote bag closer to my side. 'Hopefully she'll feel a little better about that after today.' The nurse's eyebrows rose, but I chose not to elaborate. I'd told no one what I was planning to do: not Mum, not the doctors, not even Jeff when he'd called for a brief update on my drive to the hospital. Although admittedly he'd been more interested in the date of my return than Amelia's progress. In fact, there was only one person who knew anything about my deception – a man called Nick – and as I was unlikely ever to see him again, he didn't count.

There were dark panda-like shadows beneath Amelia's eyes, even though I knew they gave her something to help her sleep at night. Fear for her health nudged the guilt aside. Nothing was more important than getting her well again.

'Hello, you,' I said, dropping my bag and coat on to one of the visitor chairs and crossing to the bed. I hugged Amelia tightly, aware that bones that used to be more deeply set were suddenly much closer to the surface.

I bent to kiss Mum's cheek, knowing from the way she squeezed my hand that the first part of today's visit hadn't been an entirely smooth ride. Well, that was all about to change.

Amelia's eyes darted expectantly from my face to my handbag. It was hard to ignore the fleeting pang of disappointment that Mum and I were no longer enough for her. Being eclipsed by a life partner would have stung but being eclipsed by one who didn't even exist hurt a hell of a lot more.

'Did you look where I said?' Amelia asked now, her voice actually trembling with urgency. 'Did you find it?'

There was one last moment to do the right thing here. Except I no longer knew what that was.

'Yes, I found it,' I said, pasting what I hoped looked like a natural smile on my lips. 'I don't know how I managed to miss it before,' I added, as I opened my bag.

I felt rather than saw the question in my mother's eyes as I pulled out the velvet box and sprang open the lid. The moment felt weighty with déjà vu as I extracted the locket and passed it to its rightful owner.

'Lexi?' questioned Mum, so softly that I only just heard her.

She was staring up at me, a worried expression on her face. I gave a small, almost imperceptible shake of my head and turned my attention back to my sister, who was clutching the locket in her hand as though scared it might suddenly be snatched away from her. I thought she'd fall eagerly on the clasp, but she was taking her time, drawing out the big reveal in an almost theatrical way.

'Now you'll see...' she said at last. There was a small secret expression on her face and for a moment reality and fantasy blurred in confusion. Amelia was positive the locket held a photograph of the man she'd fallen in love with, and suddenly I wasn't sure if I'd done something really, really stupid. But it was too late to worry about that now, as with a small click the locket sprang open.

Time didn't really stand still as she looked down at the photograph... but it felt like everything was on pause. Amelia's face gave nothing away – and I, for one, knew better than anyone how to identify every emotion on those features.

The smile, when it came, was wider, deeper and more heartfelt than anything I'd seen before. It was a bride on her wedding day smile, or the one you give when your newborn baby is placed in your arms for the first time. I'd experienced neither of those things, nor had Amelia, but that didn't seem to matter.

'Here he is. Here's Sam,' she said, her voice thick with love for the stranger in the photograph, which I'd placed in the locket just thirty minutes ago.

Mum's mouth was opening and closing like a goldfish. She was clearly struggling to know what to say. From her expression, I knew she recognised the picture in the locket as being the same man Amelia had sketched over and over again the previous day.

'Later,' I whispered softly in reply to the question in her eyes.

'And this man, this stranger, he let you take his photograph? Why would he do something like that?'

Out of all the questions my mother asked, that was the one I hadn't really considered until this moment.

'Because I asked him to?' I suggested lamely. Now that I heard the words out loud, it did seem rather peculiar. 'Maybe he's just a really decent guy who likes helping damsels in distress.'

Mum gave a classic harrumph that she'd clearly inherited from my grandmother. 'You're not exactly the helpless damsel type – nor is Amelia. Well, not usually,' she corrected sadly.

'I don't know why he did it, Mum,' I said, looking up as a

ping announced the arrival of the lift. 'I'm just glad that he did.'

Amelia had been so intent on studying the photograph of her fake husband, she'd scarcely looked up when I told her I was going to accompany Mum down to the foyer and see her safely into a taxi.

'And you're sure this man doesn't actually know Amelia?'

'As sure as I can be,' I said, shuffling closer to the far corner of the lift to make room for incoming occupants. 'There was absolutely no recognition on his face when he saw me.' Mum nodded slowly. 'Although I do think it's likely Amelia has seen him on the beach at some time, even if it was only in passing.'

'But how would she remember a total stranger in such detail?' Mum asked, playing devil's advocate. All those hours of watching TV detective shows had certainly sharpened her interrogation technique.

'I don't know. Because he's really good-looking?' I suggested. 'Or maybe it was his dog that caught her attention.'

'Barney,' said Mum.

'Mabel,' I corrected.

We reached the foyer, where beyond the revolving doors I could see Mum's taxi already idling at the kerb. 'I'll speak to the charge nurse before I go home and tell her about the locket,' I said, kissing Mum's cheek and trying to ignore the vague look of reproach on her face.

What had I done?

There was a change to Amelia that I didn't need the bank of monitors to confirm. She looked calmer and more at peace. Both her heart rate and her blood pressure had lowered and if that was in any way because of the photograph in the locket, then I could happily live with my deception.

The necklace was now around her neck, the stranger's photo as close to her heart as the spaghetti tangle of wires would allow. Every now and then Amelia's fingers would reach up and caress the silver trinket, as though to reassure herself it was still there.

'I suppose this will have to do until he gets back from New York.' A frown creased her forehead. 'Are you absolutely sure I didn't mention any details about the silent retreat place he's gone to?'

I have a habit of flushing when I lie, and I only hoped Amelia was so absorbed in staring at 'Sam's' photograph, she wouldn't look up and catch me out.

'No, you just said that he'd be out of touch for two weeks.'

Amelia shook her head. 'I can't even remember having that conversation, but Mum said exactly the same thing earlier.' She sighed and brought the photograph to her lips, kissing the stranger's face.

'I'm so glad you found the locket though,' she said, leaning back tiredly on the pillows when I later bent to kiss her goodbye. 'Thank you, Lexi. I knew you wouldn't let me down.'

'Never,' I said, embarrassed to hear the catch in my voice.

She reached for my hand and curled her fingers around mine, and for just a moment everything in the world felt right again.

The wind was howling ferociously, whistling around Amelia's cottage and reminding me of *The Wizard of Oz* right before the house went airborne. I peered through the window, but the beach was pitch-black and torrential rain made it impossible to see anything.

I returned to the comfortable settee where I'd been attempting to do some reading for work, only to glance up worriedly as the lights flickered. They'd been doing that throughout the evening and each time the electricity seemed to take a few seconds longer before deciding to come back on.

I picked up my Kindle and tried to slip back into the story, but it was a romantic thriller, with a witless protagonist who'd just gone into the attic to investigate an inexplicable banging noise. *As if anyone in their right mind would do that*, I thought, when right on cue an inexplicable banging noise echoed through the cottage.

I leapt to my feet, looking around for my trusty meat tenderiser weapon before remembering it was currently halfway through the dishwasher cycle. There was nothing in Amelia's neat and tidy lounge to defend myself with, unless I was planning on suffocating an intruder with one of her many scatter cushions.

The banging sounded more urgent now and, feeling a little foolish, I finally separated the sound from the noise of the storm and realised it was coming from the front door. The only unsolved mystery here was what anyone was doing out in this weather. Through the frosted panel on the door, I could just about make out a shape. From their hazy outline, I thought whoever was outside was probably male. But not *really tall*, I acknowledged, with an odd feeling of disappointment.

This was Somerset and not New York, but I still double-checked the security chain was in place before easing open the door.

I recognised the caller immediately. The fisherman-style waterproofs made for an easy clue, and I'd seen the same sou'wester on Amelia's neighbour earlier in the day.

'Hello,' I said, through the crack in the door, still reluctant to open it. *You can take the girl out of New York...*

'It's Tuesday,' my caller said gruffly.

Feeling foolish for my big-city caution, I released the chain and opened the door wider. Waterproofs or no, the man still looked as though he'd taken a detour to go wading in the sea on his way to my door. Raindrops were falling faster than tears down his wrinkled cheeks, and several were waiting to drip from the end of his beaky nose. At least, I hoped they were raindrops.

'It's Tuesday,' the man repeated dourly.

I stared at him in confusion. Had he really ventured out in a torrential storm simply to tell me what day of the week it was? Amelia had never mentioned that he suffered from senility, but how often had they even spoken, anyway? The man seemed to be waiting for a response. 'So it is,' I agreed pleasantly.

'You've not put the bins out. We'll get rats again,' he said in a tone that could only be described as a growl.

'Oh, I'm sorry, I didn't—'

He cut short my apology by taking one step closer and peering at me through the shadowy light.

'You're not her, are you?' It was halfway between an observation and an accusation. Even so, I was impressed. There were members of our own family who wouldn't have spotted the difference in this light.

'Your voice is different. And there's something about your mouth that looks all wrong.'

I wasn't sure if I'd just been insulted, but I chose to skip past it. Amelia's crusty neighbour might look like the old man of the sea, but there was clearly nothing wrong with his eyes.

'My name is Lexi. I'm Amelia's sister. That's the woman who lives here,' I added, unsure if my sister and her elderly neighbour had ever introduced themselves properly.

'I know that,' the old man said, his tone dismissive. 'The police mentioned her name the other day when they were snooping around here.'

Snooping wasn't exactly the term I'd have gone with, but I let it go as I suddenly realised that this cantankerous old man might be one of the few people who could shed some light on what had happened to Amelia on that fateful night.

'Do you mind me asking if you were able to tell them anything?'

'Shouldn't that be confidential information?' he asked craftily. He was clearly another armchair TV detective. He'd get on well with my mother, I thought wryly.

'Look, would you like to come in for a moment? I could make us some tea, or something,' I said, trying not to show how anxious I was for any snippet of information.

The man shook his head, inadvertently sprinkling me with water from his sou'wester. 'Saw nothing. Heard nothing,' he muttered succinctly. 'That's what I told them, and I don't mind telling you the same.'

He turned as though to go and then seemed to think better of it. 'Where is she now then, your sister?'

'She's in the hospital,' I said, hearing the unmistakable thread of concern that had crept into my voice. 'She's lucky to be alive.'

The old man's eyes might have once been a piercing blue,

but the years and the sea had watered them down. His mouth was moving, as though he was chewing over his response but couldn't quite manage to spit it out.

'Just make sure you put them bins out,' he said eventually, turning to go once again. He waited until he was at the very end of the footpath, and I'd almost closed the door, before he swivelled back to face me. 'I hope she gets better soon,' he said, and before I could formulate a thank you, he was already shuffling back towards his own cottage.

'Me too,' I said, leaning back against the front door, surprised to find an unexpected smile on my lips.

9

'So, you're *not* coming back next week, then?'
There was a good reason why I'd put off making this phone call for several days, and there was little satisfaction in hearing it play out exactly the way I'd thought it would.

'I just don't see how I can, Jeff. Not yet.'

'It's pretty easy, really. You phone up the airline, you give them your charge card number and in return they give you a seat on the plane.'

Jeff's sarcasm felt like fingernails being dragged down a blackboard.

'It's not that I don't *want* to come back,' I said, wondering how true that even was. 'It's just there's no way I can leave right now. Mum and Amelia still need me here.' *And I need them*, I silently acknowledged. When disaster strikes people you love, it's only natural for you to cleave together, to hold on even tighter to the family you have left. I remember that only too well, because that's what happened before.

'But what about your job? You've worked so hard to get this opportunity.' Jeff was bringing out the heavy artillery now. And he was right; I'd had to work twice as hard as anyone else on the team to justify every rung I'd climbed on the career ladder.

'They're being great,' I said, my smile going a little tight as I thought back to the other call that I'd been dreading to make, which had actually gone far better than this one was currently doing. 'Monica has agreed to let me work remotely on a part-time basis for the next few weeks, until we know where things stand with Amelia, and they're not pressuring me for a decision on the executive editor role.' *For now*, I added silently.

'That's reasonable of them,' said Jeff, in a way that made me think he didn't entirely mean it. 'I guess I just miss you being here in New York,' he said eventually.

I wondered if he was even aware that what he'd just said wasn't the same as saying he missed me. But did I even want him to say that when I couldn't – hand on heart – say the same?

'Perhaps we need to sit down and talk about things properly when you get back,' Jeff said carefully.

Fortunately, the line chose that moment to erupt in a crackle of static, buying me time to wonder if it was a *let's call it quits* conversation or a *let's move in together* one that he was suggesting. How bad was it that I had absolutely no idea what was in his head?

'Sure,' I said, cowardly taking the easy way out. 'We should do that when I get back.'

There was a new pattern to my days. I got up early each morning, finally conceding it was the seagulls, rather than my body clock, who got to decide when I'd slept enough. I'd splash icy cold water on my face, which brought a rosiness to my cheeks. Then, long before the sun was up, I'd pull on my borrowed sportswear and head out for a morning run. Jeff would hardly recognise this new version of me – because I hardly recognised her myself. But for the first time in my life, I began to see how running could be addictive. Pounding along the beach by the water's edge, my thoughts felt somehow cleaner and sharper. The decisions I tussled with in the middle of the night seemed to find a way of resolving themselves as my footprints scored into the unmarked sand.

I never saw a soul on my morning runs. And I told myself I didn't want to. And yet, for reasons I chose not to examine closely, each day I headed towards the mudflats and not to the nearest village. Once back at the cottage, I'd spend the morning catching up on the work emails that seemed to breed like rabbits in my inbox overnight.

But afternoons and evenings were Amelia time. I'd worked out the best shortcut to the hospital, and even had a favourite parking spot in the multistorey car park. Somehow the security guard in the main reception had discovered I lived in New York and greeted me each day with a *Friends*-style *How are you doing?*, which I still found funny, although I could see that might easily fade in time.

If I'd had even the smallest of doubts about my decision to stay, they would have evaporated the moment I told Mum I was extending my visit. I could practically see her standing a little taller, as though a heavy weight had been lifted from her shoulders.

If she'd been more her normal self, *more Amelia*, then I'm sure my sister would have been delighted I was still here.

Although a totally back-to-normal Amelia was more likely to have told me to 'get my arse back on a plane before I screw up my career and why the hell was I dithering about accepting that promotion?' She'd probably also have thrown in something cutting about it being time I flew solo and stopped using her and Mum as an excuse not to take chances. It was strange, really, that she and Jeff didn't get on better, because they clearly thought along the same lines.

The one thing I didn't think I'd ever get used to was the feeling of uncertainty as I approached Amelia's room. On her good days, I'd leave the ward with a hopeful spring in my step. But on her bad ones, I could feel despondency shadowing me like a stalker all the way back to the car.

As an editor, words had always fascinated me. But these days my laptop search history was full of ones I wished I'd never heard. *Confabulation* was currently number one on that list.

'It doesn't even sound like a real word,' Mum had complained after our discussion with one of the many doctors involved in Amelia's care. We seemed to be working our way through every medical department in the hospital, as though it were an à la carte menu. The young female physician with hair so blonde it was practically white hailed from the psychotherapy department.

'What you need to understand,' she explained patiently, 'is that someone who confabulates is not lying. They truly believe everything they are telling you. So, to Amelia this husband she talks about is very real. In her mind, he definitely exists.'

'And this confab thingy—' Mum began.

'Confabulation,' I supplied quietly.

Mum flashed me a grateful smile. 'Do you think it was caused when her heart stopped beating?'

In the space of less than two weeks, I'd learnt one thing to be true of every doctor we'd met: they hated being asked questions they couldn't answer.

'It's hard to say for sure. There are many different reasons why it occurs.' She extended a slender hand and began counting off our worst nightmares on her fingertips. 'Psychiatric disorders, traumatic brain injury, even some types of Alzheimer's have been known to cause it.'

There was a long moment of silence while we waited to see who would ask the sixty-four-thousand-dollar question. In the end, I did. 'And can you cure it?'

'We can *manage* it,' the doctor answered.

I shook my head. 'Will my sister always believe this imaginary husband actually exists, and am I making things worse by encouraging her to believe something we know to be untrue.'

The doctor's smile was so fleeting I almost missed it. 'The most important word in that sentence is that you are still *encouraging* her, rather than dismissing her claims.' She gave a small, barely audible sigh. 'Sometimes patients themselves will begin to realise that the facts they're clinging to simply don't add up. That can be a real breakthrough moment.'

'And sometimes...?' I prompted, already knowing the answer, but needing to hear it out loud.

The doctor didn't disappoint. 'And sometimes they don't.'

Physically, Amelia was beginning to show signs of improvement. For a start, she was hooked up to far less machinery than before. It meant we were able to take slow, careful walks along the hospital corridor, wheeling her trusty IV beside us as we went. She clung to my arm on these jaunts, terrified of letting go. I wondered if she remembered it was exactly how I'd been at our local lido when she was teaching me to swim. Or when she ran alongside my bike on the day the trainer wheels were finally removed.

'Don't let go,' she implored me now, echoing the words I'd once said to her as I took her entire body weight on my arm. I answered her the same way she'd done to me all those years ago. 'Don't panic. I've got you. I'm right here.'

I just wished supporting her mentally was as easy as assisting her up and down that corridor. The afternoons, when the shadows grew longer, were when Amelia's thoughts turned melancholy. In a way, it was good that Mum rarely got to see the defeat that crept over her like a second sickness as she grew increasingly tired.

'Why is Sam taking so long to get here?' It was a frequent question, posed almost daily, and I'd formulated a collection of stock replies. Some days they even worked. But not today. 'Surely he can't still be at that stupid retreat place?'

'I don't know, Mimi,' I said, feigning a sudden interest in the clouds scudding past the window. It was always easier to lie when I didn't have to look directly at her. 'One of the girls in my office went to one of those places for a week and ended up staying almost a month. Some people just need longer to recharge mentally than others.'

'Wouldn't he have asked them to let me know if that's what he was doing?'

I really wanted to say *Good point*, but of course I couldn't.

My explanations were so full of holes, they were virtually sieve-like.

'Is there something about Sam that you're not telling me?' Amelia asked unexpectedly, late one afternoon. *Like he's not real, you mean*, I thought sadly.

'Like what?'

'Has something bad happened to him that you don't want me to know? Has he been in an accident?'

'No,' I replied, crossing my fingers behind my back to cancel out the lie, because that still worked when you were in your thirties, didn't it?

Amelia lay back on the pillows, turning her gaze towards the window, where the light of day was already fading.

'Has he left me, Lexi? Is that what's happened?'

I swallowed noisily. Was this one of those breakthrough moments the doctors had said might come?

'Do *you* think he's left you?' I parried, cowardly batting the question back to her.

She looked beyond the skyline of rooftops and telegraph wires, seeing something other than the view. Slowly she shook her head. 'No. And deep down I don't think you believe that either. Not after everything I've told you about us.'

I did my best to fix a smile that felt genuine on my face. Retelling the story of her romance with Sam had somehow become part of our daily visits. Perhaps I was better at listening and pretending than Mum was. Whatever the reason, I'd been privy to an almost date-by-date account of their relationship. Her recall of something that had never actually happened was truly astonishing, as she recounted their love story in such detail that sometimes I even found myself blushing.

I knew about their first date, first kiss, even the first time they'd made love. I knew the places he'd taken her – even the clothes she'd worn. I knew their story so well, I could have given it to a ghost writer and had them pen a book about their romance.

The thought felt like a striking bell that I couldn't silence.

'But I have nothing to prove that any of it happened,' Amelia said sadly, her hand clasped around her locket. 'There are photos of us on his phone and on mine too… but you say mine is still missing, and who knows where Sam's is.'

If Sam really was a flesh-and-blood absent husband, rather than one who lived only in her head, I would have asked if she'd backed up her phone to the cloud, or we could have searched for him on Facebook. In truth, I could have suggested a dozen different ways of tracking him down, but the doctors had cautioned us about directly challenging Amelia on her confabulation. 'The doubts have to come from her,' the physicians had warned.

'There are so many things I can't remember properly,' she said now, her voice forlorn. 'There are huge gaping holes in my head that scare the life out of me. What if all my memories of Sam get sucked into them? What if everything I remember is taken away from me? What will I do then? How will I go on?'

Her tears were falling fast at just the thought of losing someone who didn't even exist. I should have been whooping at the possibility of Sam's presence finally being exorcised, but I couldn't do that. Not when I could see how it was breaking her heart.

'That won't happen. We won't let it,' I told her, gathering her up in my arms and rocking her like a lost child.

★

I waited to see if the bitter night air would knock the crazy notion from my head as I left the hospital that evening. But it was still with me as I entered the dank stairwell of the multistorey car park and climbed the numerous flights to reach my car. It remained in my head for the entire journey back to the cottage and refused to budge when I attempted to immerse myself in a box set I was currently bingeing. After thirty minutes' viewing, I gave up. I knew the plot anyway, for it was based on a book we'd published eighteen months earlier.

'Your neighbour is the murderer,' I told the guileless heroine before switching off the TV.

I drew my laptop from its case and switched it on. Opening a blank Word document, I headed up a table with two columns. The first I titled *Pros* and the second *Cons*. I spent the next hour filling them in. Cons contained angry little comments like: 'You'd be feeding her fantasy' and 'It's preventing her from seeing the truth'. But the other column was far kinder. It was filled with sentences that read: 'It would make her happy' and 'It might help her to recover'. It didn't take long to see that the Pro column was twice as long as its neighbour. But it was more than just maths that eventually decided me. It was my final notation in the Pro side. 'I have to do this, because she loves him... and I love her.'

It was one thing to have made up my mind on this bizarre course of action, but another thing entirely to execute it. First, I had to decide if I wanted to tell anyone what I was planning to do. I tried to visualise my mother's face when I told her: *I'm going to search for the man on the beach, the one who looks like Amelia's Sam, and persuade him to pose for some more photos – ones with me in them this time.* I shook my head, already knowing how that would play out. It was far better to present it to everyone if – or when – I managed to accomplish it.

And in truth, that was going to be my biggest hurdle. I was honest enough to admit finally that part of me had been unconsciously looking for the stranger on the beach on each of my morning runs. But he'd never returned to the area since that day. *Can you really blame him?* the voice of my conscience screamed out in my head. *You acted like a crazy person.* I reached for my glass of wine and tried to silence the voice with alcohol.

Come on, think, I urged my brain as I stared down at the blinking cursor on my search bar. What do you know about him? Cast your mind back. What did he reveal? I love a challenge as much as the next person, but this one seemed insurmountable. All I knew was that his first name was Nick, that he lived not far from here, and that he owned a dog named Mabel. I typed these paltry facts into the search bar and unsurprisingly got absolutely nothing. There was something else, wasn't there? Something else he'd mentioned on that day. But as hard as I tried, I couldn't summon it up from the depths of my subconscious.

Sleep on a problem, Mum always used to advise, so I did, but the solution wasn't miraculously there when the seagulls screamed me awake the next morning. It wasn't there when I cleaned my teeth, or when I swallowed a mug of strong black coffee before lacing up my trainers. But it came to me, finally, in a lightning bolt of clarity as I ran along the beach, the way I'd always suspected that it might.

I work with animals. That's what he'd said. It wasn't a lot to go on, but it was something. It was a place to start.

My feet flew across the sand in my haste to get back to the cottage. My watch recorded my time as a 'personal best'. I only hoped the same could be said of my plan.

10

The list was surprisingly long and yet I still kept adding to it. Although admittedly the last few ideas were a bit of a stretch. How likely was it *really* that the tall, dark-haired man worked in a circus or was a dolphin trainer? But the bullet-pointed professions at the top of the page in my notepad were definitely a good place to start my search.

- Vet
- Zookeeper
- Police dog handler

I could see the man in each of those professions, particularly the police one. There had been something about him that made me think of law and order or a peacekeeper.

Ignoring the work emails that I really ought to be answering, or the alarming number of submissions I was meant to read, I prepared a fresh mug of strong coffee and settled down at Amelia's kitchen table with my laptop.

I began by searching the websites of every veterinary

practice in the area, going straight to the Meet the Team tab. I found vets of every age, shape and size, but none with piercing blue eyes and jet-black hair.

With one last surgery on my list, my expectations were low as I summoned up The Willows website. I flicked quickly through the photographs of their vets, but none matched the face of the man from Amelia's drawings.

Much later, I'd marvel at how close I came to shutting down the surgery's internet window, but something was tugging at my subconscious. I clicked my way back through the photographs, ending up exactly where I'd started, with a vet dressed in surgical scrubs, wearing a theatre cap pulled so low down it was practically colliding with his dark-framed glasses. It was impossible to see the colour of his hair, but there was something about the lower half of his face... I enlarged the photograph until it filled my entire laptop screen and then took my reporter's notepad and held it over the upper half of his face, obscuring the black-framed glasses that hid his eyes from view.

My attention was drawn to his mouth with its open, friendly smile, but I'd also seen those lips twisted in wry humour. It felt almost unnecessary, but I reached for my mobile and clicked on the photograph I'd taken on the beach. I held it up beside the image on my laptop screen.

'Snap,' I said softly, astounded that I'd actually found him. Still shaking my head in amazement, I clicked on his bio beside the photograph. It told me far more than he'd been willing to reveal on the beach. I read it through several times, as though there'd be questions later. I discovered that Nicholas Forrester, BVetMed MRCVS, graduated from the Royal Veterinary College thirteen years ago. I learnt that his specialism was in small animal surgery – which explained the scrubs – and, more interestingly, that aside from being the senior vet, he owned the practice. It seemed like an impressive achievement for someone who was only seven years older than me – another fact I'd uncovered. The bio went on to reveal that his hobbies included walking his Old English Sheepdog on the beach (something I already knew) and that he enjoyed playing the guitar and reading in his free time.

I clicked on the photo gallery tab, hoping to find another one of Nick, but they were mostly interior shots of the surgery and one final photograph of the building's exterior. There was no one to hear my gasp of surprise, which sounded extraordinarily loud in the quiet of Amelia's empty kitchen. The chair legs scraped on the old quarry-tiled floor as I pushed away from the table, plucked up my car keys and ran towards the door.

I blipped the car and flung open the door, dropping to a crouch beside the footwell. The flyer was exactly where I'd stowed it days ago, in the driver's door pocket. I shivered as I reached for it, but not because I was cold. The wind tried to snatch the paper from my fingers as I slowly unfurled it. I'm not sure how long I stayed there, hunkered down beside the car, my eyes transfixed on the piece of paper in my hand. This was weird. No. It was beyond weird; it was freaky. I had been there, been at The Willows Veterinary Surgery. In a town I didn't know, in a private car park I should never have been in, I'd somehow managed to end up at exactly the place I'd been trying to find. I'd been right there, outside the surgery where Nick Forrester worked, and I couldn't even begin to calculate what the odds were of that happening.

⋆

Patience has never really been my thing. I'd always been known as the impulsive one in our family. So having to wait a full twenty-four hours before I could visit The Willows once again was a huge frustration. I even contemplated ducking out of the afternoon visiting session at the hospital. But the thought of Amelia lifting her head hopefully, the way she always did whenever she heard anyone approach her room, persuaded me that my plan was going to have to wait. I couldn't be yet another person Amelia was waiting for, who failed to show up.

At least the delay gave me time to work out how best to put forward my rather strange proposal. I even wrote it out, determined that every word should earn its place to create the compassion and sympathy I needed Nick to feel so he'd agree to help a total stranger – albeit one who believed he was her husband. I practised my speech out loud several times throughout the evening, in the way I always did before presenting an important pitch at work. I even fell asleep that night with the words running through my head.

I had a terrible night. My sleep had been disturbed by pretty much every anxiety dream in the book. It started with the one where you're up on stage and have totally forgotten your lines. Then I was driving the wrong way up a motorway and couldn't find an exit. My subconscious even had me arriving at a job interview still wearing my pyjamas.

Every minute of lost rest was visible in the mirror as I studied my reflection the following morning. Even an invigorating morning run couldn't cancel out the poor night's sleep. I'd spent a little longer than usual on the beach, scanning the horizon for a tall man with an extremely large and shaggy dog, because I would have preferred to put forward my proposition on neutral territory. But once again, the beach was entirely empty.

I took extra care getting ready for the day. I even unearthed my tongs from the bottom of my suitcase and spent time curling my hair, attempting to create some 'natural' beachy waves. Which was a bit of a joke because the real-life effect the beach had on my hair was pretty horrendous. I rummaged deep into my bag of cosmetics and found a neutral eyeshadow and my mascara wand. I applied both with care and then studied the result before giving my reflection a tiny nod of approval. A slick of soft pink gloss on my lips and I was done.

I didn't stop to question why I thought that making an effort with my appearance was going to help my case, I just knew it wouldn't hurt either. I pulled on a pair of dark indigo jeans and a fluffy red jumper that suited my colouring.

I'd checked the veterinary surgery website for their opening hours, so I expected the car park to be busier than it had been the other day, but I was totally unprepared for having to circle it several times before eventually finding a space. People were emerging from vehicles all around me, pulling reluctant dogs with tails tucked between their legs, or carrying baskets with scrabbling cats who sounded like trapped banshees. Did no one *ever* want to go inside here, I wondered, as I walked nervously towards the entrance. The pulse beating at the base of my throat revealed I might be just as reluctant as the four-legged visitors.

The surgery had a light, airy reception that was surprisingly large. It was also surprisingly full. There were three people queueing at the desk, waiting to be seen, and a quick glance at the waiting area showed that every seat was already taken. Too late, it occurred to me that turning up in the middle of morning surgery might not have been such a good idea.

I waited in line behind a woman cradling a cute-looking puppy, a teenager with a rabbit and a man with a noisily squawking bird. Finally, it was my turn.

'Good morning,' said an attractive red-haired receptionist with brisk efficiency. 'How can I help you?'

'I'd like to see Mr Forrester, please.'

Her eyes flashed across to her computer screen. 'Do you have an appointment?'

'No. I'm sorry, I don't. But I only need to see him for a few minutes.' *Six* minutes actually; that was how long it took for me to get through my prepared speech.

The woman was shaking her head as though I had just said something totally implausible.

'I'm afraid Mr Forrester's schedule is fully booked for this morning.'

I'd imagined all kinds of obstacles that I might need to get past, but naively this hadn't been one of them. How foolish of me to have thought I could simply rock up and get seen. But I hadn't come all this way to give up so easily.

'Is there no way at all that he could see me? Could you possibly squeeze me in? I don't mind waiting.'

The woman's gaze flashed meaningfully to the room full of clients and their accompanying pets, all of whom had bona fide appointments. 'As you can see, we're incredibly busy today. Is it an emergency?'

I bit my lip. 'In a way yes, it is.'

I was irritating her, I could see this, and if veterinary surgery receptionists were anything like their doctor counterparts, I realised that was a really bad thing to be doing.

'What sort of animal do you have with you?' she asked now, rising slightly in her seat to examine whatever might be sitting beside me.

'Erm, actually I don't have an animal. I don't even own a pet. That's not why I'm here.'

'Well, I'm terribly sorry, *madam*, but as you can see, we're right in the middle of morning surgery at the moment.' Back in the States, I rather liked it when people called me *ma'am*, but the receptionist had said it as though I was something unfortunate that one of the clients had done on the floor. 'Perhaps you could come back another time, but I'm afraid you won't be able to see him today.'

'Won't be able to see who?' asked a voice that made us both jump. In unison, the receptionist and I turned our heads towards a corridor beside the desk.

Nick Forrester was smiling easily at the pretty young woman on reception, and the irritated, long-suffering expression I'd been on the receiving end of evaporated as though it had never been there.

He switched his gaze to the other side of the counter and there was a moment when time seemed to stand still as his eyes fell on my face. Did he recognise me, I wondered suddenly? I certainly looked more presentable than the flushed-faced, ponytailed jogger he'd met on the beach.

'It's you,' he declared in surprise, as I released the breath I hadn't even known I was holding.

'It *is* me,' I said stupidly. I could feel the receptionist's eyes on me like tiny little lasers and I was pretty sure half the waiting room were also focused on the interesting little scene being played out before them.

'I tracked you down on the internet,' I said unthinkingly. It was a comment designed to make any sensible person run for the hills, or instantly want to take out a restraining order. 'I mean, the practice. I tracked down where you worked.' I wasn't making this any better at all.

'How interesting,' said Nick Forrester, his brow furrowing above the black-framed glasses, the ones that made him look both familiar and unfamiliar at the same time. 'Why were you looking for me, exactly?'

I was blushing now; I could feel the flush of blood rising up from my neck to my cheeks and not stopping until my face was exactly the same shade as my jumper.

'It's... it's kind of personal,' I said, glancing around at our captive audience. I'd spoken as softly as I could, but I'd definitely ignited the interest of the waiting room now.

'Oh, I see,' Nick said, taking off his glasses and bending lower to read the receptionist's computer screen.

'Is Mr Barton here with Dusty yet?' he asked, peering at what I could only assume was the appointment system.

Even when she scowled, the receptionist was annoyingly attractive. 'No. Not yet,' she said reluctantly.

Nick Forrester straightened up and gave me a fleeting smile. 'Then I can spare you two minutes.'

Two minutes wasn't going to be enough to get through my plea, but at least he wasn't throwing me out, which was better than I could have hoped for, given that I still sounded dangerously like a crazed stalker.

I followed him down a brightly lit corridor, passing several examination rooms before turning into what appeared to be an office cum staffroom at the end of the passageway.

There was an enticing aroma of freshly made coffee coming from an expensive-looking espresso machine in the corner. I would have gratefully accepted a cup if I'd been asked, but it seemed unlikely that he'd be offering me one. Instead, he turned to face me and leant back against a desk strewn with files, magazines and all manner of paperwork. His long legs were stretched out, covering half of the available space between us. My own were starting to feel a little less than steady, but he didn't ask me to sit down. I was painfully aware that the countdown on my two-minute timer was already running. And yet the first thing that came out of my mouth wasn't what I'd planned to say at all.

'Your glasses,' I said, pointing to the dark frames that he was still holding in one hand. He looked down at them, as though almost surprised to find them there, before slipping them back on his nose.

And that was when I realised why he'd looked so familiar and also why the idea of him being in law enforcement hadn't felt that far off-beam.

'They make you look like Superman – or rather, you look like Clark Kent when he's pretending *not* to be Superman.' My voice trailed away and I wondered if anyone had ever so spectacularly ruined their own plans the way my wayward tongue seemed determined to do.

But instead of politely showing me to the door, Nick surprised me by laughing. It was a rich and full sound, the kind of laugh that is almost infectious. 'That's not the first time I've been told that.'

The tension boiling inside me slowly dropped to a simmer. 'You weren't wearing them the other day on the beach. You look completely different without them,' I said artlessly.

He shrugged his broad shoulders. 'They get in the way when you're leaping tall buildings,' he said with a flash of that wry smile again, 'or when you're out running with your dog.'

He had the kind of sense of humour I liked, the type that didn't mind poking fun at himself. It was something Jeff never did. I stopped that train of thought before it even left the station. I had a feeling that comparing these two men would reveal more than I wanted to admit right now.

'As fascinating as it would be to sit here and chat about eyewear all morning...' Nick began.

I pulled myself together with a visible jerk.

'Of course, yes, I'm sorry. I know you're really busy.'

He nodded and I saw him glance surreptitiously down at his watch.

I drew in a deep breath, sad that my carefully prepared script would have to be abandoned. I opened my mouth, but before I could say a word, Nick cut in with a question of his own.

'How is your sister doing? Did the photograph achieve whatever you hoped it would?'

Time was short now, but thankfully he'd unwittingly opened the door and allowed me to fast-forward to the purpose of my visit.

'She's doing a little better,' I said, and then smiled at him. 'And thank you for thinking to ask about her – or even for remembering about our previous encounter.'

'It's not the kind of thing you forget in a hurry,' he said, which worryingly could be interpreted in several different ways. I chose to believe he meant it in a positive one.

'The thing is, what you did for her the other day – posing for a photograph – well, I was wondering if you'd be able to do it again... not just for one actually, but maybe for half a dozen or so.'

I truly don't know what I was expecting. Questions? Certainly. A request to think about it? Very possibly. Perhaps even a compliant *Sure, why not*. But I got none of the above.

'Absolutely not,' he said in a totally pleasant voice.

His refusal threw me, because I'd really thought things had been going rather well up until that point.

'I... I could pay you... you know, for your time,' I ad-libbed, instantly making things so much worse.

'No, thank you,' Nick said, straightening up from the desk. He really was incredibly tall, or was I cowering a little in defeat? At such close quarters, I had to tilt my head right back to meet his eyes. 'To be perfectly frank, it was weird enough the other day.'

I could feel my throat tightening up and my voice, when I spoke, sounded perilously close to cracking. 'My sister has "lost" someone. Someone who looks just like you.'

'You told me that, the other day,' he reminded me, already striding towards the door.

'The photograph I took last time... it really gave her a sense of comfort.'

'Surely a *false* sense of comfort,' he countered. 'How can she differentiate between fact and fiction if you keep lying to her?' It was almost as though he'd been right there in the cottage with me while I was writing out the *Cons* list.

'Look, I know this might seem like a very strange way of helping her, but you have to believe me, I *know* her, I know her better than I know anyone else on earth. And I really, really think this would help her. I wouldn't be suggesting it if I didn't.'

'And do her doctors agree with you? Have they sanctioned this course of action?'

Lie. Lie. Lie, I told myself, but somehow the command didn't reach my tongue in time.

'No, they haven't. But that doesn't mean it's not the right thing to do.'

He was at the door now, holding it open for me to go through first, but my feet had turned into dead weights on the ends of my legs.

'I know you want to do everything you can for your sister,' Nick said kindly. 'And I really admire that. But given a choice, I would always recommend going with medical advice.'

I could practically hear my hopes crashing to the floor. He was a veterinarian. A man of science and not steel. *Obviously* he was going to side with the doctors.

'And even if I didn't think this was a cataclysmically bad idea,' he said, 'it also sounds like it would be quite a heavy commitment, time-wise, and as you already saw from our reception, I'm kept pretty busy around here.'

I looked frantically around the room, searching for anything that might help me to change his mind, and that's when I saw it, on the corner of the desk. It was a double photo frame, the kind that opens like a book. On one side, a much younger version of Nick Forrester was standing beside an incredibly pretty blonde, who was holding a tiny baby in her arms. The other half of the frame held what I assumed was a far more recent photograph. Like most people without kids, I'm fairly bad at ageing them, but I thought this one looked to be about seven or eight. Instinctively, I knew the girl was the baby from the other photograph. That she was Nick's daughter was so obvious, I didn't even bother asking; she looked just like him.

Of course he wasn't going to agree to appear in a series of staged romantic poses with me. He was married. He had a family. What the hell had I been thinking? Sanity returned, and with it a feeling of shame that was going to take quite a while to fade away.

'Thank you very much for seeing me. And thank you for listening. I realise you didn't have to.'

'You piqued my curiosity,' he admitted.

'Well, I'm sorry for taking up your time. Please just forget I ever came today. I won't bother you again,' I promised, holding out my hand for him to shake it.

To Nick's credit, he didn't hesitate before gripping my hand. His handshake was warm and firm, but it was clearly terminating our meeting today.

'It was no bother,' he assured me, as our hands fell apart. 'And, like I said, this isn't the kind of thing that's easy to forget.'

We were out in the corridor now and I scuttled ahead of him, desperate to get out of there. Just before we re-entered the reception area, his hand briefly touched my elbow, stalling me.

'I really do wish your sister a full and speedy recovery.'

A huge lump suddenly formed in my throat, preventing me from replying, and by the time I swallowed it away it was already too late.

'Mr Barton,' Nick said, addressing a middle-aged man waiting on the chairs. 'Would you and Dusty like to come through now?'

11

It was a real light-bulb moment, which was ironic because it happened just seconds before the lights went out. I was curled up on Amelia's comfy two-seater, a soft, fluffy blanket over my legs and a bowl of warm, sticky popcorn beside me. On the television, Ryan Gosling was manfully rowing Rachel McAdams back to land in the middle of a downpour.

Outside the cottage, the weather was giving the on-screen conditions a run for their money. So much so that I'd turned up the volume to drown out the howl of the wind. It probably wasn't necessary, because I'd seen *The Notebook* so often I could practically quote every line in the script. But losing myself in the familiar story felt comforting, like going home. I was in my happy place – and then suddenly my thoughts were catapulted away from the action on the screen.

We'd gone out in a small rowing boat when the heavens suddenly opened up. My hair was plastered to my head and the blue dress I was wearing was sticking to me like a second skin. But none of that mattered because I knew he was going to kiss me the moment we got back on to land. I just knew it.

But those words hadn't been spoken by Allie, the fictional character in the famous Nicholas Sparks love story. They were how Amelia had described her and Sam's first kiss.

On the screen, Ryan Gosling was crushing his co-star against him, but my attention was somewhere else entirely. Had *all* of Amelia's so-called memories, the ones she'd relayed in such minute detail, originated in films or from TV? I ran through a couple of them, and now that I was looking for it, I identified at least two that I recognised from well-known movies and another with more than a passing similarity to a scene in a classic bestseller. The tapestry of my sister's love affair had been carefully stolen from the pages of fiction and a world of make-believe, and the realisation was so sad it made me want to curl up in a ball and sob for all the things I couldn't change or make better for her.

And then it happened. A flash of lightning illuminated the room through the fabric of the curtains, followed quickly by one of the loudest thunderclaps I'd ever heard, and then, with a sudden pop, the electricity went out. I froze, like a rabbit on a motorway, waiting for the lights to come back, but the seconds ticked past and the cottage remained in darkness.

Cautiously, I unfurled my legs and got to my feet. There was something eerie about the total absence of light. Without even the ambient glow of a stand-by light on an electrical device, the room felt different. I glanced towards the windows and began shuffling towards them. But my feet got entangled in the trailing ends of the blanket and as I tugged it free the popcorn bowl fell to the floor, where it shattered noisily on the old wooden boards. I crouched down to pick up the broken pieces – which in hindsight I realised was never going to end well. I'd gathered up three shards before the fourth embedded itself into the pad of my thumb. I couldn't see the blood, but I could certainly feel it running warmly down my hand and on to my wrist. Getting to my feet, I kicked a pathway through the fragments of bowl and headed towards the kitchen.

I didn't think my injury was serious but I didn't want to drip blood everywhere, and I'd left a clean tea towel folded up beside the sink that would make a handy makeshift bandage. My internal radar was clearly not functioning, because I managed to walk into the coffee table and collide with the edge of the door frame as I made my way from one room to the other. More by luck than judgement, I found the kitchen and wound the tea towel around my hand.

Standing in the middle of the pitch-black room, I felt as helpless as a mole in sunlight. I had no idea where Amelia's fuse box was, nor – let's be honest– what to do if I *did* manage to find it. More importantly, I didn't have a clue where to find a torch or candles. I thought longingly of my phone, plugged into its charger beside my bed. If I could get to the spare room without walking into any more furniture, I could at least use the torch on my mobile. I was crossing the room like a zombie in a science-fiction film, arms stretched out in front of me, when a bang on the front door stopped me.

'Is anyone there?' I called out stupidly, shuddering, because isn't that what you say at a séance? Every scary movie I'd ever seen was spooling through my head as I approached the door. I leapt back as the knocking came again.

No one in their right mind answers the door to an unknown caller in the middle of a blackout.

'Who's there?' I called out, but either they couldn't hear me above the raging storm or they didn't want to reveal themselves. My heart was thumping noisily in my chest as

I crept to one of the small hallway windows and peered through the rain-spattered pane. A sudden and convenient bolt of lightning threw the darkness into relief, allowing me to catch a glimpse of the stooped figure on the doorstep.

Rain was pouring like a waterfall from his sou'wester and cascading in busy tributaries on to his oilskin jacket. I hurried back to the door and threw it open.

'The lights are out,' declared Amelia's curmudgeonly neighbour, as though I might somehow have failed to notice it.

'I know,' I said, having to raise my voice to be heard above the shriek of the wind. 'I was trying to remember where the fuse box is.'

'That won't do you any good,' he declared dourly. 'It's not just this cottage. The power's out everywhere. Doubt it'll be back for hours.'

I couldn't decide if trudging through the rain to tell me this had been a thoughtful gesture or just the need to spread some misery, but then radically revised my opinion when the old man bent to pick up an object by his feet. There was just enough moonlight for me to make out its shape. It was an old-fashioned storm lantern.

'I thought you might be needing this.'

Igniting the burners on the gas hob to create some extra light was an obvious solution, but it hadn't even occurred to me and illustrated – if further proof was needed – that I would score very poorly on a survival skills chart. The flames burnt cobalt blue in the darkness, and through the shadows I watched as my elderly Good Samaritan began fiddling with the hurricane lamp. My nose twitched as the pungent smell of paraffin filled the room. It only took the striking of a match for the kitchen to be lit instantly with a soft warm glow.

'That oughta see you alright for the next couple of hours until they get the juice back on,' he said, sliding the lantern towards me. 'Just don't go setting fire to the old place. These cottages are timber-framed, you know.'

He had already turned towards the door, preparing to step back into the storm.

'Won't you stay for a while? I could boil up some water for tea. To say thank you... you know.'

His face was all wrinkles and shadows, but even in the flickering lamplight I thought I caught the look of surprise on it.

'I don't make much of a habit of mixing with people. I find I don't like most folks.'

I hoped the shadows hid my twitching lips. 'Well, I don't make a habit of inviting grumpy strangers to join me for a middle-of-the-night cuppa. But I'm willing to chance it if you are.'

Friendships can spring up in the most unlikely of places and usually when you least expect them. Like a field of dandelions that appear overnight, they can change a landscape in the blink of an eye. I hadn't known I'd needed anyone to fill the vacancy of confidant. After all, I had Mum – or even Jeff – if I wanted someone to talk to. And yet for some reason I hadn't chosen to unburden my secret fears on either of them. That I would find myself confiding all my worries about Amelia to a crusty old fisherman who claimed he didn't really like anyone was as astonishing as it was remarkable. It was also rather lovely.

'So, you befriended Amelia's miserable elderly neighbour?' Mum asked, for what had to be the third time the next morning, as though it didn't matter how many times I retold it, she still had trouble believing me.

'His name is Tom and actually I think it was more a case of *him* befriending *me*. And I don't believe he *is* miserable after all. I think he might just be lonely. And he's not that ancient either – in fact, he's about the same age as you. I asked.'

'Well, the salty sea air hasn't been kind to him then,' Mum said. She was clearly still worrying about my apparent lack of judgement in opening my door to a stranger in the middle of the night. In fact, I was fairly sure the whole purpose of this morning's early visit was to ensure that I hadn't had some dreadful mishap during the previous night's power cut. Admittedly, the huge plaster covering the palm of my left hand did little to reassure her.

'What on earth did you and an old fisherman find to talk about?' asked Mum, spraying copious amounts of disinfectant on to the kitchen worktops that I'd already wiped clean that morning. I wisely chose not to mention this.

'Storms. Living on the beach… and Amelia,' I added after a hesitant pause. Mum had her back to me, so I couldn't read her expression, but I saw the tension in her shoulders as she scrubbed the draining board a little bit harder.

'Hmm.' I knew without even looking that her words were coming through pursed lips. 'I'm not sure how Amelia would feel about that. She's always been much more private than you. I don't think she'd be happy with one of her neighbours knowing about her illness, and maybe even gossiping about it.'

I got to my feet to give her a quick reassuring hug. 'To be fair, Mum, I don't think Tom has that many people in his life that he even talks to, much less gossips with.'

Mum picked up the tea towel and began folding it with the precision of a professional origamist. There was an entirely different expression on her face when she eventually looked up. 'Oh, that's really quite sad. I had no idea.' And there she was: my mum, with a heart so big and generous I couldn't remember a single Christmas lunch without at least one lonely or abandoned neighbour who'd been invited to join us. It was her very best trait and the one I always hoped I'd inherit.

Despite my assurances that I'd be fine with just a slice of toast, Mum insisted that she might as well make us a 'proper' breakfast, seeing as she was here. She lifted the enormous bag she'd brought with her on to the worktop and began unloading the shopping in a way that reminded me of Mary Poppins with her bottomless carpet bag. There was far too much in the bag for a simple cooked breakfast, and I saw her surreptitiously sliding items into the fridge and store cupboards when she thought I wasn't looking. I bit my lip to hide my smile, thinking it was just as well that I was staying at Amelia's and not with her, or I wouldn't be able to fit into any of my old clothes by the time I went back to New York. Not for the first time, the thought of my return made me shiver uneasily. What was that all about? *I did want to go back, didn't I?* It was far too big a question to face this early in the day, so I parcelled it up and tucked it away in a dark corner of my mind for later examination.

Before long, the kitchen was filled with the soundtrack of a full English. Bacon was spitting noisily beneath the grill, while eggs sizzled in the frying pan. Despite my protests, I could feel my mouth watering as I retrieved the muffins when they popped out of the toaster. We were on the point of dishing up when a shadow fell over the kitchen as a shape sidled past the window.

Mum clutched a hand to her throat in a slightly over-the-top theatrical gesture. 'Oh, my goodness. Did you see that? Was that a prowler?'

I was already on my feet and halfway to the front door. I threw it open, but Tom could move surprisingly quickly for a man on the wrong side of seventy-five. He'd already covered half the distance between Amelia's cottage and his.

The wind was nowhere near as fierce as the night before, but I could still feel it whipping the cry from my lips. 'Tom. Tom. Hang on a minute. Wait up.'

There was little wrong with his hearing, I'm sure, yet he hesitated for a moment before slowing his pace and turning on the pathway to face me.

'Good morning,' I called out.

'Mornin',' he shouted back, making no move to come any closer. He stamped his feet on the path, looking decidedly uncomfortable, as though he really was the 'peeping' Tom my mother had feared.

I felt a rush of affection for the lonely old man and an inexplicable urge to draw him out of his solitude – whether he wanted me to or not. Perhaps the apple hadn't fallen that far from the tree after all.

'You were checking up on me just now, weren't you? Checking I was alright after the storm?'

Tom looked shamefaced, as though he'd been caught in the act of covering up a crime.

'Checking you hadn't burned the place to the ground, more like,' he said. But there was something new in his growled reply.

'Won't you join us for some breakfast? We've cooked far too much for just two people.'

I'm not sure who jumped more in surprise at the invitation, Tom or me. I hadn't even heard Mum leave the cottage to come and stand beside me.

Tom fidgeted on the sandy footpath, and although it was hard to tell with a complexion as ruddy as his, I thought I detected a new flush on his cheeks.

'I wouldn't want to be intruding.'

'You wouldn't be,' Mum replied, dismissing his objections as though they were of little concern. 'And besides, it's the very least I can do to thank you for looking out for my daughter – for looking out for *both* my daughters, actually.'

I turned to her in surprise. I hadn't mentioned that from the things Tom had said, he'd unintentionally revealed that he'd been keeping a watchful eye on the cottage at the end of the row, with its solitary female occupant. And yet somehow Mum had known it.

I thought there would be far more bluster and protests. I felt sure he'd conjure up some invented reason not to join us. Tom was, after all, a man who openly claimed he didn't much care for the company of others. But with a nod and a little shuffle on the pathway, for the second time in less than twelve hours he chose to accept an invitation from a member of the Edwards family to join them.

I'm not sure exactly when it happened. But somewhere

between the eggs and bacon and the numerous refills of his mug of strong, three-sugared tea, I witnessed something I hadn't expected: the birth of another new friendship. A cynic might have questioned what an old hermit of a sea dog and a retired schoolteacher might have in common. But between talk of the area where they'd both grown up, the changes they'd seen since their youth, and a shared love of birdlife – of all things – I hardly spoke a word, and I don't think either of them even noticed.

'You two certainly got on like a house on fire,' I teased, as Mum and I cleared away the breakfast things after Tom had gone.

'Stuff and nonsense,' said Mum, making it sound as though I'd lost my mind. I kept my smile hidden, because at some point during the meal I'd realised that in her own way Mum might be every bit as lonely for a friend her own age as I suspected Tom was. It was just that neither of them would ever have admitted it.

'It'll be good to have someone on hand to keep an eye on Amelia when I can't be here and you've gone back to America, that's all,' Mum said. There it was again, that sudden uncomfortable frisson I kept feeling at the idea of me leaving.

We left the dishwasher to deal with the dishes and were about to climb into the car when Tom suddenly appeared from around the corner of the cottage. Bizarrely, his arms were full of daffodils. I'd noticed there was a small, sheltered plot of land beside his cottage covered with an early flowering carpet of them, a carpet that I suspected might now be considerably depleted. He'd wrapped a bunch of the cheery yellow flowers in a sheet of newspaper, which for some reason I found totally charming.

'Thought your sister might like these to brighten up her room,' he said, holding out the flowers to me. 'They can be gloomy places, them hospitals.'

And then, with words spoken so low only the wind and my mother could hear them, he produced an identical bunch and passed it to Mum. In a morning of revelations, the most surprising thing was that I wasn't surprised at all.

12

It was ten days since my humiliating visit to The Willows Veterinary Surgery. It had taken that long for my toes to stop curling in embarrassment whenever I thought about it. Even so, I suspected Nick Forrester's polite but firm refusal would live on in my memory for some time yet – filed under the heading of *What the hell were you thinking?*

I'd altered the route of my morning run on the beach to ensure our paths didn't cross, something I imagined he'd want to avoid just as much as I did. In fact, I'd done everything I could to put the incident behind me, so the last thing I wanted or expected was to spot him right in front of me in the busy shopping mall.

There were several towns I could have chosen for my Saturday morning shopping trip. Was it just bad luck that I'd picked the same one he'd decided to visit, or was Fate determined to put us on a direct collision course? At least this time I had the chance to avoid another uncomfortable meeting. Nick was so much taller than the surrounding crowd that he'd been easy to spot, which had given me enough time to peel off from the throng and duck into the first shop doorway I came to.

'Can I help you, madam?' enquired a helpful assistant, coming to the open door to coax me inside.

'I'm just looking, thank you,' I said, glancing up and noticing that 'looking' was actually the focus of the entire window display, which was filled with a collection of mirrors in a variety of shapes and sizes. At least twenty 'me's were visible to anyone passing the furniture shop. It was, without doubt, the very worst shop doorway I could have chosen to hide inside. Through the multitude of reflections, I saw the crowd in the concourse continue to surge past. Perhaps Nick wouldn't glance this way. Perhaps he'd be distracted, or be occupied on his phone, or—

'Lexi? Is that you?'

I watched my shocked face being reflected back from a great many angles. Nick was weaving through the shoppers towards me and there was no way to pretend I hadn't seen or heard him. The mirrors proved otherwise.

I summoned up a smile as I turned, noticing as I did that Nick wasn't alone. His hand was tightly clasped in that of his companion, who was looking at me with open curiosity.

'Hello,' I said cheerily, making sure I included the girl standing at his side in the greeting.

'Who are you?' the girl asked with the unfiltered curiosity that only the very young or the very old are allowed to get away with.

Nick looked a little uncomfortable at his daughter's directness, but I was determined not to be fazed. I set down my collection of carrier bags and held out my hand to the young girl. 'Hi. My name is Lexi. And you are?'

'Holly. Because I was born at Christmas,' the girl replied, linking her hand in mine, as though we were going for a walk, rather than shaking it. I saw Nick's lips twitch, but he was too polite to say anything about my obvious inexperience with children.

'This is my daughter,' he explained, and I remembered just in time that he would have no idea I'd already identified the girl, having recognised her from the photo I'd spotted on his desk.

'It's very nice to meet you,' I said, gently disentangling my hand from Holly's when she showed no sign of letting it go. It was impossible to stop my gaze from straying into the crowd, waiting for the pretty blonde from the other side of the picture frame to complete the family group. Had Nick told her about me and my crazy proposition, I wondered? Had she been outraged by my request, or had they laughed about it – and me – together? The thought stung and made my voice sound a little sharper and brisker than it had been before.

'Well, it was very nice bumping into you again. But I'm running late so I should go. I'm... I'm meeting a friend for coffee,' I said, lying very badly indeed.

'Of course,' said Nick, stepping back and tugging his daughter to one side so I could make the hasty exit I so clearly wanted. 'Nice to see you again.'

I glanced back just once as I disappeared into the melee of shoppers, surprised to find his eyes were still on me.

Two boutiques and three shoe shops later, I'd finally stopped my thoughts from straying back to my encounter with Nick and his daughter. I'd bought more new clothes than I probably needed, but I still wasn't sure how long I was

142

staying in England and was getting a bit bored with recycling the same old outfits. And hopefully, sooner or later Amelia would come out of hospital and want to reclaim her own wardrobe.

The boots I'd worn for my shopping trip were pinching my toes and, given that my mythical friend had clearly stood me up for coffee, I decided to treat myself to an early lunch. I'd spotted a small pizza place at the far end of the concourse that looked really tempting and happily they still had several free tables. I picked one beside a gurgling fountain and a potted tree. The overhead awning was painted sky blue and dotted with fluffy white clouds, and if you shut out the milling shoppers you could almost imagine you were dining al fresco in a real Italian piazza. My *Quattro Formaggi* was delicious, and I was debating whether ordering a gelato was pushing the boat out too far when I heard a commotion coming from the upper level of the mall.

Someone was calling out loudly. Their words were distorted by the building's acoustics so I couldn't make out what they were saying, but the urgency with which they were being spoken was impossible to ignore. I glanced to one side, where the downward escalator was spilling people out on to the mall's lower level. Someone was at the top of the escalator, hurtling down the steps as though their feet weren't even making contact with the metal treads. Disgruntled shoppers were frowning as the figure flew past them, but he was beyond them in seconds and appeared too distraught to either notice or care.

I was on my feet, with no recollection of pushing myself away from the table. The figure leapt from the escalator when they were still some distance from the bottom, looking for all the world as though he was flying through the air. Something that, ironically, I'd once jested about.

He was already at a run, and initially didn't hear my cry.

'Nick. Nick. What is it? What's wrong?'

He screeched to a halt, the rubber soles of his shoes leaving actual skid marks on the vinyl. He spun around and beneath the panic on his face was a tiny flicker of relief on seeing me. At least, that's what I thought it was.

His long legs covered the distance between us in seconds.

'It's Holly. Have you seen her?' He looked like a man who didn't panic very often or easily, but he was certainly doing so now.

'Is she lost?' I asked, stupidly glancing all round as though he might possibly have missed seeing that his daughter was actually right there beside him.

His face was curiously ashen and flushed at the same time. 'I don't know,' he said, raking a hand through his hair. From the state of it, his fingers had obviously travelled that path several times already.

'I don't know if she's lost, or just wandered off somewhere… or if someone's taken her.'

I wanted to pooh-pooh his last suggestion, but from the terror on his face I didn't dare. Wasn't this every parent's worst nightmare?

'When did you last see her? How long has she been missing?'

Nick looked almost irritated by my questions, as though the time he needed to expend answering them could be better spent running up and down the escalators like a madman.

I reached out and laid my hand on his forearm. I could

feel the tension pulsating through him like voltage through a pylon.

'Think, Nick,' I urged.

'We were on the third storey. We'd been in the pet store when I got a phone call from the surgery about an emergency that had just been brought in. The phone reception was terrible, so we left the shop and Holls was right there beside me. But the call took longer than I thought it would and I... I don't know... when I looked down to check if she was okay, she wasn't there.'

I gave what I hoped was a reassuring smile, although inside me a tiny spark of fear crackled into life.

'Okay. So, did you check inside the pet shop? Could she have gone back in there?'

'Yes. No. I don't know.'

He was making no sense and his panic was starting to feel infectious. He drew in a deep breath, but I could see that all he wanted to do was bolt again.

'Yes, she could have gone back in there. But I checked and the staff said they hadn't seen her.'

'Well, what about the toilets? Have you checked in there?'

Nick thumped his forehead so hard that he knocked his glasses askew. 'The loo,' he said, as though in the company of a genius. 'Of course. She must have gone to the loo. Why didn't I think of that?'

Because you're panicking like a crazy person didn't seem an appropriate response, even if it was true.

'Okay. Well, why don't I go and check all the ladies' toilets and see if she's there.'

'Would you? Could you?' he asked desperately.

'Of course. No problem,' I said, pulling a twenty-pound note from my purse and setting it down beside my plate. It was too much, but I had no time to wait for the bill.

'Could she be with your wife? Is she here with you?'

Two expressions fought for supremacy on Nick's face. Amazement and fear.

'Natalie? No. She's gone away with friends. This is *my* weekend with Holly.'

His answer told me a great deal, but this wasn't the time to explore any of that information.

'Do you think I should find a security guard? Get them to shut down the centre?' Nick asked as we hurried from the pizza restaurant.

'Let's wait until we've checked the toilets,' I said, already scoping the overhead signs for directions to the nearest ones.

'Okay. You go do that. I'll check the Gents down here.'

I did a good job of hiding my fears as to why his young daughter would be in the men's loos.

I probably looked and sounded just as crazy as Nick had done as I ran from one Ladies to another, calling Holly's name and even dropping on to my hands and knees to peer beneath the stall doors. I got some very funny looks, but when I explained that I was looking for a little girl, everyone was very sympathetic.

'Your little girl, is she?' asked a grandmotherly type in the third Ladies I tried. According to the map of the shopping centre, there was only one left to try after this.

'No. She's a friend's daughter,' I said, running out of the room so fast my feet almost skidded on the tiled floor.

I bumped into Nick as I flew through the door. Quite

literally bumped into him. Had his hands not come up to my shoulders to steady me, I would have ended up flat on my backside.

'Anything?' he asked urgently.

I shook my head. 'No. Nothing.'

'That's it,' he said decisively, dropping a glance to the watch on his wrist. 'It's been almost thirty minutes. I'm alerting Security or calling the police.'

Acknowledging that the situation had escalated from worrying to serious was the most frightening realisation of all.

'There's one last Ladies still to try,' I said, but he shook his head emphatically.

'Go check. But I need to find her now before some pervert does.'

He'd fast-tracked to the worst possible scenario, and I wasn't far behind him. He disappeared off at a run towards the information desk on the lower level, while I ran as fast as my heels would allow to the last toilets, at the far end of the centre.

As I ran, I glanced left and right into every shop, but there was no young girl with long dark hair looking lost and confused in their doorways. I wove speedily past a group of children, all a little older than Holly, who'd just emerged from a branch of Waterstones. They were all clutching copies of *Witchery*, a book that you didn't need to work in publishing to know was going to be a *Sunday Times* bestseller. The pre-publication hype had been everywhere.

I ran on. But there was something in my head that kept buzzing like a wasp at a picnic. There was a stitch in my side, but that wasn't what brought me to a halt. Far in the distance,

I spotted a security guard reacting visibly to a message he'd just received on his walkie-talkie. Nick had clearly raised the alert, but I was no longer sure it was necessary.

I stopped stock-still in the middle of the concourse and closed my eyes, conjuring up the memory of the photograph on Nick's desk at The Willows. His daughter had been wearing a T-shirt with a very familiar raven logo on it. A logo I'd just seen ten seconds ago in the window of the bookshop and again on the front of the books in the children's hands. I ran back to the bookshop, pausing briefly to glance at the cauldron in the window, which was belching out some very realistic-looking smoke. Beside it was a collection of witches' hats, a spell book and some broomsticks. At the bottom of the window was a poster inviting you to visit their extensive in-store display in the children's section.

It was exactly where I would have wandered off to at her age, and it was no surprise to find Holly sitting enthralled in front of a mock forest, complete with swooping owls and a campfire for the junior witches and wizards to sit beside.

'Holly,' I said, dropping to my knees beside her.

She looked up from the pages of the copy of *Witchery* that she'd taken from the stack on the table.

'Oh hello. It's you. Daddy's friend.'

It was quite a stretch. But that was irrelevant. I nodded.

'Sweetheart, your daddy's been looking everywhere for you.'

Her eyes widened in surprise that quickly turned to fear.

'But I told him I was going to find the bookshop.'

'Did you?'

She nodded emphatically. 'I told him, but he was busy on the phone so he couldn't come with me.'

I nodded, aware that somewhere in the shopping centre Nick was still frantically going out of his mind. 'I don't think he could have heard you properly, sweetie. He thought you were lost.'

There was no mistaking the look of disbelief on her face. 'Why would I be lost? I'm not a baby. I'm eight now, you know.'

'Absolutely,' I said, getting to my feet and holding out my hand, this time not expecting a handshake.

'Is Daddy going to be mad at me?' Holly whispered worriedly as she placed her hand in mine. I squeezed her fingers reassuringly.

'No. He's just going to be happy to have you back.'

She scrambled to her feet, all spindly arms and legs, and with obvious reluctance put the book back on top of the pile on the table.

'Take that with you,' I said, already reaching into my purse for another twenty-pound note, which I passed to an assistant at the till as we left the shop. 'Now, let's go and find your dad, shall we?'

'I've changed my mind.'

I set down the long sundae spoon and carefully ran my tongue over my lips to catch any stray chocolate sauce before looking up. I glanced across the table at Holly, who clearly had no such worries; she was wearing at least half of her gelato over her lower face.

I'm not quite sure how Nick's suggestion of ice cream to 'calm us all down' had ended up including me. I tried to excuse myself several times, but Holly was holding on to my hand with a surprisingly strong grip for someone so small. There was still a lingering look of concern in her eyes that she might yet be in trouble with her dad. Perhaps she'd misread the gruffness in his voice when he'd dropped to his knees and folded her into a hug that went on and on.

'You *have* to come too, Lexi,' Holly had pleaded. 'Please.'

I'd glanced up at her father, running through a list of objections in my head, but they'd all evaporated when I'd seen the tension still visible on his face. A scare like the one he'd just lived through took a while before it set you free.

'Well, the ice cream at that Italian place did look good,' I admitted. Which was how I found myself back at my lunch venue, eating a dessert that could easily have fed three people.

Nick had given the menu only a brief glance before ordering just a coffee – something that, with hindsight, I really wished I'd done too. There was no sophisticated way of eating this much frozen confectionery, and I was never going to be able to finish it all. So, when Nick announced that he'd changed his mind, I immediately looked around for the waiter.

'If you don't mind sharing, we could just ask for a second spoon.'

His eyes met mine blankly.

I nodded down at my plate. 'There's more than enough here for two if you've changed your mind.'

His blue eyes looked curiously bright whenever he smiled, and right now they were positively dazzling. 'Not about the ice cream,' he said, lowering his voice, which was probably unnecessary because Holly's attention was entirely on her gelato.

'I'll do it,' Nick said, his voice practically a whisper. 'If you still want me to, I'll do the photographs.'

'What? Why?'

His eyes went back to Holly and then locked meaningfully with mine. He held my gaze for a very long moment.

'Because I owe you.'

'No, you don't,' I said, shaking my head vigorously in denial.

'Yes, I do,' Nick said, reaching across the tabletop and laying his hand over mine. Something peculiar happened in the region of my throat, tightening my vocal cords, so that my reply – when it came – sounded as though I'd inhaled helium.

'I only did what anyone would have done in that situation,' I squeaked. 'I certainly don't want you to help me out of some misplaced sense of obligation. Or worse, because you now feel guilty about saying no.'

'You're really rubbish at negotiating, aren't you?' Nick said with a smile. 'I've just agreed to do exactly what you asked of me and now you're trying to talk me out of it.'

He withdrew his hand and somehow that made breathing a little easier. I sat back in my seat, gnawing on my lower lip. 'But you don't think it's a good idea,' I said, unable to stop being the devil's very best advocate.

'That's not important. What matters is that *you do*. That's all that counts.'

'But you're so busy. You've got the practice to look after and Holly to take care of...' My voice trailed away. *What the hell are you doing?* demanded an incredulous voice in my head. Just say 'yes' and 'thank you very much'.

'If you'd still like me to do this thing, Lexi, then I'm all in. If you still want me, that is.'

I was vaguely aware that anyone overhearing this conversation was likely to totally misinterpret it.

'Then yes. Yes please,' I said, my voice surprisingly shaky. 'I do still want you.'

13

The doctors had asked us both to be there. That in itself was a worry.

'Do you really think she's ready to hear what happened yet?' Mum asked, for what had to be the fifth time since I'd picked her up. The drive to the hospital seemed to be taking even longer than usual and for once I didn't mind. I was in no hurry for this visit. In fact, I was dreading it.

'I'm just worried about how it might affect her AF,' Mum said, dropping easily into the medical abbreviations that had become part of our daily language. Unfortunately.

'I'm sure they'll have considered all the implications of telling her. And it's not fair or reasonable to keep her in the dark forever. And besides, the atrial fibrillation is something Mimi may have to live with for the rest of her life.' *As well as all the pills*, I added silently. The doctors had explained that Amelia's daily cocktail of drugs was likely to remain necessary to support her heart after the trauma it had experienced. And today was the day they'd decided Amelia should be told what had happened to her on that fateful January night.

'We'll get through this, the three of us,' I said, taking my hand from the wheel and squeezing Mum's tightly. 'We've been through worse than this.' I didn't need to say any more nor take my gaze from the road to know that my words would have brought tears to her eyes, just as they'd done to mine. Even after all this time, the shock of losing Dad never got easier, not for her or us. Perhaps if we'd had answers all those years ago, if we'd known exactly what had happened to Dad on that fateful day in the cove, it would have been easier to move on. Or perhaps not. I blinked my vision clear and flicked on the indicator before turning into the road that led to the hospital.

Dr Vaughan and a colleague – who looked, unbelievably, even younger than he did – were waiting for us at the nurses' station. I caught the tail end of their conversation as we were buzzed into the ward. They appeared to be discussing the latest episode of a reality TV show that I'd never watched. The trivial nature of their conversation shocked me more than it ought to have done. I wanted my medics to be clichés; I wanted them forever 'on the job' and obsessed with their patients. I wanted them to be exactly like *House M.D.* I shook my head as the men turned around at the sound of our footsteps. My fascination with fantasy television was almost as bad as theirs.

After a polite round of greetings, we headed en masse towards Amelia's room, our steps falling automatically in sync as we travelled the corridor, like four reluctant executioners.

'Whoa. This looks serious,' joked Amelia as she set aside the magazine she'd been flicking through.

There was a beat when someone was probably supposed to say something light-hearted. Except nobody did.

'Shit. This *is* serious.'

I still hadn't got used to hearing my sister swear so often, but that wasn't why I flinched. Almost as though we'd choreographed it, I went to one side of Amelia's bed and Mum went to the other. We both reached for a hand, threading our fingers through hers. Looking down, you'd be forgiven for thinking we were about to conduct a séance, which, given what the doctors were about to reveal, felt like the darkest of black humour.

'Well, someone say something,' Amelia said, directing her gaze at the two besuited men who'd taken up a position at the foot of her bed.

The doctors' words were quietly spoken, delivered in the most non-sensational way they could hope to find, but their impact was still devastating. I didn't look at Dr Vaughan or his companion (whose name I'd already forgotten) as they spoke. I kept my eyes on Amelia, to assess her reaction. I was on a hair-trigger, ready to pull the plug on this intervention – because that's what it seemed like – the moment I felt it was too much for her. And I knew those features too well not to recognise when that moment came, because her face was also mine.

Mystification was the first emotion to land on it, quickly followed by shock and then disbelief, before shock kicked in once again.

'I died? I actually *died*?'

I was incapable of replying, but thankfully the question was being directed towards the doctors and not me.

'Technically, yes. In layman's terms, then I suppose that could be said to be correct.'

'I wasn't breathing and my heart had literally stopped beating. That sounds like dead to me.' Old Amelia wasn't this sharp or aggressive, but then again old Amelia had never been on the receiving end of such earth-shattering news.

She stiffened suddenly, and I felt the tug of her hand as she tried to pull it free from mine. I wouldn't let her.

'You knew? You knew about this, Lexi, and you never told me.' Her words felt like accusatory bullets and every one of them found its target.

I nodded slowly.

'Why didn't you say anything? You told me I'd been unconscious when I was found.'

'Well, technically unconscious is—'

Amelia cut off the doctor's words with an angry hiss. Somehow this had stopped being about medical conditions and had crossed over into family loyalty.

'They said it would be too much for you to cope with,' I murmured lamely.

She shook her head, and the disappointment in her eyes lasered into my heart.

'They don't know me. You *do*. You should have told me everything.'

I hung my head. This was going every bit as badly as I'd feared it would.

'And do you also know what I was doing on the beach outside my cottage in the middle of the night? Are you keeping that from me too?' she asked now. Her chin was jutting forward, but above it her lower lip was trembling. The juxtaposition of defiance and defeat was heartbreaking to see.

'You weren't found outside your cottage, honey,' Mum cut in gently. 'You were on the mudflats.'

Amelia's eyes widened as she stared at our mother with an *Et tu, Brute?* expression.

All three Edwards women looked up at the sound of feet shuffling awkwardly on the squeaky lino floor.

'Perhaps it might be better if we continue this discussion a little later, when you've had the chance to absorb things properly,' suggested Dr Vaughan. No one tried to dissuade them from leaving as they practically scurried from the room.

'What was I doing on the mudflats?' Amelia asked, her voice slightly calmer now.

'We don't know,' I told her sadly. 'I'm not sure we ever will.'

'Was I alone?'

'You were when they found you,' I said, perching on the edge of the mattress and daring to reach for her hand again. This time, she didn't pull it away. 'Why do you ask? Have you remembered something about that night?'

She shook her head, and her brow fell into the furrows I imagined it would succumb to a few years further down the line. 'I wondered if Sam had been there. If he'd come back from America unexpectedly.'

Mum made a small sound that had no name, but I'd been half expecting this, or something very like it.

'Do you think he did?' Amelia persisted. 'Perhaps we argued? Maybe I ran out after him and somehow got lost in the dark.'

She was already painting a picture to fit the facts, even if everything about it was wrong.

'Maybe,' I said carefully. Sometimes the tightrope between her delusion and reality was so perilous it was best to say as little as possible.

It was all too much for Mum, who got to her feet, declaring she was going to fetch us all a cup of decent coffee from the foyer. I was fairly sure the last thing anyone's jangling nerves needed right then was more caffeine, but it was easier to agree.

The silence in the room after she left felt particularly fragile.

'I *died*, Lexi,' Amelia said softly, still feeling her way around the enormity of what happened.

'Only for a little while,' I replied, which might possibly qualify as the most ridiculous thing I've ever said.

'And do you know what the worst thing about it is?'

'What?'

'He wasn't there, and he should have been.'

'You mean Sam?' I asked gently.

Amelia shook her head and her eyes were full of tears as they met mine.

'No. I mean Dad. I've always thought that when my time was up, he'd be there. Waiting. That I'd get one last chance to see his smile. But I never saw him. And it kind of feels like losing him all over again.'

14

'I'll get this,' I said, sliding my credit card across the counter before Nick's could get there first.

For a moment it looked like he was going to object, but perhaps he saw the determination on my face for he gave in with a good-natured shrug. 'Thank you. So long as you let me buy lunch,' he said, slipping the card back into his wallet.

'Sure,' I replied with a smile that gave nothing away. There was no need for him to know it was unlikely we'd still be at the amusement park to worry about who'd be footing the bill for that particular meal. I had every intention of making this as quick and painless as possible.

Nick's call, the night before, had been perfectly timed. I'd been in a strange mood since leaving the hospital. What Amelia had said about Dad had opened the door to a carousel of memories that I hadn't allowed to roam free for a very long time. They kept spinning around my head as I prepared a microwave ready meal that I already knew I wouldn't finish, and were well entrenched as I sat straight-faced through a TV show everyone was calling 'hilarious'. Every time I closed my eyes I saw Dad as he'd been on that last morning, standing beside a car loaded with angling gear, waving up at me as I knelt on my bed watching through the window as he left for the fishing trip he would never come back from. Just before he ducked into the car, he'd pulled the keys from his pocket and waggled them at me, making me grin. Why hadn't I run down the stairs to give him one last hug? One last kiss? They were questions I'd cried myself to sleep over for a great many years afterwards.

I'd been secretly relieved when Mum had passed on my invitation to join me for dinner. 'Another time maybe, Lexi,' she said apologetically. 'All I really want is a big mug of cocoa and an early night.' That sounded surprisingly appealing, which made me wonder if returning to the UK had somehow catapulted me straight from my thirties into old age. It was certainly hard to imagine a greater contrast between the life I lived in America and the one I was living now. Perhaps I wasn't the hard-bitten New Yorker I thought I'd become after all. There was a connection to this place that I'd been denying for too long. But Somerset was patient. She was happy to quietly bide her time as she waited for me to remember just how much I'd loved growing up here and how I'd once sworn never to leave.

Muting the TV with its annoying canned laughter, I leant back on the settee and closed my eyes. I might even have drifted off for a moment or two before my phone's ring tone jerked me awake. I scrabbled for my mobile, which was never far from my side these days. My fingers jabbed anxiously at the screen, the way anyone who's ever had a loved one in hospital would instantly recognise.

But it wasn't the hospital, my New York office, or even Jeff calling me this late in the evening. I stared down at Nick's name on my phone screen for one more ring before answering the call.

'Hello,' I said, hoping the surprise in my voice would dissipate as it surfed the airwaves from my phone to his.

'Hi. I'm sorry, I've just noticed how late it is. Did I wake you?'

'No, I was just watching TV,' I lied, my eyes flicking towards the muted screen.

'I've just got back from delivering a breech foal, and I lost track of time.'

'I'm sorry. Who *is* this?' I teased.

'It's N—' he began, before breaking off when he heard my giggle. 'It's Clark. Clark Kent,' he completed solemnly.

I was smiling way more than the TV show had been able to achieve. 'I think that phrase only really works with 007,' I said, surprised at the easy banter we'd fallen into.

He laughed, but now, on listening, I could hear a thread of tiredness in his voice. I knew nothing about veterinary medicine or birthing a foal, but I imagined it had been an exhausting day for him too, just in a totally different way from mine.

'The reason I'm calling,' Nick said, fast-tracking us both back to the present, 'is to remind you that I meant what I said the other day. And to let you know that I'm free for most of tomorrow, if that's of any interest to you.'

For some unknown reason, I felt my heart skitter in my chest. I *did* still want his help, but I hadn't expected him to take the reins and volunteer his services like this. *He probably just wants to get it over and done with*, I thought. *Square the debt and then walk away from the crazy woman with her even crazier plan.* Only… it didn't feel quite like that.

'What are your thoughts on amusement parks?' I asked, momentarily stunning him into silence.

'Is this an abstract question, or are you asking me to go to one with you?'

I hardly knew him, but I already liked the direct way he approached things. Perhaps it was something to do with his profession... or perhaps it was just him.

'Amelia and Sam went on a particularly memorable date to Lassiters,' I told him, naming a well-known and much-loved family-style amusement park about thirty miles away. I recognised the absurdity in talking about an imaginary person attending an imaginary event as though it had really happened and felt certain Nick was about to call me out on it. But he didn't.

'Would you like us to go there tomorrow?'

My throat tightened convulsively, and it took a few seconds before the lump his kindness had brought to it could be swallowed away.

'If you're not too busy,' I replied.

'Like I said, I'm free until evening surgery. It's why I phoned you.'

'Then, yes please. I'd like that.'

'I can pick you up in the morning if you give me your address?' he offered, sounding a little startled when I immediately declined.

'No, don't worry. I'll meet you there at ten, if that's okay?'

I got there early, parking in the first row of bays in the largely empty car park. A couple of coaches trundled in shortly after

I arrived, and I watched as the tourists spilled out and snaked their way towards Lassiters' entrance.

I'd been to this amusement park many times as a child, but never so early in the day – nor in the year, come to that. I associated it with blistering hot summer days, dripping ice creams and sunburnt noses. My nose was certainly red right now, I was sure of that, but it was due to the wind and the cold rather than the sun, which was conspicuously absent on this chilly March morning. I cinched Amelia's sheepskin jacket a little tighter around me and wished she'd fantasised about wearing her less flattering but much warmer thick quilted coat on this date with Sam.

I kept my eyes fixed on the car park entrance, standing meerkat tall whenever a new vehicle swept in. I'm not sure why I was bothering, because I had no idea what car Nick drove. Which made it even stranger that the moment I spotted the black Range Rover in the distance, I immediately knew it was his. The tinted windows didn't reveal the driver's identity, but I was already striding towards the car as it manoeuvred into a free space. *You're going to look really stupid if it isn't him*, I thought, as I stood waiting for the driver to emerge. Luckily, my instincts had been good, and moments later Nick climbed out of the car. I noticed the thick splatters of mud on its lower panels – probably a souvenir from whichever farm he'd visited the previous night.

He saw me looking and immediately apologised.

'Sorry, I should have run it through a car wash this morning, but I had an errand to attend to and I ran out of time.'

I bit my lip guiltily, having already guessed what that errand might have been.

Could you wear a blue denim shirt tomorrow – if you have one, I'd messaged, so late at night I wasn't sure Nick would still be awake.

His reply had taken less than a minute to ping back. *Sure. No problem.*

From the brand-new, just-out-of-the-packet creases on the shirt he was now wearing, I was fairly certain what his 'errand' had been. I smiled up at him, because however disapproving Nick might be about what I was doing, it was an incredibly thoughtful thing to have done.

He reached into his car and pulled out a thick padded jacket. 'I'll take it off for the photos,' he assured me, shrugging his muscular arms into the sleeves. I was staring too much and with an effort I brought my attention back to the reason we were there. Nick wasn't my partner in crime, not really; he was just a very nice, decent man, settling a perceived debt of gratitude.

After the slight debate about who was buying the entry tickets, we went through the old-fashioned turnstile and entered the park. I'd picked up a guide map from a stand near the entrance and unfolded it now, studying it as carefully as a Duke of Edinburgh's Award candidate on an expedition. 'We should probably hit all the big rides that Amelia said they'd done fairly early on, before the crowds get here.'

Nick glanced dubiously at the grey sky, with its gathering clouds. 'Somehow I don't think it's going to get all that busy here today.'

I turned my face upwards and felt the mist of impending rain on my cheeks. 'We may have to dodge the showers,' I said with a frown. 'It was cold but dry on the day Sam and Amelia were here.' Nick said nothing, but the expression on his face was extremely eloquent. 'Except of course, I *do* realise that they were never actually here,' I added.

Nick took a step closer and gently tugged the map from my hands, looking for all the world as though it was going to lead him to buried treasure.

'How about,' he suggested, his eyes still fixed on the guide map, 'we forget to keep saying that it didn't actually happen and just concentrate on getting the photographs you want.'

This level of kindness was so new to me that I didn't know how to respond. I had no idea if he was this way with everyone, but if he was, he might truly be one of the nicest people I'd ever met.

I wonder why his wife left him?

The thought blindsided me. I hadn't seen it coming and it knocked whatever I'd been about to say clean out of my thoughts. I had absolutely no idea how his marriage had ended or who had left whom. And more importantly, it was none of my damn business.

'It really is very good of you to do this, Nick,' I said gratefully. He shook his head, batting away my words.

'If I stop thanking you for finding my lost daughter – which was a *very big deal*, by the way – how about you stop thanking me for posing for some photos on my day off, which is a very small one.'

'Deal,' I said, holding out my hand for us to shake, as though we'd just signed some sort of treaty.

His hand was warm and strong as it took and enfolded mine. I'm not sure if it was him or me who hung on a little longer than a conventional handshake says that you should. I only knew that my hand felt oddly cold when it eventually separated from his. I thrust it deep into the pocket of my sister's sheepskin jacket, as though I couldn't trust it not to reach out for his again.

'Shall we head to the carousel?' I suggested, taking back the map and noting it was the nearest ride on my 'to-do' list for the day.

He fell into step beside me. 'It's been a long time since I've been anywhere like this,' he said, looking around him with interest.

'Have you never brought Holly here?' I asked, my head still full of memories of much-loved days out here with my family when I was his daughter's age.

'Not for a long time. It's not been the most... amicable... of divorces. It's taken us a while to get past the anger and recriminations to agree on a proper visitation schedule.'

His answer ignited a great many questions that I had no right to ask, so I didn't. But my biggest takeaway was that he was no longer married. Again, nothing whatsoever to do with me.

'You should have brought her with you today,' I suggested, thinking that a pint-size chaperone might have been quite handy to stop my thoughts going off on wholly inappropriate tangents.

'I'm not sure her school would count this as a valid reason for skipping class,' he replied with an easy grin.

'Of course. I wasn't thinking. Well, maybe another time?' I said, realising too late this wasn't an outing we were likely to repeat. We weren't on an actual date. Today was just as much a fabrication as Amelia and Sam's own visit here had been.

We heard the carousel long before we saw it. The music grew increasingly loud until we rounded a corner and found ourselves standing before the ride, which looked strangely smaller than I remembered. The horses appeared more like ponies now, rather than the stallions I recalled. But everything else was the same: the rows of coloured bulbs around the canopy were just as bright, and the painted horses as vibrant as they'd ever been. The strains of the 'Carousel Waltz' blaring from the ride's speakers whisked me back into the past more effectively than a time machine.

'So how is this going to work, exactly?' Nick asked, jolting me back to the present.

'Well, you sit on one of the horses and you bob up and down as it goes around for about five minutes and then you get off.'

His lips were twitching, and it was a real struggle not to stare at them. 'I know how carousels work,' he grinned, and there was something in his crooked smile that I swear I recognised from Amelia's sketches. How had she managed to capture every little detail of his features so well from just a distant glimpse?

'What I meant was, how are we going to get a photograph of us on the ride? Are we doing a selfie?'

There *was* a collapsible selfie stick in the bottom of my bag for just this purpose, but I had a better idea. I looked around for a suitable candidate and immediately spotted one.

'Hang on,' I told him, crossing to a woman a few years older than me who was sitting on a wooden bench to one side of the ride.

'Excuse me,' I said. 'I know this is a bit of a cheek, but would you mind taking a photo of my...' – I faltered for a moment – '... of my friend and me on the ride?' I asked, pulling my phone from my pocket.

She glanced beyond me, and I swear I saw a tiny flicker of approval in the look she gave Nick. I bet he got that a lot.

'I'd be happy to,' she said, taking my mobile from me.

'Thanks,' I said, turning and running back to where Nick was waiting.

'Do you think you'll ever see your phone again?' he teased, offering me his hand to climb up on to the carousel's platform.

'Probably not,' I said, suddenly feeling so light-hearted, I didn't even care.

'I need to find a golden horse with a brilliant white mane,' I said, glancing around at the vacant horses around us.

'That'll be a palomino, then,' Nick said knowledgeably, leading me to a horse that perfectly matched the one Amelia had told me she'd ridden.

'Do you need a bunk-up?' he asked, his face dissolving into creases of amusement at my raised eyebrows. It was a corny double entendre, but it was just what we needed to keep the mood light.

'Do you think anyone has *ever* managed to ask that question without cracking up?' I said, hoisting myself up on to the back of the wooden horse.

'Probably not,' Nick said, dropping his jacket to the floor and turning towards a gleaming ebony-coloured mount beside mine.

'Oh no,' I said, stopping him with one foot already in the stirrup. 'Sam and Amelia rode the same horse. He… you… sat behind her. Sorry, I should have said… is that okay?'

I was blushing furiously, as though I'd just indecently propositioned him. But he was too good-natured to allow it to show.

'No problem,' he said, swinging easily up on to the saddle behind me. 'Do I need to put my arms around you?' he asked. *How had I ever thought that this was a good idea?* 'Uh-huh,' I replied.

Like Nick, I too had slipped off my jacket. The emerald-green cashmere jumper had been easy to find in Amelia's wardrobe that morning. I'd smiled as I'd released it from its hanger, my fingers skimming over the Saks Fifth Avenue label. All of Amelia's confabulations had a hint of truth to them, and wearing the expensive Christmas present I'd bought her a couple of years ago was just another element that made what she was saying seem so believable, even though I knew it wasn't.

The jumper was thin, and through the soft woollen fabric I could feel the heat of Nick's body as he wound his arms around my waist. The music was loud enough to make chatting tricky, which suited me just fine because the proximity of his body pressed against mine was doing odd things to my breathing.

'Anything I should be doing for the photos?' he asked, leaning even closer towards me and talking into my ear.

'Just look like you're having a really great time,' I said, tightening my hold on the brightly painted pole when our palomino began rising and falling as the ride slowly picked up speed.

He said something in reply, but the wind whipped the words from his lips, and I spent the first few rotations wondering if it had been *I feel queasy* or *That'll be easy*. I certainly knew which one I *wanted* it to be.

★

'I hope they're okay. I took quite a few, just to make certain,' said the woman from the bench, passing me back my phone.

'I'm sure they'll be great. Thank you again,' I said.

The woman's eyes slid from my face to focus on something beyond my right shoulder, which I guessed meant that Nick was now walking towards us. 'You two certainly make an attractive couple. Really photogenic,' she said. 'You looked like something out of an advert.'

'Thanks,' said Nick, smiling warmly at her. She looked totally captivated and for a moment I experienced a fleeting twinge of something that felt curiously like jealousy before common sense kicked that emotion to the kerb. *This is all pretend, remember?* For this plan to be effective, I needed to keep that fact front and centre of my thoughts at all times, otherwise I was in danger of ending up just as confused as Amelia was.

'An advert for what, I wonder?' said Nick as we walked away. 'May I?' he asked, stretching out his hand for my phone. His fingers went to the photos icon and summoned up the images of the two of us on the carousel. He tilted the phone towards me but the glare on the screen meant I had to step closer to his side to see it. His free hand settled naturally on my shoulder, drawing me nearer to view the screen. Focusing on the images was a challenge as I stood in his personal space, enveloped by the warm woodsy scent of whatever he'd used in the shower that morning.

Blissfully unaware of my inappropriate thoughts, Nick was happily scrolling through the photos. I could kind of see what the woman had been getting at. We *did* look good together... or rather, Sam and Amelia looked good together.

'I think it must be a toothpaste ad,' Nick declared finally, his eyes twinkling as he passed me back my mobile. He wasn't wrong. In practically every picture, we were either grinning broadly or laughing. We looked like a man and a woman who were poised on the precipice of falling in love. Which just proved that the old adage couldn't be trusted at all: sometimes the camera *did* lie.

We managed to cross both the helter-skelter and the swinging pirate ship off my 'to-do' list in record time. Although I doubted the selfie I'd snapped of us on the pendulum ride was worth keeping as a memory, as I was pretty green around the gills when I took it. I definitely needed Nick's helping hand as I clambered off the ride.

The ground still felt like it was swaying, and I was hanging on to Nick so tightly his fingers were probably going to bear the imprints of mine.

'Are you alright? You've gone a very strange colour,' Nick said, peering closely at my face with concern. 'Try taking some deep breaths,' he advised, his hand moving to my waist to support me as he led me away from the pirate ship.

'That ride is positively lethal. It ought to be banned,' I muttered, throwing the swinging pendulum a baleful stare over my shoulder.

'Let's find somewhere quiet to sit down for a minute,' Nick suggested, steering us towards one of the many cafés in the park. We didn't have to walk far before we found one with a collection of cast-iron tables and chairs outside. Not surprisingly, given the weather, they were all unoccupied. He pulled out a chair and lowered me on to it as though I were his frail elderly grandmother.

'Wait here,' he said, glancing towards the entrance of the café. The world was still spinning badly, and I seriously doubted I was capable of getting anywhere under my own steam right then. I nodded. 'I won't be long,' he promised.

The unmistakable hiss of a ring pull being torn free alerted me to his return. I opened my eyes cautiously as Nick set a can of ginger ale down in front of me.

'Sip it slowly. It's better for motion sickness than anything with caffeine in it,' he added apologetically, when he saw me look longingly at the coffee he'd bought for himself.

It took a good ten minutes of slow, careful sipping before I felt like me again. Nick seemed perfectly content to sit in silence, but I was aware of the concerned glances he kept shooting my way.

'Feeling better?' he asked eventually, when I was almost back to normal.

'Yes. Thank you. I'm so sorry about that. I should have just taken a selfie of us standing next to the ride, without actually going on it.'

'Why didn't you?' It was a perfectly reasonable question.

'Because Sam kissed Amelia when they were at the highest point of the ride,' I said, knowing I was opening myself up to his disapproval with those words.

'Ahhh,' Nick said, drawing out the word carefully. 'And we didn't want to recreate that memory in a photograph because...?'

He was teasing me, rather than flirting, I knew that. He was feeding me the line so I could answer it with perfect timing.

'Because there was a good chance I'd have thrown up all over you.'

Nick's laugh was rich and rumbling; it rose up as though

from a well somewhere deep inside him. He was a *throw-back-your-head*, *don't-care-who's-watching* laugher, and I was fascinated by how comfortable he seemed with the many glances that were thrown his way.

'Good call,' he said at last. 'It would probably have put me off kissing for life.'

Like a chameleon, I could feel my colour changing once again. In the space of half an hour I'd gone from pea-green to deathly white and was now a hot flushed pink. I hadn't blushed at the thought of being kissed by someone since my teenage years, but I was definitely doing it now.

Walking between the various attractions gave us time for light conversation and banter, without having to venture into anything more serious. We chatted happily about books and how I'd ended up working as an editor in New York, which segued quite naturally into why he'd chosen to be a vet.

'I've a feeling my dad would have disowned me if I'd decided to do anything else.' He smiled at my curious expression. 'Third generation veterinary surgeon,' he explained.

'Your father must be incredibly proud of you.'

'I think he is. Not that he'd ever admit it, mind you. You know what dads are like.'

I could have left the statement hanging in the air. There was absolutely no need to answer it, and no one could have been more surprised than me when I chose to do so.

'Not so much,' I said sadly. 'Mine died in an accident when I was eight years old.'

I didn't cry when I said that anymore; I hadn't done for

years. But there was such a look of compassion on Nick's face that I was in real danger of losing it.

'I'm so sorry, Lexi. That must have been very hard on you.'

I nodded, not quite ready to trust my voice for a moment.

'Amelia and I were always close – despite the age gap – but when something like that happens... well, she was the one who got me through it. She must have been hurting every bit as much as I was, but she parcelled up her pain and concentrated on helping me through mine. When I was distraught, she was always there with a hug to anchor me. And then later, when the anger of losing Dad kicked in, she passed me crockery to throw at the wall and break.' I gave a small laugh. 'And then she passed me a broom to sweep it up. She was there when I needed her. Which is why now, when she's lost and confused about everything—' Damn it, those tears were much closer than I'd realised after all.

Nick surprised me by reaching out for my hand. 'It's okay,' he said, squeezing my fingers gently. 'You don't have to say anything else. But it's easier to understand now why you're doing this. Why you're willing to try absolutely anything to help her.'

Our conversation had slipped way off course and there was only one way I knew to get us back to the easy camaraderie of before.

'But you still think I'm a little crazy?' I said, smiling so he knew I was joking.

'Oh, absolutely,' he replied.

We were two-thirds of the way round the park and the camera reel on my phone had more than enough faux memories of

Amelia and Sam's date at Lassiters. It was probably time to set Nick free to enjoy the rest of his day off. And yet whenever I tried to summon up the words to release him, they were hard to find. I was honest enough to admit the reason: I was having a surprisingly good time and I didn't want it to end. And perhaps I wasn't the only one feeling that way, because Nick seemed to be enjoying himself too.

We walked in companionable silence, the only sound being the distant rumble of carriages thundering on a track, accompanied by a series of shrieks.

'Are you hungry? We could grab some lunch,' Nick suggested, consulting the map, which he was now holding. 'There's a pizza place near the exit.'

We were at a junction on the pathway, standing beside a signpost with two arrows: one directing visitors to the way out, the other to the park's only roller coaster.

'There's one last ride I'd like to go on, The Cobra. Amelia mentioned she'd bought a souvenir photo of them on it.'

I'd already explained to Nick that unlike the photograph I'd taken of him on the beach, today hadn't been about recreating specific snapshots.

'So, what are you going to do with all these photos?'

'For now, I'm going to put them away in a memory box. One of Amelia's greatest fears is that she'll lose every memory she has of Sam.'

'I thought that's what you *wanted* to happen?'

He'd got straight to the heart of the dilemma that kept me awake each night. 'I want her to realise that none of it ever happened; that it was all some crazy glitch in her head. If she does that, then I'll happily destroy every last photograph. But what I *don't* want is to see her struggling to remember Sam's face, or the places they visited, or how much she loved him.'

'Which is why we're creating a collection of photographs of events that never really happened, with someone you're still hoping she'll forget?'

I stared at him for a long moment, like a school kid lost for words in front of their teacher.

'I never said it was a perfect plan.'

He laughed then, and I couldn't help but join in. I didn't expect him to understand my logic, especially when most of the time I scarcely understood it myself. But amazingly he did.' 'You must love your sister an awful lot.'

'I do,' I said softly.

Nick's eyes were warm. 'You make me wish I wasn't an only child.'

It was one of the nicest things anyone had said to me in a very long time.

The Cobra was the park's most popular attraction, and it was the first time we'd had to queue for a ride all day. As we neared the front of the line, Nick slipped off his glasses, as per the instructions on the warning posters. Instantly, he morphed from mild-mannered Clark Kent to Superman before my eyes. Only this time I had better control of my tongue and didn't mention it. Instead, I turned my attention to the track, which rose skywards at an alarmingly steep angle.

'Are you okay with heights?' I belatedly thought to ask, suddenly not entirely sure whether I was.

'It would make "leaping tall buildings in a single bound" kind of tricky if I wasn't,' Nick quipped back.

How on earth had he known that I'd been struck once again by his resemblance to the comic book hero? I only hoped *all* my thoughts about him weren't that transparent, or I could really be in trouble.

We took the front carriage because that's where Amelia and Sam had sat. I tried to tell myself that the nervous thrill thrumming through me was anticipation for the ride and had nothing to do with the proximity of Nick's thigh against mine as we sat shoulder to shoulder and hip to hip in the tiny cart.

'We should probably hold hands on the ride,' I said as the operator walked along the line of carriages doing a final safety check.

'We should?' Nick asked, turning as far towards me as the safety bar would allow.

'For the photo. Sam and Amelia were holding hands,' I added awkwardly.

'Oh. Of course.' Nick held out his hand obligingly and I placed mine within it. His skin felt warm to the touch and even though I wasn't worried about the ride, I felt instantly calmer with his fingers curled around mine.

With a clank of gears, we pulled away from the platform.

'Is it okay?' Nick asked, peering over my shoulder at the souvenir photo as we walked away from the counter.

'It's perfect,' I said, studying the mounted photograph in my hand.

It definitely wasn't my best look. My mouth was open in a wide scream, and my hair was flying wildly in the wind, just as my sister's had been. The photo had captured Nick and me with our arms raised, in classic roller coaster fashion, exactly as Amelia and Sam had done. But there was one subtle difference between the print in my hands and the one Amelia had described. In mine, the couple in the front carriage were holding hands, and the more I thought about it, the more certain I became that Amelia had never said anything about that at all.

15

'I'm sorry. This wasn't how I wanted our date to end.'

'That's okay,' I said, brushing back my hair, which the wind was currently whipping across my face. 'And besides, it's not a *real* date, remember?'

Nick gave his crooked grin, which was growing on me a little more than it should.

'True. Although to be honest, it's been way more fun than many of the *real* dates I've been on lately.'

Interesting. I stored that one away for later.

'I really didn't think they'd shut this early,' Nick said, glancing again at the 'Closed' sign on the pizza restaurant door, as though if he looked at it hard enough it would magically change to 'Open'.

I gave a shrug, which I hoped hid my disappointment that our time together was coming to an end sooner than I'd expected.

'It's half past three,' I said, amused by the surprised expression on his face as he double-checked his watch. If nothing else, at least it proved the day hadn't dragged by for either of us.

'We could try and find somewhere to grab a bite in a nearby town,' he suggested.

I shook my head. 'I'd need to leave almost as soon as we got there to make it to the hospital in time. And besides, don't you need to get back for work?'

Nick nodded, and I like to think there was a smidgeon of regret on his face as we began making our way towards the exit. He walked me to my car and even though he must have been in a hurry to leave, he showed no sign of it as he stood by my open driver's door, waiting for me to climb in.

'So, what's next?' he asked. His bright-blue eyes were mesmerising behind the window of his glasses. I found myself having to concentrate extra hard when we were standing in front of each other like this, because there was something about his face... his eyes... that kept making my thoughts wander.

'Next? Well, you go to work, and I go and visit my sister.' Glib was definitely the way to go, I decided, pleased to hear just the right amount of nonchalance in my reply.

And yet Nick still showed no signs of leaving. 'I meant what's next on Sam and Amelia's schedule? Where's our next date?'

This was the moment to release him from his obligation. I'd found his missing daughter in the shopping mall, and he'd given up his day off to help me achieve something he probably still thought was crazy. Whichever way you looked at it, we were definitely quits.

Except Nick was having none of it. 'You'll only have evidence of a single date if we stop now. Don't you need photos from some of the other memorable occasions?'

'That *is* what I'd originally intended. But I can see now that I wasn't being sensible. This is going to take up way too much of your time.'

'Let me worry about that,' he said.

Let him go, I told myself. *Let him leave before you start catching feelings that don't belong to you. They're Amelia's, not yours.*

'What else did they do together?' Nick asked, interrupting those dangerous thoughts. For a moment, some of the very explicit details my sister had shared flashed through my thoughts – only it wasn't Amelia and Sam in those intimate images, but two people who looked an awful lot like them. I felt an incipient blush.

'They went horse riding at sunset,' I said on a rush, before anything more risqué came out of my mouth. 'Do you happen to know anyone with a couple of horses?'

Nick raised a single eyebrow, and I felt the warmth of a pink tinge flood my cheeks. What a ridiculous question to ask a veterinary surgeon.

'That would be a strong yes,' he replied, his eyes twinkling. 'Can you ride?'

'That would be a strong no,' I said, biting my lower lip to stop the smile that seemed determined to take over my mouth.

'This should be interesting,' he said, stepping back finally to allow me to slide on to my seat. 'Leave it with me, I'll arrange it,' he promised.

There was more than enough time to stop him, to tell him I'd changed my mind, but I appeared to have lost all my good sense somewhere in the amusement park that day.

'See you soon,' Nick said, as he firmly closed my car door.

It was strange how three perfectly ordinary words could suddenly become so important.

'You're wearing my jumper.'

I had an instant flashback to my early teenage years, when I was forever getting caught raiding my big sister's wardrobe. *Same crime, different reason*, I thought, as I looked down at the emerald-green sweater that I'd intended to change out of before going up to the ward. How distracted had I been to have totally forgotten?

'Sorry. I had an important Zoom call with an author just before I left the cottage and none of my decent stuff was clean,' I lied.

'Oh, okay,' she said, sounding a little disappointed with my answer. 'I thought maybe you'd been out somewhere for lunch.'

At least this time I could tell the truth. 'No. I definitely didn't go out for lunch,' I said, my thoughts straying to the meal Nick had wanted us to share.

'Earth to Lexi,' said Amelia, snapping her fingers and my attention back to her hospital room. 'Where did you go? You were miles away.'

'Sorry,' I said. 'I was just thinking about work things.'

I instantly regretted my words as a troubled look crossed the face that looked so much like mine.

'Don't you think you should be back in New York by now?'

'Don't you think it's time you stopped asking me that?' I batted right back.

'They're not going to wait forever for a decision from you,'

Amelia pointed out reasonably, unaware this was something I'd already considered and made my peace with. 'And what about Jeff?' she persisted. 'He can't be happy you're staying here to look after me – which incidentally I don't need, in case you were wondering.'

'I thought you didn't like Jeff?' I asked, slipping easily back into the sisterly banter that came as naturally to both of us as breathing.

'I never said that.'

'You didn't have to.' I grinned at her and touched my forehead and then pointed at hers. 'It's a twin thing.'

'It's a good taste in men thing,' she shot back, just as one of the nursing team came in to take her obs.

I didn't need to ask for the results to know that Amelia was getting better. Maybe the end to this whole awful ordeal really was in sight.

Perhaps because Amelia had mentioned him, or perhaps because I'd spent the best part of the day with another man, Jeff was on my mind more than usual on the drive back to the cottage. Our relationship had slipped into a coma, and if I was being honest, it had probably started long before I'd got on a plane to be with my family. We were sleepwalking through something that wasn't old enough to be comfortable and taken for granted. And yes, the physical attraction was still there, but sex – even the great kind – can only carry you for so long. You couldn't and shouldn't build a future on it. The cold hard truth was that Jeff and I had been happily travelling along two parallel tracks that were now slowly veering off in different directions. It wasn't the first time one of my relationships had run out of steam. In fact, for a romantic fiction editor, I didn't seem to have a clue how to find my own happily ever after.

Less than forty-five minutes after getting home, I would find out just how true that was.

Despite the lateness of the hour, the message from my assistant, Kacey, in New York wasn't entirely unexpected... but the first line was definitely an attention grabber.

I've thought long and hard and I still don't know if I should tell you this...

They've offered the job to someone else, I thought immediately. They're going to reassign my authors to another editor; they're making cuts, they're letting me go. My worst-case scenarios just kept on coming, each one making me feel a little queasy. I typed back:

You can't start a message like that.

The blip of my sent message sounded extraordinarily loud in the empty lounge.

Okay. I have something to tell you. But you didn't hear it from me.

Except I patently did, I thought, as my lips twisted in concern.

Fine. What is it?

The dancing dots of her typed reply went on and on, creating their own telephonic torture. I was already wondering how up to date my CV was and who I should send it to first, when her reply finally landed on my screen.

Do you remember me telling you I was going to my cousin's wedding in The Hamptons?

I stared in bewilderment at my phone. What did this have to do with the team restructuring? Kacey's question was clearly one I wasn't expected to answer, because she followed it up with her first revelation.

Well, I was worried I wouldn't know anyone there. But it turns out that actually I did…

Kacey stopped typing, and a tiny wave of irritation swept through me. This was *not* the moment to pause for dramatic effect, but she was doing so anyway. I typed:

Who?

And even before I'd pinged the question to New York, I think part of me already knew the answer.

Jeff.

I sat back in my chair, gripping the phone in both hands as though it was a grenade and my hold on the pin was slipping. I was waiting for the next message but instead four images flew across the Atlantic and landed on my phone screen. It seemed to take an eternity for Amelia's slow internet to download them.

The woman in each of the photographs was so close to Jeff, she might actually have been superglued to his side. I recognised her immediately as one of the assistants in his firm. I knew very little about her, except that her name – Tallulah – seemed to crop up in conversation more frequently than his other colleagues. I tried to remember what else he'd told me but could only come up with the fact that her family were extremely wealthy, and that she'd gone to Harvard. Both things were likely to have impressed Jeff.

I jumped and almost lost hold of my mobile when it suddenly rang in my hand.

'Screw it,' Kacey said on a rush. 'You need to hear this in person, although I feel terrible telling you, what with your sister being so sick and everything. But if it was me... well, I'd want someone to let me know if my boyfriend was playing around behind my back.'

I scrolled back through the images she'd sent me. There were entwined arms, and bodies pressed up together on a dance floor, and heads resting on shoulders they shouldn't be on, but that was hardly conclusive evidence. Although perhaps it was enough to cause anyone in a serious relationship to be worried.

So why wasn't I? Is this how you know when something is really over? When it flatlines right in front of you but you carry on breathing and your eyes stay dry?

And yet despite that, my pride was bruised... just a little. Which was why I answered Kacey the only way I knew how.

'It's sweet of you to be worried. But I knew Jeff was going

to the wedding as Tallulah's plus-one. He checked I was fine with it first.'

For a basically honest person, I was beginning to grow concerned about how many lies I'd been telling recently.

'And are you?' Kacey asked. Was there a trace of disappointment in her voice? There'd be no water-cooler mileage out of this conversation.

'I am, Kacey. I really am. So, what's going on at work?'

Telling Kacey I was okay wasn't a lie, but I was human enough for my feelings to be a little hurt, even if my heart wasn't. Of course, there was a chance that the photographs were misleading. After all, hadn't I just spent an entire day recreating something on the screen that didn't exist between Nick and me? Wasn't that the same thing?

Entirely different, my reflection contradicted, as I wiped the make-up from my face and climbed into bed. My mind was racing too much to lose myself in a book, so I reached for my phone and began scrolling through the photographs I'd taken that day at Lassiters. My motives had been pure, but didn't the photographs with Nick's arms around me, or of us holding hands on the roller coaster, appear every bit as damning as the ones of Jeff and Tallulah at the wedding? If my photos were entirely innocent – which they were – then it was only reasonable to assume theirs could be too.

My dreams that night were confused and disturbed and for once I was delighted when the noisy cawing of the seagulls on the beach pulled me out of them.

16

Kippers. I could definitely smell kippers. My nose twitched like a rabbit's as I pulled the duvet from my face. Rain had been falling heavily when my seven o'clock alarm had woken me, and one look at the windswept beach had been enough to persuade me I'd rather grab a few extra hours of sleep on a Saturday morning than go jogging in a deluge.

Without the filter of duck down and feathers, the aroma of smoked fish intensified. How was that even possible? I reached for my dressing gown and swung out of bed. The old oak floorboards felt cold beneath my bare feet, but I didn't bother hunting for socks. I paused at the top of the stairs, where the smell of fish was even stronger. Was it coming from the sea?

'Hello? Is anyone down there?' I called out as I began to descend the creaky treads, never for a moment expecting a reply. I jerked in shock when a figure emerged from the shadows.

'Well, finally. I thought you were *never* going to wake up,' said Mum from the foot of the staircase.

'Jesus, Mum, you scared the life out of me. I thought you were an intruder.' Which she kind of was, because I'd had no idea she was planning on visiting that morning. *What if I hadn't been alone in the guest room double bed?* I shook my head, wondering where on earth that ridiculous thought had come from.

As my eyes adjusted to the shadowy hallway, I noticed Mum had an old-fashioned apron knotted around her waist. There was a cleaning cloth in her hand and the sleeves of her paisley shirt were rolled up for business.

'What are you doing here, Mum?' I asked. Her answer was interrupted by the warning siren from the kitchen's smoke alarm. With a speed that belied her years, she hurried back to whatever was spitting and sizzling beneath the grill.

While she attended to the oven, I silenced the alarm before throwing open both windows to let out the worst of the smoke. Sadly, the smell of fish wasn't so easy to dispel. I cinched my dressing gown more tightly around me and watched as Mum slid two large herring fillets on to waiting plates. I was wondering if this was the right moment to tactfully remind her that I didn't eat kippers when she reached for the roll of plastic wrap, covered one of the plates with it, and carried it to Amelia's back door.

I wondered then if I might actually still be asleep, because this was beginning to feel like an incredibly vivid but totally surreal dream.

'Where exactly are you going with that kipper?' Surely one of the strangest questions I'd ever asked anyone.

Mum paused by the open doorway, a slight flush colouring her cheeks. 'I'm just taking it down to Tom,' she replied, ducking through the opening before I could ask one of a great many questions.

In her absence I made us both tea and then, when ten minutes had passed and she *still* hadn't reappeared, I slid her breakfast plate back beneath the grill. I was halfway through a bowl of muesli when she let herself back into the kitchen, bringing a strong March breeze in her wake.

'Is this like a Meals on Wheels or Help the Aged kind of thing?' I asked, nodding my head in the direction of Tom's cottage.

Mum's face flushed again, which really ought to have alerted me. In my defence, I'm really not a morning person.

'It's a friend doing a favour kind of thing, actually,' Mum replied in a tone I hadn't heard for a great many years. 'Tom brought the kippers round as a gift, and I offered to cook them. And for your information, he's only a couple of years older than I am.'

There was a lot to assimilate in her reply and for once I was glad that muesli took longer to chew and swallow than other cereals.

'So, are you and Tom friends now?' I asked, trying very hard to keep the incredulity from my voice, but it crept in anyway.

'Perhaps we are,' Mum replied enigmatically. 'Would that be so very strange? After all, *you* were the one who introduced us.' She made it sound as though I was guilty of matchmaking, and truly nothing could be further from the truth. I felt like someone who'd picked up a book, only to discover they'd somehow skipped several really important chapters.

'And it will certainly be a comfort knowing there's someone

close by who can keep an eye on Amelia when you go back to New York,' she continued.

I was used to the way my stomach contracted whenever I thought about going back. I thought the queasy feeling was because I was homesick for Manhattan, but lately I was beginning to wonder if it was because I was already missing Somerset, even before I'd left it.

'You still haven't explained what you're doing here at the crack of dawn on a Saturday morning.'

'Now we know Amelia could be out of hospital in a week or so, I wanted to make a start on getting the place ready for her. And it's hardly the crack of dawn, Lexi,' Mum added, her eyes dropping to her watch. 'It's after eleven.'

That surprised me almost as much as Tom and her being new 'besties'. I reached for my phone to verify the time, but never got as far as registering it because the message on the screen brought me up short. *Missed call. Nick.*

Whenever I visited Amelia in the hospital, I automatically switched my phone to silent, and I must have forgotten to turn the ringer back on last night when I left the ward. It had been three days since our trip to the amusement park. Three days for me to interpret Nick's lack of contact as a change of heart. I'd almost called him at least half a dozen times, but so far good sense had kicked in when I was still one number away from connecting to his phone. And now, on the day he calls, my phone was switched off. Was that just bad luck, or was the universe trying to tell me something?

My fingers itched to call him back, but with Mum sitting less than a metre away, I was going to have to wait. I still hadn't told her what I was doing, and I wasn't sure I was ready for the disappointment I was afraid I'd see in her eyes when she knew about it.

Mum was giving the kipper on her plate far more concentration than it probably deserved, and I wondered if I'd somehow hurt her feelings about her new friendship. Despite Tom's prickly barnacle exterior, I really did like him. Some years ago, Amelia and I had asked Mum if she'd ever thought of remarrying, because we'd wanted her to know that if she did, we'd both be okay with it. I can still remember the sadness in her voice when she replied. *Not everyone is lucky enough to find their true soul mate in life. But if you do, you realise you're one half of a miracle. And miracles rarely happen more than once in a lifetime.*

'I'm glad that you and Tom are friends,' I told her now, as she got to her feet and began gathering up our dirty dishes. 'And I'm sure Amelia will be too – just as long as you don't end up moving in three doors down from her.' I crossed to the sink to give her a hug, so she knew I was teasing. 'Seriously, Mum, Mimi and I just want you to be happy. She'll be as pleased as I am that you've made a new friend.'

'Speaking of new friends,' Mum said in a neat segue, 'I met one of yours this morning.'

She tossed me a gingham tea towel before plunging her arms into the sudsy water, her attention seemingly on nothing more than the dirty dishes. But she didn't fool me for a minute.

Very slowly, as though each word needed to be carefully excavated, I turned to face her. 'What friend? Who?'

She had exactly the same look on her face that she'd worn when I'd broken my grandmother's heirloom flower vase and hidden the shattered pieces at the bottom of the wheelie bin. Two decades on and she'd lost none of her knack.

'I think you can guess who I'm talking about.'

I swallowed noisily.

'I must say, Amelia's drawings of him were uncannily lifelike.'

'Nick? Nick was here?'

Mum withdrew her arms from the suds and folded them across her waist. Never a good sign.

'It might have been nice, Lexi, if *you*'d told me what you were up to, rather than having to hear it from a total stranger – albeit a perfectly charming one,' she added, with just enough censure in her voice for me to know I was unequivocally in the wrong here.

'He told you everything?'

'I worked it out for myself from the things he said. I don't think he realised that you'd not told me what you were up to.'

'Why didn't you wake me up when he was here?'

'I wanted to. But he insisted that I let you sleep.'

She was looking at me very closely. 'He seems like a very nice young man. With an extremely friendly dog.'

I'd been absently twisting the tea towel in my hands. Glancing down, it looked exactly like the rope I was busily hanging myself with.

'Are you mad at me, Mum? Do you think what I'm doing is crazy?'

Mum took the tortured tea towel from my grip and held my hands in her warm sudsy fingers. 'Yes to the latter, no to the former.'

Her eyes were bright as they met mine. 'You're one of life's natural-born fixers, Lexi – when you see a problem, you're compelled to sort it. And you love your sister. There's a bond the two of you share that's stronger than your dad and I could ever understand. She'd walk through fire for you, and I know you'd do the same for her.'

Unexpectedly, I found myself crying. Tears were running down my cheeks and I made no effort to wipe them away.

'If you really believe this madcap thing you're doing with this man is the right way to help Amelia, then I have to trust your judgement. You know her heart better than I do.'

There was a huge lump in my throat that was making it almost impossible to swallow.

Mum smiled gently and there was love and trust on her face. 'Just make sure that whatever you're doing with your friend Nick, you're doing for the right reasons.'

My friend Nick. My mother's words followed me as I climbed back up the stairs and jumped into the shower. I turned the water up to its highest temperature – having finally solved the conundrum of the boiler – and stayed under the jets until my skin turned the colour of a lobster. Nick wasn't my friend, not really. I hardly knew anything about him. *But isn't that the way it goes with a new friendship*, I reasoned, playing devil's advocate with myself. You meet someone. You connect with them on whatever level and then you get to know them better. Little by little. But could you really be friends with someone when the only reason they're in your life is because they look like someone else? Even though Mum had unofficially given my plan her blessing, was I guilty of callously using Nick? The thought made me shiver, despite the heat of my shower.

My phone was sitting on top of my bed, waiting for me to return its last missed call. And yet still I hesitated.

*

In the end, it was the sound of Mum busily vacuuming the lounge that had me dialling Nick's number. Having changed Amelia's heart medication once again, the doctors felt confident that, with careful monitoring, she could be discharged from hospital as early as the beginning of next week. The news sent us into panic mode: Mum's mission was to get the house as sterile as an operating theatre, while mine was to complete the memory box of photographs in a little over a week.

Determination made me swallow down my nerves and find the courage to place the call.

'Ah, good morning. You're awake now, are you?' It was the second time today I'd been greeted with that comment, but Nick's words left me more flustered than Mum's had.

'Yes. I'm so sorry I missed your phone call and that I was still asleep when you came round. I wish you'd asked Mum to wake me. I feel terrible that you had a wasted journey.'

I could hear the smile in his voice. 'Don't worry about it. Mabel appreciated the extra-long walk, and it was good to meet your mum. Although I don't usually do the "meet the parent" thing this early in the dating process.'

He was teasing me, I knew that, but it was impossible not to rise to the bait.

'Don't forget, it's just *pretend* dating, Clark,' I reminded him.

His laugh was low and warm, and I liked the way our private joke showed no signs of getting old just yet.

'The reason I was trying to get in touch,' said Nick, 'was to let you know that I've managed to line up a couple of horses for our next date.' My gulp was way noisier than I'd intended. It travelled with perfect clarity down the phone line. 'That *was* the plan, wasn't it?' he queried uncertainly. 'You wanted to recreate Amelia and Sam's sunset horseback ride?'

'Yes. I did. I do. That's great,' I said, hoping he couldn't hear that my enthusiasm was about as real as our relationship.

'The horses belong to a farmer friend of mine. The one you'll be riding is owned by his thirteen-year-old daughter and it's really docile.'

'Docile is good.'

'You'll be absolutely fine,' Nick assured me, hearing the nerves in my voice. 'I won't let anything terrible happen to you.'

'I'm going to hold you to that,' I said as I reached for a notepad to scribble down the address of his friend's farm.

We agreed to meet at six that evening, a full hour before the sun was due to set. I spent most of the drive trying to guess how many times I was likely to fall off during a sixty-minute period. Riding wasn't my thing; it never had been. Amelia had been the typical horse-mad teenager in our family, while I'd been far more obsessed with books and boy bands. The closest I'd got to an interest in horses had been my Jilly Cooper obsession.

Now that Mum knew what I was doing, it had been easier to swap our usual hospital visiting slots. I was even hopeful that if we finished our ride early enough, and all my bones were still intact, I might have time to make the end of the evening session.

My heart began beating faster the moment I spotted the

signpost for the farm. I was clearly more nervous about getting on a horse than I'd realised, I thought, as I swung my car down the farm's long dirt-packed driveway.

I certainly looked the part though, with my oldest, comfiest jeans and a thick flannel checked shirt that I'd found in the back of Amelia's wardrobe. She hadn't specifically mentioned what she'd been wearing on the day she and Sam had gone riding, but I figured that anyone whose Spotify playlist consisted almost entirely of country music would probably have favoured a cowboy look.

It was only when I pulled into the yard that I began to question my choice of outfit. This was no dude ranch, the kind my American friends always raved about; this was a real working farm and I probably looked just this side of ridiculous. I quickly pulled off the bandana scarf that I'd tied around my neck, but there was nothing to be done about the shirt or the cowboy boots.

Nick was standing on the far side of the yard, chatting to a man who looked to be a couple of years older than him. He was leaning casually against the bonnet of his car, one foot resting on the bumper. He looked like an advert for something outdoorsy and expensive. My heart gave a small lurch, but that was probably because I'd just spotted two very large horses standing beyond the men. The animals were both saddled up, and from the way they were pawing the ground, they were obviously impatient to go. Both horses were being restrained by a young girl. She leant closer to the smaller, dapple-grey one and whispered something into its mane. I had a horrible feeling it was probably an apology.

Nick straightened up the moment I climbed out of the car. There might have been the merest twitch of his lips as he made his way towards me. His friend, the owner of the farm, wasn't nearly so restrained.

'Well, howdy, ma'am,' he said, doffing an imaginary Stetson by way of a greeting.

I gave a rueful smile. I really had no one to blame but myself for the ribbing. I looked up at Nick, waiting for a jibe, but he held up his hands as though in surrender.

'I have nothing,' he said.

I grinned and turned to face Nick's friend, who I instantly liked.

'Hi. I'm Lexi,' I said, holding out my hand. 'Thank you so much for letting us borrow your horses.'

'Doug,' he said by way of introduction, as his calloused fingers gripped mine. 'It's the least I can do, considering the number of times I've dragged this one out of his bed in the middle of the night.' He paused just long enough for me to conjure up a totally inappropriate visual, which meant I completely missed his next comment.

'...and Nick tells me you've not done much of this before.'

I took a long shot that we were talking about riding and not impersonating my sister.

'Not at all, really,' I said. I *definitely* didn't imagine the worried expression that flitted across his daughter's face.

'You're probably going to need to wear that jacket,' Nick advised, looking down at the quilted garment I was carrying. 'It's going to get chilly once the sun goes down.' He was wearing a dark cable-knit jumper that made his already broad shoulders appear even wider. 'And you'll also need to wear this,' he said, picking up a riding hat and passing it to me. He saw my hesitation and perhaps mistook it for vanity.

'The hat is non-negotiable, Lexi,' Nick said firmly. 'You don't wear it, you don't get to ride.'

'Where's yours then?' I asked, looking around for a second hat and failing to spot one.

Nick's crooked grin put in its first appearance of the day. 'I don't need one. I'm not going to fall off.'

'I thought you said I wouldn't either,' I shot back, reaching for the hat and putting it on my head.

'Are you sure this is only *make-believe* dating?' Doug asked, his eyes flitting between me and his old friend. 'Because you certainly bicker like a real couple.'

I could hardly blame Nick for telling his friend the truth about what we were doing, but it wrong-footed me even more than the idea of climbing on to a horse did. A change of subject was needed, so I turned to the young girl who was waiting patiently beside the horses.

'Hi, I'm Lexi. Thank you so much for letting me ride your horse. I'll take good care of him.'

'Her,' the girl corrected, with a very teenage eye-roll.

'I'll look after Dotty,' Nick assured the girl, whose expression transformed into one of undiluted adoration as she looked up at him. Were they aware that she had a king-size crush on her dad's friend, I wondered?

Getting on the horse was actually much easier than I'd feared, thanks to the mounting block they'd thoughtfully provided. Nick obviously needed no such assistance and had swung himself up easily on to the black horse.

'Could you take a photo of us on Lexi's phone, Pippa?' Nick asked the young girl when we were both settled and ready to go.

I pulled my mobile from my jacket and passed it to the

teenager, who expertly rattled off a variety of snaps from different angles. After passing me back the phone, I was surprised when she took a couple of steps backwards and began heading towards the farmhouse.

'Oh, I thought you'd be coming with us,' I exclaimed, feeling a tiny frisson of panic. This far from ground level, it was hard to work out if it was the ride that I was worrying about or being alone with Nick. At Lassiters we'd been on neutral territory, but here he was very much in his natural element, and I very much wasn't.

'Pippa's got homework she needs to finish,' Doug answered on behalf of his daughter.

'We'll be just fine,' Nick said, turning to me in his saddle. 'I've got you.' As we began a slow and gentle walk out of the yard, I couldn't decide if his words made me feel safer or even more nervous.

We took a bridleway that led from the yard to open farmland, and happily both horses seemed very familiar with the route. I realised there was very little I actually needed to do as far as riding went, so revised my objective to just staying on.

'Are you okay? You're doing really well,' Nick commented a few minutes later, when the farm was well behind us.

'Try telling that to my bottom,' I said unthinkingly, before realising I'd drawn his attention to a part of my anatomy I really didn't want him thinking about at all.

'Sitting down might be a little uncomfortable tomorrow,' he admitted. 'And you'll really feel it in your inner thighs.'

I definitely didn't want him thinking about my inner thighs either.

'Were you working at the practice today?' I asked, trying to steer us back to polite conversation.

'No. I'm not rostered on this weekend. I had Holly for the day, but she's gone to a sleepover tonight with ten girls from her class.'

I grinned. 'That'll be fun when you have to return the invitation.'

A look that was hard to identify crossed his features. 'I think that'll probably be her mum's department, not mine.'

I considered not probing, but my curiosity was too strong. 'Do you and your ex not get along? If that's not too personal a question to ask.'

Who was I kidding? It was *way* too personal. I was stepping well outside of acceptable boundaries, but thankfully Nick didn't appear to take offence.

'Well, we certainly don't get along as well as we once did,' he replied with a rueful smile.

'At least you can joke about it.'

'I can now. But it wasn't so funny at the time.'

'What happened?' I asked, shocked by my own curiosity. It was as though I'd forgotten how to filter my thoughts before they came tumbling out of my mouth. 'You don't have to answer that,' I added on a rush.

Nick shrugged and I searched his face carefully. I could see the lingering scars from an old painful memory. 'It's not an original story. Boy meets girl at university. They marry too young, too soon, and get pregnant too early. And then six years later she calls out another man's name at a moment when she really ought to have known who she was with.'

The bitterness of the old betrayal was still in his voice.

'Oh God, Nick. I'm so sorry. That must have been awful.'

'More so because it was my best mate's name,' he said, his lips tightening on the words.

'Doug?' I asked on a horrified gasp.

Thankfully, Nick seemed to find that amusing.

'I'm pretty well adjusted, but I think that would be pushing it. No, it was another friend. Strangely, he and I lost touch after that.'

'Are they still together?' My tongue appeared to be on a mission to embarrass the hell out of me.

Nick shook his head. 'She told me afterwards she'd only had the affair to get my attention.' He urged his horse forward, making it impossible to read his face as he completed his sentence. 'I guess it worked, although perhaps not in the way she'd expected.'

I suddenly wished I knew him better, because if I did, I might have found the right response to his open honesty. But I didn't, so it was easier to remain silent. I was searching for something to say that would lighten the moment or create a diversion and fortunately the sun helped out by starting its slow dip towards the horizon, bathing the sky in a palette of reds and mauves.

Nick glanced up. 'Photo op time?' he asked, pulling his black horse to a halt.

I nodded and watched as he leant across and gently pulled on Dotty's reins to bring her to a stop.

'Shall we go for a selfie?' he asked, skilfully repositioning both horses so we'd be backlit by the descending sun. He took my phone and held it aloft, as he leant into the gap between the two horses.

'Can you come a little closer?' he asked.

I did as he asked, until we were shoulder to shoulder in the frame. If I'd been more experienced in the saddle, that was the moment when I might have felt my right foot slip out of the stirrup. But I was too distracted by Nick putting an arm around my shoulders and pulling me closer towards him.

The photographs, when I examined them later, told their own story, although not necessarily the one I'd intended. We were smiling in the first three, happily unaware that in photo number four our expressions would be entirely different. Neither of us saw the squirrel scamper down the tree and run directly in front of us. But Dotty did. I'd never been on a rearing horse before and if there's a trick to not being unseated, I didn't know it. I'd been so preoccupied creating the perfect photo of Amelia and Sam that I'd even relaxed my hold on the reins. What happened next was inevitable. One minute I was sitting on the horse and the next I was airborne, while Dotty was galloping away at speed.

Nick's reactions were fast, but nothing was going to save me from connecting with the ground. Luckily, his arm had still been around me when the squirrel spooked my horse, and he managed to grab a fistful of my jacket when she reared up. It wasn't enough to hold on to me, but it definitely broke my fall. Everything took on a slow-motion quality and it seemed an eternity before my bottom connected heavily with the soft, muddy earth as I landed with an embarrassing squelch.

Nick leapt from his horse and was crouched down beside me in an instant. 'Don't move,' he urged, his hands already running up and down my legs in a way I might have enjoyed in other circumstances. 'Are you hurt?' he asked, taking his eyes from my legs and darting them to my face. 'Did you hit your head?'

'No, I'm fine,' I said, as the hands moved from my legs and began travelling down the length of my spine. *He's a medic... kind of*, I told myself firmly. *There's nothing at all inappropriate in him running his hands over you.*

Fortunately, the examination was soon over and Nick sat back on his haunches. 'The good news is nothing appears to be broken or sprained,' he declared with a satisfied nod. It was all very professional and businesslike until he added, 'How's your bottom?'

'Bruised and sitting in several inches of cold mud at the moment,' I replied.

If he offered to examine it, that was definitely where I'd draw the line, but he didn't. Instead, he got to his feet and held out his hands. He lifted me up and out of the muddy ground with a huge plopping sound.

'Do you think you can walk?' he asked, still holding fast on to both my hands.

'Sure,' I replied and then proceeded to take a couple of steps that made Bambi look like an expert figure skater.

'Perhaps you'd better hang on to me for a bit,' he said, letting go of my hands and offering me his arm.

I took it and it was only then, as I scanned the clearing, that I realised we were down one horse.

'Where's Dotty?' I cried, doing a full 360-degree turn as though I might possibly have missed the dapple-grey mare.

'Halfway back to the farm by now, I should imagine,' Nick said. He seemed strangely unconcerned, but his answer threw me into a total panic.

'What if she isn't? What if she's lost? Oh God, I promised Pippa I'd take good care of her and look what's happened. I'm a horrible person. *And* I'm a shit rider.' I turned to Nick, who seemed to be doing his best not to laugh. 'I *told* you I'd fall off.'

'You did,' he agreed solemnly, pulling out his phone. I watched, transfixed, as his fingers rattled off a speedy text. He received a reply almost immediately.

'Doug's going to look out for her. He said to tell you not to worry. Dotty knows her way back home.'

My gait was stronger now and although my bottom still felt curiously numb, at least I could walk more easily.

Nick's borrowed horse had been happily munching on the grass throughout the drama, and luckily hadn't bolted off after his stablemate. It was only when Nick took hold of its bridle and brought the animal towards me that I realised what was on his mind.

'Uh-uh,' I said, shaking my head as he bent to position one hand at my knee and the other by my ankle to give me a leg-up. 'I'm done with riding for today.'

'I'll be right behind you in the saddle,' Nick said. 'You'll be perfectly safe.'

'You're going to have to stop saying that,' I told him, 'because I don't believe you anymore. Your superhero skills are about as good as my jockey ones.'

There was a moment of silence and then suddenly we were both laughing. It was the kind of laughter that brought tears to your eyes and made your ribs ache – it was out of proportion to the humour of the situation, and yet neither of us could seem to stop. And then something happened, while we were holding on to each other, incapable of speech. I don't know how it began, or when, or whose laughter stilled first, but suddenly our eyes connected and everything slowly went quiet and very, very still. It was a moment spun out of delicate glass and I think both of us were too shocked to shatter it.

Who knows how long we might have stood there in the twilight, just looking at each other, unsure of what was happening, if Nick's horse hadn't interrupted the moment with a very impatient whinny. The feeling – whatever it had been – disappeared into the dusk as though it had never been.

'Let's walk back then,' Nick said, and there was something in his voice that told me the 'thing' – whatever it had been – still hadn't entirely left him either.

17

Doug was waiting for us in the yard. Pippa was over by the stables, nose to nose with her beloved Dotty, who, as predicted, had made her way safely back to the farm. The two men exchanged a few words as Nick passed the black horse back to Doug, who gave a cheery wave in my direction and then headed towards the stables.

I waved back and then turned towards Amelia's car.

'Well. This was… fun,' I said, pulling a comical expression so he didn't think I was blaming him for how our faux date had ended.

I unlocked the car and paused as my eyes ran over the vehicle's pale beige upholstery. I glanced back over my shoulder at my mud-caked jeans, which were stuck to my legs like a second skin. Even the bottom of my jacket was covered in a thick sticky residue.

'Do you think Doug might have an old towel I could borrow to sit on?' I asked Nick, staring after the retreating farmer, who was now out of earshot.

'Probably,' Nick said, 'but I've got a better idea. My place is only ten minutes from here. If you like, you could get cleaned up there and then I'll drop you back here to collect your car.'

His suggestion was practical and sensible and yet still I hesitated. 'But then I'll just dirty up *your* car,' I said.

'Lexi, I'm a vet who works in a rural area. Trust me, my car's seen much worse than a bit of mud.'

Dusk had dissolved into darkness and the farmyard's floodlights flickered on just in time for Nick to see me shivering in my cold, muddy clothes. The thought of getting out of them was what sold it for me. That's what made me say yes. It had nothing whatsoever to do with a desire to prolong our time together.

'Well, so long as I'm not messing up your evening plans, then yes please. I accept the offer. Thank you,' I said, falling into step beside him as we headed towards his Range Rover.

His car certainly wasn't as pristine as Amelia's, but I still felt guilty about making it dirty, so I slipped off my jacket and balled it up, inside out. Without it, I immediately shivered; the temperature had dropped dramatically in the last hour.

'Here,' Nick said, without hesitation. Before I had a chance to object, he was tugging off his thick cable-knit jumper.

'Oh no, Nick... that's alright. You really don't have to—' I began, but the jumper was already in my hands and, damn, it felt so wonderfully warm.

'Lexi, please just put it on,' he said, pulling his car keys from the pocket of his jeans. Beneath the jumper, Nick was wearing a grey marl T-shirt, the kind that had seen so many washing-machine cycles it was almost gossamer thin. It clung to him so closely that the muscles of his back and shoulders were outlined as clearly as if he were bare chested.

I was horribly aware that I was staring and the easiest way

to stop doing that was to pull the thick jumper over my head and block out the view. Although the relief was short-lived, because the smell of him was suddenly all around me as I burrowed into the folds of the borrowed garment. It was a tantalising teaser of what it must be like to be held in his arms, which was an avenue my thoughts definitely shouldn't be taking, but they were going there anyway.

'Are you warm enough?' Nick asked as we drove down the bumpy farm track that led to the road. He'd turned the heater to its highest setting, which meant the car was slowly filling with the aroma of hot dried mud.

'It's like a spa day gone terribly wrong,' I told him, pleased to see how that made him smile.

'You're really funny,' he said, his eyes still on the road. 'You make me laugh more than anyone's done in a very long time.'

That was either one of the nicest things he could say to me, or one of the worst. I decided I'd take it as a compliment.

'I'm here all week,' I quipped. But the stand-up comics' catchphrase only served to remind me that my time here in Somerset, with my family, and also with Nick, would soon come to an end.

He surprised me by being on the same wavelength. 'We don't have long, do we?'

Such a big question, with really only one answer. I replied on a purely superficial level. 'No. Not long. The doctors seem confident Amelia will be home next week.'

Nick nodded thoughtfully and fell silent for a while, his attention focused on the winding country roads, or so I thought. He cleared his throat twice before eventually speaking. 'I have a small confession to make,' he admitted hesitantly.

I turned in my seat to face him. 'That sounds ominous. What did you do? Bribe that squirrel to jump out so you could lure me back to your place?' I was joking and totally unprepared for the look of guilt that flashed across his face.

'Not exactly,' Nick said, turning down a driveway and pulling up outside a building surrounded by open countryside. The house was in darkness and there wasn't a neighbouring property in sight.

I'd watched enough true crime TV shows to know this was the moment I should probably start feeling nervous. But *nothing* about this man scared me, which in itself was a little worrying.

'I was sort of hoping that our date might extend beyond our ride, so I booked us a table at an Italian restaurant in town.'

I was still searching for an appropriate facial expression when Nick added with a boyish shrug, 'I know. I should have asked you first.'

You do know I'd have said 'yes', don't you? I practically had to clamp my lips together to stop the admission from escaping.

'Why didn't you?'

'I thought you might say no.'

Either Nick was rubbish at reading body language or I was far better at hiding my feelings than I realised. Either way, I was secretly glad that the man pretending to be my boyfriend didn't have a clue that I was attracted to him. Because if he did, things could get really weird.

'Well, I would have accepted, but I don't see how I can now,' I said with genuine regret as my gaze dropped to my mud-caked jeans.

Nick nodded and climbed out of the car. I was all fingers and thumbs with the unfamiliar seat belt clasp, and he'd already walked round to the passenger side and opened the door for me by the time I'd freed myself.

'You're a very hard woman to buy a pizza for,' Nick said, subtly steering our conversation back on to a more casual footing. 'Every time I try, something gets in the way.'

'We could try ordering a takeaway and see what the universe throws in our path?' I suggested.

'I'm up for that challenge if you are,' Nick said, placing a hand at the small of my back and guiding me towards his front door.

Nick's home was surprisingly modern. I hadn't realised from the outside, but it was actually a barn conversion – albeit a small barn. 'More of a *shed* conversion, really,' he joked. The architect had done a great job, marrying the old oak beams and exposed brickwork with bleached wooden flooring, gleaming chrome, and huge walls of glass that in daylight probably afforded spectacular views of the open countryside. It was totally different from Amelia's fisherman's cottage and a whole world away from my New York apartment... but I loved his home from the moment he opened the front door.

Nick kicked off his boots while I loitered on the doormat, worried about leaving a muddy trail on the immaculate floor. Suddenly there was a joyous yelp followed by a frantic skittering as roughly seventy-five pounds of highly excitable Old English Sheepdog came hurtling across the room towards us. Mabel initially had eyes for no one but Nick, greeting him as though she'd not seen him for at least a month.

'How long have you been gone?' I laughed. The dog was literally whimpering with joy as he fussed her.

'Only a couple of hours, but she has no concept of time,' Nick replied, scratching the dog between her ears and staring deep into her dark-brown eyes. I shook my head because there was something extremely wrong in feeling envious of a dog. Mabel was generous with her affections and then spent several minutes greeting me, although I suspect the smell of my jeans and what I'd landed in was of more interest to her than I was.

I pulled off my boots and stood them beside Nick's on the mat, telling myself to stop being ridiculous for thinking how good they looked side by side like that.

'The shower room is at the top of the stairs. You'll find clean towels in the hall cupboard and help yourself to any of the toiletries.'

'Thank you,' I said, heading towards the modern open-tread staircase, which looked like it belonged in an art gallery.

'I'll dig out something for you to change into and leave it outside the door. But it's all going to swamp you, I'm afraid.'

'Anything will do,' I assured him.

I was halfway up the stairs when he stopped me again. 'Are you hot and spicy, or more of an anchovy person?'

My nose automatically wrinkled at the mention of the small salty fish fillets.

'Thank goodness,' Nick declared, 'or I was going to have to break up with you on the spot. Hot and spicy pizza it is then.'

My stomach was already growling in anticipation as I located the shower room and began peeling off my dirty clothes. I was undressed and about to step into the shower when I heard Nick's footsteps echoing along the upstairs corridor. I froze as they came to a stop outside the bathroom door. Ridiculously, I covered my breasts with my arms, as though he really *was* a superhero with X-ray vision.

'Are you alright in there? Did you find everything you need?'

I could feel myself blushing. Standing naked so close to him, albeit with an inch-thick door between us, felt disturbingly erotic.

'Yes. All good in here,' I replied breezily. Beneath my left breast, I could feel my heart thumping like crazy.

I waited until I heard his footsteps retreat before crossing to the walk-in closet, which was filling the bathroom with clouds of steam. I stepped beneath the hot jets, wondering if it might have been better to opt for an ice-cold shower instead.

As promised, there was a small pile of clothes outside the bathroom door, and a carrier bag for my dirty ones. I unfolded a pair of pale-grey joggers and a matching hoodie. I smiled as I stepped into the joggers, already knowing I was going to look like a circus clown. They were miles too long – I could pull them up almost to my armpits – and even tightened to the max, they kept slipping down from my waist.

I took one last look in the mirror before leaving the bathroom. The make-up I'd applied so carefully earlier was gone, and my damp hair fell to my shoulders in a beachy, dishevelled kind of way. I didn't think Nick's invitation to 'help myself' had extended to his comb.

He must have heard me coming down the stairs, for he called out to me from the kitchen. 'Did you find the clothes I left for you? Do they fit?'

I paused on the bottom tread, still hidden from view. 'Well, you know that scene at the very end of the Tom Hanks' film *Big...*' I began, rounding the corner to enter the kitchen.

He was leaning back against the worktop, smiling even before he saw me.

'It was the smallest thing I could find,' he apologised.

'Honestly, it's fine,' I repeated, hoicking up the joggers once again.

His eyes dropped to my hips, knocking my pulse rate up a notch. 'Do you think they'll stay up?'

'Who knows?' I said with a shrug. 'It certainly adds an element of excitement to the evening though, doesn't it?'

I liked the easy banter we seemed to fall into so naturally. We found the same things funny. We made each other laugh. It was, I realised, something I'd never really had with Jeff. It was strange how the distance had allowed me to see just how many things had been missing from my relationship with him, and how very inconvenient it was to find *all* of them in someone I was never going to be involved with.

'The pizza will be here in about ten minutes,' Nick said, crossing over to a huge American-style fridge. 'Would you like a drink while we wait? I've got wine, beer, or—'

'Beer, please.'

I know I didn't imagine the look of approval in his eyes at my choice. He pulled the caps from two bottles and brought them over. He was reaching for glasses from a cabinet, but I shook my head and took one of the bottles from his hand and lifted it to my lips. I could feel his eyes on me as I swallowed down the ice-cold brew. It's a miracle I didn't choke.

With excellent timing, the doorbell rang right then, affording me an opportunity to give myself a strict talking-to while Nick went to answer it. I was in danger of forgetting what I was doing here, and that could only end badly for all of us.

Nick returned to the kitchen, carrying a flat box roughly the size of a paving slab.

'Just how hungry are you?' I teased as he set it down on the breakfast bar and flipped it open to reveal a cheesy feast that could easily have fed half a dozen people.

'Famished,' he said with a grin.

'Me too,' I admitted, pulling out one of the highly polished chrome stools and climbing on to it.

Nick was busy slicing the pizza, but he still caught my slight wince as I settled myself on the hard seat.

'Would you like a cushion?'

'No. I've enough natural padding down there,' I said, wondering how yet again our conversation had returned to the topic of my bottom.

'Gluteus maximus,' Nick said as he sunk his teeth into a slice of pizza.

'Wasn't he the guy in *Gladiator*?' I joked.

We laughed more that night than I'd done in months.

'So, what's left on Amelia and Sam's bucket list of incredible dates?' Nick asked, when all that remained in the pizza box were a couple of slices that I'd put money on him eating for breakfast.

'There are loads. More than we can get through in just a week.'

Nick leant back on his stool and pushed the pizza container to one side, replacing it with a notepad and pen. 'Okay. Well, what are the "must-do" ones then?'

My thoughts spooled back through my conversations with Amelia. I immediately censored the skinny-dipping escapades, or anything she'd mentioned that had made me blush. Once the more risqué ones were ruled out, there were only three more memorable dates that I wanted to include in the memory box.

'Sam surprised Amelia on the night of her birthday by turning up at her door bearing a cake alight with candles.'

'I like this guy's style,' Nick said admiringly, jotting down something illegible beside a bullet point. 'We can easily recreate that one. What else?'

'They picnicked on the beach in the middle of a heatwave. That was the date when Sam proposed.' I paused, as though we were in a court of law. 'Allegedly.'

Nick nodded thoughtfully. 'The picnic, the beach, and the proposal we can definitely do. But the heatwave will be harder to create, given that it's only the beginning of March.'

His pen flew across the page, but even squinting I couldn't decipher a single word. It had to be a medic thing, I decided.

He was still scribbling away, head bowed, which made it easier to reveal the final item for his list. 'The last one is entirely dependent on the weather.'

Nick looked up curiously.

'It needs to be raining – pouring, actually. And I'll have to wear a blue dress and you'll need to be in a white shirt.' Nick's head tilted to one side and there was the beginning of a frown on his forehead. 'I think Amelia "borrowed" a famous scene from a film and her subconscious spun it into a memory of her and Sam.'

'What film? What memory?' It was a reasonable question,

and yet for the first time in Nick Forrester's company, I suddenly felt shy. And warm. Really, really warm.

'It's called *The Notebook* – you've probably never seen it. And this particular scene is—'

'When they kiss in the rain,' Nick completed, his expression unreadable.

His eyes met mine, and as worried as I was about what he'd see in them, I couldn't look away. Nick was the first to break eye contact.

'We live in the UK so it shouldn't be hard to find a rainy day,' he said, jotting *Rain, Blue dress, White shirt* down on the pad. It was the only bullet point he underlined and scrawled a large question mark beside.

It wasn't late when Nick took me back to my car, but I was so tired I knew I'd have to drive home with every window wide open.

'I have Holly with me all day tomorrow and I'm working late on Monday. But we can do the picnic thing on Tuesday lunchtime if you like,' he said as we stood side by side next to my car.

'That would be great. I'll get the food and sort out a picnic blanket and everything.' I shuffled nervously before adding on a rush, 'Do you think you could dress as though it's summer?'

'We'll freeze, but sure,' he said easily.

It was impulse that drove me to do what I did next. Good sense played no part in my actions. I leant forward, rested my hands on his broad shoulders and pressed a hurried kiss on to his cheek. It was over in a split second, but my lips still registered the warmth of his skin and the fleeting scratch of stubble.

The driver's door was already open, and I ducked rapidly into the car as though seeking sanctuary.

'Do you have any special requests for the picnic? Anything you really like to eat?' I asked, horribly aware I was babbling and talking nonsense to cover my embarrassment.

Nick was polite enough to play along as though it was a perfectly sensible question.

'I have a thing for those marshmallow biscuits, the ones covered in coconut,' he replied. 'I've been known to eat two packets at a single sitting.'

'That definitely confirms your superhero status,' I said with a smile. 'I'll get you some.'

As I drove back down the farm track towards the main road, I could still see Nick in my rear-view mirror, standing in the middle of the yard. He made no effort to get back into his own car but stood watching mine, until it became just red brake lights in the distance.

18

Amelia was gripping my hand so tightly her nails were digging into the soft flesh of my palm. I glanced across the room at Mum, who was sitting bolt upright in the other visitor's chair. She was staring intently at the doctor and I could see no visible reaction to his words until my eyes dropped to her lap, where she was twisting the straps of her handbag so fiercely I doubted they'd ever spring back into shape.

'So, let me get this right. You want to administer an electric shock to my heart?' Amelia managed to sound both scared and incredulous at the doctor's suggestion. 'After everything that happened the last time it stopped, you want to do it *again*?'

I thought I was going to have to be her advocate at this meeting, to speak for her, but as it turned out she was doing just fine without me.

'You have heart failure,' the doctor explained carefully and deliberately.

It didn't matter how many times I heard that phrase, it never failed to send a shiver through me. I'd read enough books and researched the internet sufficiently to understand those words weren't as dire as they initially sounded; that in medical terms, it just means that your heart isn't functioning as it should. But still.

Amelia's heart might be the one that was failing, but mine was the one in danger of breaking.

'From what I've read,' I said, turning to Dr Vaughan, who'd arranged this meeting, 'people can live perfectly normal lives with managed atrial fibrillation.'

If there was one thing I'd learnt over the last few weeks, it was that physicians really don't like being challenged by well-meaning family members who've spent too much time in the company of Doctor Google.

To give him his due, Dr Vaughan was remarkably patient. But the muscle twitching at the corner of his eye gave him away.

'That's quite true, Lexi.' I could never decide if it was a good or a bad thing that Amelia's entire medical team now knew all of us by our first names. 'But in the long term, AF is a strain on the heart, and if we can restore your sister's heartbeat to a regular rhythm it will offer her a much better outcome.'

'But it still sounds so dangerous,' I said.

I looked down at Amelia's hand, linked so tightly with mine it was impossible to see whose fingers were whose. They were as identical as the rest of us. Mum was now holding Amelia's other hand. We formed a chain, but a broken one. We needed Dad here to complete the circle, but that hadn't been possible for a very long time.

'I can assure you that cardioversion is an extremely common and safe procedure.' He was speaking to a trio of sceptics. 'I often liken it to the advice they give you when your computer isn't working properly. You need to turn it off and turn it on again to fix the problem.'

'No disrespect, Dr Vaughan,' I said, 'but I find it hard enough to believe that one when the man at PC World says it. But if *he*'s wrong, all I have to do is buy another computer.' I looked over at my sister, and the love on her face shook me a little. 'I can't buy another sister.'

'Amelia will be in very safe hands. It's a controlled environment and there will be a room full of cardiac specialists with her. Her heart will not stop, it will be reset.'

There was a long moment of silence as his words found a place in each of us.

'It's an outpatient procedure, so you'll be back home in just a few hours,' Dr Vaughan said, his tone gently cajoling. I could have told him he was wasting his breath, from the set of Amelia's jaw.

'No, thank you,' she said perfectly pleasantly, as though passing on another slice of cake.

'Amelia, honey, maybe we should talk about this,' I said.

Ignoring me, she turned to Dr Vaughan. 'I assume as it's *my* heart, I still have the final say?'

Dr Vaughan swallowed noisily and nodded.

'Then I say no.'

This clearly wasn't going the way the consultant had planned, and he directed his gaze to Mum.

'We could possibly defer it for a little while; schedule it for when Amelia has had time to settle back home. But I must stress it would be far better to undergo it as an elective procedure rather than an emergency one further down the line.'

'I said no.' There was steel now in her voice, like a sword had been unsheathed. 'I've heard what you said, and I've made up my mind. I'm not going to agree to anything until Sam gets back. As my husband, he has a say in what happens to me, so he needs to be involved in the decision-making.'

A helpless message telegraphed from the doctor's eyes to Mum, who then relayed it on to me.

'When Sam is back, then we'll talk again,' Amelia said firmly. 'If he agrees, then and only then will I give my consent.'

It was Tuesday morning. Day two of a week I already knew I was never going to forget. The cawing seagulls no longer bothered me; my brain had learnt to tune them out as effectively as it did the constant sirens in New York. I pulled apart the bedroom curtains and peered through the breaking dawn at a nondescript sky, hoping yet again the weatherman might have got it wrong. I'd been checking the forecast obsessively on my phone, the radio and the television, moving from one source to the next when I failed to find an answer I liked. I was hoping for sun and praying for rain. But according to the meteorologists, neither was on the cards for the rest of the week.

I swung out of bed and headed straight for the bathroom. Nick would be getting here at noon, and I still hadn't shopped for our beach picnic. Breakfast was a quick slice of toast that I munched on distractedly as I stood at the kitchen counter, running my eye down my shopping list.

Half of my attention was on the TV weather girl, who kept flashing cheeky grins at the camera and telling us it was a thick jumper kind of week but at least we weren't going to need our umbrellas. I switched her off mid-sentence and reached for my car keys.

My shopping list was probably over the top and extravagant, but I was trying to compensate Nick for asking him to sit on a freezing cold beach in a pair of shorts. I still wasn't sure that fancy olives, artisan bread and expensive French cheeses were sufficient recompense for pneumonia, but if all else failed we could always wrap ourselves up in the picnic blanket. Except I didn't have one of those either, I realised, as I quickly added it to the bottom of the list.

The local general store didn't stock everything I wanted, so I'd need to venture further afield to a larger supermarket in the next town. A quick glance at the kitchen clock confirmed I was cutting it fine for time, so I made a snap decision not to bother with make-up or even to run a comb through my hair. What did it matter if I looked a little scruffy? I wasn't going to bump into anyone I knew.

Except I did – even before I got to my car, in fact. Tom was slowly climbing up the sandy footpath from the beach. There was a fishing rod over his shoulder and a hook with his morning catch in his hand.

'Mornin',' he said, lifting his free hand to the brim of his cap in greeting.

'Hi, Tom,' I said, pointing my keys at the car, which beeped back and obediently unlocked its doors. 'You're out early.'

Tom's reply was a small snort of amusement. 'Call this early? This is the middle of the afternoon for a fisherman. The fish don't sleep, you know.'

I eyed the deceased ones on his hook. 'Well, those certainly won't be doing so anymore.'

It wasn't a great joke, but Tom laughed so heartily his eyes began to water. I was about to turn away when a thought suddenly occurred to me.

'I suppose as a fisherman you have to be good at predicting the weather.' I glanced up at the sky. 'Are you able to tell if it's going to rain this week?'

A few more lines joined the concertina of those already on his face, as Tom looked up and frowned. With a small grunt, he set down his rod and catch. I watched in fascination, expecting him to stoop down and sniff a piece of seaweed, or sprinkle a handful of sand into the wind. Instead, he reached into the pocket of his trousers and withdrew an iPhone, which happened to be the next model up from mine. His gnarled fingers moved quickly to a weather app.

'Not according to this, it isn't,' he said with a grin.

This time, it was my turn to laugh. You'd have thought as an editor I'd know better than to judge a book by its cover, but I kept underestimating Amelia's neighbour. From the expression on Tom's face I'd clearly made his day, and all at once I was really glad he was going to be here for Mum and Amelia when I wasn't.

'And while you're asking me for pearls of wisdom,' Tom continued, 'then you probably shouldn't be doing that.'

He was referring to the handful of burnt toast crusts that I was about to scatter outside the cottage for the gulls. 'That's summertime tourist nonsense,' he said disparagingly. 'City dweller foolishness.'

I dropped the crusts anyway with an impish shrug. 'But

that's what I am, Tom, remember? I'm just a crazy New Yorker.'

He looked at me speculatively for a long moment before slowly shaking his head.

'No, you aren't. You're a Somerset girl, down to your bones. You've just forgotten it for a while, is all.'

There was a very good reason why I preferred supermarket shopping late in the evening, and I was reminded of it the moment I saw the crowded car park. The aisles were busy and seemed to be teeming with children, either running amok among the displays or screaming for release from the front of a trolley. It took me a while to work out that the schools must be closed for a staff training day.

Keeping a close eye on the time, I began speed-shopping, throwing items into my trolley like a game-show contestant. It was probably way too much food, and yet I still kept loading up the trolley. I'd managed to locate everything on my list and had even found a picnic hamper on the shelf beside the plaid blankets. *Almost done*, I thought, as I plucked up two bottles of Prosecco and slotted them in among the rest of my shopping.

I ducked down a relatively empty aisle to check my list one last time. With a satisfied smile I straightened up, and then felt my lips part in surprise when I saw I'd come to a stop directly in front of the marshmallow biscuits Nick had said were his favourite. I pulled a couple of packets off the shelf... and then added two more, just for the hell of it.

In my head, I was already whistling through the checkout

and was back outside, loading the bags into the boot of my car. So, when a voice I didn't recognise called out my name, I didn't initially react.

'Lexi! Lexi!'

I didn't turn around. It was surely a different Lexi they were hailing, although admittedly it isn't a particularly common name. The third call of my name caused my steps to falter, but it was the fourth that made me stop and turn around.

For a moment I stared at the face of a stranger standing a short distance away, wondering why she looked so familiar. Was she a celebrity? Or maybe an author I'd met once? Even while my brain was throwing up possible suggestions, I already knew they were wrong.

'I *knew* it was you,' a young voice cried out as a small shape emerged from behind a supermarket trolley. The figure left the blonde woman with the hauntingly familiar face and ran towards me. They cannoned into me with enough force to almost knock me off my feet. And then a pair of spindly young arms wrapped themselves around me in an unexpected bear hug of a greeting.

'Holly,' admonished the attractive blonde. I'd recognised Nick's daughter at the exact same moment that I finally placed her mother. The last time I'd seen her face, she'd been in a picture frame beside the man I was planning to spend the afternoon with. The knowledge wrong-footed me and I felt immediately guilty, as though I'd been caught in a crime.

'Holly, come away,' Natalie Forrester admonished. 'You know better than to bother people we don't know.'

'But I *do* know Lexi. Don't I?' she asked, looking up at me with Nick's eyes.

'You do,' I confirmed with a smile, my hand ruffling Holly's dark curls. I looked up, intending to introduce myself, but the cool reception in Natalie's eyes froze the words in my throat. Perhaps Holly sensed there was something less than welcoming in her mother's attitude, and she attempted to fix things by introducing me herself.

'This is Lexi, Mummy,' Holly said guilelessly. 'She's Daddy's new best friend.'

She meant well, of course she did, but it was hard to imagine a single worse description she could have given to her mother.

'Oh, I wouldn't say that, exactly,' I interjected hurriedly. 'We really don't know each other that well. Hardly at all, in fact.' I was flustered and could feel my face flushing in exactly the same way it did so often in Nick's company. For an entirely different reason, of course.

I could feel the sweep of Natalie Forrester's eyes and knew I was on the receiving end of a comparison with what she'd seen in the mirror that morning. In a strange way, I was kind of glad that my hair was awry and my face freshly scrubbed. Surely she could see I was no contest for her *not-a-hair-out-of-place* blow-dry and immaculate make-up? Perhaps she did, because she seemed to relax a little, which would have been fine if only her gaze hadn't dropped to my shopping trolley. Her lips tightened and I knew why. Those bloody marshmallow biscuits. They told their own story.

'It was Lexi who bought me my new book when we had ice creams at the mall, after they lost me.'

Natalie's head jerked up and you didn't need to be a genius to realise Nick had been sparing in the details about what had happened on that Saturday morning.

'I'm sorry. You *lost* my daughter?' I'd never fully appreciated the phrase of being 'between a rock and a hard place' the way

I did at that moment. Natalie automatically assumed I was responsible; she *wanted* me to be responsible. I realised I had no choice now but to admit to something I didn't do, because I certainly wasn't about to drop Nick in it. Besides, his former wife already looked like she hated me.

'I took my eyes off her for just a moment. I found her very quickly.' The last at least was true.

Natalie was shaking her head in disbelief. 'Nick and I agreed we wouldn't introduce our... *friends*... to Holly without clearing it with each other first. So you can understand why I'm less than happy to be having this conversation.'

You and me both, I thought with feeling.

'It appears that you know my husband quite well, and yet he's never mentioned you to me. Not once.' It was a neat and very effective put-down. And the fact that she'd dropped the 'ex' and had referred to Nick as her husband was not lost on me.

'There was no reason for him to mention me. We really *are* more acquaintances than friends, and we did just bump into each other that day at the mall. It wasn't planned.'

It was impossible to tell if she believed me and I sent up a silent apology to Nick in case I'd just made the situation even worse.

'Lexi Edwards,' I said, holding out my hand to her over the width of the supermarket trolley. For a long moment, I thought she was going to ignore it.

'Natalie Forrester,' she eventually replied in kind. She placed extra emphasis on her surname, which she had clearly retained, although I noticed there were no rings on her left hand.

'Do you live around here?' she asked. I sensed this wasn't just polite curiosity.

'No, I don't. I have family in the area, but I live in New York. I'll be returning there very soon.' *Finally* a glimmer of a smile emerged. She clearly liked that much more than anything else I'd said so far.

'I'm so sorry,' I said, making a big show of looking at my watch, 'but I really do have to go. I have a... an appointment... and I'm running late.' The guilt came again like a tidal wave, as I realised I'd very nearly called it 'a date'. I felt like there should be a huge scarlet letter 'A' emblazoned on my forehead, which was ridiculous because Nick and Natalie had been divorced for some time.

'It was so nice meeting you,' I lied to Natalie. 'And seeing you again, Holly,' I added, which was entirely true.

Natalie inclined her head slightly. 'I'm sorry if I came across a little frosty,' she said, 'but as a parent you have to be *so* careful about who your child associates with.'

I nodded and gave a tight smile, as though the icicles in her glare hadn't been the least bit uncomfortable. I didn't exactly run towards the checkouts, but I walked fast enough to be out of breath by the time I got there.

'I'm so sorry,' Nick said, for what had to be the fourth time in just ten minutes. 'She had no right to be rude to you.' To be fair, I hadn't once said that Natalie *had* been rude. But perhaps that was his ex-wife's default setting.

Nick ran a hand through his hair, which was already dishevelled from the strong westerly breeze blowing in from the sea. 'I should have told her everything to begin with. It wasn't fair of her to blame you for something that was entirely my fault.'

'I've got broad shoulders,' I said, with an *it really doesn't matter* shrug. And I wasn't exaggerating. With the amount of clothing I was wearing for our beach picnic, it was safe to say I had a broad *everything*. Somewhere, several layers below the jumper, hoodie and thick fleecy jogging bottoms, there was a very small, insubstantial bikini. But every time I thought about peeling off my clothes to reveal it, I shivered, for reasons that might have absolutely nothing to do with the weather.

I was reliably informed that beneath his own warm clothes, Nick was also wearing something more suited for a heatwave than the biting chill of the wind we were currently experiencing.

'I didn't want to get you in trouble,' I said, leaning forward to lift a few more food containers from the picnic hamper.

'That's not something you should have to worry about.'

Was that a very polite way of saying *you need to mind your own business*, I wondered?

'I'll have to find a way to make it up to you,' Nick said with a smile, passing me the tray of olives. 'To thank you properly.'

I plucked up a meaty kalamata olive and popped it into my mouth. 'What you're doing today more than squares us up.' I burrowed a little deeper into the folds of my chunky jumper. 'Although I'm really sorry about the weather. I had no idea it was going to be this bracing today.'

'Is it cold?' Nick asked, his eyes twinkling. 'I never noticed.'

Warmth briefly flooded through me, despite the fact that the sun hadn't even put in a passing appearance so far. I reached for the pair of oversized sunglasses I'd brought with me and slipped them on my nose, grateful that their lenses covered so much of my face. I'd always been hopeless at hiding my feelings. *You're an open book*, Amelia used to say, which always struck me as a great description for an editor. But right now, I'd give anything to be just a little more mysterious.

Our lunch was every bit as delicious as I'd hoped it would be, and with the dedication of a magazine stylist I'd managed to create the image of a picture-perfect summer's day. But the inviting picnic hamper and plaid blanket couldn't disguise the fact that it was bloody freezing.

'This is crazy,' I said, as I saw Nick surreptitiously rubbing his hands together in an attempt to restore his circulation. My teeth were chattering against the plastic champagne flute, and I was probably spilling more Prosecco than was making it to my lips. 'Let's just call it a day and go back to my place.'

'No. We've got this,' Nick said. It was a phrase he'd used before, and I liked the feeling it always gave me, like I was in safe hands. He set down his plate of food and got to his feet, holding out his hands to me.

'On your feet, Lexi Edwards. Let's get you out of those clothes.'

As cold as it was, his words still had the power to ignite a small flame somewhere inside me.

'Do you have much success with that line?' I asked, going for humour because anything else felt way too dangerous.

'Absolutely none.'

I might have continued the banter, but my train of thought was derailed as Nick peeled off his thick hoodie. With it came the T-shirt he had on beneath it, leaving him bare chested in the sharply biting March wind. I'd guessed he'd be muscular by the width of his shoulders, but the fine dark hair on his chest that arrowed down from his torso and disappeared into the waistband of the joggers was a surprise.

His hands went to the white drawstring cord and as hard as I tried, I couldn't drag my eyes away as he undid the knot and began to tug them down. A muscle was throbbing so violently at the base of my throat he could probably see it, even across the width of the blanket between us.

'You're not chickening out on me, are you?' Nick asked, looking up as he kicked his clothing to one side. He was wearing a pair of darkly patterned board shorts that sat low on his hips and clung to his thighs in the wind.

'No, of course not,' I said, suddenly embarrassed, because he must surely have seen me staring at him as though he was a present being unwrapped. *Don't you dare objectify him*, I told myself sternly. Guilt is a powerful motivator and it had me pulling off my own clothes, several layers at once, until the pile of garments at my feet grew into a small mountain. I gasped when I pulled the T-shirt over my head and although I can't be certain, I thought maybe Nick did too... or it might have just been the wind. I could feel the heat of his eyes on me as my joggers hit the pile, and for a second or two I felt the blaze of it on my bare limbs, but then the wind picked up again, sand-blasting our bare skin and making it impossible to think of anything except getting back into our clothes as quickly as possible.

I picked up my phone and ran over to a nearby low crop of rocks that I'd already checked out for suitability. Nick straightened up the picnic blanket, while I fumbled with the settings on my phone, setting a ten-second timer on the camera.

'Are you ready?' I called out to him, checking my mobile was securely propped up on the rock.

'Just get over here, woman,' he called back.

I was laughing as I ran towards him. We hadn't discussed how we'd pose. But when he held out his arms to me, I fell straight into them. I clasped my hands together around his body and the smell, the feel, and the goddamn sexiness of him was so potent I almost forgot to turn to the camera and smile.

We took it in turns to run back to my phone and set up the next shot. My favourite was the one where we laughingly fed each other olives. I was so busy trying to recreate Amelia's memory, I was totally unprepared that the touch of Nick's fingertips against my lips was scorching an entirely new one into my own head.

The final photograph, before our limbs turned blue with cold, was the one that had made this date so memorable for my sister. Almost shyly, I pulled the small velvet ring box from my bag.

'Do you think you could...?'

With an unreadable expression, Nick took the box from me. 'Of course.'

My legs were trembling as I left him on the blanket and raced over to my phone one last time. The laughter that had been present throughout this whole crazy photo shoot was suddenly gone. The seconds were ticking. It took five to run back to the blanket, two to position myself in front of Nick. Somewhere in the remaining three seconds he dropped down to one knee and reached for my left hand, holding it gently in his as he flipped open the box and looked up at me. I never heard the multiple clicks of the camera shutter, nor the wind, nor anything at all apart from the low throbbing beat of my heart. Seconds became hours, as I looked down at the man kneeling at my feet.

When I look back on that moment, I can no longer tell

if the memory is mine or Amelia's. But what I *do* know is that this was when I first realised I was caught somewhere between fact and fantasy... and that I was beginning to fall in love with my sister's husband.

19

Bumping into Tom twice in one day was unusual enough for me to wonder if Mum might have something to do with these seemingly random encounters. Either she'd asked her new friend to keep an eye on me or Tom had embarked on a keep-fit regime that had him walking up and down the footpath all day. I knew which one my money was on.

As luck would have it – bad luck, that is – we bumped into Tom as we raced across the sand towards the cottages. The sky had darkened ominously, although I knew from persistent checking that rain wasn't forecast for today. Even so, when the wind had whipped up fiercely, we hadn't lingered on the beach, but had gathered our belongings and headed for Amelia's home and the promise of warmth and a hot drink. I was cradling a bundle of clothes, some of them Nick's, while he carried the picnic hamper, the blanket and my beach bag.

You have to admire an elderly man who doesn't blink or even raise a curious eyebrow when two scantily dressed people come bounding towards him. There wasn't even a hint of incredulity in Tom's voice as he paused his walk and deadpanned, 'Afternoon. Nice day for it.'

I shot him a meaningful look that he pretended not to see.

'You're probably wondering what we're doing, dressed like this, Tom,' I said, flashing a quick apologetic glance at Nick.

'Catching pneumonia was my first guess,' Tom said, leaning against the wooden post-and-rail fence that ran the length of the footpath. 'Other than that, it's none of my beeswax whatever shenanigans you've been getting up to on the beach.'

'It's not often you hear the words "beeswax" and "shenanigans" in the same sentence,' Nick said with a grin as I closed Amelia's front door a few minutes later. I'd performed quick introductions and had to admire Nick for not looking the least bit fazed as he shook the elderly fisherman's hand, dressed only in a pair of board shorts.

'Tom's not like other people,' I said by way of explanation as I wriggled back into my jumper. 'If I read him in a book, I'd probably edit him for being too much of a cliché.' I sighed gratefully as I pulled my socks back on. 'But Tom's the real deal. I like him a lot.'

Nick paused midway through zipping up his hoodie. 'I think the feeling is mutual. I like that there's someone close by and that you're not here totally alone until Amelia gets home.'

'Have you forgotten where I live? We New Yorkers are a pretty resilient bunch.'

'I haven't forgotten,' Nick said carefully.

His words put a silly old grin on my face as I made our tea, and it was still there when I carried the mugs into the lounge.

Nick was standing beside the window, looking out as the wind whipped the sea into a new frenzy. Like many cottages, Amelia's had fairly low ceilings, but I swear they must have dropped a good six inches since that morning. It wasn't just Nick's height that made the room seem so much smaller. It was him. His presence seemed to fill every centimetre of space. I'd never before been so hyper aware of someone the way I was of him. I'd experienced sexual attraction before, of course I had, but this was a whole other level. It was physiological, as though the atoms I was made of somehow shifted and realigned whenever I was near him.

In reaction, I took a step away from him after setting down his mug on the coffee table. I kept retreating until my back bumped into the wall on the opposite side of the room. He must have noticed my slightly bizarre behaviour, but politely chose not to mention it. What I was feeling didn't make sense, because just fifteen minutes ago I'd been posing in his arms for the photos, wearing nothing but a skimpy bikini and a cheesy smile. But now, fully clothed, with a whole room width separating us, I felt the pull of him.

He cupped his mug with both hands and unconsciously I mimicked him. He leant back on the wall beside the window, exactly mirroring the way I was standing. A body language expert could have written an entire case study on all the things we were saying to each other without speaking a single word.

We must have found some innocuous topics of conversation to discuss, because I can't remember there being any awkward silences between us, but then again I also can't remember what we talked about. It felt like a mammoth underground seam had suddenly opened up, and it was growing fast.

When Nick pushed away from the wall a short while later,

saying that he needed to go home and shower before evening surgery at The Willows, I felt almost relieved. I stopped myself just in time from offering him the use of my own bathroom. I'm not sure which one of us I thought couldn't be trusted if his clothes were to come off again. But I had a horrible feeling it might be me.

When you've made up your mind to do something, something important, it's beyond frustrating having to wait for something as mundane as the other half of the world to wake up.

A night of restless tossing and turning had left me with a new set of dark circles beneath my eyes and a curious determination that confused me with its intensity. I needed to speak to Jeff. It was a conversation that could no longer wait until I returned to New York.

Nick had given no indication that the attraction I felt for him was reciprocated. *Which probably means it isn't*, intoned a gloomy voice in my head. But irrespective of what he felt for me, there were ends that needed tying before I could allow myself to take a single step forward.

I watched the minutes tick past until we reached a time that was almost acceptable to place my call. I'd chosen video calling, because it's only right you look someone in the eye if you're intending to say goodbye to them.

I had no doubts that this was the right thing to do. There'd be some people – Amelia, for one – who'd probably say it was in fact long overdue. But that didn't mean I wasn't nervous when I did one last calculation of the time difference and dialled Jeff's number. He wasn't an early riser, or a morning person, so I wasn't surprised that it took five rings before he picked up.

'Hello.' His voice was thick and still blurry with sleep. I should have waited an hour or so until he was properly awake. I was annoyed with myself for my impatience, and he sounded a little annoyed too.

'Hi, Jeff. Sorry to call so early. Did I wake you?' I heard the rustle of sheets and knew that I had.

Although my camera was turned on, Jeff had yet to switch his phone to video.

'Yeah, you did,' he said, his voice losing its edge as he thought to ask, 'Is something wrong? Is Amelia okay?' I made a mental note to remind myself that his first thought had been to ask about her, which was going to make this a whole lot harder to do.

'Yes, she's coming out of hospital at the end of the week.'

'Oh.' The word came out weighty, as though it was supporting a hundred thoughts. 'So does that mean you'll be coming back home then?'

Was there a hint of apprehension in his question? It was so hard to pick up on nuances on a transatlantic call. It was why I'd wanted to do this over video.

'Not straight away. We'll need to see how she copes to begin with.' I pulled the collar of my shirt away from my throat, as though it was suddenly choking me. 'Look, can you switch your camera on.'

'I don't think that's a good idea. A bunch of us went out last night to a bar and we all got pretty wasted. Believe me, it's not a pretty sight this morning. And besides, the apartment is a mess.'

He was making this unintentionally hard for me. 'Jeff, I honestly don't care. Just turn your camera on. Please.'

Perhaps he heard something in my voice, or perhaps he'd simply run out of excuses. Either way, I heard the sound of him getting to his feet and walking across the hardwood floors of his loft. He moved from the bedroom to the open-plan lounge before eventually switching over to video call.

I hesitated for a moment as the pixels grouped together to reveal the man I'd woken with and fallen asleep beside enough times to still feel sad about what I was about to do.

'The thing I wanted to say is—' I began, before a sudden movement behind him cut off my words mid-sentence. Jeff was sitting at his breakfast bar, but another shape had come in and out of frame beyond him. I knew the layout of his place as well as I did my own. The figure had been moving at speed from the bathroom to the bedroom. But not so fast that I hadn't seen the tanned bare limbs, or the towel wrapped around her body.

'Who's that?' I asked, which was a redundant question, because I'd already identified the running figure as Tallulah, the assistant at Jeff's firm who'd taken him to the wedding in The Hamptons.

'What?' asked Jeff, curiously deciding that gaslighting was the way to go. 'There's no one here but me.'

I gave a small humourless laugh. I'd been worrying needlessly about this being hard. In the end, Jeff had made it remarkably easy.

'Jeff, I can still see her trail of wet footprints on the floor.'

His head shot around, looking not at the polished hardwood but at the entrance to his bedroom. Neither of them seemed aware that, backlit by the morning sun, the shadow of a woman's figure was projecting on to the wall.

When Jeff turned back to the camera, his face was a kaleidoscope of shifting emotions, as though he couldn't quite decide which one to pick.

'I'm sorry, Lexi. It's just that you've been gone for so long—'

'Six weeks, Jeff. It's been just *six weeks*.'

He was obviously still looking to spin things his way, apparently unaware that the only way they were spinning was out of his control. 'We never said we were exclusive, you and me,' he mumbled.

Even though this break-up was my decision, that still felt like a punch to the stomach.

'No, you're right, we didn't. I guess we both thought we didn't have to.' I gave a small wry laugh. 'Although perhaps for entirely different reasons.'

'You're angry with me.' At least he had the grace not to put a question mark at the end of that sentence.

'Actually, no. I'm not, Jeff. Truly I'm not. We had some good times together and I don't want to ruin the memory of them by turning this into a mud-slinging contest. We weren't each other's forever person, and deep down I think we both always knew that. Tallulah's a far better fit for you than I ever was.'

He winced then, clearly surprised that I knew the name of the woman who'd shared his bed the night before.

He ran a hand through his hair, a gesture I'd once found endearing, but today it was just an attractive man, staring guiltily into his phone, wondering how he'd screwed things up so badly.

'I'll see you around, Jeff,' I said, pressing the button to disconnect the call before he could reply.

20

We'd walked down this same corridor every day for the
last six weeks, but this afternoon there was a lightness
to our steps that hadn't been there before. Mum had got to
the hospital first but had chosen to wait for me in the foyer.
It was as though we both felt a curious need to re-enact that
first night when we'd hurried to Amelia's bedside, when her
fate still hung in the balance.

It certainly felt much easier to breathe this time around as
we rode the lift to the ward than it had on that first dreadful
night. The nursing staff greeted us by name or with cheery
waves as we walked towards the room that would soon be
occupied by another patient.

'Well, don't you look nice,' Amelia said as I slipped off my
coat and threw it over the back of a chair.

Mum, who'd claimed her regular seat on Amelia's left side,
looked across the hospital bed with a puzzled expression.
'You *do* look very smart, sweetheart. Is that a new dress?'

'Uh-huh,' I murmured, bending down to drop a kiss on

Amelia's cheek. I should have known I wasn't off the hook when I saw my sister's nose twitch like a rabbit's.

'So, what's the special occasion?'

'There isn't one. Apart from celebrating the fact that you're coming home tomorrow, of course.'

Amelia wriggled herself higher against the pile of hospital pillows and shook her head. 'No, that's not it. You've tonged your hair, done something different with your eye make-up, *and* you're wearing your favourite perfume.'

Her heart might not be functioning as it should, but there was clearly nothing wrong with her powers of observation. She was totally wasted as an accountant; she'd have made a great detective.

She flapped her hand in my direction, to encompass the soft wool dress with its deep V neckline. 'That's not how you usually dress when you visit me. You're normally much scruffier than this.'

I took my usual seat on the opposite side of the bed and tried to laugh off her scrutiny, which was starting to make me feel uncomfortable.

'How rude.'

Mum would probably have let it drop there, but not Amelia. She was as relentless as a Canadian Mountie.

'Okay, okay,' I said, when I realised she wasn't going to let it go. 'I'm meeting an old friend for a drink when I leave here.'

A little late in the game, Mum finally realised where I was going, but by now Amelia's interest was piqued. She nodded encouragingly for me to continue. 'More, please,' she asked, like Oliver holding up his empty bowl. 'I'm starved of anything remotely juicy in here.'

'There *is* no more,' I said firmly. 'And what there is, is far from juicy. I happened to bump into someone I knew in the supermarket the other day and we said we'd catch up over a drink.' It was a loose version of the truth, and I should have left it there, but when you're not very good at lying, there's always the temptation to over-embellish. 'It's their birthday tomorrow, so we're celebrating that.'

Amelia's face took on the familiar wistful expression it wore whenever anything reminded her of Sam. Her eyes met mine, and I knew she was thinking about the night he'd allegedly surprised her on her doorstep with a cake alight with candles. It was the reason there was currently a bakery box, two packets of candles and some matches on the back seat of Amelia's car. Tonight's event would be the final one that I'd recreate for the memory box of photographs. It would have been nice to have included the 'kiss in the rain' scene from *The Notebook*, but the weather had remained annoyingly dry. Perhaps that was just as well, because I still wasn't entirely sure whose benefit that photograph would have been for: Amelia's or mine.

'Does this man – I'm assuming it's a man – have a name?'

'Nick,' I said, diving into the bag I'd brought with me and withdrawing a bottle of champagne. I hadn't intended to produce it so soon, but I was desperate for a diversion. 'Do you think we'll be in trouble if we have a sneaky glass of this?' I asked, pulling three plastic champagne flutes from the bag.

'I'm willing to risk it,' Amelia declared, already holding out her glass as I popped the cork as quietly as I could.

Happily, somewhere between the toasts to getting out of hospital and a life free of bedpans and commodes, my plans for the latter part of the night were forgotten.

★

It was eight o'clock, and Nick had assured me that evening surgery at The Willows would be over by the time I arrived. But when I pulled into the practice's car park, I realised he was still working. Through the reception window I could see him talking to an elderly man, who I assumed was a client.

I had one hand on the car's door handle, but I stopped short of pulling the lever. There was something about the way Nick was standing as he spoke to the older man that kept me in my seat. Despite the fact I hadn't known him for long, I found Nick's body language as easy to read as the pages of a familiar book. Whatever he and the other man were discussing, it looked serious, and definitely shouldn't be interrupted by an intrusive outsider – especially one bearing an enormous birthday cake with enough candles to set off a smoke alarm.

I watched as Nick laid his hand briefly on the old man's shoulder and saw the man's head droop a little lower. Without knowing why, I shivered. The two men walked slowly to the surgery doors. Nick held them open as the old man shuffled out, leaning heavily on a walking stick. Around his other hand was a lead belonging to a dog who looked every bit as frail and aged as its owner.

Transfixed, I remained in my darkened car and watched as the two men and the dog made their way slowly towards the only other vehicle in the customer car park. I was glad I'd parked in the shadows beneath the sprawling branches of a tree, because the scene playing out in front of me looked private and painful, in every sense of the word. The old man's gait was stiff, but his dog's was even worse. Before the trio were even halfway across the car park, Nick bent down and gently scooped the animal into his arms. The dog lifted its head worriedly and I saw Nick's lips move, presumably giving the animal some words of comfort.

The client unlocked his car and Nick bent low to set the dog gently on the back seat. By the time he'd straightened up, the old man had extracted his wallet. Nick shook his head firmly and once again laid a hand on the other man's shoulder. This time I was close enough to see the dog's owner was crying... and I wasn't far behind him. This was a story that could only have one ending.

I didn't get out of my car straightaway when the old man drove off. And I wasn't the only one not to move. Nick remained motionless for several minutes in the middle of the car park, simply staring into the darkness. He moved only when he heard the click of my car door opening, turning towards me as I crossed the space between us. He was standing in a pool of light from a security lamp and my steps faltered for a moment when I saw the unusually bright glisten of his eyes. He looked sad and a little defeated, and the impulse to run to him and throw my arms around him was so strong, it took genuine restraint to continue walking in slow and steady strides towards him.

I greeted him with a hesitant, 'Hey, you.'

'Hey,' he replied with a smile that didn't manage to reach his eyes. They still looked sad. He glanced in the direction his customer had taken and then back towards me.

I nodded slowly, letting him know that I'd seen their exchange and understood. This time his smile managed to travel a little further north. My heart ached, not just for the old man and the fate of his beloved pet, but also for the man standing before me. The man who looked like a superhero fashioned from steel, but who cared deeply and wasn't afraid to show it. It just about broke me when he lifted a hand and brushed it across his eyes, looking almost surprised to discover his fingers came away damp.

'It never gets easier. You'd think, after all these years, that it would.'

'Perhaps it never should,' I said, slipping my hand through the crook of his arm.

With unspoken agreement, we headed back towards the surgery and went inside. Nick looked down at me with eyes that were dry now, but still sorrowful.

'Even when you know it's absolutely the right thing to do, it's still so hard. But telling Charlie tonight that Digger had got to the end of the road…'

I didn't imagine the crack in his voice, and in the absence of finding the right words to say, I simply reached for his hand. It was the first time our fingers had threaded together when we weren't pretending, and it felt so unbelievably right, as though of all the hands in the entire universe, I'd finally found the one I wanted to hold on to for ever.

'Charlie's wife passed away last year, and I've been nursing Digger along for months now, but it's finally time to let the old boy go. It's always heartbreaking, but more so this time because that dog's the only family Charlie has left.'

Nick might be holding back his tears, but mine were falling freely and I didn't even know the old man or his dog.

'Will he be okay? Charlie, I mean?'

Nick nodded slowly. 'In time. But I'll keep an eye on him.'

'I want to go straight out and buy him a puppy,' I said between inelegant sniffs.

Nick smiled sadly at my words and shook his head. 'That's not always the answer. Some people need time to let go and say goodbye in their own way.'

I had no doubt that was why Nick had encouraged Charlie to take his old companion home, so they could spend one last night together. His compassion dwarfed me. Like iron filings to a magnet, my attraction to him kept growing stronger every time I was with him. It was just as well that I'd be leaving soon, because even now I knew our goodbye was going to leave a scar.

'Losing something you love is always painful, but the good memories you're left with are proof that it was worth it.'

His words struck a chord, because wasn't that exactly what I'd been doing with Nick all this time? I'd told myself the 'memories' we'd been creating were all for Amelia, but it was only now that I questioned if they might also be for me.

'Do you mind if we wait a bit before we do the cake thing?' Nick asked as I followed him down the corridor to the staffroom. 'I'm going to need a moment or two to reset.'

I didn't skip a beat, nor spare a thought for the very expensive gateau I'd bought earlier that day from the fancy patisserie in town. 'Oh, I'm sorry, Nick. I should have messaged earlier to let you know. I couldn't find a suitable cake, so there won't be a photo op tonight.'

For a poor liar, I must admit I sounded pretty convincing. Nick certainly didn't appear to doubt me. I saw the flicker of relief in his eyes and knew I'd made the right call. He was in no mood for that kind of frivolity, and if truth be told, neither was I.

He crossed to the coffee machine and held up the jug in an unspoken question. I nodded my reply. I suspected his thoughts were once again back with Charlie as he passed me a cup. Nick's day had left its mark on him. It was there in the twin furrows between his brows, and the way he dropped heavily on to the staffroom's only couch. He leant back against the cushioned seat with his long legs stretched out in front of him. I searched the room for somewhere to sit, preferably somewhere that didn't require joining him on the couch.

Something felt different tonight. A door had swung open that I wasn't sure we could close, or even if I wanted us to. And through the gap I could feel something new arcing between us, something combustible. It scared me a little.

I sat down on an old faded armchair covered in short wiry hair, which probably meant I'd stolen the dogs' favourite seat. Nick had closed his eyes and was absently rubbing at the muscles on the back of his neck. I got dangerously close to offering him a neck massage, before good sense silenced me.

When he finally sat up and opened his eyes, he looked recharged. 'So apart from the missing cake photo, do you have all the others that you wanted?'

My stomach clenched at his words. With a jolt, I realised that our final photograph had already been taken and that my mission was now over. A feeling of panic ran through me, knowing this was probably going to be our last evening together. Nick had upheld his end of the deal and then some. It wasn't his fault that I suddenly wanted so much more than we'd ever agreed to.

He was staring at me curiously, presumably waiting for my answer. 'Yes. I've got more than enough photographs. I've had them printed up and they're tucked away in a box beneath my bed... just in case Amelia needs them.'

Nick nodded slowly, his expression unreadable.

'I can't thank you enough for being such a good sport about everything and agreeing to do this for someone you don't even know.'

'I know *you*,' he said evenly.

Our time together might be drawing to a close, but it was never too late for one last blush. And it was a big one. Flustered, I paid far more attention than was needed to setting down my empty coffee cup. This was the second goodbye I'd delivered in the space of a few days, and on paper this one should feel a lot easier than Jeff's had done. Only it didn't.

'I know you've had your doubts all along about what we were doing, and it really meant a lot to me that you still went along with it anyway.'

There was a serious look in his eyes that was hard to pull away from. 'I wanted to help you.'

'You did.'

I hated how everything we were saying was now slipping into the past tense. This really was all coming to an end, and I wasn't ready. Not even close.

'I guess you'll be pretty occupied over the next few weeks, taking care of Amelia?' Nick's eyes had annoyingly dropped to his coffee, making it impossible to read them. But from the way he was rotating the mug within the circle of his palms, it almost looked as though he was nervous.

'Fairly busy, I imagine.' Was he asking if I'd have time to see him again? Surely if that was what he wanted, he'd have come straight out and said it?

'And then you'll be going back to the States.'

There was definitely no question mark at the end of that

sentence. It felt like a thick black line was being drawn beneath the story of us.

'That's the plan.' Three words, and yet I could hear the reverberation of a thousand doors closing as I uttered them.

It felt like my cue to leave, and I took it, springing to my feet as though a starting pistol had been fired. 'Well, it's getting late, and I have to be at the hospital early in the morning.' My words came out in a rush, as though they were planning on racing me out of the building to my car. 'I should probably go.'

Stop me. Say you don't want me to leave just yet.

My telepathy was clearly faulty because he didn't pick up on any of the signals I was silently screaming across the room at him.

'I'll walk you to your car,' Nick said, getting to his feet.

'No, that's fine. I can see myself out.' I was hoping for a quick, clean exit before I did or said anything to embarrass myself, but he was having none of it.

'I'll walk you,' he said in a voice that brooked no argument.

The reception was in darkness now, and he didn't turn on the lights as we passed through it. By the glow of two flickering computer screens, we made our way to the door. Tension thrummed between us. It hummed like a generator whose gauge was tipping slowly towards the red side of the dial. Did Nick feel it too? Perhaps he did, because just before unlocking the door he cast a quizzical look around, as though sensing something in the air had altered. The ions between us felt like they were fizzing in freefall as we stepped out into the cool night air.

I wasn't wearing a jacket, so was immediately aware that the temperature had dropped in the last thirty minutes and that a strong wind had whipped up. Those conditions were a precursor to something that definitely wasn't supposed to happen tonight. Perhaps in more ways than one.

I felt the first drop of rain on my face. It landed on my cheek like a tear. It was followed quickly by another. And then another. We'd almost reached my car, and Nick was walking so fast I was practically trotting to keep up with him. He got to the vehicle and turned to face me. Raindrops were falling, faster and faster. His dark hair glistened with them. They spiked his lashes, glittering there like diamond fragments.

'It's raining,' I said, stating the glaringly obvious.

Nick glanced up as though seeking confirmation and a few more raindrops found their way on to his lashes. The urge to rub them away was almost irresistible.

'It is,' he declared solemnly.

Say it, a voice in my head screamed at me. *Say it now, or you're always going to regret letting this moment slip away.*

I dug in my bag for my phone and pulled it out. 'Maybe we could take one last photo? *The Notebook* one,' I suggested in an unsteady voice that didn't sound like mine at all.

I counted my heartbeats as I waited for him to reply, until they grew too fast to record. The rain had intensified, and I was halfway towards the drowned-rat look, which average mortals couldn't pull off as effectively as Hollywood actors. And yet still Nick said nothing. When I was just about as embarrassed as it's possible to get without imploding, he held out his hand for my phone. He held it aloft in a classic selfie pose and waited for me to close the distance between us.

I'm not sure how many people I'd kissed before him, but I do know that I'd never been this nervous, nor wanted someone's mouth on mine as much as I did his in that moment. It might not be real; it might just be for the camera, but I didn't care. All I knew was that I wanted this.

Nick was so close I could feel the heat of his body, despite the rain. I'm glad I hadn't already closed my eyes, for I'd have hated to have missed the look on his face or the expression in his eyes as he deliberately set my mobile down on the roof of my car.

My eyes flew to the abandoned phone and then back to him.

'This isn't Amelia's first kiss,' he said, his voice low and throaty. 'It's ours. Yours and mine. And we don't need a photograph to mark this moment, because I don't think either of us will ever forget this.'

And then his hands were on my shoulders, drawing me closer. They slid upwards with slow deliberation, as though he was giving me time to stop this if I wanted to. He got his answer as my arms went around his body.

Nick's hands cradled my face and then his fingers were sliding through my hair, as he lowered his mouth to mine. There was nothing tentative or hesitant in his kiss. It was everything it should be... and so much more. His lips moved with just the right amount of confidence and skill, teasing out my response. When his tongue began its exploration of my mouth, I met it with an eagerness that was frankly embarrassing.

I could no longer feel the rain. However hard it fell, it wouldn't extinguish this fire, not with our bodies welded together as though we'd been through an inferno. One of Nick's hands had dropped to the small of my back, supporting me. The other had slid lower and was cupping the curve of my bottom. It held me against him in a way that left no doubt that he was as turned on by our kiss as I was.

I didn't even realise he'd spun us around until I felt the cold wet surface of my car behind me. Our kisses were growing more ardent, and if there were security cameras in the car park Nick was going to need to erase the tapes before his colleagues saw them, because neither of us was holding back or taking it slowly.

His hands were on my bottom, and I gasped softly against his mouth as he lifted me easily from the ground. My legs went around him, anchoring me against him in the place we both craved. The rain was beating relentlessly on my bare thighs, and I shivered as his hands skimmed over the damp flesh.

I don't remember him walking us through the car park or pushing open the surgery door, but we made the journey somehow without collision or mishap. The first thing I became aware of was the soft cushions of the staffroom couch as he gently lowered me down on to it.

I can remember murmuring something about getting everything wet before we found an easy solution to that problem. My fingers began working on the buttons of his shirt, pulling and yanking them fervently. When they were freed, I tugged the garment free from his waistband. My eyes were heavy with desire as I looked up at him. Nick was breathing hard, clearly trying to rein in something that was about to escape. He held his body away from mine, as though doing planks in a gym.

'This isn't how it should be, Lexi. You deserve better than this.'

I shook my head, terrified this was all about to stop. 'This is perfect,' I breathed against his mouth.

'You should have a bed,' he said hoarsely, as his fingers finally found the clasp of my zip and tugged it slowly down. 'Silk sheets,' he murmured against my throat as he gently eased the dress off my shoulders. 'And champagne,' he said, nipping gently on the sensitive skin at the side of my neck.

'I don't need any of that,' I said on a groan, as his mouth returned to claim mine. 'I just need this.'

The buckle on his belt was digging uncomfortably into my stomach but that too was easily sorted as my fingers went to the fastening and slipped it free.

This time it was his turn to gasp.

'We can stop. If you want us to, we can stop,' Nick said throatily.

'No, we can't. *I* can't,' I said with an abandon I'd never known before.

Stopping simply wasn't an option. Until suddenly it was.

I didn't hear the phone ring, though the handset was right on the desk beside us. I was so lost in the heat of desire I was deaf to every sound apart from the low moaning I couldn't repress as Nick's fingers skimmed lightly across the lace of my bra.

His fingers were scorching me and then suddenly they were gone, and so too was the weight of his body.

I don't think I've ever seen a face so full of tortured regret as he looked down at me for a very long moment before sadly shaking his head. 'I'm so sorry, but I have to get this.'

I looked around, still too lost in the moment to realise that somewhere close by a phone was ringing and Nick was about to answer it.

'I'm the only vet on call. I *have* to answer it,' he said, swooping down to press a brief, hard kiss on my lips before plucking up the handset.

He looked away from me as he took the call, as though he couldn't entirely trust his resolve not to weaken.

I heard several *Uh-huhs* and quite a few *I sees* from him, as I straightened up my underwear and zipped up my dress. By the time he got to the point in the call when he was saying *That's okay. Don't worry. Bring her straight down to the surgery. I'll meet you there in ten minutes*, I was entirely presentable, apart from the tell-tale flush of desire still staining my cheeks.

21

When you've loved someone your entire life, you see things that the rest of the world misses. When your connection runs even deeper, like mine does with Amelia, their pain and disappointment becomes yours too. Which meant that on the morning she left hospital, I had a ringside seat to every moment when my sister's hopes were lifted before they crashed and burned.

She hid it well. If Mum had been there, I'm not sure if even *she* would have seen how her elder daughter's hands had tightened on the arms of the wheelchair as the orderly propelled her out of the lift and into the hospital foyer. Would anyone else have realised there was nothing casual in the way her eyes swept the vast reception area? Would they have spotted how she sat up straighter, as alert as a meerkat, when she spied a man in the far corner of the room by the vending machine? His face was hidden, but his hair was almost the right shade, and he was nearly tall enough, although possibly not as broad shouldered. Either way, the similarities were close enough for Amelia's fingernails to curl into the cushioned vinyl armrests of her wheelchair. Her neck was craned as far as it could go and I think she was seconds away from calling out his name, when the man bent to retrieve his drink from the dispenser and turned around. It wasn't Sam, of course it wasn't. And it wasn't Nick either. As we walked towards the car park, my heart ached like a stone in my chest... and it wasn't only for my sister.

She thought she saw him again at a crowded bus stop. Out of the corner of my eye, I saw her fingers paw at the passenger window as we drove past and then slide slowly down the glass as once again she realised it wasn't the face she was looking for. Her disappointed sigh filled the car with a melancholy that even the radio couldn't erase, but I turned up the volume anyway.

Because she'd mentioned Sam much less over the last few weeks, and had stopped asking when he was going to leave the retreat, we'd all hoped her confused fantasy was finally fading. But now I wondered if she'd simply been biding her time, convinced he'd be waiting for her when she left the hospital. It felt like we'd taken two steps forward and three back.

'Have you booked your return flight yet?' she asked, finally turning her gaze from the window when we left the suburbs – and strangers who weren't Sam – behind.

'Are you trying to send me packing already?'

Even her smile looked tired. 'You've got a life to get back to, Lexi. You've put it on hold for long enough.'

'Here I am, looking forward to us being roomies, and you can't wait to get shot of me,' I teased. 'And this is *before* you've tasted my terrible cooking or found out I've been borrowing half your wardrobe for weeks.'

Too late, my words reminded me of the reason for that and the man I was doing my best not to think about. Although to be fair, pretty much everything had made me think of Nick since the moment I'd opened my eyes that morning.

He'd been front and centre of my mind, a spot he'd occupied since I'd driven away from the surgery the night before. I'd reached for my phone to check the time and with a jolt had seen his name on the screen. It would appear that at 2 a.m., he'd sent me a message. It must have arrived just minutes after I'd finally given up on hearing from him and had fallen into a restless sleep. My fingers had felt less than steady when I clicked open the inbox, unaware I was holding my breath until it escaped me on a long, exhaled stream as I read his three-word message.

I'm so sorry.

Sorry. What was he sorry for? For kissing me? For allowing things to go so far that we'd been only two heartbeats away from making love when we were interrupted? Or was he apologising for answering the phone call?

It was weird that two men with the exact same face occupied our thoughts as we drove closer to Amelia's coastal cottage. By the time we caught our first glimpse of the sea, it was hard to know whose relationship was the greater fantasy: Amelia and Sam's, or mine and Nick's.

I caught one more fleeting look of disappointment as Amelia scoped the parking area next to her cottage and saw only Mum's car there. Phantom husbands don't have cars, and it's only in cheesy films that you'll find them waiting inside, beneath a Welcome Home banner.

It was a strange day. We were like three actors in a play, saying the right things, doing the right things, but somehow failing to sound authentic.

'It feels good to be home,' Amelia said, her fingers grazing the walls, the door jambs and even the wooden banister rail in the hallway. But her eyes looked anxious as they flitted left and right as though something was wrong. I'd followed her into the cottage, after winning a brief dispute over who should carry the small holdall containing her belongings and the far-from-small carrier bag containing her medication.

Mum was excelling in her role of thankful parent. On hearing the front door open, she'd emerged from the kitchen carrying a cake she'd baked to celebrate Amelia's homecoming. It made me think of the one I'd bought from the patisserie, the one I'd given to the charge nurse on Amelia's ward that morning for the staff to share.

Amelia's exhaustion was clear. We'd been warned it would take time for her to regain her strength, but it was only now, seeing her outside of a hospital environment, that I realised just how long a journey that was going to be. Even the short walk between the front door and the lounge had winded her and stolen some of the colour from her cheeks.

She managed only a couple of sips of the tea Mum had insisted on making before leaning back against the settee cushions mumbling something about 'resting her eyes'. I glanced over at Mum as Amelia's chest rose and fell at a rate that looked a little too fast for my liking. Mum quickly tidied away the worried expression she'd been wearing, but I'd still seen it.

With a stage whisper that probably wasn't needed, for Amelia was already softly snoring, Mum said she was going to pop round to Tom's to let him know that Amelia was back. I managed to hide my smile and resisted pointing out that he'd probably have worked that out himself seeing as he'd been outside his cottage, ostensibly weeding his weed-free plot, when I'd pulled up. I didn't understand her coyness about their friendship because I certainly didn't mind – in fact, I wished she'd found someone years ago. Dad wouldn't have wanted her to be lonely.

After Mum left, I spent longer than I should have done watching my sister sleep, with a hawk-eyed scrutiny that could easily spill over into obsession. Was her breathing always this shallow? I never thought I'd miss the reassurance of hearing the familiar bleeps from a bank of monitors, but I did. I even spent ten minutes googling the price of defibrillators and wondering if Amelia would like one for an early birthday present, before good sense finally made me close that window on my laptop. We'd laugh about my foolishness one day, I promised myself, as I tiptoed out of the room to let her rest.

But it was hard to dismiss just how much damage her poor heart had sustained as I unpacked the assortment of pills she would need to take every day. I didn't like seeing them lined up like that on the kitchen counter, so I rearranged the lower shelf of a cabinet so they could live there.

It was ostrich-like behaviour: out of sight, out of mind. And it was just the type of thing Amelia would have ridiculed me for... back in the day. And she'd have had a positive field day over my indecisiveness on how to reply to Nick's message. I worked with words all day long, so you would have thought I'd be able to arrange a half dozen or so of them in the right order to reply to him. But I had no idea what to say. The problem was that I didn't want him to apologise for something I really wanted us to do again. But I also didn't want to say anything that would embarrass the hell out of both of us if he didn't feel the same.

In the end, I sent an amusing shrugged shoulders GIF. I waited for a response, but none came. *He's probably just busy at work*, I told myself. Even so, much as I'd done while Amelia was in hospital, I made sure my phone was never far from my side. I was actually checking if I still had signal when Amelia walked into the kitchen, startling me so much that I almost dropped the phone on the quarry-tiled floor.

I was pleased to see that the nap had restored some of her colour.

'I think I'll have a shower before lunch. I smell of hospital,' she said.

'Good idea,' I replied. 'Would you like a hand?'

She gave me a withering look that was so 'old Amelia', I couldn't help but smile.

'Even on the ward, they let me do that myself,' she said with a shake of her head. 'Remind me, when are you going back to New York again?' she asked over her shoulder as she turned towards the stairs.

I laughed, but still followed her like an anxious Border Collie as she began to slowly climb the treads.

'This is going to get old very, very quickly,' Amelia said when she was halfway up the flight, aware that I was keeping a vigil, two steps behind her. Her snipe would have carried more weight if it hadn't been delivered between short, panting breaths.

'Hey, I'm just trying to get upstairs, lady, but there's a slow-moving object up ahead of me.'

It was good to hear her laugh.

Amelia went into her room, while I peeled off into the one I'd occupied long enough for it to now feel like mine. It was quiet for a long time, and I wondered if she'd experienced any flashbacks to the last time she'd been in her bedroom. Maybe she'd even be able to answer the puzzling question of *why* she'd gone wandering on the beach in the middle of the night.

I tidied away some laundry, checked my phone a couple more times, and eventually ventured back out into the hallway. I found Amelia there, staring into the airing cupboard where the boiler was housed. She was frowning.

'There's no hot water,' she said, turning towards me. I was slow to realise that the expression in her eyes was confusion rather than irritation.

'No, there wouldn't be by now. You'll need to override the current settings,' I said, heading for the stairs.

'Oh yes, of course,' she said, still looking at me rather than the boiler. Something about her response felt vaguely off, but I couldn't pin down what it was.

'You have no idea how long it took before I eventually made friends with your bloody boiler,' I said.

Amelia smiled vaguely and looked back at the unit. She raised her right hand, but her fingers didn't make contact with the control panel, they simply hovered in the air beside it.

An unexpected frisson of fear ran down the length of my spine.

It was no big deal. She probably hadn't had to tweak the settings in ages; it was hardly surprising that she couldn't immediately remember how to do it.

'Here. Let me,' I said, nudging her gently aside as my fingers went to the panel and punched the correct sequence of keys.

It wasn't the fact that I'd had to show my sister how to

operate the boiler in her own home that bothered me, it was more the look of relief on her face as she turned towards the bathroom. That was the thing I couldn't quite shake off.

It was nine o'clock, not late by any standard, but the cottage was dimly lit and in silence. It was three hours since we'd eaten, and two since Mum had returned home and Amelia had gone to bed. It left me with more free time than I really wanted to run through all the reasons why I hadn't heard back from Nick all day. I'd gone through every imaginable scenario – including a few frankly ridiculous ones – but my thoughts kept circling back to the one glaringly obvious answer: Nick felt so uncomfortable about what had happened the previous night, he'd probably never get in touch again.

I switched off the television, plunging the room even further into the shadows. I'd tried and failed to get into three different programmes this evening, before finally acknowledging the problem wasn't the TV at all, it was me.

This is ridiculous, I murmured. Why the hell was I staring at my phone like a heartsick teenager? I was a twenty-first-century independent woman and if I wanted to speak to a man this much, I should get my shit together and call him myself.

At almost the exact moment I'd made up my mind to do precisely that, my phone buzzed on the settee cushions beside me and Nick's name flashed up on the screen.

'Hello, Lexi. Is this a good time to talk? I'm not interrupting your dinner or anything, am I?'

I laughed. 'Amelia's body clock is unfortunately still set to hospital hours. She insisted we eat hours ago. Actually, I was just about to call *you*.'

'Were you?' he asked, and I could just tell by his voice that he was smiling. 'I'm sorry, I know I should have called you earlier, but it was totally manic at the surgery today.'

'That's okay. I've been pretty busy here with Amelia and probably couldn't have talked until now,' I said, rolling my eyes at the lie.

'Of course. How's she doing?'

'She's okay, I guess, or at least I hope she will be. She's so much weaker than I was expecting her to be and she's still not quite... herself.' I could explain it no better than that.

'That's hardly surprising, though. She's been through a huge ordeal, and it's bound to be hard for her readjusting to being home again after so long.'

His words were reassuring, and I clung to them like a life raft. He *was* a medical professional, after all, albeit one more used to dealing with hardpad and distemper than human cardiac issues.

'Is she there right now? In the room with you, I mean.'

I frowned. 'No. Not right now. She's gone to bed. She went out like a light. Why do you ask?'

'Because I'd really like to see you. I think we need to talk about last night.'

I swallowed loudly. We'd been on the phone for a minute or two, and neither of us had yet mentioned the large grey elephant that was sharing the line with us.

'Mum's gone back home now. I can't go out and leave Amelia. Not on her first night back.'

'Of course not,' Nick said, sounding genuinely shocked at

my reply. 'I wouldn't ask you to. But I was hoping that ten feet or so from your front door might be okay.'

His meaning clicked into place like a puzzle piece, and I immediately leapt to my feet and went to the window. It was a journey of only seven steps, but it was long enough for me to be glad I'd put on make-up that morning and sorry that the jumper I was wearing wasn't my most flattering.

I pulled back the curtains and waited for my eyes to adjust to the dark. Initially, I could see nothing but a blanket of black, but gradually shapes began to form out of the darkness. In the distance, a shimmer of white sharpened into the roll of an incoming wave. Dunes materialised on the sand and beside one, a short distance from the footpath, I saw the glow of a phone.

'Can you meet me outside?' Nick asked. I still couldn't see him, but the clouds obscuring the moon were on the move, and gradually a tall shape morphed from the shadows. Backlit by the table lamps in the front room, I was far more visible to him than he was to me.

I glanced in his direction and then up towards the staircase and the bedroom where my sister lay sleeping. 'You can't come in,' I said, sounding genuinely panicked at the thought. How would Amelia react if she walked down the stairs and found her missing 'husband' in the lounge, in the arms of her own sister? Because let's not kid ourselves here, that was what was going to happen if I invited him inside.

'I get that, and I totally understand. It's the reason I didn't knock on your door when I got here.'

In reality, I was staring at Nick through the window, still separated from him by the thick stone walls of the cottage and about ten metres of sandy beach. But in my head I was already running barefoot through the sand and into his arms.

He pulled me like a magnet. But then so did Amelia.

'Okay,' I said, my voice dropping to a totally unnecessary whisper. 'Wait there, I'll be out in a minute.'

I crept up the stairs like a burglar, automatically avoiding the third and seventh steps that always creaked. My heart was thumping so loudly in my chest as I eased open Amelia's door, it was more likely to wake her than anything else ever could. She was curled up on her side, facing away from the door and towards the window. Her room was at the front of the cottage and looked directly out on to the beach, and she hadn't drawn the curtains. I bit my lip worriedly. There was no way I'd be able to close them now without disturbing her. All I could do was trust that she wouldn't wake up and that if she did, she wouldn't decide to look out of the window. I turned back to the hallway and gently pulled her door to a close behind me.

I paused for a moment as I passed the mirror at the bottom of the stairs. There was no time to hunt for a comb, so I ran my fingers through my hair until it looked a little less like I'd just got out of bed. It was impossible to disguise the sparkle in my eyes or the rosy flush on my cheeks, and I wasn't even sure that I wanted to. As much as I'd like to play it cool, my body was having none of it.

I slid my feet into the first pair of shoes I found on the rack beside the front door and slipped out into the night. Without the guiding light from Nick's phone, it was difficult to see him on the inky black beach. I didn't want to risk calling out his name, so I stepped blindly off the path and on to the sand, trusting instinct that I was heading the right way. A memory that wasn't even mine flashed through my thoughts. Was this what had happened to Amelia on the night she collapsed on the mudflats? Had she believed she was on her way to meet Sam, and then somehow got turned around in the dark?

I glanced back at the cottage, suddenly wishing I'd had the foresight to leave some lights on to guide me... just in case. And then all thoughts of getting lost disappeared, as a pool of light from a phone torch flicked on and then off. My steps quickened and I turned towards the light that was guiding me towards Nick.

He had moved a little further away from the cottage, mindful of my fears that Amelia would spot us. His eyes must have been better adjusted to the darkness than mine, and I didn't see him approach until he was right there in front of me.

'Hi,' I said on a whisper, which was ridiculous because our voices would surely be drowned out by the sound of the surf.

'Hi.' His voice, like mine, was hushed; he was taking his cues from me. I took a half step towards him, as though we were playing chess and the next move would be his. He made it, reaching out and drawing me towards him. There was a latent urgency in the way his arms circled my back and pulled me close that excited the hell out of me. It was so dark I still couldn't see him properly and I only knew his head had lowered to kiss me when I felt the warmth of his breath on my face. A sensible person might have had a moment of concern that they'd still not visually identified the man they were about to kiss. But I'd left sensible and cautious back in the cottage. I recognised the feel, the smell and finally the taste of him, as Nick's lips moved on mine. The kiss went on for so long that when we eventually separated, I was breathless from it... from him.

'I've been thinking about doing that all day,' he confessed, sounding almost embarrassed by the admission.

I smiled up at him, hoping there was enough moonlight for him to see how happy his words had made me.

'It's felt like the longest twenty-four hours of my life,' he continued. His hands were spanned against my back, not pulling me in, but holding me close. 'God knows what I did at work today, because I don't think there's been a single minute when my thoughts haven't found their way back to you.'

He was laying out his feelings, allowing himself to be vulnerable before me, without even looking for the safety net that would tell him I felt the same. It was bold and it was brave of him, and for that he deserved my honesty.

'Ditto,' I admitted. The guard I normally kept raised had dropped so easily I was quite shocked by my reply.

Several more minutes were lost as our mouths found each other again, our lips and tongues speaking a language that needed no translation.

'This is crazy,' I said at last, finally finding the self-control to push him gently away from me.

'Crazy good, or crazy bad?'

I leant forward, allowing my forehead to rest on his chest, where I could feel the increased tempo of his heart pounding against me. 'Both,' I said softly. He must have heard the regret in my reply. It prepared him for the words that I didn't want to say but knew that I must.

'We can't let this happen, Nick.'

'We can't let this not,' he countered.

I smiled sadly, because it wasn't as simple as what he

wanted or what I wanted. We weren't the lead characters in this story of ours and it was only tonight that I finally appreciated that.

'I'll be going back to New York in about a month,' I said. It wasn't the true reason why I was applying the brakes even before we'd started, and I think he understood that.

'That's not insurmountable, Lexi, you know that.'

'No. Maybe not. But it's not ideal. Your life is here right now and mine is over three thousand miles away.'

'People do long distance. They make it work.'

I shook my head sadly. 'You've got ties here that I'd never ask or expect you to sever.' We both knew I wasn't talking about his job or the practice.

Nick's voice was suddenly several degrees sadder. 'It's true, I could happily live or work anywhere, but I could never leave Holly.'

'And I'd never ask you to,' I said fervently, reaching for his hands and gripping them tightly. 'I know what growing up without a dad feels like, and I wouldn't wish that on anyone... especially not Holly.' I smiled gently. 'I don't have much experience with kids, but I'm kind of smitten with yours.'

'The feeling's mutual. Holly talks about you a lot. When she likes someone, she doesn't hold back.' My breathing was perfectly alright until he added softly: 'Neither do I.'

My heart gave a leap as he looked down at me with eyes that were full of what he was about to say next. I shook my head fiercely, stopping him. *Don't put it into words that I'll never be able to unhear*, I silently implored him. Nick was surprisingly good at reading me, for after the longest moment he slowly nodded.

'But that's not the real reason you don't want to see where this could go, is it?'

I shook my head sadly.

'It's because of Amelia,' he said.

I swallowed down my disappointment, but it had left a bitter aftertaste in my mouth. 'I don't see how there's any way I could be involved with you. Not now. Not ever. We can't have a relationship that my family don't know about.'

'Because I look like someone who doesn't exist.' Nick might be doing his best to hide it, but I could hear the frustration in his voice.

'For Amelia, you *do* exist. You're the man she believes she's married to.' I reached up and allowed my fingers to gently touch his cheek. 'This is the face she loves.'

'And what about you?' he asked, making it so much harder to reply when he turned his head and gently kissed the hollow of my palm.

'I love my sister. I'd never do anything to hurt her.'

'Of course you wouldn't. But what about you? Would Amelia really want you to sacrifice something that could be very, very real, for something that isn't? Surely she'd want you to be happy too?'

'I'm sure she does. But not if the place I find that happiness is in the arms of the man she loves.'

'Who doesn't exist,' Nick repeated sadly, as though either of us could ever have forgotten that fact. His sigh was long and deep, carrying away all our *what might have been*s in its wake.

'I guess all we can do then is make the most of the next four weeks,' he said. 'We could meet whenever you're free – even if it's only for a quick coffee, or something.'

'It won't be enough,' I said gloomily. 'And it'll just make it harder to say goodbye.'

He pulled me into his arms again, silencing my protests with one more kiss.

'Let's at least try,' Nick said. He was making it very hard to say no, or even think straight, with his body pressing against mine in all the right places.

I glanced back anxiously towards the cottage. 'We'd have to meet in secret. Amelia could never, ever find out. It would destroy her.'

'I understand that.'

He reached for my hand and lifted it to his lips, while his eyes stayed locked on mine. 'I'm not ready for this to end yet,' he said.

'We're going to break each other's hearts,' I predicted softly.

'No, we won't,' Nick said with a confidence that was surely misplaced. 'We've got this.'

22

'I had the craziest dream last night.'

I paused in the act of whisking eggs in a Pyrex bowl to give Amelia my full attention. 'If it's an erotic one, I'd just as soon not hear it.'

She gave a snort of laughter, but then her face grew more serious. 'It could easily have gone that way, although I was a voyeur rather than a participant.'

'Kinky,' I said, picking up a fork and turning my attention back to the eggs.

'Don't you want to hear it?' she asked, pushing her sleep-tousled hair back from her face.

'Go on then,' I said, switching on the hob and tossing a slab of butter into the frying pan. I made sure my features were suitably neutral, wondering why everyone always thinks the random images conjured up by their sleeping brain are as fascinating to other people as they are to the dreamer. They never are.

Except today, they were.

'I dreamt I saw you walking on the beach in the middle of the night.'

I swallowed noisily, but luckily the butter was sizzling loudly enough to hide it.

'I wasn't skinny-dipping, was I?' I asked, trying to joke my way out of what was fast becoming a really uncomfortable conversation.

'No. But it looked like you could easily have ended up naked.'

My thoughts were spinning, trying to imagine how a *not-guilty* Lexi would react to those words. She'd be interested, of course she would be.

I poured the eggs into the pan and then turned my attention back to my sister, who was watching me from her seat at the kitchen table.

'Go on then. Spill the beans. Tell me what I was doing in this dream of yours.'

'You were kissing Sam.'

The fork slipped from my hand and clattered noisily on to the quarry-tiled floor. I was glad I had to bend down to retrieve it and wipe up the messy eggy trail it had left. It meant that by the time I finally straightened up, my face was wiped clean of panic. But my hands still felt shaky as I returned my attention to our scrambled-egg breakfast.

'Yes,' continued Amelia, her brows furrowing as though she could still see the scene replaying in her head. 'The two of you were getting really hot and heavy on the beach, and I was rapping on the window, trying to let you know that I was right there and that I could see what you were doing, but you couldn't hear me.'

I felt sick. Had Amelia seen us? Had she woken, confused

and disorientated from her high-dosage sleeping pills, and wandered over to the window? Or was this just a horrible – and very accurate – coincidence? I'd checked in on her as soon as I got back inside, after leaving Nick to walk back to his car, which he'd parked further down the lane. Amelia had been in the exact same position as when I'd left, facing away from the door. Which meant I hadn't seen her face. I couldn't swear she'd been asleep. What if she'd been lying there, her cheeks wet with tears after witnessing the ultimate betrayal by two people she loved?

'Dreams don't mean anything,' I said decisively as I slid the eggs from the pan on to waiting slices of toast. 'And given the number of drugs they've got you on, one of me making out on the beach is actually fairly mild.'

Amelia took the plate from me and gave a small shrug. 'I guess so. But it felt incredibly vivid.'

I'd been intending to message Nick when Amelia went upstairs to shower and dress, but I set my phone aside and busied myself instead with tidying up the kitchen. My guilt-driven cleaning frenzy spilled out into the hallway, where it came to an abrupt stop. The shoes I'd grabbed to wear on the beach the night before were still there on the mat. They were Amelia's and the soles were caked with clumps of damp sand. Had she seen them on her way into the kitchen, I worried? With a furtive glance at the staircase, I eased open the front door and vigorously wiped the shoes clean with my hands. *I'm not cut out for a life of subterfuge or deceit*, I realised, as I scrubbed my hands beneath the kitchen tap under water so hot it was practically scalding. If I was serious about continuing this thing with Nick, I was going to have to be a hell of a lot more careful going forward.

*

The days that followed had a curious quality – like the ones between Christmas and New Year, when you really don't know what day of the week it is anymore. I'd turned on my out-of-office, having agreed I'd be taking a few days' vacation time. But that felt like entirely the wrong name for it. Vacations are a time when you kick back and relax. And I wasn't able to do that, for a great many reasons. With each passing day, it became clear that the story we'd concocted about Sam and the silent retreat was perilously close to its use-by date.

A lot of watching went on in those early days. Amelia watched the windows whenever a shadow fell across them. She watched the post when it fell on to the mat, searching for an envelope with familiar handwriting. And she watched the beach and the incoming waves, like the wife of a sailor who'd been widowed by the sea.

I did my fair share of watching too. I watched Amelia with an obsession that sat just this side of unhealthy. I counted her breaths when she wasn't looking and was transfixed by the readings on the home blood pressure monitor that I'd presented her with.

'Worst gift ever,' she'd declared with unusual pithiness as she fastened the cuff around her slender upper arm. 'And I don't remember the hospital saying I needed to do this every day.'

She was right; they hadn't, but seeing her readings sit comfortably within the normal range took the edge off my anxiety. Given my general stress levels, my own results were probably far higher than hers anyway.

Mum was part of the watch patrol too, although her

attention was divided equally between her daughters. 'Are you sure you wouldn't like me to stay here for a week or so?' she asked, not for the first time, as I walked her to the door one afternoon. 'It's a lot to take on, looking after Amelia on your own.'

'I'm right here,' Amelia sang out from the lounge.

'If it's a matter of space, I'm sure I could always stay at Tom's,' Mum continued.

'Ah... *now* we're getting to it,' Amelia called.

I smiled at that and stepped closer to give Mum a reassuring squeeze. 'Honestly, Mum, it's all fine. Let me take up the slack for these first couple of weeks. There'll be time enough for you to take over when I've gone back home.'

'I can still hear you both, you know. And for the hundredth time, I don't need looking after.'

Mum and I exchanged a meaningful glance. Whatever she might think, Amelia still needed our assistance – even though she'd never admit it.

The hospital had recommended 'gentle exercise', so we'd been taking short walks along the beach twice a day. But it worried me how quickly and frequently Amelia needed to stop and rest. As much as I liked the feel of her arm linked through mine, I'd have liked it a whole lot more if it had been there for companionship rather than support.

The final type of watching that went on was much less worrisome, and involved a great many hours spent curled up on the settee bingeing through films we'd missed. We quickly worked our way through the good ones and were now dipping into the kind that would definitely be categorised as B list.

It was late afternoon, and we were halfway through a romcom that was so cheesy it should have been served with crackers. The dialogue was poor and the plot implausible, and yet Amelia and I were still somehow sticking with it.

'Do you know what this movie needs?' Amelia said.

'A decent scriptwriter?' I guessed.

She giggled at that, and it made me want to bottle the sound.

'No. What it needs is ice cream.'

'I think there's a box of Magnums in the freezer,' I said, already unfurling my legs from beneath the fleecy throw I'd snuggled beneath.

'No. We need the really good stuff, the kind you eat straight out of the tub with a couple of spoons.'

'I don't think we have any of that,' I said with regret.

'Yes, we do,' she said, groping on the settee for the TV remote to pause the film. 'There's a tub on the bottom shelf, right at the back behind a big bag of ice cubes.' She picked up a device and pointed it at the screen. 'I had to hide it there to stop Sam from finding it. He loves ice cream.'

My lips felt cold as the smile on them froze. 'Oh, right. Okay. I'll see if I can find it then, shall I?'

Her reply was an angry growl as she repeatedly pressed on a button that failed to halt the film playing on the screen. 'What's the matter with this bloody thing?' She was quicker to anger these days, and it always caught me by surprise. But this time, I just laughed.

'It might help if you had the right thing in your hand,' I said.

She looked down at what she was holding, and I heard every tick of the clock on the wall as I waited for her to laugh, but she continued to stare at the piece of technology in her grip as though it had personally offended her.

'That's your calculator, not the TV remote,' I said, laughing because it should have been a funny moment, even though I was starting to feel that it wasn't.

She recovered well, with a laugh that sounded like she'd borrowed it from someone else. '*Of course* it is,' she said, throwing her calculator down impatiently on the cushions as if punishing it for deliberately tricking her.

We looked at each other for a long moment. Was this another of those things I was meant to brush under the carpet? Because it was starting to get pretty crowded down there.

'Ice cream,' I said decisively, as I strode from the room and into the kitchen.

Since moving in, I'd only used the upper shelves of Amelia's freezer; I certainly hadn't bothered investigating the lower sections. I crouched before them now, engulfed in a wave of cold air from the open cabinet door.

'Hidden behind the ice cubes, so Sam couldn't find it,' I said softly as I pulled the bag aside and saw the tub of expensive ice cream. I reached for it, and as I plucked it out something thin and black slid into the space it had just occupied.

I was cold. Really cold. And it had absolutely nothing to do with crouching in front of the open freezer. I reached for the dark object and pulled it out.

Its surface was encrusted in tiny particles of ice that looked like snow. I brushed some of it clear. The glass beneath my fingers resembled a windscreen that had been in a really bad accident.

All thoughts of the film and the ice cream were forgotten as I returned to the lounge with the object in my hand. I set it down carefully on the coffee table. It was still covered in freezer snow, which was melting fast.

'What's that?' Amelia asked.

'Unless I'm very much mistaken,' I said, sounding like a character in a whodunnit, 'that is your missing iPhone.'

That at least got her attention. Amelia sprang forward and plucked up the mobile, mindless of the puddle of icy water that was now dripping from it.

'Where did you find it?'

It felt like an almost unnecessary question.

'It was in the freezer, behind the ice cream tub.'

'What was it doing there?'

'That was going to be *my* question,' I said.

Her face was genuinely puzzled, as though I'd presented her with an intriguing conundrum that she'd quite enjoy solving. I didn't feel anything except a sensation of impending dread that I could neither explain nor understand.

'I suppose it must have got caught up when I was putting the ice cream away and I never noticed.' She gave a *what am I like* laugh, and looked happily towards me as though expecting me to join in. 'This is the very best thing that could have happened.'

'It is? How?'

'Because now you'll be able to see all the photos of Sam that are on it,' she said, cradling the phone in her palm.

My smile felt stiff and awkward as I took the ruined mobile from her. 'I'm not sure, hon. It might be too badly damaged to pull anything from it,' I said, really hoping that was true.

'But we have to send it away somewhere. We have to try,' Amelia pleaded.

'Of course we do,' I said, my thoughts spinning like tyres on ice. 'I tell you what, one of the guys I went to uni with started up his own mobile phone repair company. How about

I send him the phone? If anyone can retrieve the photos from it, it's him.'

'Could it be the medication she's on? Could that be why Amelia is so... *befuddled*?' It was an old-fashioned word, but I could think of none that was a better fit for the collection of strange incidents in Amelia's behaviour.

'Veterinary pharmacology isn't quite the same as the human type,' Nick said patiently, 'so I'm no expert. But it's certainly possible. You should mention it to her doctors.'

'I will,' I said, speaking softly, the way I did every night on our phone calls. I fell silent and I loved how Nick knew I needed a moment before continuing. 'It's feeling so helpless that gets to me. I know it's a terrible thing to say, but it was all so much easier when Amelia was still in hospital.'

Nick was far kinder to me than I was to myself. 'Don't beat yourself up,' he said. 'You're doing a great job and statistically it's well documented that patients get better quicker in their own home environment.'

'You're talking about dogs and cats again, aren't you?'

'Maybe,' he said, drawing the word out.

I didn't think I'd ever tire of making him laugh. It was like discovering you had a secret superpower. Our nightly phone conversations had quickly become the highlight of my day. Sometimes Nick made the call, sometimes I did. I liked the reciprocity of it. We talked about everything and absolutely nothing. It wasn't unusual to hang up and realise we'd been speaking for over an hour and yet I couldn't remember a single topic we'd covered. It wasn't the same as seeing him in person; but in a way it was strangely better. The physical distance between us allowed us to talk – really talk – without the combustible sexual attraction getting in the way. And the more I got to know him... the deeper I began to fall.

23

I woke earlier than usual the next morning, driven from my bed by a feeling of nervous energy that only one thing could cure. Exercise. Even as I splashed cold water on my face and brushed my teeth, I could hear the call of the beach amid the cries of the swooping gulls. It felt good to be reaching for my running clothes once again, after neglecting them for nearly a week.

I paused to stick my head around Amelia's door, surprised to discover that she too was awake and sitting up in bed, trawling through something on the replacement phone I'd bought her weeks ago.

'I'm going for a run before breakfast, if you're okay with that.'

Amelia set down her mobile and turned to me with an exaggerated expression of surprise.

'Who are you, and what have you done with my sister?'

I laughed. At moments like this, it felt like I was worrying about nothing.

'You'd be surprised; I'm all about the running now.'

'Your lips are moving, but I don't understand the words,' she deadpanned.

'Are you sure you don't have a problem with me going?' I asked.

Amelia lifted her eyes from her phone screen, which had once again claimed her attention.

'The only problem I'd have was if you expected me to go with you. Now go.' She shooed me away with a flap of her hand.

It was chilly and the sun was still low in the sky when I set off along the beach. I turned left out of the gate, towards the mudflats, my feet finding their rhythm as I ran to the beat of the music from my headphones. It was a route I'd scored in the sand many times before, but when I reached the point where I normally turned around, I decided to press on.

I was heading into the sun, which was now high enough in the sky to be dazzling without sunglasses. With them, I'd probably have spotted the figure at the water's edge far sooner.

I slowed my jog to a stop, resting my hands on my thighs as I squinted into the glare, waiting for my eyes to adjust. Someone was sitting on the sand, at the point where it changed from wet to dry, but they were looking out to sea and not at the beach. It was obvious they hadn't seen me, and I was still too far away to identify them. But then a volley of barks filled the air, sending seagulls soaring higher, as the waves split and Mabel bounded through them to retrieve her ball.

The memory of our first encounter on the beach was very much in my thoughts as I changed direction and headed towards Nick. It was impossible to shake off the feeling of serendipity as I closed the distance between us, made stronger because – as far as I could tell – he was sitting in the exact same spot where we'd first met.

Nick got in two more throws of the tennis ball before he became aware that someone was approaching. He swivelled from the waist, and I watched a huge grin replace the thoughtful expression on his face when he recognised it was me. I already knew I'd be playing that moment on repeat for the rest of the day.

'There you are,' Nick said, smiling up at me from the sand, as though he'd been waiting for me all along and this wasn't just some happy coincidence.

He patted the space beside him, and I dropped down on to it.

'Good morning,' he said, leaning over and pressing a brief but firm kiss on my lips. That was new for us and even now I realised that however long we had together, it would never get old. It was also the first time I'd seen him looking anything less than clean-shaven. Dark stubble covered his cheeks, making him look even more attractive than usual – something I'd have argued was actually impossible to achieve.

Mabel was happily frolicking in the waves, and I smiled at her doggy antics as she repeatedly dropped and then recaptured her ball. I drew up my knees and rested my chin on them, turning my head to one side to look at Nick.

I was aware there was a big old Cheshire cat grin on my face that I could do nothing to hide. It somehow managed to stretch even wider when Nick reached inside a paper carrier and pulled out a takeaway container of coffee. For a moment I thought it was his, before noticing there was already a cup wedged in the sand by his feet.

'Flat white with two sugars,' he said, reciting my drink of choice as he passed me the coffee.

I took it from his hands, my grin faltering slightly.

'That *is* how you take it, isn't it?' he asked.

I nodded, cupping my hands around the container, which was still hot enough to warm them. 'I don't understand. How did you know I'd be here this morning? *I* didn't even know I was going for a run.'

I'm normally quicker at joining up the dots, but in my defence it *was* fairly early, and I was still a little wrong-footed to find him here on the beach. 'Have you...? Did you...? Have you been coming here every day?'

The stubble camouflaged his blush, making it hard to spot – unless you were looking very closely. And I was looking very closely.

Nick gave a shrug that missed nonchalant by a country mile. 'We agreed that we'd meet for coffee whenever we could... so this seemed like a good place to start.'

'But we've spoken every day since that night on the beach. Why didn't you say anything? Why didn't you tell me you'd been here every day? With coffee,' I added enthusiastically, as I took a long sip.

Nick reached for my free hand and threaded his fingers through mine. 'Because there's a lot going on with you right now, and I didn't want to complicate things.'

Was he kidding me? We'd spent the last few weeks with me pretending to be my own sister and him her non-existent husband. How much more complicated could we possibly make it?

Perhaps he heard the flimsiness of his reply, for he shook his head as though his own words had disappointed him. 'No.

It's more than that. As much as I wanted to see you, I didn't want you to feel pressured or obligated in any way. Your focus is on Amelia, which is exactly where it needs to be. So, I just decided I'd come to the place where we met and wait to see if Fate would step in. And today it did.'

I was silent for a long moment, not because I couldn't think of what to say, but because I couldn't trust my voice not to wobble. 'That might just be the most romantic thing anyone has ever done for me.'

His dark brows drew a little closer together at that. 'Well, that's just all kinds of wrong. It makes me think you've been going out with entirely the wrong sort of men.'

I smiled at him, holding nothing back. 'I'm beginning to think that myself, and you'd certainly get no argument from Amelia on that one.'

As tempting as it was to linger on the beach, we both knew we couldn't stay for long. Nick had to go home and shower before work and I needed to get back to Amelia. But that brief interlude on the sand had shifted the course of us. We sat on the shoreline, taking turns throwing the ball for Mabel, and when my head dropped to his shoulder and his arm found its way around my waist, it felt like the most natural thing in the world. Nick didn't kiss me – not in the way I wanted him to – but in a way that felt right too. Whatever this thing was, it was bigger than lust and had foundations that were stronger than I realised.

It was with real reluctance that I finally got to my feet to leave. 'You've no idea how much I needed this,' I said, gathering up my empty cup. I wasn't referring to the coffee, or the apple Danish he'd also produced for me. 'I was starting to feel a bit overwhelmed, but this has been like a reset.' I gave a rueful smile. 'It turns out there's a good reason why I work in publishing and not nursing. According to my current patient, I fuss too much and panic too easily. It makes me think I'll be a terrible mum one day.'

Nick didn't miss a beat. 'I don't believe that for a single minute.'

I knew he was only being polite, but my reckless heart was having none of it. It was already chasing after dreams that could never be.

'Same time tomorrow?' Nick asked, pulling me in for one last hug.

'Tomorrow,' I agreed happily.

It was one week later, and we were once again walking along the shoreline of the deserted beach at dawn. It was cold, but with Nick's arm holding me close to his side, I felt only the warmth of him. I already knew that long after I returned to New York, Somerset and this beach would hold the memory of us in the palm of its hand.

Every now and then we'd stop to examine pieces of unusual driftwood or shells, or when it felt like too long since our last kiss. I'd never had a relationship before where I enjoyed the comfortable silences almost as much as the conversations. But then, the longer I spent in Nick's company, the more I came to realise that I'd never really had a meaningful relationship before. I used to think that I'd never connect with anyone the way I connected with Amelia. And the pain of knowing that I couldn't tell her what I'd finally found, without breaking her heart in the process, was destroying me.

Nick was holding a length of bone-white driftwood that

I'd admired and was fiddling with it like a baton as we strolled along the sand. If I didn't know better, I'd have said he was nervous. But Nick didn't do nervous, or at least he hadn't until now. Without warning, he came to a sudden halt and turned towards me. The sun was still low in the sky, its reflection glinting in his glasses, making it impossible to read the expression in his eyes.

'I have a question I want to ask you.'

'That sounds awfully serious and important.'

'It's semi-serious,' Nick said. For once, the amusement was absent from his voice. 'But it *is* kind of important... to me.'

Now I was the one who was nervous. 'Okay.'

'Lexi Edwards, will you go out with me? On a date. Our *first* date.'

I'm not sure what I'd been expecting him to say, but it certainly wasn't that. 'We've already been on loads of dates together,' I said. 'How can it possibly be our first?'

He reached for my hand and slid his fingers through mine. 'Those dates were Amelia and Sam's, or they've been snatched meetings on a windswept beach. I'd like to do it properly this time.' The piece of driftwood he'd been twirling slipped from his grip and fell to the sand.

'Could you be free on Saturday, and would you come to a wedding with me?' he asked, dropping to his knee to retrieve the stick.

'It's not going to be mine, is it?'

I have no idea why I thought this was the right moment to go for a quip. I think seeing him down on one knee and talking about weddings had rattled me a little. 'Obviously, that was a joke,' I said, biting my lip awkwardly as I looked at him. 'And not a particularly funny one,' I mumbled, as I dropped my gaze to my feet because it was more comfortable than meeting his eyes.

'Not your best,' Nick agreed. 'But interesting that that was where your thoughts went.'

He hadn't made me blush for quite a while, but he didn't appear to have lost that skill at all. He picked up the driftwood and laughed, but there was a muscle twitching at the base of his throat that I swear hadn't been doing that a moment ago.

'A good friend of mine from university is getting married next Saturday and I'd really like you to come with me. As my date, my *plus-one*,' Nick added with emphasis, seeing as I'd proved myself to be in need of clarification. 'I'd like you to meet my friends,' he added, 'the people I went to uni with.'

'I've already met one of them, haven't I?' I said, remembering only too well how little I'd enjoyed that particular experience.

'Natalie isn't going to be there,' Nick was quick to assure me, before adding softly, 'but I really hope *you* will be. Do you think your mum would be able to stay with Amelia?'

'I'm sure she would,' I said, my thoughts already turning to the logistics. It would be tricky to arrange, but not impossible. Didn't we deserve the chance to have one normal day together?

'Yes,' I said impulsively, grinning at him. 'We'll make it work somehow. I'd love to come with you. Consider it a date.'

'Our first,' Nick said, leaning forward and dropping a light kiss on the end of my nose.

'If you say so,' I said with a mock long-suffering sigh, glad that our normal banter had been restored.

We had turned around and were retracing our own footsteps in the sand when Nick threw one last curveball in my direction.

'It would have been a very poor proposal, wouldn't it?

Just randomly asking you while we were on a walk, with no flowers or champagne or anything.'

'Those are just trimmings, they're not essential. I happen to think a beachside proposal is rather romantic.'

Nick's laugh was soft and low. 'Well, I'll bear that in mind, then. Just in case.'

As I slipped my arm through his, I wondered how many times I would replay this conversation in my head over the next few days.

More than I could ever have imagined, as it turned out.

24

It was the fourth time I'd read the email, and each time my finger hovered over the button to reply and then fell away. The email was hardly a surprise; in fact, I'd been expecting it weeks ago. My office in New York had been incredibly understanding, but I'd always known they would eventually press me for a decision about the new job.

The clock counting down my return had begun ticking once they knew Amelia was out of hospital and making good progress. It was time to go home. Except I wasn't so sure where home was anymore. My head said it was back in New York and the life I'd made there, doing a job I had worked my butt off to get. But my heart... my heart was pulling me in an entirely different direction.

'Are you decent?' Amelia called from the hallway and then came in anyway before I could answer. I hurriedly closed my laptop and stuffed it back into its case.

'How do I look?' I asked, getting to my feet. I wasn't fishing for compliments, just trying to throw her off the scent.

Even so, I was pleased with the admiring wolf-whistle she attempted.

'You *do* know you're not meant to outshine the bride, don't you?' Amelia asked, taking a step back to get the full effect of the dress I'd always intended to return because it was more 'red carpet' than I'd expected. Catching sight of my reflection in the full-length bedroom mirror, I was very glad I'd kept it. The shimmering floor-length gown was one-shouldered in design, with delicate silver embroidery over ink-navy tulle. It was easily the most glamorous dress I'd ever tried on – let alone owned.

'I guess it's not a registry office and then off to the pub kind of a "do" then?' Amelia asked, as she tweaked the swirling fabric of the skirt into place.

'I hope not, or I'm going to look really stupid.'

Amelia ran her eyes over me, from the hair pinned into a loose chignon that showed off my neck and bare shoulder, down to the sparkly navy shoes that I'd borrowed from her wardrobe – with permission this time.

'You look gorgeous,' she said, closing the distance between us and enveloping me in an unexpected hug. 'My wonderful, exceptional sister,' she whispered, squeezing me tightly, as though trying to imprint this moment into her memory. I squeezed her back just as hard, wanting to do the same. My carefully applied make-up was suddenly in jeopardy as my eyes tingled at her words. They'd sounded uncomfortably like a goodbye.

'Right back at you,' I said, leaving a faint outline of pink lipstick on her cheek as I kissed her.

She stepped back, giving me one final head-to-toe sweep of

approval, but not before I'd seen her swipe a hand tellingly beneath her eye.

'What you need is a silver evening bag,' she declared, looking down at the small black clutch I had laid out on the bed. 'I've got a gorgeous beaded one somewhere that I've never even used,' she said, her eyes screwed up in concentration. 'God, where is it? I haven't seen it in ages.'

'I've not come across it in your wardrobe,' I said, realising too late the implications of my words. But my big sister was used to her younger sibling rifling through her clothes, and luckily didn't pick up on just how well acquainted I was with her closet.

'It's in a dark-grey box... I think,' Amelia said, shaking her head. 'Crap, I hate the way I can't remember things as well as I used to.'

I gave her shoulder a gentle squeeze. 'Don't worry about it. My cab's going to be here in a minute anyway, so I wouldn't have had time to swap bags.'

It was the second comment I'd made that caused her to frown.

'I still don't understand why your friend Nick can't pick you up himself, rather than expecting you to make your own way there.' It wasn't the first time she'd voiced this opinion and it was getting harder to find a believable excuse to offer.

'He just can't,' I said, which did nothing to put her off the scent.

'But why? Are you ashamed of us, is that it? Or is it that he doesn't want to meet your family?'

I was pondering which of those two alternatives to shoot down first when I saw a look of dawning horror cross her face.

'Oh my God. I know why you don't want him to come to the house.'

My throat tightened, making breathing suddenly really difficult.

'You do?' My voice was a nervous croak.

'You're bloody right I do,' she said, her tone now several degrees colder. 'He's married, isn't he?'

'I... I... No. No, he isn't,' I said, but my stammer and hesitation betrayed just how close she'd come to a version of the truth.

'Jesus, Lexi. Are you stupid enough to be fooling around with some other woman's husband?'

If her words weren't so terrible and damning this would almost be funny, in a very dark, sick, black humour kind of way.

'I would *never* do that,' I said, trying to drown out the voice in my head that was saying, *Really? Wouldn't you, Lexi? Isn't that effectively exactly what you are doing?*

Amelia was looking at me with such disapproval that I almost wanted to tell her the whole truth about Sam and Nick and even the box of stupid photographs that I now wished I'd never taken. Although if I hadn't, I would never have met Nick and that was also too terrible to contemplate.

I took a deep and steadying breath and reached for Amelia's hand. 'Mimi, I promise you my friend Nick is not married. He was, but he's divorced now.'

'So he *says*,' she said sarcastically.

'So he *is*.'

It was the closest we'd come to an argument for a long time, and I didn't like the idea of leaving her on an angry note.

'If you say so,' Amelia said, which as everyone knows

actually means *I don't believe you, but I'm not going to push it right now.*

Thankfully, at that moment three short bursts of a car horn made us both turn towards the window.

'My cab is here,' I said with genuine relief.

Amelia nodded, and perhaps she too wanted to pull back from our cross words. She swept her eyes over me one last time. 'You really do look beautiful, Lexi.' Once more she shook her head. 'I only wish I'd found that silver evening bag for you though.'

Before running down the stairs to the waiting cab, I swept my gaze around the bedroom one last time, checking I'd left it neat and tidy, because tonight my mother would be the one sleeping in this room, while I might possibly be... elsewhere. I shivered, the way I did every time I thought back to Nick's comments about the overnight arrangements.

'Some of the guests have made plans to stay at the hotel overnight,' he said.

'Are you one of them?' I asked.

His eyes found mine before he answered. 'I was, but I let the room go when you agreed to come with me.'

My raised eyebrows asked a question. There was a whole other conversation going on beneath the seemingly innocuous one about hotel rooms.

'The hotel was fully booked, and I couldn't get you a room of your own.'

What made you think I wanted one? my eyes asked, when my lips were incapable of forming the words.

He stepped closer and pulled me into his arms.

'I had no hidden agenda when I asked you to come to this wedding with me, Lexi. I didn't want you to think that I had any expectations. Keeping that hotel room made me feel uncomfortable... so I let it go.'

I lifted my arms and wound them around his neck. 'That was either really respectful of you, or a cunning way of telling me you don't fancy me.' I was teasing him, although beneath the humour I was asking a very real question.

'I think you know the answer to that one,' he said, pulling me closer and letting the proximity of our bodies settle the debate. '*If* something happens between us, I want it to be because we're both there in the moment, deciding it's the right thing to do, not because there's a hotel room upstairs waiting for us.'

I kissed him slowly, leaving the taste of me on his tongue as I asked, 'Do you think you might live to regret this decision?'

He gave a very satisfying groan as he gently released me. 'I already do.'

Nick was waiting for me by the lychgate of the charming country church where his friend was getting married. The cab swept into an adjacent gravelled forecourt, but Nick didn't see it arrive because another tuxedo-wearing guest had just spotted him. Through the window I could see the two men shaking hands as I paid the driver and climbed out of the taxi.

I didn't say a word. I didn't call out his name, or raise an arm in greeting, but somehow Nick knew I was there. I saw him tense, bid farewell to the man he'd been talking to, and then slowly turn to face me. On legs that inexplicably felt like jelly, I began to make my way towards him as he began walking to meet me. His eyes stayed fixed on my face as I drew step by step closer to him.

His hand was held out and waiting for me when we finally met on the driveway.

'You look...' He shook his head as though in a daze. 'I don't have the words to tell you how beautiful you look,' he said, sounding genuinely awed.

'I think you just found the right ones,' I said, smiling so broadly it made my cheeks ache.

It was a very British wedding, the kind where you keep expecting Hugh Grant to pop up suddenly. It was quaint and charming, but also surprisingly emotional. Nick had already told me the story of how his friend Will had met his bride in very unusual circumstances when they'd been involved in an accident that had left her in a wheelchair. So, when Bella had shakily got to her feet and walked slowly down the aisle towards him, a collective gasp had run through the church and there hadn't been a dry eye in sight. But perhaps what I loved even more was when Nick had reached for my hand and held it warmly as the couple exchanged their vows.

The country house hotel where the reception was being held was impressive without being starchy. We were ushered into a large reception room with floor-to-ceiling windows. Through them, I watched Will scoop Bella from her chair as the photographer took a picture that I already knew would end up in a frame.

'Here you go,' Nick said, handing me one of the glasses of champagne he'd lifted from a tray. He followed the direction of my gaze and smiled.

'I don't even know them,' I said, watching as the bride and groom exchanged a tender kiss, 'but I'm so pleased they found their happy ending.'

Nick shook his head. 'It's not their happy ending,' he corrected, 'it's their happy beginning. And it just goes to prove that whatever challenges life throws at you, love always finds a way.' He grinned. 'Was that a little too Hallmark?'

'A bit,' I admitted, 'but I kind of liked it.'

It was a conversation I'd have liked to continue, but we were interrupted by one of Nick's friends who he'd not seen in years, followed by another, and then another. Some people were better than others at containing their curiosity when Nick introduced me simply as 'Lexi'. No label. No title. I sipped thoughtfully on my champagne and wondered if there even *was* one that would fit our situation. I wasn't his girlfriend, and he wasn't my partner. We weren't lovers, but we were so much more than friends. We travelled a curious no man's land as we teetered on the edge of falling for each other and saying goodbye. No wonder there was no name for what we had.

There were enough telling glances from Nick's university friends to realise that some of them had been expecting to see Natalie at his side today. Perhaps that wasn't surprising, for she *had* once been part of their friendship group.

Over the next few hours, I laughed hard enough to bring tears to my eyes as I listened to Nick's friends regale the table with stories of their past, which frankly made my own university exploits sound decidedly tame. Their reminiscences revealed another side to Nick, a more playful, light-hearted version. I liked the boy he'd once been almost as much as I did the man he'd become.

It was no surprise to discover that I liked Nick's friends a lot too. With a different throw of the dice, these people could have been *my* friends, and it made me nostalgic for all the times I'd never get to share with them.

The bride's dad gave a speech that made me cry. I thought I'd done a good job of hiding my emotions, but Nick still noticed.

'Are you okay?' he asked, bridging the space between our chairs to whisper into my ear.

'Yes, I'm fine,' I said, as I scrabbled in my small but virtually useless evening bag for a tissue. Nick took the folded handkerchief from the breast pocket of his suit and pressed it into my palm. 'It's a wedding thing,' I explained, taking the silk square and dabbing the corner of my eye. 'It's bad form not to cry at least once.'

'You don't have to explain,' he said. And when I lifted my watery gaze to his, I realised he was right. I didn't have to. Because he understood me, in a way that no one – except possibly Amelia – had ever done before. Was I really going to walk away from a connection this strong? Could I be making the biggest and most stupid mistake of my life?

'Okay, there's something about me I really ought to have told you before now.' Nick's tone was suddenly serious and snapped my thoughts back to the present. He waited until he saw he had my whole attention. 'I can't dance. No rhythm, no co-ordination, no style or grace whatsoever.'

His eyes were on my lips, waiting for the amusement to appear, which of course it did.

'Is this your way of telling me you won't be taking to the dance floor tonight?'

He surprised me then by springing immediately to his feet as the first chords of the band struck up. He held out his hands and pulled me from my chair.

'Hell no. I love dancing. I'm just bloody awful at it.'

I'd like to say he had exaggerated, but I had two bruised toes that would beg to differ. You had to love someone who threw themselves with such enthusiasm into something they were patently crap at doing. I faltered midway through a spinning twirl that could easily end with me flat on my back.

You had to love someone.

You had to love someone...

The words were ricocheting in time to the music, the beat of which Nick consistently failed to follow. He didn't care. He was laughing and smiling at me, and I knew then that I would always remember this, because it was the moment I realised I loved him.

When the music eventually slowed down, and the smoky voice of the band's vocalist began to sing about him and Mrs Jones, I went into Nick's arms as though I'd never been held by him before. Everything felt new and fragile and incredibly precious. The curves of my body fitted perfectly against the planes of his as he pulled me closer. I could feel the warmth of his breath against the side of my neck, and the graze of his lips as his mouth brushed against my pulse point, which was hammering like crazy.

Two or three songs in, and I had to keep reminding myself we were in a public venue and that the thoughts running through my mind had no place among a roomful of strangers. When I lifted my head from where it had settled on Nick's shoulder, I saw a cobalt flame flickering in his eyes. It scorched all sense from me.

'Can we get out of here?' I asked huskily.

Nick seemed to struggle to formulate a reply, which I took as a very encouraging sign. He simply nodded, his eyes never leaving my mouth.

'Let's go,' he said at last, his voice a mixture of velvet and gravel.

He led me from the dance floor, weaving a pathway between couples who were now gyrating to a well-known banger, guaranteed to get everyone on their feet.

'Shouldn't we say goodbye to your friends?' I asked, suddenly aware he'd already collected my bag from our table, and we were now in the hotel foyer.

'I love that you think I have enough control to handle a round of goodbyes as well as the twenty-minute drive to get back to my place.'

He was looking down at me, and my already erratic pulse broke free from its moorings and began to race.

'Twenty minutes?' I asked, my voice weirdly breathy.

'Eighteen, if I'm lucky with every set of lights.'

'Are you feeling lucky?' I asked, biting my lower lip. I wasn't usually this provocative, but Nick was bringing out a whole new side of me.

He pulled me to him and kissed me with a preview of the passion I knew we'd be sharing in roughly twenty minutes – eighteen, if all went well.

I hardly remember the drive. I know the radio was playing, but I'd be hard pushed to tell you if the music was low, sexy jazz or 'Baby Shark' on repeat. I *do* remember being present enough in the moment to hurriedly rattle off a message to

Mum and Amelia, letting them know I wouldn't be coming home that night. But my fingers were far from steady, and it was probably so full of typos it would take them until morning to decipher it.

My admiration for Nick grew enormously as we travelled the lanes towards his home. He was driving fast, perhaps a little above the speed limit, but he was never reckless. He kept his eyes on the road the entire time – later confessing that if he'd allowed them to stray to me, we could have ended up wrapped around a tree, or upside down in a ditch at the side of the road.

However composed Nick might outwardly appear, there were still clues that gave him away. He parked at an oddly slewed angle on his driveway and left the keys dangling in the ignition. He was out of the driver's seat and beside my door while I was still fumbling with the seat belt. He leant over me to release the clasp and I heard the breath hitch in his throat before he pulled me free and into his arms. Then his lips were on mine in a kiss that started on the driveway beneath a canopy of stars and continued all the way through his front door and into the hallway. I was vaguely aware of Mabel looking up sleepily from her dog bed and then studiously turning away.

Nick's suit jacket ended up on the hallway floor, quickly followed by his tie and my sparkly stilettos, which were abandoned on the stairs. We left a treasure trail of clothes on our way to his bedroom. By the time we got there, every button on Nick's shirt was undone and I'd tugged it free from the waistband of his trousers.

He cradled my face in his hands as he kissed me passionately in the upstairs hallway. Our tongues met, exploring, probing, and deepening the kiss until I was groaning softly against his mouth. His hands were still in my hair, but mine had slid down his shoulders to travel across the contours of his chest... and then dip lower. This time, Nick was the one who groaned. He ran one hand down the curve of my spine, his fingers stalling when they found the zip of my dress. I held my breath, waiting. With every second he delayed, the ache between my legs became almost unbearable.

My hands went to his hips, and I pulled him against me, firmly enough for there to be no misunderstanding. For a moment, he hesitated.

'You're sure about this, Lexi? If you've changed your mind, it's not too late to stop.'

'I don't want to stop. Do you?' It was going to destroy me if he said 'yes'.

In answer, he finally tugged down my zip and slipped his hand inside the opening of my dress. I moaned and pressed myself against him; he was so hard he felt like granite against me. Nick dropped his hands to my hips, and in a movement so fast it made me gasp, he lifted me up and against him. My legs went around him and locked behind his back. We half stumbled, half fell through the bedroom doorway and somehow made it to the bed.

The rest of his clothes were gone in seconds; I was *that* impatient, *that* greedy. But Nick took his time, laying down a fiery trail of kisses that started at my throat, moved down across my bare shoulder, and then followed the curve of my breast. The strapless bra that had taken me ages to fasten earlier came off much faster with Nick's fingers working the clasp. He looked down at me for a long moment before almost reverently brushing my exposed flesh. The agony of waiting for his caress was quickly forgotten as he cupped my breasts, before lowering his head to tease each nipple gently with his lips and tongue.

What followed was a blur of sensations so far beyond the realm of what I'd experienced before, I honestly wondered if I'd been doing it wrong for my entire adult life. We explored each other slowly, inch by tantalising inch, as though on a journey we'd always wanted to take but had never found the right companion to travel with. Until now. The foreplay alone confirmed that I was ruined for any other man. I never wanted to do this with anyone but him.

When Nick finally steadied his weight on to his arms and eased himself between my legs, my eyes were open and so were his. Neither of us looked away. When he pushed himself inside me, I could feel his body trembling beneath my hands.

'God, Lexi, I've wanted this for so long.'

He matched his pace to mine, reading every movement and sound I made as though we'd done this a thousand times before. He knew exactly when I was close, and I saw the urgency on his face intensify as he finally tipped me over the edge. I came with a cry I couldn't suppress, and seconds later Nick shuddered against me, calling out my name as he spilled into me.

It was like nothing I'd known before, and as he gathered my body into his arms and tenderly kissed my forehead, I knew it had been every bit as incredible for him as it had been for me.

25

'This is *not* how I intended our first morning together to play out.'

Nick was still apologising. He'd been doing it ever since his phone had woken us as the first light of a new day began creeping in through the window. He kept saying 'sorry' as he moved through the semi-darkness, gathering up his clothes in a well-practised sweep. And he was still doing it now as he stood beside his bed looking down at me. I was acutely aware that the bed sheets were still tangled and pooled around my waist.

'How am I expected to walk out the door with you looking like that in my bed?' he said with a groan.

I brought up my hands to cover my boobs. 'Better?'

He shook his head and took hold of my wrists to move my hands, raising them up and pressing them into the pillows by my head, holding me prisoner. Admittedly, a very willing prisoner. He knelt on the bed and then laid his body on top of mine. My breath caught in my throat as I felt him hardening through the sheets.

It was just as well Nick managed to find some control from somewhere, because I was running on empty.

'I can't do this. I've got to get to the farm,' he said, releasing me.

I nodded, kissing him hard and fast before pulling up the sheet to prevent any further distractions.

'Go back to sleep, if you can,' Nick urged as he shrugged into a thick hoodie and jerked up the zip. 'If it had been anyone else but Doug, I'd have told them to call the practice. I'm not even on call this weekend.'

'Honestly, Nick, it's fine. *I'm* fine,' I assured him.

I'd known it was serious from the moment his frown of annoyance had changed into one of concern as his friend apologised for calling him at such an ungodly hour. There had followed a brief conversation during which Nick had fired off a series of questions, none of which I'd understood. But I realised they were all equine related. Whatever answers Nick had received dialled up the concern on his face.

'I'll be there in fifteen,' he told his friend.

Nick climbed out of the bed and, sandwiched between numerous apologies, told me that Dotty, the horse I'd ridden on our visit to the farm, was seriously unwell with colic.

'Doug said Pippa is half out of her mind with worry. She loves that horse more than anything else in the world. Honestly, Lexi, if it was anyone else but them—'

'Go,' I interrupted him. 'I understand.'

'You could probably do with getting some rest,' Nick said from the bedroom doorway. He was at least five metres away from me, but I swear I could feel the heat from his eyes as he added, 'Neither of us got much sleep last night.'

'I know,' I said, sharing a look that new lovers anywhere would recognise.

'I had such big plans for this morning,' Nick admitted, forcing himself through the doorway with visible effort. 'And none of them involved either of us getting dressed.'

I giggled, wondering when I'd last felt this light-hearted, and then felt immediately guilty when I thought of the desperate teenager waiting at the stables for the only vet she trusted to save her horse.

'Make yourself at home while I'm gone. I'll be back as soon as I can.'

'I'll be here,' I promised. And then, because I couldn't resist, I dropped the sheet and gave him one last quick flash.

Nick was still laughing as he ran lightly down the stairs and out into the early morning.

Surprisingly, I did manage to go back to sleep. Nick must have been gone for several hours by the time I woke the second time, for the sunlight filtering through his bedroom window was in an entirely different spot on the polished wooden floor.

I stretched lazily in his bed as memories of the night before played through my head like an X-rated movie. I smiled as I surveyed his bedroom floor, littered with our discarded clothes. Over by the door was Nick's shirt, which I'd impressively managed to toss clean across the room. Pulled by the need for coffee, I swung out of bed and slipped it on. Nick had told me to make myself at home, but I didn't think that offer extended to wandering around his house stark naked.

As I headed for the kitchen, I discovered more discarded clothing. I scooped up the sparkly stilettos from the staircase and picked up my black clutch bag from the bottom tread. I set the shoes down, but for some reason my fingers tightened on the slim evening bag.

Just moments earlier, the only thought in my head had been the espresso machine in Nick's kitchen. But now, as I stood in a shaft of morning sunlight, I suddenly shivered. Something felt wrong... something to do with my handbag. I flipped the catch and peered inside. Everything that should be there *was* there. But I couldn't shake the feeling of ill ease.

It was still there as I stepped into Nick's kitchen and set the bag down on the gleaming countertop. Amelia had been right; a silver bag *would* have looked better with my outfit. There it was again, that feeling of something being off kilter.

Distracted, I turned towards the cupboard where Nick stored his mugs, but I never got to pull one down. With the impact of a lightning bolt, the memory I'd been grappling to catch hold of slowed down enough for me to snag it.

I've got a gorgeous beaded one somewhere.

I could hear Amelia's voice as clearly as if she was standing right there in the kitchen beside me.

It's in a dark-grey box... I think.

She'd been talking about her missing silver evening bag, and I'd been too distracted to pay much attention to her words. But I did now, because I knew *exactly* where that grey box was. It was beneath the bed in the guest room. I'd seen it every single time I'd knelt to slip another bundle of photographs into the memory box.

My heart was pounding against the wall of my chest and the sound of blood rushing in my ears made it difficult to think straight. There was absolutely no reason to think that Amelia would have remembered the location of the grey box overnight. Or that she'd decided to look for it at all. But what if she had?

Could I risk her finding the memory box? I asked, and answered my own question by racing back up the stairs to Nick's bedroom and pulling on my clothes much faster than he had removed them. Those photographs should never have been taken, and seen out of context they could do nothing but harm.

The Uber driver wanted to chat, but all I wanted was for him to drive faster. Every red light and busy junction felt like it had been put in our path deliberately to slow us down.

'Do you think you could go a little quicker?' I urged him.

'In a bit of a hurry, are you?' It was the second redundant question he'd asked so far, the first being 'Off somewhere nice today?' when I climbed into the back of his car at ten o'clock in the morning dressed in my wedding finery.

I felt bad breaking my promise to Nick that I'd be there when he returned, and I shut my mind to the image of him running up the stairs, only to find my hastily scrawled note in the place where he'd left me.

Nick, I'm really sorry but something has come up and I have to leave. I'll call you later. I hope Dotty is okay. L x

I leapt from the car almost before it had come to a stop on the sandy lane and threw a hurried thank you over my shoulder to the driver. I burst through the front door as though on a rescue mission, glancing left and right as I ran through the hallway, hoping to find my sister in one of the downstairs rooms. But both were empty.

I ran up the stairs, tracking damp sand from the soles of

my stilettos as I went. As I crested the top tread, I saw the door to my bedroom was open. Feeling physically sick, I took a tentative step forward.

'Amelia?' I called out, straining my ears in the hope that I'd hear the drum of water from the shower, but her reply came, as I somehow had known it would, from my own bedroom.

My legs felt leaden as I crossed the hall. She was exactly where I feared I would find her, kneeling on the floor beside my bed. Surrounding her, fanned out on the wooden boards, was a sea of glossy photographs from the memory box.

Her head turned very, very slowly to face me. 'What the fuck are these?'

'I can explain,' I said hurriedly, which was an outright lie, as I had absolutely no idea how to do that.

She had no interest in hearing my explanations. She led with an anger that I suspected had been brewing for several hours.

'You lied.' Her voice didn't even sound like my sister's. 'You lied to me. I asked you if your friend had been able to get the photographs off my phone and you stood there, right in front of me, and lied your head off, telling me he hadn't been able to retrieve them.'

'I... I...' I had nothing. I wasn't prepared for this argument. But Amelia certainly was.

'Every last treasured memory I have of Sam was on that phone. You *knew* how important those photographs were to me and you bloody lied about having them. And then you printed them off and hid them from me. What the fuck is wrong with you?'

I shook my head, every inch of my body scorched by the flaying I was getting. The flaying I deserved.

'But worse than hiding these from me,' Amelia said, placing a trembling arm on the bed to help her stand, 'worse than the way you deceived me, was the way you made me doubt everything I knew to be true. You made me think I was going crazy. I searched every inch of this cottage for signs of Sam, but I couldn't find any. And now I know why.'

Because he isn't real, I desperately wanted to say, but she wasn't allowing me to speak yet.

'You've hidden every last trace of him away from me, haven't you? Just like you hid these photographs. But what I can't for the life of me work out is why. Why, Lexi?' she asked, her whole body trembling with emotion. 'Why would you do this to your own sister? Your flesh and blood. Your twin.'

'Please, Mimi, let's just calm down and think about all of this rationally.' I looked around the room desperately. 'Where's Mum? She'll back me up on this.'

'She's at Tom's,' Amelia snapped. 'And leave her out of it. This is just between you and me.'

'Okay,' I said, holding up my hands as though surrendering. 'But please, don't think I did anything here to hurt you.' My voice wobbled as tears began to course down my cheeks. 'All I wanted was to make you well again.'

Amelia's eyes were glittering, but it was rage that had put the sparkle in them, not tears. 'You wanted to be the only one who could make me better,' she said, her voice that of a stranger.

I shook my head. 'What? No. What do you mean?'

She looked down at the photographs scattered at our feet. 'You can see what Sam and I feel for each other. It's there in every single bloody photograph from my phone. And you couldn't stand that, could you?'

'What?' She was so far off beam I had no idea how to pull the conversation back into the realms of sanity. 'I'm not jealous of you and your relationship with Sam,' I denied, overriding the voice in my head that insistently reminded me he didn't exist.

'Well, I think that's exactly what you are. You're jealous of having someone be as close or closer to me than you are. And you're jealous of having someone who looks at you the way Sam looks at me in these photographs.'

I couldn't help glancing down and catching a snapshot of Nick and I smiling at each other on the beach. My tears began to fall even faster.

'You've probably been envious ever since I met him. He was always more your type than mine.' She made a good point. Nick was exactly the type of man I'd always been attracted to.

'Maybe you couldn't stand it that I'd made a relationship succeed in the way you never have.'

Her abrupt change of direction left my head spinning.

'What's that supposed to mean?'

'The way every relationship you've ever had has come with a built-in self-destruct button. You've not been unlucky in love, the way you like to believe.' I shook my head at the venom I'd never once heard before, spewing out of this stranger who looked like my sister, but clearly wasn't.

'You've deliberately made sure you don't find love by picking the wrong men over and over again. You've self-sabotaged your life ever since Dad died.'

If she'd taken out a dagger and sliced it straight into my heart, she couldn't have hurt me more. She was the only one who knew the guilt I still carried deep inside me for what had happened on the day our father died, and hearing her use it as a weapon just about destroyed me.

'And now you don't want anyone to love me, or care for me either, except you. You've done nothing since you've got here but keep Sam away from me.'

I was shaking my head, helpless to know how to convince her that she was a million miles from the truth.

She suddenly sat down heavily on the mattress, as though struck off her feet by a revelation.

'Oh my God. You've been *keeping* Sam from me all this time. That's where you've been going when you were supposedly meeting your friend "Nick".' She air-quoted the name of the man I loved. 'I don't believe there even *is* a Nick at all. You've just made him up, haven't you?'

The accusation, turning the tables on which one of us was in love with a man who didn't exist, was so ridiculous I actually laughed out loud. Too late, I realised that was absolutely the worst thing I could have done.

Amelia was shaking her head, putting all the pieces together and coming up with entirely the wrong picture. 'Every time you met this Nick, you were really seeing Sam, weren't you, telling him he couldn't come and see me, that it was bad for my recovery if he came back before I was well again.' She thumped the mattress in triumph. 'I always knew that bloody ridiculous story about him being at a silent retreat was a load of bollocks. Sam would never have done something like that.'

I really wanted to tell her that our mother had questioned

exactly that, but of course I couldn't. I shook my head slowly. 'I can't talk to you when you're like this.'

'What, seeing things clearly for the first time in months, you mean?'

'Seeing everything wrong. Seeing *me* wrong. I love you, Amelia. With all my heart and with every sinew of my body, I love you and I would never, ever do anything to hurt you.'

Amazingly, some of my sincerity managed to pierce the miasma of anger and rage.

'You do love me. I know that. But so does Sam, and you've stopped him from coming back to me. And I can't let you do that anymore.'

A cold feeling of dread swirled through me.

'What does that mean?'

She hesitated. I held on to that thought for a long time. At least she had hesitated before saying the words that sliced through our relationship like a sabre.

'I want you to leave. It's time you went back to your own life in New York and let me get back to mine. When you've gone, Sam will come back to me. I know he will.'

26

I stood for a long time in the guest bedroom, still dressed in my wedding outfit, trying to make sense of what had just happened. I'd never rowed with Amelia like that; I'd never been on the receiving end of such anger. I couldn't see how we'd ever be able to fix our shattered relationship after this, and the thought it might be irretrievably broken made the tears fall even faster down my face.

Amelia wanted me gone, not just out of her home but out of the country, and even though I'd always known I'd have to leave soon, I'd thought it would be when her confusion had cleared and the confabulation about a man who didn't exist had finally faded away.

But Sam was still here in her thoughts and somehow Amelia had convinced herself that I was the one preventing him from being by her side. The only way left to prove he *wasn't* real was for me to leave and wait for her to finally understand that he was never going to come back to her... because he didn't exist.

But the worst realisation of all was that while Sam lived

on as my sister's phantom partner, Nick could never be mine. Our fledgling relationship and all the hopes that had sprung into life after last night had to be put aside now. I couldn't, I wouldn't, build my own happiness on my sister's broken heart. It would ultimately destroy us both.

I tore off the dress, left it as a pool of tulle on my bedroom floor and reached for my laptop. I'd been mentally composing this email for weeks, with two different replies. It wasn't until I typed the words accepting the job offer that I realised I'd been intending to turn it down all along. Instead, I signed off by assuring my manager that I'd be back at my desk in Manhattan by the end of the week.

I clearly wasn't thinking straight, or I'd have checked with the airline to see if I could even find a flight at such short notice. But luck was with me. There was one seat left on a direct flight to JFK in two days. Technology made it all too easy to burn bridges before you had time to change your mind. You simply rattled in your credit card details and with a single click you had altered your own destiny.

The irony wasn't lost on me that I was flying back across the Atlantic with almost the same degree of urgency with which I'd crossed it several months ago. And yet in the space of that short period, everything had changed. Well, to be fair, most of the important events changing my future had occurred only in the last twenty-four hours.

'I've managed to get a flight for the day after tomorrow.'

'I think that's for the best,' Amelia replied tightly.

We hadn't said much to each other since our row that morning and when we did, the words had sounded stiff and uncomfortably polite, like a conversation between strangers. A chasm of ice had opened between us, and I had absolutely no idea how to bridge it.

The only glimmer of hope was Amelia's reaction when I suggested moving back into Mum's for the next two days.

'You don't need to do that,' she shot back. 'You can stay here until you leave.'

It wasn't exactly an olive branch, or even a twig, but I took it as an encouraging sign anyway.

It was mid-afternoon before I finally heard Nick's voice. He'd sent several apologetic messages throughout the day, but I hadn't replied to any of them. I didn't want to distract him while he was working, but if I was being totally honest, I had needed those extra hours to strengthen my resolve, which I already knew he'd challenge.

Amelia was pretending to read a magazine, but the speed with which the pages were being turned gave her away. We were miles apart, despite being in the same room. I'd moved to the window and was staring at the incoming waves as they crashed on to the beach, realising how much I was going to miss this place when I left. When my mobile rang, I knew it would be Nick's name on my phone screen and my stomach flipped over and seemed to collide with my heart, which was already beginning to sink. This was it.

Amelia looked up, her eyes following me suspiciously as I turned away from the window, headed towards the hall and slipped out of the cottage. The wind felt sharp, like a slap on my cheeks as I crossed the pathway and stepped on to the beach. I should have stopped to pick up a jacket, I realised, as I shivered in my loosely woven jumper. Or perhaps it wasn't the weather that was making me tremble. It took two attempts before my unsteady fingers managed to answer the call.

'Hey,' Nick said, and even though I'd locked my emotions behind a steel wall, he almost took me down with that one word. He sounded so happy, and I was about to ruin all of that.

'Hello.' My voice sounded as tight as my grip on my mobile.

'Is everything all right? I've just got back and found your note.'

'Everything is fine,' I said. It was the first lie, but I doubted it would be my last of the day.

'Oh, good. You had me worried for a moment. I thought something had happened to Amelia.' The relief in his voice was palpable and I felt like a monster for hurting a man this caring.

'Is Dotty okay?' I asked.

Nick sighed, and I heard the exhaustion in the sound. 'She will be, but it was touch and go for a while. I'm sorry it took me away from you, but at least the outcome is positive.'

It might be for the horse, but sadly not for us.

'I'm glad, really glad,' I said, my voice cracking unexpectedly.

'Lexi, what is it? What's wrong? Don't tell me everything's okay because I can hear that it's not.'

'We need to talk, Nick.'

I heard his single hard swallow, as though the lump in his throat was almost as large as the one in mine.

'You're starting to scare me here. Is this something I should be worried about?'

'I... I really don't want to get into it on the phone.'

His sharply indrawn breath told me he was already on the right page of the book I'd never wanted to open.

'Where are you? At Amelia's?'

'Yes.'

'I'm leaving right now.'

I went back into the cottage and pulled a quilted jacket down from the hook beside the door and then, as an afterthought, grabbed a handful of tissues and stuffed them into my pocket. I had a feeling that however many I took, it was never going to be enough.

I don't like to think how fast Nick must have driven to get to me so quickly. It brought back the memory of our speedy drive the night before, although it would be hard to find two more contrasting situations.

Twenty minutes after ending our call, Nick pulled up amid a shower of gritty sand. He parked his car some distance from the row of fishermen's cottages and climbed out without even glancing towards them. Somehow, he knew exactly where he'd find me. I dug my hands deep into the pockets of my jacket and watched him cover the distance between us. His stride slowed and then faltered when he got close enough to read the expression on my face.

He shook his head slowly, as though in disbelief.

'I'm so sorry,' I said, longing to run to him and take it all back, to unsay the terrible words I'd yet to utter, to unbreak the heart I was about to shatter.

'Why?' It was a sorrowful question and one I couldn't properly answer.

I shook my head. He deserved so much more than I was giving him.

For a long time, neither of us spoke.

'I've fallen in love with you, Lexi.' It was the one thing I wanted to hear more than anything, and the last thing I ever wanted him to say. 'I just wanted you to know that before you say anything else.'

There were two Nicks standing before me, then four, and then a whole army of them as my vision blurred with tears. *Me too* was right there on my lips; but telling him that would only make an impossibly painful situation even harder.

'I've booked my flight back home. I leave in two days.'

I watched him flinch beneath my words as though they were knives.

'Let's walk,' Nick said, his voice gruff. He offered me his arm and for a moment I hesitated, but the pull of him was too strong. Even across an ocean, it still would be. I slid my arm through his as we set off across the sand.

'Why now? Why today? Was it something I did... or didn't do?'

I couldn't allow him to think that, even if it would have given me an easier exit.

'There is not one thing about last night that I'd change. It was perfect.'

'So perfect it's made you want to hurry back to the other side of the world?'

'It's where I live,' I said simply. 'I was always going to go back. We both knew that.'

'Has someone said anything to you?' he asked.

'No,' I lied, on a knee-jerk reflex.

'You just woke up and had a change of heart?'

'My heart hasn't changed,' I told him, my voice solemn. It was the most honest thing I'd said so far.

'I thought we had a few more weeks until you had to leave.

I've been trying to think of ways we could make this thing work ever since I left you this morning.'

While I'd spent my day trying to cut him out of my life, he'd spent his trying to carve me a place in his own. I'd be shedding tears over that dichotomy for a long time to come.

'Long-distance relationships never work,' I declared, coming to a sudden stop and forcing him to face me.

'How do you know? Have you ever had one?'

I wanted to lie, but there was a look in his eyes that wouldn't let me.

'No. But I know it wouldn't work for me.'

He reached for my hands, trapping them inside his.

'You can't say that for sure. Don't we deserve to at least give it a try?'

My eyes dropped to the sand, because looking at him while I stamped out all hope was just as hard as I'd always known it would be. *Of course I want to try*, I screamed silently.

'I could fly out for the weekend every fortnight,' Nick suggested, his voice still hopeful. 'And then when Holly is away with her mum, I could come and stay longer.'

'You'd be forever on a plane, and it would cost a fortune.'

'Do you think I care about that? You're worth it. *We're* worth it,' he said, pulling me towards him. I wanted to resist but my feet had run out of willpower. I collided with his chest and buried my face there so he couldn't see how close I was to wavering.

'I've accepted that big promotion at work.' I mumbled the excuse into his hoodie. 'It's a huge step up for me. Lots more responsibility. I'll be working all hours, including weekends,' I added meaningfully. 'We'll end up ruining the memory. Can't we just leave it as a single perfect moment in both of our lives? I know what will happen if we don't. You'll get frustrated that I'm too busy to spend time with you, or I'll get angry that you're always dashing back to the airport. Our schedules will never be in sync, and we'll have to resort to kinky phone sex between visits.'

For the first time, a fledgling smile flickered on his lips. 'See, you finally found the upside.'

I smiled sadly and stepped out of his hold. It felt symbolic.

'Please let me have this wonderful memory of my time with a man I met under the most incredible of circumstances. If we keep trying to find a way to stay in each other's lives, it's going to destroy everything good about you and me.'

I saw him stiffen as my words struck him like blows. I tilted my face to look at him. His eyes appeared damp, and as much as I wanted to believe it was the wind making them water, I was horribly afraid it was me. There's a special place in hell reserved for those who hurt someone this kind, and that was where I was heading.

'There's something more to this. Something you're not telling me. None of these reasons would have made you suddenly decide to give up on us. What happened after I left you in my bed this morning?'

I didn't want to tell him, but how could I leave things like this, with him thinking I didn't care enough to find a way for us to be together?

'Please, Lexi. If you're walking away from me, don't I at least deserve to know why?'

So, I told him. I told him everything. He didn't interrupt me. He didn't say a single word, he just stood beside me, staring out to sea while I systematically destroyed something that had only just begun to live. When I finally finished talking, he turned slowly to face me.

'If you'd chosen another man over me, I would have fought for you.'

I felt my heart swell in my chest at the sincerity in his voice.

'If you had chosen Amelia and her happiness over me, I would have somehow come to terms with it, because I know how much you love her.'

Tears were stinging my eyes again, but I blinked them away.

'But what I can't fight and what I can't understand is that you're choosing Amelia's happiness over your own. You're enabling her fantasy to destroy your own reality. And I'm powerless against that. There's nothing I can say, because the only person who can change the way you're thinking... is you. I will put you first. Always and forever. You and Holly are the most important things in the world to me and I will put you both before everything else. But you need to put yourself first too. You need to put Lexi and Nick before Amelia and Sam.'

'I can't, Nick. I can't do that to her.'

He was quiet for the longest time. I couldn't tell if he was furious, frustrated, or heartbroken. Perhaps all three.

'Will you let me come to the airport with you?'

I reached for his hand, trying to memorise the feeling of his fingers curled around mine, because I knew it was going to be the last time I ever felt them there.

'No, Nick. It would be too hard. Please let's end it now, here on the beach where it first began.'

He drew me back into his arms again, and for a moment I thought he was going to kiss me, which would have been my undoing, but Nick was too honourable for those tactics. His arms tightened around me in a hug that said everything we both felt. It went on and on, as though we both knew that something precious would be gone the minute our arms fell away.

Time seemed to stretch endlessly as the world went quiet. The gulls stopped shrieking, the wind ceased its whistle, and the surf grew muffled.

'I'm not going to stop hoping that you'll find a way back to me,' Nick whispered into my hair.

'I leave in two days. That's not going to change.'

'I know.'

I'd done all I could to shut the door on our future. But Nick was still there, standing on the other side of it, hoping for a way to break it down.

27

'This is ridiculous, Lexi. You *have* to let me talk to her.'

I shook my head. 'No, Mum. We've been over this again and again. You can't say anything.'

I reached across the kitchen table and took hold of her hand, keeping my voice low so it wouldn't carry to Amelia's room, where she was taking yet another nap. There'd been quite a few of those over the past two days. She was clearly avoiding me.

'Right now, Amelia thinks I'm the only one to blame.'

'I know,' Mum said sadly, 'and that's why I want to put her straight. It's so unfair.'

'It would be more unfair if there was no one here she could trust after I've gone. As it stands, I'm the only villain in this story. I'm the one keeping Sam from her and making her believe he isn't real. It would devastate her if she thought you were stopping him from coming back too.'

I saw by the tears filling Mum's eyes that she understood exactly what I was saying.

'The only way to fix this is for me to go back to New York

and clear the way for Sam to come back to her. And when he doesn't, when Amelia finally realises that he was never real, then maybe she can start to get better. And that's all I've ever wanted.'

'Is it, Lexi? What about you and Nick?'

Would it always hurt this much whenever I thought of him? I had a horrible feeling that it probably would.

'There is no Nick and me. There never can be while Amelia still believes there's a Sam.'

'This is all so messed up,' Mum said, shaking her head as she tried to make sense of the tangled chaos our lives had become. 'You're giving up too much for her. I'm not so old or blind that I don't recognise love when I see it right before my eyes.'

I met her gaze and smiled gently and meaningfully. 'Me neither,' I said, allowing my eyes to travel to the window and the fisherman's cottage beyond, where Tom lived. Mum blushed like a teenager, and it was the only bright moment in a day full of darkness.

'We're not talking about me. I don't want to see you walking away from someone who cares about you and wants you in his life.'

'It's hard to share a life with someone when you are thousands of miles apart,' I said, opting for the easy excuse.

'Did Nick say the distance made it impossible?'

I thought about lying, but she'd brought me up better than that.

'No. He wanted us to try.'

'So why won't you?'

'How can I, Mum?' I cried, my voice rising. 'To Amelia, Sam and Nick are the same man. Until she realises that she's never been in love with him, then I can't be either. In some ways, leaving now is as much for me as it is for Amelia. Perhaps when she sees things clearly, Nick and I could try again – if he still wants to by then, that is.'

If I haven't broken his heart into so many pieces that he'll never forgive me, I add silently.

My last morning in the fisherman's cottage began the same as my first, with a chorus of cawing seagulls. I was going to miss waking up to their strident cries and the sound of the tide. I was going to miss a great many things.

I swung out of bed and caught sight of my reflection in the dressing-table mirror. It was *not* the face of a happy traveller. Nor was it one of someone who'd enjoyed much sleep over the last few days. There was every chance I'd be charged excess at the check-in counter for the bags beneath my eyes.

I glanced at my watch and then, in a reflex I was powerless to resist, my gaze went to the bedroom window and down the sandy track that led to the road. I'd made it very clear to Nick that I didn't think we should see each other again before I left. I told him that I wanted to spend the time with my family. What I hadn't told him was that one of them could barely speak to me without getting teary-eyed and the other one could barely speak to me at all.

Amelia was already in the kitchen, nursing a cup of cold coffee, when I entered the room. There were dark circles beneath her own eyes that would have given mine a run for their money.

'Good morning.'

Her head jerked up, but she didn't reply, she simply nodded.

In front of Mum she put on a better show, but when it was just the two of us she made it very clear that she had little to say to me. I poured myself a coffee from the jug on the counter and pulled up the chair that had been mine for the last three months.

After a farewell dinner that no one except Mum had wanted, we'd said our tearful goodbyes on the doorstep, with a promise that I'd phone her when I got to the airport. You'd have thought that having lived abroad for so long, I'd be better at leaving my family behind by now. But everything felt harder this time around. Amelia's illness and our current estrangement was a horrible reminder that you never know when your last goodbye really will be *your last goodbye*.

'My taxi will be here soon,' I said quietly.

For a fleeting moment I thought I glimpsed a look of panic in Amelia's eyes, but she quickly blinked it away. She nodded yet again.

My suitcase and carry-on luggage were ready and waiting beside the front door, yet my steps were slow and reluctant as I walked out of the cottage when the cab pulled up just moments later. While the driver loaded my bags, I paused to take one last mental snapshot of the beachside tranquillity I was leaving behind. It was hard to believe that in less than twenty-four hours I'd be back in the hustle and bustle of noisy New York City.

Amelia surprised me by following me out of the cottage. Perhaps she wanted to ensure I was definitely leaving, although it didn't look that way as she leant on the low wall beside her cottage, watching me closely as my eyes once again went to the deserted sandy lane.

You were the one who told him not to come. You made

it perfectly clear that you didn't want him to see you off, I reminded myself. Besides, he'd be in the middle of morning surgery right now. I wondered how long it would take to forget Nick's schedule and stop trying to picture exactly where he was and what he was doing at any given moment of the day.

Amelia was also looking hopefully down the empty lane, waiting for an entirely different man to arrive. With a heavy heart, I realised both of us were destined to be disappointed.

'Well, I guess this is it,' I said, turning to her as the driver pointedly looked at his watch. I held out my arms and for a very long moment I thought she was going to turn away from me. But instead, she took a half step closer. That was enough for me. I bridged the remaining distance in two quick strides, holding her tighter and longer than I knew she wanted.

'We'll get past this, Mimi, I know we will,' I whispered into her hair.

Her arms fell away, and she stepped out of the hug as though she'd done her duty.

'Maybe. Maybe not,' she said quietly.

It left me with nowhere to go, and I could already feel the sting of tears as I turned from her.

'You need to leave now or you're going to be late.' She sounded a little breathless, almost as though she was trying not to cry, which I knew wasn't true. I, on the other hand, had given up on any chance of remaining dry-eyed. There was a very good reason why I'd worn waterproof mascara today.

'Please, look after yourself; you're my favourite sister,' I told her solemnly. 'So don't go doing anything stupid. No more midnight strolls on the beach. Remember to take your pills on time and do what the doctors tell you.'

'You don't have to worry. Sam will look after me.'

I gave a watery smile and climbed into the back seat of the cab. I corkscrewed in my seat as we pulled away from the cottage, watching out of the rear window as my sister grew smaller and smaller. How long would she stand there, I wondered, not seeing me off but waiting for her missing husband to arrive?

Her hope was almost as irrepressible as mine, because I didn't stop looking for Nick to put in a last-minute appearance until the taxi had left the slip road and joined the motorway for the long drive to the airport. It was only then that I finally admitted he had done exactly what I'd asked of him. He had stayed away.

28

The terminal was too everything: too bright, too noisy and far too busy. Three months of coastal living had softened the sharp edges I needed to survive in one of the busiest cities in the world. I was going to get trampled underfoot in Manhattan. I dodged one passenger with a piled-high trolley only to stumble straight into the path of a besuited businessman who tutted loudly in annoyance as he swerved to avoid me. I hurried from the terminal entrance before I single-handedly caused a domino-style avalanche of falling passengers.

It had been a mistake not to grab a trolley and I lost count of the number of times I murmured *Excuse me* and *I'm sorry* as I wheeled my cases through the crowds. Finally, I managed to slalom my way to the Departures board. It flicked through several screens before reaching my flight. No gate had been allocated, but at least check-in was open.

Weaving through the crowds, I arrived at the row of desks I needed, only to find a great many people had beaten me to it. The line of passengers was enormous, snaking back and forth on itself like a Chinese dragon in a parade. *Why on earth hadn't I checked in online last night?*

I paused for a long moment and then peeled away from the chicane and wheeled my luggage towards a nearby café. Ten minutes later I was at a table with a latte and a baguette that I nibbled on half-heartedly as I watched the queue shuffle forward without me. There was no reason to delay joining it, but still I hesitated. Neighbouring tables all around me filled and then emptied, but I never moved.

Playing 'chicken' with a flight is a dangerous and curious game and if I didn't know better, I'd think I was deliberately trying to miss my plane. *Enough of this nonsense,* I told myself sternly, getting to my feet just as my phone buzzed with a message. I was in such a rush to read it that I tore a fingernail pulling the mobile from my pocket. Guilt and disappointment flooded through me when I saw it was Mum's name on the screen and not Nick's. I should have called her by now, but I was stalling over that too. *I'll message when I'm airside,* I promised myself as I forced my reluctant feet to take me back to the airline desk.

I took my place in the queue behind a young couple who'd obviously come straight from a registry office. There were still pieces of confetti caught in the woman's hair and they both kept looking down at their bright, shiny wedding bands and smiling. *That could have been you, you know.* For once, the voice in my head didn't sound like Amelia's. It was mine. I looked away, the way you do from the sun for fear it could hurt you.

Behind me was a family with a mountain of luggage and three young children who'd yet to discover the joy of queueing.

'Would you like to step in front of me?' The harassed mum cut her trolley into the space faster than an F1 driver.

Two minutes later I made the same offer to an elderly couple, and then again to a group of girls who were clearly part of a hen party.

Twenty minutes after joining it, I was actually further back in the queue than when I'd started. I was un-queueing, if such a thing even existed.

'Are you quite sure, my dear?' queried a middle-aged woman, unable to believe there was no catch in my offer.

'Yes, I'm... er... waiting for someone and they're running late,' I said, embellishing the falsehood by staring across the terminal as though trying to spot my mythical travelling companion. It was a curious lie that felt strangely true. Was that what I was doing? Was that the cause of this feeling of unease that I couldn't seem to shake off? Was I really expecting Nick to make a last-minute dash through the airport to stop me from leaving, just like they do in the movies or the books I edit? If so, I was even more deluded than my sister.

Eventually, I ran out of people to give my place to. Worse, I think my backward progression had alerted the interest of the airline staff. When I was one of only a handful of people left in line, I had no choice but to go forward when a check-in officer beckoned me up to the desk.

'You've cut it very fine,' he informed me, his hand already outstretched for my passport. 'Check-in is about to close.'

I stared down at his outstretched hand for several seconds, as though I was thinking about reading his palm.

He sighed. I guessed it had been a long shift. 'I'm going to need to see your passport, ma'am.'

The maroon document was in my hand, but I didn't push

it through the opening. Instead, my fingers tightened on its cover, as though this could well end up in a tug of war.

'Actually, no, you don't,' I contradicted. I was aware that, somewhere to the left of me, a female security guard had taken one step closer to the counter.

'Ma'am, if you don't give me your passport, then I can't check you on to this flight.' He enunciated each word carefully, as though English and common sense might be equally unfamiliar to me. 'And as I already explained, you're cutting it extremely close to the wire, time-wise.'

'Yes. I understand. I just need a few more minutes,' I said, once again stepping aside and hauling my suitcases with me. 'I just need to make a quick phone call before I check in.'

'Ma'am, you're in danger of missing your flight to New York.'

I nodded. 'I know. I'm sorry, but I have a really strong feeling that I'm not meant to get on that plane.'

A middle-aged couple who'd been queuing behind me looked up in alarm.

'Are you psychic?' the woman asked, with a degree of fear that told me she was not a happy flyer. 'Have you had a premonition that there's something wrong with our plane?'

The security guard took another step closer towards me.

I raised my hand in what I hoped looked like a calming gesture. 'No. It's nothing like that. I'm not psychic,' I assured her, ignoring the memory of all those inexplicable occurrences Amelia and I had shared. 'I just meant that I think my boyfriend might be coming to see me off.'

'Well, unless you check in within the next five minutes, you're *both* going to be able to wave the plane goodbye,' said the check-in officer dourly.

I dragged my cases out of the way of the middle-aged couple, who were still regarding me nervously. Perhaps if I phoned The Willows to find out if Nick was there or not, it would silence this stupid feeling that getting on the plane would be a terrible mistake. I didn't need to speak to him, but at least then I'd know. One way or the other.

I dialled the number of the practice, but while it was still ringing against my ear, I heard something that made me disconnect the call. It was hard to be certain. The terminal was noisy, and the loudspeaker system was far from clear. But I thought I'd heard my name being paged.

My first thought was Nick. Had he come here after all, even though I'd told him not to? Had I somehow sensed his presence close by, and *that* was why I hadn't wanted to go airside?

I scoured the milling crowds, looking for a tall, dark-haired man wearing glasses that made him look like a comic-book hero. But he was nowhere to be seen. I shifted my weight anxiously from one foot to the other, ears pricked to hear if they would repeat the page.

In my peripheral vision I could see the officer at the check-in desk looking my way as he pointedly tapped his watch. Less than thirty seconds later, the overhead speakers crackled into life once more.

'Will passenger Lexi Edwards travelling to JFK from London please proceed immediately to the nearest information desk.'

My head shot up. There had been no mistaking it that time. In a world of largely incomprehensible airport announcements, that one had been as clear as a bell.

I have no recollection of crossing the terminal. My pace was probably that of a professional speed walker as I headed towards the information desk. Fifteen metres from my destination, I broke into a run.

'My name is Lexi Edwards. You were just paging me,' I gasped out on a garbled string of words that I could tell the woman behind the counter hadn't caught.

'Lexi Edwards,' I repeated, forcing myself to speak more coherently. 'I've been paged.'

Part of me had been convinced that Nick would be standing here at the information desk, but as he clearly wasn't, my brain was already jumping ahead to worst-case scenarios while the woman rattled my name into her computer. After what felt like an eternity, she looked up from her screen.

'The message is for you to call your mother.'

Mum? It was Mum? I tried to calm my racing heart by telling it she was probably concerned because I'd forgotten to call her. But was that really a sensible reason for paging someone when they were meant to be on a plane already? As I stepped to a quiet spot beside a pillar to place the call, I knew it was more serious than that. I was all fingers and thumbs as I pulled my mobile from my pocket.

I swiped away the accusatory 'Three missed calls' message on my home screen. I should have phoned her back. I fumbled dialling her number, like someone who'd never seen a mobile phone before, much less placed a call on one. It took three attempts before I finally succeeded in putting the numbers in the correct order and making the call. My heart was pounding as I listened to the ring tone trilling in my ear.

'Lexi.' It was Mum's voice, and she was crying.

My knees immediately started to give way. The busy airport was receding as I found myself hurtling back through time to that first, middle-of-the-night phone call in my New York apartment all those months ago. It was the worst kind of déjà vu to hear Mum confirm my greatest fears.

'It's Amelia. She's back in the hospital. They think she's had a heart attack.'

It felt like time had folded back on itself as I travelled from the airport to the hospital. I scarcely allowed the needle on the dashboard of the new hire car to drop below the speed limit throughout the three-hour journey.

I spent most of the drive lost in my thoughts. The question I kept circling back to allowed me no peace. *Is this my fault? Did our argument cause my sister's relapse?*

I'd been too shocked to ask Mum anything remotely sensible on the phone, so I had no idea what had happened after I'd left Amelia standing beside her cottage, waiting for Sam. I'd been so absorbed in my own personal drama I could have missed the early clues that she was starting to feel unwell. She had been a little breathless, I remembered now, but I'd put that down to her still being upset with me. And all those naps when I'd thought she'd been avoiding me – were they a symptom of exhaustion because her heart was failing again?

It was the same hospital but a different ward to the one Amelia had been on before. I searched the direction signs for the one that would lead me to the Coronary Care Unit. Even the name of the ward scared me.

The hospital wasn't cold – they never are – yet I was shivering when I stepped into the lift. It felt like every drop of blood in my veins had been replaced with liquid dread. I stared at the numbers on the overhead panel as they carried me up to the seventh floor. Five... Six... the breath hitched in my throat. *I'm so frightened.*

The first person I saw was Tom. He was bent low, muttering something that sounded menacing to a vending machine that appeared to have stolen his money. He gave it a punishing smack that I'm sure hurt his hand far more than it did the drink dispenser. Either way, it worked, and a bounty of items clattered into the drawer. Tom didn't take them, for he'd heard my footsteps. He shot a glance down a corridor I couldn't see.

'Esme, she's here. Lexi's here.'

As though responding to an onstage cue, my mother emerged into the main corridor. Her eyes flew straight to mine and stayed there as we closed the space between us. I thought I was comforting her, but just seconds into the hug I realised it was probably the other way around.

'How is she?' I whispered. Amelia's heart might be the one in trouble, but my own refused to beat until Mum answered that question.

'She's sleeping now. They've got her hooked up to all kinds of monitors and machines. Again.'

I hugged Mum tightly. 'She got better before. She'll do it once more,' I said with a conviction I wished was real. 'I'm so glad you didn't have to wait here alone this time,' I continued, shooting Tom a grateful smile.

'Tom was here before I was,' Mum said, turning to the fisherman with a look that told me more about their relationship than she'd yet revealed. 'He came in the ambulance with Amelia. He refused to leave her.'

I crossed over to the elderly man and pressed a grateful kiss on to his weather-beaten cheek. 'Thank you for that.'

He shook his head, looking embarrassed to be the focus of attention.

'Can you tell me what happened?' I asked.

Tom lowered himself stiffly on to one of the plastic chairs that lined the corridor.

'She said she'd been feeling poorly all morning,' he said, employing a euphemism that seemed woefully inadequate to describe a suspected heart attack. 'She decided to get some fresh air, to see if it helped.'

He dropped his gaze to his gnarled hands, seeming surprised to find them trembling. 'It didn't,' he said gruffly. 'I found her on the pathway, panting and gasping like she'd been out running or something. Her phone was in her hand. She'd already called for an ambulance.'

I'm not sure what was worse – to hear that Amelia had to dial 999 herself, or that she'd had to go through the entire ordeal without a single member of her family beside her. I glanced up and saw a single tear roll down Tom's cheek and realised I was wrong. My definition of 'family' had just expanded.

'I didn't know what to do to help her, so I put my jacket around her and sat down on the path beside her until the ambulance folk arrived.'

He looked across at Mum, as though apologising he'd not been able to do more. She shook her head with a teary smile, wordlessly telling him he'd done plenty.

'It sounds like you did everything just right,' I told him. 'What time did all this happen?'

'Just after three o'clock.'

It was the exact same time that I'd experienced the weird reluctance to catch my flight to New York. Amelia had been in trouble and, hundreds of miles away, I'd sensed it. She might claim to want me out of her life, but the ties that bound us were stronger than any argument. They'd pulled me back to her.

At just after midnight, they allowed Mum and me into the unit to see Amelia. Whatever sedative they'd given her was clearly doing its job for she seemed completely unaware that we were there, even when we held her hand or kissed her cheek. For us, just being able to see her, to watch the rise and fall of her chest and hear the reassuring blip of the heart monitor, gave enough comfort to last until morning.

A duty doctor, who frankly looked too young and tired to be the physician in charge of the ward, approached the bed.

'Amelia is stable and comfortable,' he said gently. 'The best thing you can do for her now is to go home and try to get some sleep. The cardiologist will be able to give you a clearer picture of her condition tomorrow.'

I was about to protest, to insist that we stayed; then I caught the anxious glance the young medic had given Mum. He was right. A woman her age shouldn't be spending the night on uncomfortable hospital chairs.

'That sounds like a sensible idea,' I said, slipping my arm through Mum's and gently steering her away from her elder daughter's bedside.

'You can phone throughout the night for updates, but I'm confident Amelia will get a better night's rest than either of you.'

He wasn't wrong.

*

I pulled out of the virtually empty hospital multistorey and pointed the car in the direction of the beachside cottages. Mum sat beside me, looking like the dictionary definition of exhausted. I covertly glanced her way each time we travelled through a pool of light from a streetlamp. Not covertly enough, as it turned out.

'Stop worrying about me, Lexi,' Mum said, laying a hand on my arm. Her joints looked misshapen, and the skin was not as supple as it had been, but it was still the hand I'd held throughout my childhood.

'I'm as strong as an ox,' Mum declared. It was the first time I'd laughed in hours.

'Sure. In a world where oxen are five foot nothing tall and as slight as a stick insect.'

She smiled wryly. 'If you both didn't look so much like your dad, I'd have thought they'd brought out the wrong Petri dish all those years ago,' she joked.

In the quiet warmth of the car, Tom had nodded off in the back seat, but spent several minutes insisting that he hadn't when we finally pulled up at the fishermen's cottages.

'I'll walk you to your door,' I said as I climbed wearily out of the driver's seat.

'I've been walking up and down this pathway unaided for the last fifty years. I think I can manage it alone,' Tom responded with some of the acerbic humour I would forever associate with him. Even so, I noticed he didn't offer any further protest when I fell into step beside him on the sandy path.

He paused at his threshold, withdrawing his front-door

key on a length of old frayed string, which inexplicably made me want to cry.

'You look after your mother now,' Tom said, his voice even gruffer than usual. He reached for my shoulder and gave it an awkward squeeze. 'And yourself too, my girl.'

Fortunately, Mum had a key for the cottage, because the one I'd been using for the last three months was still sitting on a table in the hallway. I picked it up now and slipped it back into my pocket. I had an inkling I was going to be needing it again for a while.

'Why don't you have Amelia's bed tonight?' I suggested.

Mum nodded wearily and I suspected she'd be asleep the moment her head touched the pillow. Yet she paused with one foot on the bottom tread of the stairs.

'You didn't mind Tom being there tonight, at the hospital? You didn't think it was disrespectful to your dad?' she asked hesitantly. It was probably the wrong time to be having this conversation, but she had enough to worry about currently. This, at least, was one concern I could easily dismiss.

Sometimes the right words come to you just when you need them. 'Dad's been gone a long time, Mum. And he wouldn't want you to be facing any of this alone. And besides, I think he'd approve of Tom.'

'I just wish you had someone too,' Mum said sadly. 'Will you call Nick to let him know what's happened today?'

It was a question that had been circling in my head for hours, but my mind was made up.

'No. As far as Nick is aware, I'm halfway over the Atlantic right now. There's no need for him to know I never left.'

29

'What did they say again?'

If I needed confirmation of how nervous Mum was, it was there in the number of times she asked me to repeat the overnight update I'd been given from the hospital.

'They said she had a pain-free night and was resting comfortably,' I replied, pulling out of a junction and into the stream of morning traffic. I felt far more comfortable being back behind the wheel of Amelia's car again rather than the hire one, which was being collected later that day.

Amelia's cardiologist had finished his morning rounds but was waiting on the ward for us to arrive. It was a reminder that what had happened to her all those months ago had been truly unique. I doubted every patient's family received this kind of preferential treatment.

'Lexi, Esme, it's good to see you again,' Dr Vaughan said politely, extending his hand as we approached.

'I'd like to say the same,' I told him as we shook hands, 'but I was kind of hoping we'd never meet again. No offence intended.'

'None taken,' the consultant said with a smile. He swept an arm, like a waiter ushering us to a table. 'Shall we continue our conversation in Amelia's room?'

Dr Vaughan stepped to one side at the doorway, allowing us a private moment together. I was so determined not to cry. I lasted a good twenty seconds, which all things considered was pretty good going.

'You should be in New York,' Amelia said, her eyes narrowing, as I finally released her from a hug.

'And you should be at home watching something cheesy on Netflix... with Sam,' I added. It was a white flag. I was asking her for a truce.

She nodded slowly, understanding perfectly. Perhaps being blue-lighted to hospital in an ambulance makes you reassess which battles are worth fighting.

'There was nothing worth bingeing.' Her sassy retort was ruined by the breathless catch I could once again hear in her voice.

Beneath the banter, I could see the fearful expression in her eyes. I reached for her hand. Wherever the next half hour or so would take us, I wanted her to know she wasn't going there alone.

None of it was easy listening. To hear that my thirty-nine-year-old sister had suffered a heart attack was shocking enough, but to learn that the resultant damage was such that surgery, or even a transplant, might eventually be her only option was terrifying.

'But in the interim, I believe we need to revisit the question of cardioversion,' Dr Vaughan said, his voice grave. 'Amelia's erratic heartbeat is putting too great a strain on her heart, which, despite her medication, is still struggling to work as it should.'

My eyes went to my sister. She'd been so insistent that she wouldn't consider the procedure until Sam returned; how were we going to persuade her to agree to it now?

'Can we delay it at all?' I asked, earning a grateful look from Amelia, whose complexion was still the colour of old parchment.

'In an ideal world I would prefer to leave it a few days, but I really don't think we have that option now.'

There was a long moment of silence. I wondered if I was the only one holding their breath, waiting for Amelia to insist yet again that Sam should be present to make this decision with her.

'When?' she asked, her voice thready with fear. 'When would you do it?'

'Today. As soon as possible,' Dr Vaughan replied.

Before responding, she turned to me, her eyes huge and bright with tears. 'Can you try to reach Sam and let him know?'

I think we all heard my nervous swallow, but I never broke eye contact with my sister. 'Of course I will.'

Amelia finally turned to face the physician.

'Alright,' she said quietly. 'Do it.'

'What time did they say they were coming to get me?' Amelia asked, as her gaze continued to shift from the clock on the wall to the door to her room.

'Still one thirty,' I said gently.

'Oh, right,' she said, nodding as though this was new news,

despite the fact she'd asked the exact same question at least four times in the last thirty minutes. That's how I knew she wasn't just nervous, she was terrified.

'It's all going to be fine, Mimi. The procedure has a very high success rate,' I assured her, quoting from the many articles I'd read online. It didn't feel appropriate to add that in about fifty per cent of cases, the patient's heart refused to stay at its new 'normal' rhythm and reverted to the abnormal one. As our dad always liked to say: *We'll cross that bridge when we come to it.*

Please let Amelia be one of the successful cases, I silently pleaded to any god who might be listening. *Surely my sister deserved one lucky break?*

It didn't help knowing that I was the reason she kept checking the time and the hospital corridor. She believed Sam had been told what was happening, and she was waiting for him to join us. In a film, this was the bit when the hero would come bursting through the door at the very last minute. It was a white knight on a charger kind of thing. And nothing I could say would convince Amelia that Sam wasn't going to show up. Consequently, it seemed best to say nothing.

The hospital café was buzzing with activity. Mum and I had to do two circuits of the room before I eventually found us a free table. I set down the tray with the cups of coffee neither of us wanted and checked my watch again. Amelia had only been gone for twenty out of the sixty minutes her procedure was supposed to take, and I was already itching to return to the ward.

'Your family can go for a walk or visit the café when we

take you down to the lab,' the arrhythmia nurse specialist had informed Amelia as she passed her the consent form to sign. Amelia's mind was clearly wandering, almost as much as her eyes. It made me wonder how much of the nurse's information she'd even heard, let alone absorbed. Her attention had been focused only on the doors of the ward and who was coming through them. Or, more importantly, who wasn't.

'Do you have any questions?' the nurse asked with a cheery smile as she took back the clipboard after Amelia had scrawled her name on it. Even her signature looked different these days; the loops were bigger and untidy, and her name had spilled out of the box she was meant to write in. It was no longer the neat, meticulous script of an accountant. And I'd seen the way she'd hesitated before writing her surname, as though unsure whether to write Wilson or Edwards. In the end, she wrote both.

Amelia waited until the nurse had excused herself before looking up at me with an expression that nearly broke my heart. She looked little and lost inside the ill-fitting surgical gown. After weeks of practice, I thought I was inured to the sight of my sister in a hospital bed, but it turned out I wasn't, not at all. I realised with a jolt that I'd give anything to swap places with her, which was ironic, seeing as I'd spent the last few months doing precisely that. Not that Amelia knew about that, of course. And she never would, I resolved in a moment of belated clarity. Those staged photographs of her and Sam had been the cause of us falling out. The only good thing to have come out of them was that without them I'd never have met Nick, or known I was capable of the kind of love I'd truly stopped believing in.

I had Amelia to thank for that. Was that the payoff? Were

our lives still so inextricably linked that she had to lose her soulmate for me to find mine? We rarely read each other's thoughts anymore, so it startled me to find that perhaps that uncanny ability wasn't entirely lost.

'Don't go feeling sorry for me, Lexi,' she said, reaching for my hand.

'I'm sorry for *anyone* who has to wear a hospital gown like that,' I said, trying to lift the serious look from her eyes with a feeble joke.

She shook her head. 'Don't pity me because I still believe Sam is coming.'

'I... I don't... I never said...' My lies were unravelling between us like pulled threads.

'It doesn't matter now why you did what you did. Because I knew the truth. In here, I knew it,' she said, covering the erratically beating heart in her chest. 'Sam is real, and he *will* come back to me. I know he will.'

I shivered as I was struck with a horrible premonition. What if something went wrong during the procedure? What if this was the very last conversation we'd ever have? Did I really want the last words I said to my sister to be a lie? Hell yes I did.

'I think he will too,' I said as they began wheeling her bed away. 'In fact, I'm sure of it.'

We beat Amelia back to the ward by a good fifteen minutes. I left Mum in the café and raced back to the car, where I pulled a large bag from the back seat. An instinct I didn't totally understand had told me to collect the memory box of photographs from their new home in Amelia's bedroom. I couldn't conjure up her phantom husband to be at her hospital bedside when she came round, but I could at least make sure she had photographs of the two of them close at hand.

I watched the doors to the corridor even more avidly than Amelia had done, jumping to my feet in relief when they finally wheeled her back through them. She was still more asleep than awake, mumbling utter nonsense as they positioned her bed back in the bay.

'The doctor will be along later to explain everything to you both when Amelia is a little more awake,' the arrhythmia nurse informed me with a kindly smile. 'But it all went very well. She went straight back into sinus rhythm after just one shock.'

That was the Amelia I knew and loved, the one who aced every test and exam and who never did anything wrong. Failure simply wasn't part of her vocabulary.

Amelia dozed for the next hour or so while Mum and I took it in turns to rise from our chair whenever she murmured fretfully in her sleep. Her long dark hair was splayed out across the pillow, and I gently touched the silky chestnut strands, being careful not to disturb her. She was mumbling something I couldn't quite make out, but whatever it was made her forehead furrow into a stave of lines.

'I'm so sorry Sam wasn't with you today, Amelia,' I said softly. 'But I'm really glad that I was.'

Ironically, both Mum and I had nodded off when Amelia came fully awake. I guess our broken night's sleep had finally taken its toll. I'm not sure what woke me, but I jerked upright in my chair to find my sister sitting up in bed, looking far better than she had when they'd wheeled her down to the lab.

While we slept, Amelia had clearly found the memory box of photographs that I'd set down on the bedside cabinet, for they were now tipped out all over the blanket that covered her legs.

'How do you feel?' I asked, my throat dry and scratchy, and not just from the overheated ward.

'Better,' she said succinctly.

On the other side of the bed, I saw Mum too was now awake. She shot me a worried glance as Amelia's hands rifled through the photographs.

'What are these?' my sister asked.

Photographs seemed too facile a response, so I substituted it with one that I hoped she would appreciate more.

'I brought them from the cottage for you. I thought you'd like to have them here when you came round.'

A tiny frown creased the smooth skin of her forehead. 'Why?'

I swallowed awkwardly. This was where I was going to have to explain why Sam still hadn't turned up, despite me asking him to. But I never got the chance to offer up the lie, because she reached among the photographs and plucked one up, holding it towards the light shafting in through the window.

'Who is this?' she asked, her face unreadable as she turned to me. 'Who is the man in these photographs?'

There were a thousand ways I'd imagined today might play out, but I can honestly say that I hadn't for a moment considered this would be one of them. Was this the moment when Amelia finally realised the photographs were of two imposters?

I swallowed several times before attempting to use my voice. Even so, it still came out squeaky.

'He doesn't look familiar to you?'

Her forehead crumpled in concentration as she reached for yet another photo. It was one taken on our horse ride. 'Hmm… not really. Do you mean an actor or someone famous?'

I shook my head. 'No. Someone you know. Someone you know *very well.*'

Another frown, this one genuinely puzzled.

'No. I don't think so. Why do you ask?'

The moment was here, and I felt like I was about to pull the pin out of a grenade that would explode everything. 'You don't think that man looks like Sam?'

It was the longest ten seconds of my entire life before Amelia set down the photograph and turned to face me.

'Who's Sam?'

30

'That's ridiculous. I'm sorry, but what you're saying makes no sense whatsoever.'

I glanced across at Mum, but she appeared to have developed a sudden fascination with the threads of the hospital blanket. Amelia's gaze was focused on me anyway, waiting for an answer or an explanation that I'd been searching three months to find.

'Why would I have claimed something crazy like that? Didn't anyone question the total lack of evidence?' Amelia lifted her hand and began counting points off on her fingers. 'You say there are no clothes of his, no belongings at the cottage, there's no wedding ring, nothing at all to suggest that I'd secretly got married and hadn't told either of you about it.' She gave a derisive *as if I'd ever do anything like that* eye-roll. 'And how was this supposed "husband"' – she air-quoted the word – 'meant to have disappeared off the face of the earth?'

I drew in a deep breath, knowing that I was walking through a virtual minefield here. 'Mimi, hon, we asked you all of those questions and a thousand more.'

'So why did you believe this nonsense, then?'

Mum lifted her head, and it nearly broke me to see the tears in her eyes. 'We didn't, sweetheart. But *you* did. You believed it with all your heart.'

Mum's words took the wind from Amelia's sails, but we were still in choppy waters.

'In the early days when you were very poorly, the doctors thought the delusion was a result of the hypothermia,' I said, reaching for my sister's hand and squeezing it. It was one of only a few times I could remember when she didn't squeeze mine back. 'They hoped it would fade away as you grew stronger. But it never did. It was so *real* to you, and you were so unwell. It would have been cruel to keep insisting you were wrong. The doctors kept telling us the false memories would eventually become less real to you, and that you'd stop believing you were married.' I gave a small humourless laugh. 'I guess they were right about that one after all.'

Amelia was still shaking her head as though at any moment I was going to burst into giggles and say *Ha ha, April Fool.* Except it wasn't the first of April, and I'd never found anything less funny in my entire life.

'If it had been *you* this had happened to,' Amelia said, with a hint of challenge in her voice, 'I'd have insisted that you showed me proof. I'd have wanted to see your marriage certificate, Facebook posts, or photos of the two of you together.'

I swallowed down a throatful of guilt as I waited for the other shoe to fall. It did so with an almost audible thump.

'Oh my God. Is *that* the meaning of this memory box? Were you trying to fool me into believing a fantasy?'

She made me feel like I'd failed her all over again. Tears stung my eyes, but I refused to let them fall. 'You were terrified of forgetting Sam. And your memory has been a bit... *unreliable...* lately. The photographs were my misguided attempt to help you keep him real.'

'Even though he wasn't,' she countered, but the fire had left her argument now. Thank God, something I'd said had managed to extinguish it.

The memory box full of photos was still upended on the hospital bed. In a court of law, it would probably be referred to as Exhibit A.

'But it's not *me* in those photos, even though the person in them looks like I do *and* appears to be wearing all my clothes,' Amelia said, with just a hint of sass in the jibe. Something inside me slowly began to relax. 'Those photos tell a story for sure, but it's not one of me and a man named Sam. They're the story of how my sister finally fell in love.'

Back in the courtroom scenario, this was the point when someone ought to be leaping to their feet and shouting out 'Objection'.

I gave it a shot.

'I never claimed I was *in love* with Nick. We're just having... a thing.'

Finally, Amelia smiled, even if it was sardonically. 'You might be able to lie to yourself, Lexi, but you can't lie to me. You never could.' She ran her hands over the scattered photographs. 'The truth is there in every single one of these. You're not that good an actress. I should know – I've sat through enough of your school plays.'

She blurred in my vision as I laughed and cried at the same time.

⋆

Long after I dropped Mum back at her house and returned to Amelia's cottage on the beach, my head was still spinning at the turn of events. To be honest, Amelia totally forgetting her insistence that she was married to a man called Sam was almost as hard to grapple with as her having invented him in the first place.

'You do know what this means, don't you?' Mum asked, with one hand still on the door handle of the car when we pulled up outside her home. It was telling that she hadn't wanted to ask me this question while I was driving.

'What does it mean?'

'It means there's now no obstacle to prevent you and Nick being together,' she said, with such joy that it brought a lump to my throat.

'Except maybe the three thousand miles that separate his home from mine,' I reminded her.

'Pwah,' she said expressively. 'That's a minor detail when you think about the one that previously stood in your way.'

'I'm too tired to think about any of it tonight,' I lied, reaching across the centre console and pressing a warm kiss on her cheek.

But *of course* I was going to think about it. All night long, and then some, I imagined. But that didn't mean I was going to *do* anything about it. I was very aware that Amelia's return to normality might be short-lived. Something had clearly happened to her during the cardioversion therapy, something other than the resetting of her heartbeat. Her true memories had somehow been restored when her heart had been shocked today. In the same way that the false ones had taken seed when it had been shocked that night on the beach all those months ago.

But the effects of cardioversion were known to fail in half of all cases. If that happened to Amelia, might she once again believe she was Mrs Sam Wilson? I had no intention of reaching out to Nick just yet. To raise his hopes only to crush them again would be beyond cruel. I needed to wait until Amelia was discharged from hospital and was back in her own home once more before I even considered speaking to him.

But the thought that there might miraculously now be a chance for us was the reason I eventually fell asleep with a smile on my face.

'It still feels like they're letting you out of hospital too soon,' Mum fretted, watching as I packed Amelia's bulging bags of medication into a holdall.

'Not to me, it doesn't,' said Amelia, who was swinging her legs impatiently on the bed as we waited to be given permission to leave. 'I can't wait to be back in my own home.'

'Why do the doctors need to speak to us again?' I asked, with an anxious glance at my watch. The car park ticket was only valid for another twenty minutes and getting a fine would definitely take the shine off a day that I hoped would be life-changing. I was going to phone Nick as soon as we got back to the beach. I planned on walking to the spot where we'd first met and telling him that things had changed. I only hoped the way he felt about me wasn't one of them.

For the last two days, my mind had kept wandering off in directions it had never travelled before. It kept showing me glimpses of a future that might one day be ours. I'd be loading the dishwasher, but suddenly I didn't see Amelia's quaint little kitchen, I saw a spacious New York loft with views over the Hudson, the place we called home. Or I'd be pushing a trolley up the aisle of a supermarket, but just for a moment it changed into a pram, where a tiny dark-haired baby with bright blue eyes giggled up at me.

I wasn't foolish enough to believe they were premonitions, but they were glimpses of a potential future that might become our reality. For the first time since I'd told Nick I was leaving, I was daring to dream. And damn, it felt good.

Dr Vaughan gave a peremptory knock on the door frame and walked into the room, followed by an older man I'd never seen before. I gave Mum a quick reassuring smile that did little to disguise my concern that this meeting required more than one doctor. The older medic turned and gently closed the door. I shivered. This was not good.

Dr Vaughan began with a round-up of the successful cardioversion treatment and once again touched on the need for Amelia to undergo heart surgery. He felt a bit like a warm-up act, and from the way my sister's eyes had narrowed, I knew she thought so too. I looked at the doctors and noticed what appeared to be a subtle shift in power between the cardiologist and the other senior physician.

My head swivelled to Amelia. 'Do you know what this is about?'

She bit her lip, looking suddenly apprehensive. 'I think they have something else they want to tell us.'

'You're scaring the shit out of me,' I said, not sure who I

was addressing that remark to, but feeling like it applied to practically everyone in the room.

The second consultant, who I'd incorrectly assumed was here because of Amelia's heart attack, took a small step forward as Dr Vaughan took one in retreat.

'Amelia, I'm not sure if you remember me. My name is Mr Robinson. I'm a neurologist. We met in the early days of your previous hospital stay.'

'I remember,' Amelia said. There was a new dull note in her voice.

'I understand that the confabulations – the false memories – you experienced before have now disappeared, but other troublesome symptoms still remain.'

'I'm not so sure they were false memories after all, doctor. They've started to feel more like premonitions.'

I swallowed noisily and didn't dare look at Mum.

The neurologist appeared unfazed, plucking the folder he'd been carrying from beneath his arm and flipping it open to a page covered with test results.

'Your initial symptoms were baffling to us.' He paused to give Amelia a wry smile. 'We doctors don't like admitting when we're stumped about something, and you presented us with a conundrum. As you know, we conducted many tests at that time.' His expression switched to one of sympathy and I knew then, with a horrible, sickening clarity, that whatever he was about to tell us was going to change everything.

'This isn't anything to do with my heart, is it?' Amelia asked, directing the question to the cardiologist, who was standing behind his colleague.

'No, Amelia, it's not,' Dr Vaughan confirmed.

The neurologist surprised me then by stepping forward

and perching on the foot of Amelia's bed. It didn't look like a pose someone would adopt when they were about to give you good news.

'Most of the tests we ordered told us nothing, but we've now had the results from a particular blood test that we took several months ago.'

'What is it? What have you found?' Had my voice ever sounded that scared before?

The neurologist surprisingly turned not to Amelia, but to Mum.

'Mrs Edwards, has anyone in your family ever been diagnosed with Alzheimer's disease?'

Mum's expression was as confused as I imagine my own was.

'Alzheimer's?' she repeated. 'No. We have nothing like that in our family.'

'Are you saying I have Alzheimer's? How is that even possible? I'm only thirty-nine years old, for God's sake.'

The neurologist turned back to face Amelia. 'The blood test we ordered was a shot in the dark, really – it was more to rule *out* a diagnosis. But I'm afraid what it has revealed is unequivocal. You have a condition known as FAD, which stands for familial Alzheimer's disease. It's an extremely rare type of Alzheimer's that affects only about one per cent of people who suffer from the disease. It's a very specific anomaly caused by an inherited defective gene, which was why I asked if anyone in the family had ever suffered with similar symptoms: memory loss, forgetfulness, confusion. Can I ask about your father? I see from medical records that he passed away.'

'He died in an accident over twenty years ago, and he

definitely didn't have dementia,' I said. My response was pricklier than I'd intended, but I felt like we were under attack, and I'd gone straight into defensive mode.

'Why are you so convinced this is what I have?' asked Amelia. 'Couldn't your tests be wrong?'

The neurologist was clearly not used to families ganging up and refusing to accept his diagnosis. 'We ran them several times. I'm afraid they're conclusive. This particular mutated gene presents itself again and again in affected families. There is *always* a traceable link from generation to generation. When someone has this faulty gene, they have a fifty per cent chance of passing it on.'

'Well, there you are then. You're clearly on the wrong track. Dad didn't have this illness.' I turned to Mum, expecting her to be nodding in agreement. What I didn't anticipate was the tortured expression on her face as she turned towards the doctors.

'My husband was adopted as a baby, so he never knew his biological family.'

The information seemed to float in the air, settling on everyone in the room like a contamination.

'Well, okay,' I said, already grappling for a solution. 'That's not an insurmountable problem. There'll be adoption records somewhere. I know these things are sealed, but I'm sure, given the importance of finding out if this thing really *is* in Amelia's genetic make-up, we'll be able to get them unsealed.'

'Not just *my* make-up,' Amelia said quietly.

I turned slowly towards her, amazed that it had taken me this long to grasp the implications of what the neurologist had said. *Any child of an affected parent has a fifty per cent chance of inheriting the gene.* If Amelia had this thing, then there was a chance that I did too.

'There *are* no records of his biological parents,' Mum said, her voice heavy with sadness. 'Your dad was what they used to call a foundling. An abandoned baby. He was left in a cardboard box on a piece of wasteland. There's no way of knowing if anyone in his family ever suffered from Alzheimer's disease.'

I wasn't aware that I'd sunk down on to a chair until I felt it beneath me.

'We knew Dad was adopted, but why did no one tell us about the circumstances before?'

'I wanted to, but he didn't want you both to know.'

'Why? Because right now it seems pretty fucking important that we know our own family medical history.' Amelia was angry and I was only a step or two behind her.

'He was embarrassed, Amelia. He didn't want you to know he'd been unwanted.'

A long moment of silence settled on the room. Eventually, it was broken by the question the neurologist had been patiently waiting to ask.

'Is it possible, in hindsight, that your husband had any of the early symptoms of FAD?'

'No,' I said, too quickly to have thought my answer through. 'He died in a stupid accident when he...' My voice trailed away.

'...Forgot to check the time of the incoming tide. Dad drowned because he forgot to give himself enough time to get out of the cove,' completed Amelia.

My eyes found hers and then my mother's, as the implication of what we were saying finally struck home. For over twenty years, we hadn't understood how Dad could possibly have made the stupid mistake that cost him his life. Could the reason he forgot to check the tide have something to do with FAD? Was that any more or less ridiculous than his own daughter walking on the mudflats in the middle of the night wearing only her nightgown?

Suddenly I began to cry.

'His keys. The morning he left to go fishing in the cove, he couldn't find his car keys anywhere.'

'Losing objects like your keys or a phone is very often an early symptom of the condition,' Mr Robinson said quietly.

Amelia's eyes were filling with tears because she knew exactly what I was about to say.

'Dad wouldn't have gone fishing that day if I hadn't stupidly helped him look for his keys. I was the one who found them. If I hadn't, he wouldn't have been able to drive to the cove, so it wouldn't have mattered if he'd forgotten about the tide or not. He'd have been safe.'

Mr Robinson was shaking his head. 'It's impossible to be certain, but it sounds very much as though your father's forgetfulness might have been a symptom of the early stages of FAD.'

There was a question on all our lips. I didn't want to ask it, because I was afraid I already knew the answer.

'Is there… is there a cure for this thing?'

Very slowly, the doctor shook his head. 'We know much more about it now than we did back then, and one day we *will* find a cure.'

The room fell silent. All I could hear was the thundering of my heart.

Amelia was the first to speak. 'If all that's true, then Dad got lucky, didn't he?'

My head shot up like a deer who'd just heard a rifle being cocked.

'He got to die before this thing had the chance to take him down.'

The rest of the meeting went by in a blur.

'Amelia, we'll arrange for you to speak with a counsellor, who'll be able to help you navigate your way through the next few weeks. I'm sure there will be a great many questions you want to ask.'

'There's only *one* I want an answer to right now. Lexi and I were born from the same round of IVF. Genetically, we're almost identical. So, if *I've* inherited this fucked-up gene, does that mean she has too?'

I watched Amelia's face as she waited for the doctor to throw me a lifeline. She wasn't even asking about her own prognosis, or how the disease would progress; all she was thinking about was me.

'The odds remain at fifty-fifty,' Mr Robinson said, shooting me a sympathetic glance. 'One sibling having the gene doesn't affect the chances of the others getting it.'

Bile rose in my throat and for an awful moment I didn't think I'd be able to swallow it back down.

'Could the IVF have helped? Lexi was cryo... cryo...' It was a bad moment for the word to have been stolen from her.

'Cryogenically frozen,' I said softly.

Amelia nodded gratefully. 'Could that have killed off the faulty gene? Could that have helped protect her?'

'I'm afraid it wouldn't. IVF embryos are unaffected by the freezing process.'

The doctors fell silent for a moment, allowing us all to absorb their words. Amelia was the first to speak and I should have known by the look on her face that I wasn't going to like what she was about to say.

'Lexi, you need to get tested. You need to have the blood test done as soon as possible and find out if you have this too.'

Four heads turned in my direction. I truly didn't know the words were even in my head, much less that they would fall from my lips with such conviction.

'Absolutely not. I do not want to know.'

31

I stormed out of the cottage, slamming the door pointedly behind me. Ten minutes of staring with unseeing eyes at the incoming waves did little to calm me down. I heard the crunch of footsteps on the sand behind me and moments later a shadow joined mine on the beach. I didn't turn around.

'I'm so angry. I could throttle her.'

Tom's wiry eyebrows rose in surprise.

'Didn't take you for the violent type,' he murmured, leaning forward to rest his elbows on the top rail of the fence. I got the sense he was waiting for my rage to cool from boiling to a less homicidal simmer.

'You might have to get used to it. Unless I can make my idiotic sister see sense, I'll probably be like this for a while.'

'Reckon she's just as mad at you,' Tom said, bending to pick up a piece of seaweed and examining it carefully, as though it held the answer to all our problems.

'I know,' I said, brushing a lock of windswept hair from my eyes. 'I hate where we are right now. I'm not used to fighting with her... well, not over something this important.'

Tom dropped the seaweed and briefly covered my hand with his gnarled fingers. 'You both need to stop trying to swim against the tide. You'll never get to shore that way.'

I smiled gently. 'Good advice. If I was a trout, perhaps.'

Tom chuckled, his whole body shaking with mirth. 'You'll both find a way through this. I'm sure of it.'

It had been four weeks since we learnt that Amelia had FAD and I still felt physically sick every time I thought about it. I'd be standing in the supermarket, trying to decide what kind of pasta we wanted for dinner, and suddenly the realisation would hit me all over again and I'd find myself crying, right there in the middle of the grocery aisle.

Or I'd wake in the night and feel compelled to check on her. I'd tiptoe across the hallway, ease open her bedroom door and stand in the shadows, not moving until I'd seen the steady rise and fall of her chest.

Not surprisingly, she called me out on that one. 'Will you please stop doing that,' she said a few mornings ago. 'You're really freaking me out. The next thing I know, you'll be holding a mirror in front of my mouth to check I'm still breathing.' I swallowed uncomfortably because that idea had already crossed my mind. 'How would you like it if I crept in on you every night?'

'It's not *every* night,' I retorted, passing her a plate of toast, which she waved away. Her appetite had been slow to put in a reappearance since she'd come out of hospital. 'You know perfectly well why I'm doing it *and* what you need to do to make me stop.'

Amelia sighed and ran her hands through her hair in

frustration. 'For the hundredth time, Lexi, I'm not having cardiac surgery.'

'And I'm not having the blood test,' I countered.

We stared at each other across the kitchen table, like angry halves of a Rorschach test. Somehow, every conversation – even the seemingly innocuous ones – always led us back to this same argument.

'You're not thinking about how your decision affects us.'

'Ditto that,' she shot back.

'My decision not to be tested for FAD is hardly the same as you refusing life-saving heart surgery. A treatment that you *know* will extend your life.'

'Don't you see, Lexi, that's exactly *why* I don't want it,' Amelia said with passion. 'I've been dealt two really shitty hands. Both have terrible outcomes. All I'm doing is deciding which one I want to play.'

'You're not playing, you're folding,' I said, continuing with the poker analogy.

'I'm choosing how I want to spend the time I have left. You were there when the doctors told me what to expect from FAD.'

It felt like she'd stabbed me with the memory. We'd asked them not to pull their punches, and heaven help us, they hadn't.

'That is not how I want to end up,' Amelia said sadly. She cupped my cheek tenderly. 'I don't want to look at this face and not know it belongs to the most amazing sister in the world. I don't want to lose everything I know about you and Mum and everything I know about me.'

'I just want you to fight like hell to stay with us,' I said, my lower lip trembling like a two-year-old's. 'There could be a cure right around the corner, and you'll never know because you gave up too soon.'

'I'm not giving up. I'm still taking my medication, I'm doing the cardio rehab, but I won't have surgery or go on a transplant list. I've decided to let my heart decide what's best for me and when it's had enough.'

I had a horrible feeling she meant those words in their most literal sense.

'You certainly went to a lot of trouble creating these.'

I'd left Tom to return to his own cottage and had silently let myself back into Amelia's. She was sitting at the kitchen table, on to which she'd upended the memory box of photographs. Too many smiling images of Nick were looking up at me.

I strode to the sink but could still feel the warmth of his gaze following me.

I missed the twinkle in his eyes, or the way he'd look at me over the top of his glasses, making something inside me melt. I missed the smell, the sight and the taste of him. It was like all my senses were going through the worst kind of withdrawal.

I thought I'd seen him in the distance on my morning run two days ago and could have qualified for the Olympics with the speed I'd run the other way. It was naïve to imagine our paths wouldn't cross during my compassionate leave of absence from work. But it was too soon and too raw to see him yet.

'Why haven't you told him that you never left Somerset?'

I stared at Amelia across the width of her kitchen.

'You know why.'

'Don't you think he has a right to make his own major life decisions?'

Her words were like well-aimed poisoned darts, each one perfectly placed. No one knows how to wound you better than your own sister.

'No. This is one decision that only I can make.'

'You'd rather live without him than give him the chance to spend his life with you, just in case you might have FAD. Which, incidentally, you could bloody well get tested for... but won't.'

My smile was twisted. We'd taken hardly any time at all to get back there.

Amelia shook her head sadly. 'You do know you're doing it again, don't you? Even now, when we know Dad would have passed away anyway from this illness, you're still doing it.'

'Doing what?'

'Punishing yourself for what happened on that last morning. Blaming yourself for finding those bloody keys. Making sure you don't have a happily-ever-after ending, because you've managed to convince yourself you don't deserve one. Every time you start a relationship, you're looking for a way to end it. This time, you're using an illness that you might not even have.'

I drew in a deep breath and, for what felt like the thousandth time, firmly reminded her of my decision.

'I won't contact Nick. I won't get tested. And I won't stop trying to change your mind about having an operation.'

Her smile looked wry as she began gathering up the photographs.

'You're so bloody obstinate.'

'Got it from my big sister,' I replied.

⋆

It was Amelia who suggested the Sunday lunch idea.

'I think Mum might still be worried that we're not totally on board about things between her and Tom,' she said, dropping her voice in case either of the septuagenarians walking a short distance ahead of us overheard her. From the level of the volume when they watched TV, that seemed highly unlikely. Even so, I leant in closer.

'I think it would be nice to invite him to a proper family meal. A kind of welcome-to-the-family sort of thing.'

I groaned softly. 'Oh God, you're not going to quiz him about his finances or ask if his intentions are honourable, are you?'

Amelia gave a mischievous shrug. 'That's one of the few benefits of being sick. You can practically get away with murder and everyone forgives you.'

Mum was totally on board with the plan. In fact, I seemed to be completely out of the loop with the arrangements. She'd hurried away muttering something about shopping lists and sorting out the 'good china'. Sunday was only two days away and she was a woman on a mission.

'Is this really a good idea?' I asked when my sister and I were alone once again.

Amelia smiled. 'A family dinner with our mother's seventy-five-year-old suitor. What could possibly go wrong?'

32

The cottage was filled with the smell of roasting beef. It took me straight back to Sunday lunches of my childhood and would normally have triggered a feeling of nostalgia and comfort. But not today, because for some reason something about this lunch was making me nervous. Amelia seemed concerned about nothing except what to wear, and Mum's only fear appeared to be overcooking the meat or burning the potatoes. I was the only family member freaking out about today – and I had no idea why.

Amelia wasn't the only one stressing about her wardrobe choice. I'd changed outfits three times, and nothing felt right.

'You could always borrow something of mine,' Amelia suggested as she passed my open bedroom door, before adding with a touch of sarcasm, 'Oh no, I forgot, you've already done that.' She disappeared into her bedroom, chuckling at her own joke.

I stared at her door as it clicked to a close. She was more Amelia and yet somehow less Amelia than before all of this happened. Sometimes it felt like a darker, evil twin had infiltrated her psyche and kept putting in unexpected and unwelcome appearances. I shook my head at such nonsense, because it sounded like the plot of a poorly drafted science-fiction novel. Amelia already had a twin – me – and neither of us was dark nor evil. But it was probably true that none of us were entirely ourselves right now; we were scarred and bruised by the events of the past few months and scared about the future.

I didn't like the direction my thoughts had taken and looked for a distraction among the sea of tissue paper on the bed. I'd stumbled across an online sale from one of my favourite clothes shops and had given my credit card an energetic workout. I'd promised myself I'd only keep one of the dresses I'd bought, but they all looked so good it was hard to choose.

In the end, I went for my favourite: a soft caramel-coloured sheath that looked deceptively simple on the hanger but found the contours of my body and accentuated them perfectly. It was the kind of dress that hinted, rather than shouted, at what was beneath. The neckline stopped short of revealing any cleavage, and yet it still made me feel sexier than anything in my sister's closet had done. I finished off the look by slipping silver hoops into my ears and threading a collection of colourful bangles on to my wrist, neither of which were Amelia's style. These days, it felt important to stress the differences between us rather than the similarities.

I did one last check of my make-up before pulling the clip from my hair and shaking it free, so that it tumbled down over my shoulders.

'What can I do? Shall I lay the table?' I asked as I walked

into a kitchen filled with steam from the collection of pans bubbling away on the hob.

'That would be great, Lexi,' Mum said gratefully. 'Amelia was going to do it, but she's busy looking for something at the moment.'

I glanced into the hallway and caught a glimpse of my sister moving from the lounge and heading towards the stairs. I paused for a moment, frowning as I saw her stop to catch her breath halfway up.

I was just setting the last dessert spoon into position when Amelia joined us in the kitchen. She was wearing a pair of smart black trousers, a silky long-sleeved red shirt, and an expression of immense frustration.

'What's up?' I asked, as I began folding paper serviettes into something resembling a pyramid shape.

'I'm looking for something,' she replied, clearly distracted as her gaze travelled the four corners of the kitchen. 'I swear I've looked absolutely everywhere, and I can't find it.'

I gave up in my attempt to turn the serviette into a recognisable shape.

'What have you lost? I'll help you find it.'

Amelia smiled gratefully, opened her mouth, but then stopped as though someone had pressed a pause button.

'It's um... it's my... it's...'

'Dying of suspense here,' I said, which was meant to make her laugh. Only it didn't. And when I saw the first flicker of confusion in her eyes, suddenly I didn't find it funny either.

She raised her left arm and looked down at it, like an actor who'd written their lines on the back of their hand. But there were no scribbled cues scrawled on her smooth skin.

'It's my wrist clock,' she declared at last, with a small, relieved laugh.

It was hot in the kitchen with the oven going and the hob at full blast, and yet I felt an icy shiver travel down the length of my spine.

'Your what?'

'My wrist clock,' Amelia said, her eyes going from me to Mum as though we were being exceptionally dense.

I caught the look on Mum's face and knew my own was wearing an identical expression of concern.

Amelia glanced meaningfully back at her bare wrist.

'Do you mean your *watch?*' I asked, aware that my voice didn't sound entirely normal. 'Is that what you're looking for?'

'Yes. That's what I just said,' Amelia replied, sounding impatient with me in a way she seldom did.

'No, actually you didn't. You called it your "wrist clock".'

She gave me a long stare, as though daring me to take back what I'd just said. But I didn't, because this felt like something we couldn't and shouldn't ignore. Amelia gave a casual shrug. 'Yeah, whatever. You knew what I meant. I just couldn't think of the word for a moment. So, have you seen it? Have you seen my *watch?*' She emphasised the word pointedly.

'It's in the bathroom, on the window ledge,' I said, biting my lip worriedly as she left the room to retrieve the missing item.

I waited until she was safely out of earshot before saying anything, but Mum beat me to it.

'It's nothing, Lexi. She's just overexcited about the lunch today, that's all.'

'Mum, she forgot the word. You could see her struggling to look for it, and she just couldn't access it.'

'Maybe it's the heart pills she's on,' Mum said.

'Or maybe it's starting to get worse,' I countered darkly. She didn't get a chance to respond to that because there was a timely knock on the front door, telling us our lunch guest had arrived.

My first surprise was the sight of the old fisherman in a suit. It made him look entirely different. He smelled different too. He entered the hallway on a cloud of Old Spice and mothballs. The suit was shiny in places, the way fabric goes when it hasn't been set free from the wardrobe for a very long time.

'Hi, Tom,' I said with a broad smile, genuinely happy to see him. He was clutching a bunch of shop-bought flowers, and somehow that said more about how fond he was of Mum than anything else. 'Are those for me?' I asked playfully, putting out my hand to relieve him of the bouquet.

'Don't be daft. They're for your mother,' he said, shuffling a little awkwardly in a pair of shoes I bet hadn't been on his feet for many years.

I surprised him by leaning over and dropping a light kiss on his weather-beaten cheek. 'She'll love them,' I whispered. 'And you're looking very dapper today.'

'Dapper,' he said, with what was probably meant to be a dismissive snort, but I could tell from his quicksilver smile that he was pleased with the description.

Tom headed to the kitchen, where Mum's squeal of pleasure told me he'd hit a bullseye with the flowers. Giving them a moment of privacy, I'd turned towards the stairs, my thoughts still troubled about Amelia, when the sound of a car pulling up outside the cottage stopped me in my tracks.

I glanced towards the front door and then at Amelia, who was descending the stairs. Ignoring my panicked expression, she looked beyond me at the dining table.

'You've done it wrong. You've only set four places. There's five of us for lunch.'

Swallowing was suddenly really, really difficult.

'What do you mean? Amelia, what have you done?'

She gave me a tough-love stare, seemingly unaware how close I was to killing her.

'Someone had to do it.'

I heard the sound of a car door slamming.

'Do what? Who is the extra place for?'

She shook her head, looking almost disappointed in me.

'Don't be dense, Lexi.'

A knock behind me caused the blood to drain from my face.

'Go on then,' she urged, nodding towards the front door. 'Let's see this guy I was meant to be married to.'

Still blindsided, I opened the door. Nick was standing before it, looking so impossibly handsome that the breath caught at the back of my throat.

His face lit up in a long smile when he saw me. There must have been hundreds of people who'd smiled at me in my lifetime – maybe even thousands. So what was it about Nick's – *and only Nick's* – that had the ability to ignite this inferno within me? I slipped through the front door and pulled it to a close behind me, shutting out the members of my family who had crowded into the hall.

Nick looked like his alter ego today, with his black hair

377

neatly combed and his dark-framed glasses in place, rather than the contacts he sometimes favoured. He wasn't dressed as formally as Tom, but the trousers and blue shirt combo were a world away from the casual attire I was more used to seeing him in.

'Hello, Lexi.'

God, how I'd missed that voice.

'I'm guessing by the shocked expression on your face that no one told you I was coming today?'

I shook my head dumbly, wondering when the ability to speak might return.

Nick reached across and gently pulled my hand away from my throat, where it had flown the second I'd seen him. He didn't release it from his own but threaded his fingers through mine.

'I... I... I didn't... I wasn't...'

'I'm guessing it wasn't her scintillating conversation that first attracted you to my sister,' said a voice behind me.

I spun around to see that Amelia had opened the front door and was standing in its frame with an exceedingly smug look on her face. I could see Tom and Mum craning their necks in the background, trying to get a better view of what was going on.

'I'm Amelia. Lexi's big sister,' Mimi said, unbelievably shoving me to one side and holding out her hand to Nick. 'It's nice to meet you in person. You didn't sound this tall on the phone.'

Nick's lips twitched but his eyes kept flashing back to my face, which was probably still cycling through from shock to dismay and back again.

This was a huge moment. Not just for me but for Amelia

too. It was one thing for her to dismiss her confabulation about being married as nonsense. It was easy to look at a photograph and say: *I've never seen that man before.* But how did she feel when the man she'd been able to draw from memory with perfect accuracy was standing right there in front of her?

Her eyes travelled the length of the man I loved.

'So, you're Nick,' she said artlessly, shaking his hand.

'I am,' Nick said, and for a moment I could sense a change of pressure in the air. Perhaps that's what happens when five people simultaneously hold their breath.

'They told me I dreamt of you.'

'I heard that too,' Nick said.

I was starting to feel light-headed from either lack of oxygen or suspense.

'Is it rude to say I genuinely have no memory of you?' Amelia asked.

'It's not rude at all,' Nick replied, his eyes kind as they looked at my sister.

Every cell, fibre and sinew in my body that had been set to high alert received the signal that it was safe to stand down. A bubble of relieved laughter escaped from one of us – or maybe all of us. It was interrupted by the ping of the oven timer. I flashed a look of panic over my shoulder at my mother. I couldn't sit down across the table from Nick, not with my entire family hanging on our every word.

But it would appear I'd seriously underestimated my mother's Machiavellian capabilities.

'That timer doesn't mean lunch is ready. It means you have forty-five minutes before I need to serve up. I imagine you two must have quite a lot to catch up on.'

Still feeling like I was floating through a dream, I watched as Amelia reached past me and relieved Nick of the flowers and bottle of wine he'd placed on the low wall beside the door.

'I'll take these, shall I? Enjoy your walk,' she said, giving me a gentle shove away from the door as she closed it behind her.

Alone again, although probably still being observed through the cottage windows, I turned to Nick.

'I've rehearsed this moment a thousand times. I knew exactly what I was going to say to you if I ever saw you again.'

'Was it good?' he asked, smiling down at me as though he was never going to take his eyes off me again.

'Yeah. It was excellent.'

'Do you remember any of it?'

'Not a single word.'

His laugh was soft and low and everything I thought I'd forgotten.

'Well, that's alright, because I've got a lot I want to say too. Shall we walk?' he suggested, offering me his arm.

We stepped from the pathway on to the sand and somehow his arm slipped around me, pulling me against his side. I went willingly.

His opening words startled me. 'I went to the airport that day, you know.'

'You did?'

There was a sheepish look on his face that tore at every single one of my heartstrings.

'I wasn't going to try to talk you out of leaving. I just wanted you not to be there alone. I stood in the terminal, watching your plane as it took off.'

'I wasn't on it.'

His smile was wry. 'I know that now. But I wouldn't if your sister hadn't told me. Why didn't you let me know you were still here, Lexi?'

Here was the moment I'd been dreading. The words were all there, clawing their way up my throat, but I couldn't bear to do this to him. Not again. So instead, I said the ones I never thought I would, because if I didn't say them now, I'd never get another chance.

'Before I say anything else, I want you to know that I've fallen in love with you too,' I told him, repeating the declaration he'd made to me on this very beach. 'I'm sorry I never said it back to you that day.'

Behind his glasses, I saw tears welling in his eyes. I'd made him cry. Damn. I promised myself I'd never do that again. How many more times was I going to break this man's heart?

Nick brought us to a stop and took both of my hands in his. 'I need you to know that Amelia has told me everything. I know about the FAD and the reason you don't want to let me back into your life.'

This time it was my turn to cry.

'I can't do that to you, Nick.'

His hands slid up my arms, coming to a rest on my shoulders.

'That's not your decision to make. You can decide not to have the test. You can decide to live in New York or Somerset or any damn country in the world. But you don't get to decide who I want to love for the rest of my life, because only *I* can do that. And I've already made up my mind. That person is you.'

I placed my hands on the solid wall of his chest, trying

to harness some strength from the reverberating beat of his heart. I didn't dare look at his face. Seeing the impact of my words would have derailed me.

'It's not fair to you,' I told his shirt buttons. 'You have a right to know if the person you're thinking of spending your future with actually has one.'

Nick flinched at my words. I felt it in every cell of my body.

'Whether you choose to have the test or not is *nothing* to do with me,' he said, his voice hoarse. 'If you want to find out, then great, I'll support you in every way I can. I'll come with you for counselling and be by your side whether the result is negative or positive. But know one thing: it will make absolutely no difference to how I feel about you.'

'It will, Nick. It *has* to. Looking after a partner with Alzheimer's isn't what you signed up for.'

'There's only one thing I'm signing up for,' Nick said, his voice cracking with the intensity of his feelings. 'And that's loving you for the rest of my days and yours. There's only one reason for you to walk away from me, and that's because you don't love me the way that I love you.'

He pulled me gently into his arms. 'No relationship comes with a guarantee, Lexi,' Nick whispered. 'There are no crystal balls. When you love someone, it's a huge joyous leap into the unknown. And I'm leaping with you.'

In every lifetime, there will be one moment that you know you'll remember until the day you die. This was mine.

Nick's head was slowly dipping towards me.

'Are you going to kiss me now?' I breathed against his lips.

'I am,' he replied.

And then he did.

33

Forty-five minutes after we left, we were back at the row of beachside cottages, stamping the sand from our shoes.

'I have no idea how this is going to go down,' I told him, glancing worriedly towards Amelia's home. In reply, Nick reached for my hand and squeezed it gently. His thumb swept back and forth across my palm as we walked the short distance to the front door. When we were out of view of every window, he kissed me again, hard and fast.

'We've got this,' he said, releasing my hand and capturing my heart in the same moment.

Everyone was gathered in the lounge when I led us back inside. Nick possessed the kind of easy charm that I suspected always went down well with mums, and mine was no exception. She greeted him warmly and even expressed disappointment that he hadn't brought Mabel with him today.

'Her table manners still need a little work,' he said, his eyes twinkling.

'Oh well, maybe next time,' Mum replied.

With old-fashioned good manners, Tom got to his feet

when we walked in and gripped the hand Nick extended in greeting.

'Nice to see you again,' Nick said.

'Almost didn't recognise you with your clothes on, lad,' chuckled Tom.

My eyes met Mum's as the two men shook hands. It felt as though we'd all been drawn together by an invisible thread and stitched into a strange patchwork tapestry. For a moment I wondered if I was the catalyst that had brought us together, but then I looked over at Amelia, smiling with satisfaction from the settee, and I realised the thread drawing us together wasn't me at all, it was my sister.

With perfect timing the oven pinged from the kitchen, this time announcing that lunch was ready. There was an awkward little shuffle as we took our seats, with Nick and me on one side, Mum and Amelia opposite us, while Tom hesitantly took the position at the head of the table. My eye caught Amelia's and it wasn't just a twin thing to realise that we were sharing the same thought. Dad had been gone for many years now and all we wanted was for Mum to be happy. As unlikely as Tom might be on paper as a candidate for that role, there was something about the elderly fisherman that had brought a new sparkle to our mother's eyes.

There were two things I hadn't had to worry about today. One was the food, which was delicious. Mum blushed delightfully with every compliment received, although perhaps a little deeper when the praise came from Tom. The second was whether we'd find anything to talk about. Thankfully, between Nick and Tom there were enough amusing stories and funny anecdotes to last a whole month of Sunday lunches.

It was all going well until Amelia decided that polite

boundaries no longer applied to her. Midway between passing Nick the Yorkshire puddings and Tom the gravy boat, she casually asked, 'So, are you and Lexi a thing again now?'

'Amelia,' I hissed, hitting every single syllable of her name.

'What? I'm only asking the question we're all thinking. Are you and Nick...'

Her hands fluttered, and for one dreadful moment I thought she was going to elaborate with graphic gestures. If she had, she'd have been wearing the lunch she'd so far only pushed from one side of her plate to the other.

'We're together,' Nick confirmed, giving me a long, slow smile that, God help me, made me blush like a teenager.

'And how's that going to work out transatlantically then?'

'That's not even a word,' I said, my eyes pleading with her to drop it. Nick and I hadn't discussed the logistics yet and I didn't really want it served up for a group debate around the dining table.

'We'll figure it out,' Nick said, sensing my discomfort far better than my sister had done. I wasn't used to having someone know me better than she did. I kind of liked it.

Amelia still looked vaguely disappointed. She wanted everything all sewn up and I thought I knew why. The reason made my eyes sting with tears. She wanted to know we were all going to be alright when she wasn't with us any longer.

'Actually, I might be done with New York for now.'

Four pairs of startled eyes flew my way. I couldn't blame them. I don't think I'd known it myself until the words were tumbling from my lips.

'If I'm good enough to do that job in New York, then I'm good enough to do it anywhere.' Nick looked like he was about to interject, but I cut him off. 'Everyone I love most in the world happens to live in one tiny corner of Somerset and the idea of being anywhere else right now is just plain crazy.'

We made it all the way to the apple pie and ice cream without any further awkwardness. We were almost home free, but then the elephant in the room, the one we'd all been studiously ignoring, finally broke free.

'Did you know, Nick, that Lexi thinks I must have seen you walking your dog on the beach at some point and somehow the memory of it got lodged in my subconscious.'

Nick nodded slowly, as unprepared as the rest of us were for the way Amelia emphatically shook her head. 'I don't believe that. I know my memory has been a bit flaky recently, but I doubt I'd have forgotten seeing you – you're a pretty distinctive-looking guy.' She took another sip from her wine glass before continuing. 'I imagine you've heard the "Man of Steel" thing before?'

Nick's eyes flashed to mine and there was a smile in them that belonged to me.

'Once or twice,' he replied, his voice warm.

Amelia took it all in: our shared look, and the secret smile that passed between us. She gave a small, satisfied nod.

'And if I'd been close enough to have committed your features to memory, it stands to reason you'd have remembered seeing me too?'

It was a simple question and one I'd asked Nick myself, so it was hardly surprising that Amelia had homed in on it.

'Probably,' Nick replied with understandable caution. Like the rest of us, he wasn't entirely sure where my sister was going with this.

'As far as anyone can tell, this fantasy of mine began when

those two doctors found me on the beach and restarted my heart after it had stopped beating.'

There was a lot of clinking of cutlery and shifting in seats as we collectively stepped into an area we weren't comfortable occupying. Beneath the table, the serviette that had never quite made it to a pyramid was clenched tightly in my fist.

'My body received one hundred and fifty joules of electricity and I woke up convinced I had a whole history with a man who looks just like you. And that belief stayed with me for months, until my heart was shocked again to restore its rhythm. And then it simply disappeared.'

'That's it in a nutshell,' I said, getting to my feet to begin clearing the table.

I had an armful of crockery and glassware and I have no idea how I didn't drop it when Amelia shared her bizarre conclusion.

'I've spent the last few months living inside an elaborate false memory of something that never happened without any of you realising it wasn't *my past* I was seeing at all. It was *Lexi's future.*'

'Okay. Just for the record, I would like to make it perfectly clear that insanity does not – to the best of my knowledge – run in my family.'

Nick stopped drying the plate in his hands. Mum's good crockery was too delicate for the dishwasher, so we'd volunteered to wash up. It was a good opportunity for a debrief of the Sunday lunch that had started perfectly normal but ended up in *The Twilight Zone*.

'You don't think there could be anything in Amelia's theory, do you?' I asked with a nervous laugh, because those words really had no business being spoken out loud.

To his credit, Nick didn't throw back his head and laugh at the very strange women in the Edwards family – which Jeff most definitely would have done in his place.

'I'm a vet, Lexi, which means I'm a man of science. I spent years studying things that can be proved and explained. I look for answers in reality and in the everyday world. And I always find them there. So, in answer to your question, no, I don't think Amelia had a prophecy about your future.'

He was so pragmatic, it made me feel foolish for even giving the idea air to breathe. 'We made Amelia's visions come true, you and me, by doing the things she believed she'd "seen" in her past.' He air-quoted the word, making it clear that his viewpoint was immovable on this one. I smiled weakly. Nick was a scientist by profession, and it was natural for him to deal in cold hard facts that were either black or white. But I worked in a world of fabrication and make-believe. I saw far more grey than he did in Amelia's words.

Had Amelia found me the perfect soulmate because I'd done such a poor job of doing that myself?

34

'Are you awake?' Something in Nick's voice made me think it might not be the first time he'd asked me this.

'I am now,' I mumbled sleepily, stretching out an arm to lift my phone from the bedside table. 'It's so early,' I said, squinting at the numbers on the screen, feeling sure I must have misread them.

Nick was propped up on one elbow, looking down at me with an excited smile and eight hours of stubble on his face. 'I couldn't sleep. I've been waiting ages for you to wake up.'

I arched my back, bringing me close enough to kiss him. 'Just for future reference, are you always like this on Christmas morning?'

'Like what?' he asked, his hand slipping behind my back and keeping our naked bodies skin to skin.

'Like you're six years old,' I said, my laughter cutting off as he suddenly moved and slid between my legs. All at once, being woken before the sun had even risen didn't seem that bad after all.

A little later, when we were still a tangle of limbs, Nick

pushed the damp hair from my forehead and said tenderly, 'Happy first Christmas together, Lexi.'

'Was that my present?' I teased, tasting the salty tang of sweat as I kissed his shoulder.

His eyes twinkled in the way that still made me feel like a lovestruck teenager. 'I wanted to give you something you couldn't return,' he joked.

I smiled, thinking of the pile of glossy beribboned gifts already stacked beneath the Christmas tree in Nick's lounge. *Our* lounge, I mentally corrected.

So much had changed in the last seven months, it was hardly surprising my brain had trouble keeping up with the pronouns. And moving in with Nick was still a relatively recent development.

After Amelia's diagnosis, I couldn't imagine ever wanting to leave her beachside fisherman's cottage. When your time together is finite, you don't want to squander a single second of it. *But everything is finite, Lexi,* Amelia had said with a calm acceptance that had astounded me. *Every relationship has an end date – but people are like ostriches, they choose not to think about that. Something like this knocks all that crap to the kerb and forces you to focus on the things that really matter: family, friendship and love. Which is why,* she said with a wry smile, *I'm formally giving you notice that I'm evicting you.*

'You're what?' I said, turning away from the mirror where I was styling my hair before my date with Nick.

'You heard me. I'm done with having you and Nick here for half the week and Mum here for the rest of it. You people are treating my home like a bloody hotel.'

I set down the curling wand before I burnt myself. 'Mimi, I don't think—'

'That I can cope without help?' she completed with a hint of the old feistiness I hadn't seen for a while. 'You're right. I *do* need help. Which is why I asked Mum to get in touch with some home care companies.'

I shook my head. 'Those places charge a fortune, hon, and you don't need them when you've got family right here.'

'I know how much they cost, and we don't need to worry about that. I'd have been a pretty rubbish accountant if I hadn't been investing my money wisely for all these years,' she said. 'And as much as I love that you both want to look after me, I truly don't want that. *Anyone* can be my carer but only *you* can be my sister, and that's why you no longer have the job.'

'Evicted and fired on the same day? That's got to be some sort of record,' I said, attempting a laugh that fell short by a country mile.

'Come here,' she said, holding out her arms for a hug I think we both needed.

Things were moving fast, much faster than I wanted to admit. Each horrible milestone was a marker on the highway to somewhere no one wants to visit. There was an oxygen canister beside her bed these days, and another in the corner of the lounge. She didn't need to use them every day, but her reliance on them was definitely increasing. And we were probably single-handedly responsible for a huge spike in the sale of Post-it notes. They were all over the house, reminding Amelia to do hundreds of things she once would never have forgotten. The important ones were written in red: **Check there's water in the kettle before you boil it. Turn off the oven. Make sure the back door is locked.** But it was the ones written in blue that broke my heart. **Your underwear is in the** third drawer of the dresser. You have two sugars in your tea. Clean your teeth before you go to bed.

It had been a relief when we'd finally stopped arguing over our differing viewpoints. I think we both realised we were in danger of ruining the precious time we had left by being so angry with each other.

While Nick went downstairs to let Mabel out, I took advantage of the unexpectedly early start and jumped into the shower. There were several hours before everyone arrived for Christmas lunch, but still about a hundred things on my 'to-do' list.

'Everything will be fine,' Nick had soothed, seemingly forgetting that I rarely cooked anything that didn't set off every smoke alarm in the house.

'I just want to make today special,' I said. Nick knew me well enough to understand my concerns ran deeper than ruining the turkey or running out of Baileys. I wanted everything to be perfect because I was achingly aware that it might be the last Christmas when Amelia was still Amelia and not a stranger with a memory full of holes.

'We'll make it unforgettable, I promise,' he said, pulling me into the circle of his arms. 'We've got this.'

And maybe we had. The house was decorated with enough lights to be visible from space, or so Nick had teased. And yet he'd uncomplainingly spent hours up various ladders, stringing up 'just one more set of lights' whenever I asked him to.

In a surprising act of seasonal goodwill, Natalie had agreed that Holly could spend half of the day with us, which meant the world to Nick. I loved seeing him in all his many guises – compassionate vet, supportive friend, tender lover – but it was watching him as a dad that never failed to melt my heart. Sadly, it was a role he was unlikely to play again if I *had* inherited FAD. Although Nick had never once pressured me to take the test, there had been times when my decision not to felt as shaky as a stack of dominoes on the verge of collapsing.

He was waiting for me in the bedroom with a steaming mug of tea and the same excited expression he'd worn on waking me. I took the hot drink gratefully and sipped it while snuggled deep into the folds of my thick towelling robe. A heavy frost had settled overnight on the trees that neighboured the bedroom window, transforming the view into one straight off a Christmas card.

'Have you finished?' Nick asked when my mug was still half full. 'Because I've got something I want to give you.'

'Again?' I teased with a wicked grin, my eyes going to the tangle of bed sheets.

'This is a *real* present,' he said. There was something in his voice that was hard to define. It fell halfway between excitement and nervous anticipation.

'Don't you want to wait until everyone gets here?'

Nick shook his head emphatically.

'Ohhh, it's *that* kind of gift, is it?' I said, immediately imagining something risqué. 'Okay, hang on a minute and I'll just pull some clothes on.'

My hands went to the belt of my robe but his were faster, stopping me from undoing it. 'You're fine just as you are.'

Nick was acting weirdly and was clearly in a hurry for us to go downstairs, although I noticed *he'd* found time to pull on jeans and a navy T-shirt. He'd also been busy while I was in the shower. The Christmas playlist I'd compiled was playing softly from every downstairs speaker, and he'd even switched on the lights on the huge Norwegian pine standing in one corner of the lounge.

Five hundred fairy lights beckoned me across the room. There's something particularly magical about a twinkling Christmas tree in the early dawn light. Ours was positioned beside the floor-to-ceiling windows that looked out on to the dense woodland behind Nick's home. It was hard to say which looked more spectacular, the icy boughs outside or the illuminated pine.

Nick left my side and, ignoring the pile of presents beneath the tree, crossed to the oak dresser. He glanced back over his shoulder and shot me a smile as he slid open the top drawer. From it, he withdrew a large, flat, gift-wrapped parcel.

'I wasn't going to give you this yet,' he said, his eyes dropping to the present in his hands. 'I was going to wait until New Year's Eve.' My curiosity was definitely piqued. He gave a boyish grin that lit his face and knocked about twenty years off his age. 'But I can't wait any longer.'

He walked towards me, and I was suddenly aware that my heart was thudding hard against my ribcage. Whatever he'd bought for me, it clearly meant a lot to him.

'I love it,' I declared enthusiastically as he placed the gift in my hands. 'It's absolutely perfect.'

He flashed me a crooked grin. 'You don't even know what it is yet.'

'I don't need to. It's already my favourite, because you gave it to me,' I said, kissing the grin he was still wearing before my fingers went to the tape securing the gift wrap. Nick moved to stand behind me, his hands resting lightly on my shoulders as my fingers worked to release the gift. From the weight of it, I already knew my initial guess of sexy lingerie was way off beam. It felt like a framed painting.

It took just two tugs for the gold foil paper to flutter to the floor. Behind me, I could sense Nick holding his breath as I turned the frame over and tilted it towards the light.

'Oh Nick, it's wonderful,' I said, bringing the sketch closer to examine it better. I recognised it immediately as a copy of one of our staged photographs. For a moment I wondered if Amelia might have drawn it, but it far exceeded her modest talents. I peered closely at the name written in the lower right-hand corner, but didn't recognise it.

'I found a local artist and commissioned her to recreate the photo of the day we picnicked on the beach in the freezing cold weather.'

I looked down at the drawing in my hands and smiled at the memory.

'I know we have the photographs we took that day, but they were always for Amelia, not us.' Nick's arms slipped around my waist, drawing me back against him. 'I wanted something that was our own memory, because that was the day when everything changed for me. It was the day I first realised I was falling in love with you.' His voice was little more than a whisper in my ear.

'Me too,' I said, unable to tear my eyes away from the two figures in the picture. They were a good likeness and when I looked at them, I didn't see Amelia and Sam, I saw only Nick and me.

'It really is perfect,' I breathed, 'although it's not quite accurate...' My voice trailed away as I looked more closely at the picture. There were several discrepancies now that I studied it better. First, there was no sign of the beach or the sea in the sketch, for the artist had drawn us against a forest backdrop. And there were other differences. The illustrated figures were accurately posed, but the artist had swapped out the skimpy bikini I'd been wearing that day for a far less revealing robe, and Nick's board shorts had been replaced by a dark T-shirt and jeans, much like the outfit he was wearing this morning.

I looked down at the towelling robe I'd put on after my shower and almost dropped the framed drawing as I finally realised what I was holding. This sketch wasn't capturing a memory that had happened nine months ago... it was happening right now, right this minute. I slowly turned around, my eyes filling with tears when I saw two Nicks: one in the frame in my hands and the other right there in front of me. Both were down on one knee, holding out a ring box. Against the forest backdrop beyond the lounge window, Nick reached for my left hand and flipped open the velvet box to reveal a beautiful pear-cut diamond ring.

'I didn't realise you could live your whole life never knowing something was missing until the day you unexpectedly find it. And when you do, everything falls into place and you know you're exactly where you were always meant to be, with the person you're meant to share your life with. I love you, Lexi, and always will whatever your answer is, but I really hope it'll be a yes. Will you marry me?'

'Yes,' I said, my voice caught between laughter and tears. Nick's eyes were locked on mine as he slipped the ring on to my finger. It slid in place as though it had always been there.

★

THE MEMORY OF US

Most of the things on my Christmas 'to-do' list didn't get done after all. It was hard to concentrate on anything when I kept stopping every few minutes to gaze in wonder at my left hand. I was engaged. Nick and I were getting married, and I couldn't wait to share the news with my family. But there was someone else to consider too, someone who was already very close to my heart.

'I think you should tell Holly first, before I say anything to Mum and Amelia.'

Nick had been watching in amusement as I slid the turkey into the oven with a whispered 'good luck'. His smile faded slightly.

'Are you worried Holly won't be happy about this? Because I know for a fact she will be. She's been begging me to ask you for weeks. If I'd waited much longer, she'd probably have asked you herself.' He dropped his voice, as though sharing a secret. 'I think she might be angling to be a bridesmaid.'

'The job's hers,' I said, abandoning the oven and joining him on the other side of the room. 'But I still think it'll be a big adjustment for her. I don't want her to feel left out or worry that you won't have as much time to spend with her now – because you absolutely will.'

'And *that* is why I love you,' Nick declared, pulling me against him and kissing the side of my head.

'Not for my domestic goddess skills?' I teased, my eyes going to the mess I'd made in the normally tidy kitchen.

'Strangely… not so much,' he said on a laugh.

A little later, dressed in the cheesiest Christmas jumper I'd been able to find, I ran a comb through my hair and did one last check of my make-up. As I slid the dressing-table drawer shut, my eye fell on the white envelope nestled among the cosmetics and toiletries. *Where you'd hidden it*, said a voice in my head. *Where you'd put it for safe keeping*, contradicted another. Curiously, they both sounded like me. I pulled the letter from the drawer. The envelope was a little crumpled, which was hardly surprising given how many times I'd read the letter inside it.

I could hear Nick finishing up in the bathroom and hurriedly dropped the letter back into the drawer, but something stopped me from sliding it shut. It felt like the wrong day to be keeping secrets from each other, especially one this huge.

Nick came into the bedroom and even though my mind was still on the envelope with the NHS logo in the corner, I couldn't help the breath from catching in my throat. He looked devastatingly attractive, dressed in black jeans and a slim-fitting shirt of the same colour.

'I promise I'll wear the reindeer jumper for lunch,' he said, mistaking the look of concern in my eyes.

'It's not that,' I said, biting my lower lip guiltily as I reached once again into the drawer for the letter.

'What's that?'

'Open it,' I said, putting the envelope into his hands. His eyes flickered when he saw my name and the familiar blue logo.

'It's addressed to you,' he said.

I nodded. 'I was going to tell you about this after Christmas… but now, because of what's happened today…' My eyes slid down to my hand and despite the sudden seriousness of our conversation, I couldn't help smiling. 'I want you to know sooner rather than later.'

His dark brows had drawn together, and a tiny muscle was twitching at the corner of one eye, magnified by the lens of his glasses. He pulled out the single sheet of paper and I know I wasn't imagining the way it trembled slightly in his hand.

Nick was a fast reader, usually reaching the end of a page even quicker than I did, but he took his time over the letter, as though needing to be quite sure he understood what he was reading.

'Are you sure, Lexi?' he asked at last. There was a look on his face that spoke of relief and in hindsight I realised I should have pre-empted the situation with a little more information.

'I am sure,' I said, moving away from the dressing table and coming to stand beside him to read the letter again, as though I couldn't already have recited it verbatim. 'I'm having my first genetic counselling session in the New Year.' It was the first step on the road to having the test to discover if I'd inherited the faulty gene.

'What made you change your mind?' Nick's confusion was understandable. I'd not told anyone that over the last few months I'd started to question my insistence that I didn't want to know what the future had in store for me.

'Lots of things. Not all of them huge, but it felt like they were growing and that perhaps *not* knowing was a greater weight to carry than actually discovering the truth. What do you think?'

'I think I want whatever you want. There's no right or wrong decision for you to make here, only what is right for you.'

I nodded because he was saying exactly what I'd told myself a thousand times over.

'I'm still not committing to anything. I just want to talk

it through with a counsellor and *then* make an informed decision about what I want to do, rather than follow my knee-jerk one of saying no one should ever know their own future.

'But what I *didn't* want,' I said, taking the letter from Nick's hands and sliding it back into its envelope, 'was for you to think that I'd made this appointment because of what happened today. That's why I wanted to show this to you now, so that you knew you hadn't forced my hand. I'd already decided to do this.'

He looked at me then with more admiration than I deserved.

'I still might not have the test. Only forty per cent of those who go to a geneticist actually go through with it.'

Nick shrugged, as though nothing could be of less importance. If it was possible to love him even more than I already did, it happened right there in that moment.

'I'd like to come with you – if you want me to, that is.'

I nodded just as the sound of tyres crunching on gravel came from the driveway. Our guests had arrived.

While Nick was busy taking coats and relieving Amelia, Mum and Tom of a ridiculous number of Christmas presents, I took a moment to slip the diamond ring from my finger and transfer it on to a long silver chain hung around my neck. I dropped it down inside my jumper and smiled when the ring settled right next to my heart. A spot already claimed by the man who'd given it to me.

'I couldn't manage another mouthful,' Tom declared, even as he rummaged through the tub of Quality Street for his personal favourite.

Christmas lunch had been an enormous success, thanks to Nick's assistance and several glasses of champagne, both of which seemed to make everything far less stressful. With unheard-of restraint, Mum hadn't attempted to take over and had even claimed that sprouts taste better when you overcook them and *everyone's* gravy has lumps in it.

Now, with the dishwasher humming through its first cycle, Nick got to his feet and laid his hand on Holly's shoulder. 'Feel like keeping me company on a dog walk?' he asked, managing to sound impressively casual.

I held my breath, not sure I was capable of holding in our secret much longer if Holly decided the book I'd given her for Christmas was more enticing than a walk with her dad. Thankfully, she didn't.

'Are you okay?' Amelia asked when they'd been gone for about twenty minutes. 'You seem awfully on edge.'

'Probably because I've just lived through the Yuletide equivalent of the *MasterChef* final,' I said, my glance going to the settee where Mum was now quietly snoring.

Amelia's frown told me she didn't entirely believe my reply.

'Have you had a good day?' I asked her, because when all was said and done, that was all that really mattered. It was all for Amelia.

'I have. You've made it absolutely perfect,' she said, swivelling on the settee to face me. 'If this is the last Christmas I ever properly remember, then I can't think of a better one to go out on.'

Tears stung my eyes, but her fierce glare stopped them from falling.

'None of that. Not today. Today is only for making happy memories.'

My ears pricked up when I heard the sound of the back door opening, followed by the skitter of Mabel's claws on the tiled floor. They were back.

I didn't need to ask Nick if he'd spoken to Holly. The answer was right there in her ear-to-ear grin and the way she positively skipped into the room. I matched her smile with one of my own and gave her a secret wink.

'I'll put the kettle on,' I said, ducking into the kitchen where Nick was already pulling a bottle of champagne from the fridge. 'I thought we might want to toast our news with something a little stronger than PG Tips,' he said with a grin.

I loaded a tray with glasses and then pulled the silver chain out from its hiding place beneath my jumper. For the second time that day, Nick slipped the diamond ring on to my finger.

'Let's do this,' he said.

Mum was now awake but so engrossed in her conversation with Tom she failed to spot the extremely unsubtle way I flaunted my left hand as I set the tray down on the coffee table.

'More fizz?' Tom queried. I suspected he'd have preferred a bottle of stout or a glass of rum.

'I thought we should,' Nick said, his eyes going to his daughter, who looked as though she was in serious danger of exploding.

Nick popped the cork on the bottle with the efficiency of a barman, while I held out the waiting glasses with my left hand. I'd set two back down on the table before an excited squawk from Amelia told me she'd finally spotted my ring.

'Oh my God, Lexi,' she cried, leaping off the settee at a speed that belied her heart condition. 'Are you...? When did you...? Are you two...?'

'Ever going to finish a sentence?' I prompted with a laugh. I truly have no idea what happened next, but we were suddenly involved in a group hug that felt more like a rugby scrum as everyone – even Tom – joined in. I never thought of joy as being tangible before, but I swear I could feel it in the air at that moment.

Holly hung on the hardest, fastening her skinny arms tightly around my waist. I hugged her back just as fiercely, already loving her as I'd done from almost the first day I met her.

'I didn't think today could get any better,' Amelia declared, her eyes going from me to Nick, who'd come to stand beside me. 'But it just did.'

'I thought you said there'd be no tears today,' I teased, as she wiped her hand roughly beneath her eyes.

'Happy ones don't count,' she said, looking more excited than I'd seen in months. For that alone, I'd get engaged every single day if she asked me to.

Holly looked up at her dad and then turned her face to me. 'I dreamt about this happening,' she admitted on a shy whisper.

'Do you know what, sweetheart, so did I,' Amelia said.

35

I remember reading somewhere that, on average, couples take twelve months to plan a wedding. We did ours in just six weeks.

'Folk will think it's a shotgun affair,' Tom commented when we informed him of the imminent date.

'Only if they've been teleported here from the nineteenth century,' I replied, giving the old fisherman a friendly hug.

I slid the last invitation into its envelope and added it to the very small stack on the table waiting to be posted.

'Will it be soon?' Amelia had wanted to know, a few days after she'd learnt of our news.

'As soon as we can make it happen,' I told her, understanding perfectly why she'd asked that question.

She nodded and her eyes clouded with a fleeting sadness.

'Are you thinking of having a church wedding?'

'To be honest, Mimi, I'd happily marry Nick in the middle of a field, but I can't see Mum being best pleased with that. Besides, Holly has her heart set on walking down an aisle scattering rose petals everywhere. Hopefully with you standing right there beside her.'

Amelia shook her head firmly at my suggestion.

'Nothing on earth will persuade me into some peach-coloured froufrou meringue dress, not even for you,' she said. 'And I don't need to be your bridesmaid or – God forbid – your maid of honour,' she added with a dramatic shiver. 'All I ask is that you try to make it happen soon, so that I'll know whose wedding I'm at.'

She did that all the time, trying to turn her worsening Alzheimer's into something to laugh about. It was a coping mechanism, I knew that, but it didn't make it any easier to hear.

'I'm sorry you never got to be my bridesmaid like I promised you all those years ago,' she said, reaching for my hand. 'But on the bright side, at least Mum gets to see *one* of her daughters walk down the aisle.'

A lump roughly the size of a golf ball lodged in my throat, making it impossible to do anything other than nod fiercely in acknowledgement.

It had felt wrong to splurge too much on the wedding, and although I knew Nick would happily have gone along with whatever I suggested, I wanted to keep things modest.

'You can't buy your wedding dress on eBay,' Amelia had protested when I'd swivelled my laptop towards her to show her a gown I'd just found listed there.

'You can if it's this pretty,' I said, hitting the icon to enlarge the picture until it filled the screen. The dress was a strapless, sweetheart neckline gown, with delicate silver embroidery and a Milky Way of tiny crystals scattered across the sheer fabric. If I'd tried on a hundred dresses in every fancy bridal boutique in town, this would still have been the one I'd have chosen.

Amelia spent a long time looking at the photos, and I could tell by the smile playing on her lips that she could already visualise me in the gorgeous pre-loved gown.

'You're going to be such a beautiful bride,' she said, sounding choked.

'And you're going to be the most beautiful guest,' I countered.

'With my oxygen tank in tow,' she said, shooting a begrudging glance at the black cylinder beside her. Then she flipped the mood completely by adding, 'Which I'll only be bringing along because you're going to take Nick's breath away when he sees you.'

I hadn't known what to expect from my first counselling session, although the image of lying on a couch while someone scribbled away on a clipboard beside me had been hard to shake off. The reality was very different.

The first surprise was discovering that genetic counselling wasn't *actually* counselling in the psychological sense of the word. It was more of a learning process where I'd be given all the facts and options so I could make an informed decision about whether I wanted to go ahead and get tested.

I attended the first session alone, but Nick came with me to the second one some weeks later. That was the day I learnt about preimplantation genetic testing, a complicated type of IVF that gives couples like us the chance to have children, if they want them.

'I feel I ought to have known about that pre diagnosis thingy before now,' I admitted as we walked back to Nick's car.

'PGT,' he said, the abbreviation slipping easily off his tongue.

'You knew about it already?'

'Most vets are science nerds,' Nick said with a sheepish shrug. 'And we use something very similar with cattle.'

'I'm not sure if that makes me feel better or worse.'

Nick smiled and paused halfway through reversing out of the parking space to squeeze my hand. 'PGT doesn't and shouldn't alter whether you decide to get tested. It's still one hundred per cent your decision. Have you told Amelia about the counselling sessions yet?'

I shook my head. 'I want to wait until I've decided one way or the other. I don't want to get her hopes up only to disappoint her.'

'You do know that nothing you do will ever disappoint your sister, don't you?' Nick said gently.

In the end, the decision was easier than I thought it would be. I wanted to know. Not for Amelia, or Mum, or even for Nick. I wanted to know for me. I'd never understood people who skip to the end of a book because they need to know how it ends, but perhaps now I was starting to. Knowing would bring its own kind of comfort. Pandora's box was right there in front of me and even though I was terrified, I still wanted to open it.

I told Amelia my decision two days before the wedding, and I truly don't think she could have been more ecstatic if I'd won the lottery.

'It's going to be alright, Lexi,' she cried, reaching for my hands and gripping them. 'I just know your test will come back negative.'

'You don't know that, hon. No one does.'

'*I do*,' Amelia insisted. 'It's the same as how I knew you and Nick were destined to get together.' It seemed inappropriate to remind her that initially she'd 'seen' him as *her* husband rather than mine. 'And now I'm just as certain that the faulty gene will have skipped you. You and I were in a Petri dish lottery when Mum and Dad had IVF, and the only thing that makes any of this bearable is knowing *I* was the one who inherited this thing and not you. I don't think I could've coped if it had been the other way around.'

Welcome to my world, I thought sadly.

'This is a very tame hen night,' Mum observed as she squeezed a sachet of vinegar over her chips.

I looked around at the beach, which, although a little chilly, looked particularly beautiful this evening.

'What had you been expecting, Mum?'

'I'm not sure. Perhaps something a bit livelier?' she suggested tentatively.

I'd been to plenty of hen parties that were lively enough to raise anyone's blood pressure, and I wasn't sure how Amelia or Mum would have coped with an evening of baby-oiled strippers and bottomless cocktails.

'Well, this is exactly what I wanted,' I said, munching contentedly on a particularly long chip. 'My favourite takeaway, in one of my favourites places, with my two favourite mother hens.' I picked up the bottle of chilled

Prosecco that I'd planted in the sand and waved it aloft in an unspoken question.

'Better not,' Amelia said, answering for them both. 'If you get Mum tiddly, I'm not going to be able to help you carry her back to the cottage.'

Beneath the joke was an ever-present reminder. Amelia's home was only about fifty metres away, but that was about as far as she felt comfortable walking these days.

We stayed on the beach until the sun slipped slowly into the sea and then gathered up our belongings and threw our leftovers on the sand for the waiting gulls.

'Better hope Tom doesn't find out you did that,' Amelia teased, knowing it was sure to bring a blush to Mum's cheeks. I hid my smile and resolved that tomorrow, when I threw my wedding bouquet, she would be the one to catch it.

Mum's taxi arrived not long after we'd returned to the cottage and Amelia and I walked her to the car, our arms wound around each other's waists.

'Twins?' the driver enquired with the kind of delight we used to get all the time when we were younger. It was dark enough for him not to have seen the difference in our ages, which her illness had made more noticeable lately.

'Kind of,' Amelia said.

'Absolutely,' I countered.

I'd have loved to have sat up for half the night reminiscing with my sister about the past, but I could see that the evening had wiped her out. It was hard to reconcile how arbitrary FAD was with Amelia's memories, leaving the ones from twenty years ago virtually intact while obliterating what had happened just a few hours ago.

'I'm going to get an early night, Lexi,' she said, pausing at the foot of the stairs as though summoning up the energy to scale Everest rather than climbing to the upper floor.

'Do you want a hand?'

She shook her head, still as fiercely independent about accepting my help as ever, although she happily leant on the carers who visited the cottage each day.

She paused on the second tread and turned back to face me.

'I've left a little something for you on the pillow in your old room,' she informed me. 'An early wedding gift.'

'Should I wait and open it with Nick tomorrow?'

Amelia shook her head. 'No. This one is just for you. And before you tell me it's too much, it isn't, and I really want you to have it.'

I was intrigued enough to want to follow her up the stairs right there and then, but she insisted I wait until later.

'Phone that fiancé of yours. From the number of times you've checked your mobile this evening, you're clearly having withdrawal symptoms about being away from him for just one night.'

I accepted her teasing good-naturedly, mainly because she knew me well enough to realise I was indeed missing Nick. It was our first night apart in months and I scarcely waited for the sound of Amelia's bedroom door to click shut before calling him.

'I am not enjoying this,' he said.

'Charming,' I heard Doug say in the background over the easily identifiable soundtrack of a pub.

'I meant being apart from you,' Nick said into the phone, dropping his voice a little lower so that his friend couldn't join in our conversation. I didn't want to keep him long, so we only spoke for a few minutes, but just hearing his voice centred me.

'I'll see you in church,' he murmured softly as we said our goodbyes.

'I'll be there,' I promised, feeling suddenly emotional. 'I'll be the one in the big white dress.'

'I'll find you,' he replied. 'I'll always find you.'

I'd actually forgotten all about the mysterious gift Amelia had left for me by the time I went to bed. But I saw it the moment I flicked on the lights in my old bedroom.

'Oh, Mimi,' I said on a sigh, when I saw the item sitting squarely in the middle of my pillow. I was shaking my head as I crossed to the bed, knowing now why she'd already warned me that she wouldn't take the gift back.

I lifted the engraved locket from its spot on the pillow, the chain falling like a silver snake into the palm of my hand. The locket had been Amelia's since her eighteenth birthday and was our grandmother's last gift to her. It was too much to accept, but Amelia was one step ahead of me, for there was a note beside the pillow.

Yes, this was given to me by our grandmother and now I'm giving it to you. Call it your something old, or your something new – but not your something borrowed, because I want you to keep it. Wear it for me and I'll always be right there beside you... even when I'm not.

Tears were already falling down my cheeks as my trembling fingers fumbled awkwardly with the clasp before the locket sprang open. I smiled nostalgically as I looked down at the photo of Nick on the beach, taken on the day we'd met. I tilted the locket to inspect the second image. My breath caught as I stared down at one of my favourite photographs of Amelia and me. It had been taken three years ago on a breezy day in Central Park. One of us – I couldn't remember who – had cracked a daft joke just as the shutter clicked. The photo caught the moment and somehow it captured every best memory I had of us. Two identical faces, both smiling the same smile as our hair tangled together in the wind; we were the same, but still uniquely and wonderfully different. I hadn't seen this photo in years and had no idea how Amelia had managed to find it, but I was very glad that she had.

I already knew that in a burning house, this locket was the thing I'd rescue before all others, and that I'd be wearing it with pride and love at my wedding the next day.

36

It should have been raining that day. The sky should have been ominously grey with lightning spearing across it like a scar. But the sun was shining through the bedroom window, giving no clue that this would be the day when the world would change forever.

I'd woken, as I always did, locked safely in Nick's arms. I could never remember inching towards him in the night, but every morning I'd find myself right there, curled into the curve of his body.

'Good morning, wife,' he whispered into my ear, his breath warm against the back of my neck. It was how he'd greeted me every day for the last two months, and even though we were technically edging out of the honeymoon phase, his words never failed to start my day with a smile.

Despite Nick being on call, his phone hadn't rung during the night, and I remember feeling as though the day had already begun with a small victory. He got out of bed and pulled on old joggers and a sweatshirt, pausing at the bedroom door to watch me stretch like a lazy cat in a beam of sunlight that was hitting the mattress.

'What are the chances that Mabel doesn't feel like a walk this morning?' he asked hopefully.

'Slim to none,' I replied on a laugh, loving the reluctance to leave me that was written so clearly on his face.

It was a perfectly ordinary Wednesday morning. A nothing special or remarkable middle-of-the-week day in spring. Later, I'd wonder why I'd had no presentiment that this day would be the gatepost between 'before' and 'after' and why I hadn't somehow been aware of it.

We grabbed a quick breakfast the way we always did, sitting on stools in the sunny kitchen. Cereal for me, toast for Nick, and a bowl of kibble for Mabel. Nick's thoughts were already on the busy morning of surgery ahead of him at The Willows, while mine were straying to the complicated edit I was halfway through. Deciding to go freelance had been a huge gamble, but one that happily appeared to be paying off. It allowed me to continue doing the job I loved without having to compromise on the amount of time I got to spend with Nick or my family.

We kissed goodbye in the hallway, and perhaps I held on to him for a few moments longer than normal. Maybe a feeling of unease had already filtered into the day, and I just didn't know why yet.

'I'll call you at lunchtime,' he said, pressing one last kiss on to my lips.

I nodded, unaware that I wouldn't be here to take the call.

I loaded the dishwasher and tidied the kitchen before pouring one last coffee to take with me into the lounge. There were enough spare bedrooms to have claimed one as a home office, but I'd chosen to set up my desk in this corner of the room, right beside the wall of windows where Nick had proposed. I suppose there would inevitably come a time when I'd pull out my chair and not think of the day when he'd dropped to one knee before me on this very spot, but I wasn't there yet.

I was quickly engrossed in the edit, pleased with how it was slowly shaping up. I was so lost in the author's words that when my mobile vibrated silently on the stack of papers where I'd left it, I was reluctant to tug myself out of the story.

But when the name 'Linda' lit up on my phone screen, all thoughts of the novel were swept from my mind. I snatched up the phone, my fingers clumsy as I accepted the call.

There were three erratic heartbeats before Amelia's carer spoke my name. Three beats for me to hope she was asking me where the bin bags were kept, or something equally trivial that Amelia could no longer remember.

'I don't want you to panic,' Linda began, her soft Scottish burr sounding more pronounced than usual. A small, distracted part of my mind wondered why anyone ever bothered to preface a sentence with those words. It had to be the most useless phrase in the entire English language and was the ultimate self-fulfilling prophecy. I panicked.

'What's happened?' The words felt like bullets, fired from a place of absolute fear.

The thing I liked most about Amelia's carer was her straight-talking, no-nonsense attitude. So, it was strange to hear her picking carefully through a minefield of euphemisms to answer me.

'Your sister's had a "bit of a turn".'

I was fairly confident that phrase wasn't one you'd find in

any medical dictionary. And as a former nurse, I doubted it was one Linda herself would normally use.

'What does that mean exactly, "a turn"?'

'It means I'm a wee bit concerned about her breathing.'

'Have you tried her on oxygen?'

It was an insulting question, but Linda was as good at handling panicked relatives as she was their ailing loved ones.

'Of course, and it's helped her… some. But not enough for my liking. Which is why I've called for an ambulance.'

'An ambulance?' I parroted, as though I wasn't entirely sure what one of those might be.

'Just to be on the safe side,' Linda said carefully, before totally destroying the moment of calm she'd created by adding, 'I think you should make your way straight to the hospital, Lexi.'

I'd had this conversation before – a thousand times or more. It usually ended in me jerking myself awake, bathed in a sheen of sweat and fear. But this was no dream. This was real and it didn't matter how many times I'd rehearsed my lines, I wasn't ready for this scene to play out in real life.

'Have you called my mother yet?' My thoughts were spinning like a centrifuge, and I was grateful to have managed to snatch and grab a useful one.

'Yes. I have. Luckily, Mr Tom was with her. He's called for a taxi to take them to the hospital. They'll meet you there.'

I had a hundred questions to ask but they were all silenced when I heard the sound of a distant siren trilling down the phone.

'I'm sorry, Lexi, I have to go now. The ambulance is almost here. Will you be alright? Can you make your way to the hospital?'

A sound escaped me. I'm not sure what I'd been aiming for, but it came out halfway between a sob of despair and a humourless laugh. *Of course* I was alright. It wasn't *my* heart that was failing. Mine was thumping against the walls of my chest, obscenely reminding me just how well it was able to pump the blood around my body. Unlike my poor sister's.

I have no recollection of ending our call or propelling myself from the lounge, but I must have done, for I found myself back in the bedroom, pulling on shoes and reaching for a jacket and my bag. I ran at reckless speed back down the stairs, lucky not to have slipped and ended up arriving at A & E in an ambulance alongside Amelia.

I tried reaching Nick as I hurried through the house, between letting the dog out into the garden and tipping an excessive amount of food into her bowl. She looked up at me curiously, in the way dogs do when their owners are acting weirdly out of character.

'I'm sorry. I don't know when I'll be back,' I explained, crouching down beside her. I only realised I was crying when Mabel's long pink tongue swept over my cheeks to dry my tears. I buried my face in the thick fur of her ruff and she leant her weight against me, somehow understanding how much I needed a hug right then.

Nick's phone kept going to voicemail – which was no great surprise when he was in surgery – so I dialled the main practice number and left a message with a receptionist who was so new to the job I couldn't even remember her name.

'Who shall I say called?'

'Tell him it's Lexi. Ask him to meet me at the hospital as soon as he can,' I said as I reached for my car keys and slammed the front door shut.

'Which hospital is that? Do you want me to add anything else?'

'No. He'll know where and why,' I said, my voice so unsteady it was practically tripping over itself. 'Just... just ask him to hurry,' I said, before severing the connection and throwing my car into gear.

It was the same as the first trip I'd made to the hospital, a little over fifteen months earlier. Although this time minus the transatlantic flight and the lengthy cross-country drive in a hire car. But the feelings of helplessness and terror were all horribly familiar.

I parked in the hospital multistorey, as I must surely have done a hundred times before, but even as I ran from the car towards the hospital, I knew something felt different. *This is the last time you'll do this.* The voice in my head sounded so real I could practically hear it echoing in the stairwell, ricocheting off the concrete walls. I tried to outrun the words, but they followed me down every level until I reached the ground. I forced myself to take a moment to steady my breathing before barrelling through the hospital's revolving doors.

Mum and Tom could only have beaten me there by a matter of minutes. They were still at the information desk, waiting to be told where Amelia had been taken. I fell into Mum's arms, while Tom stood by wringing his weather-beaten hands in a way I'd never seen anyone do in real life.

'Do we know how she is?' I asked Mum, somehow managing to include the woman behind the desk in the question.

'Only what Linda told me on the phone. Amelia was... *poorly*... when she got there this morning.'

Poorly. A bit of a turn. All the euphemisms were coming out today and I could blame no one for using them when the words they stood in place of were so bloody scary.

'She's been taken to Milton Ward. It's on the—'

'Seventh floor. Yes, we know,' I told the young woman behind the desk. We were probably more familiar with the geography of the hospital than she was.

Mum and I turned towards the bank of lifts, failing to notice that Tom was now lagging several steps behind us. I jabbed at the lift call button.

'Perhaps it's best if I stay down here,' Tom said, his voice gruff and hesitant and nothing like his usual brusque tone. 'You don't want the likes of me cluttering up the place. You'll want to be alone with Mimi.'

It was the first time I'd heard him use the diminutive version of Amelia's name, which only her family used. It sounded perfectly at home on his lips. Perhaps that's what brought the tears to my eyes, or it could have been the lost and terrified expression in Tom's.

'I know she'll want to see you too, Tom,' I said, reaching out and clasping one of his restless hands in my grip. 'You're family, after all.'

Tears don't come easily to men of Tom's generation, and to see the gnarly old mariner crying unashamedly in the busy hospital foyer broke the tiny pieces of my heart that weren't already quietly shattering.

I knew things were bad even before we stepped out of the lift. Dr Vaughan was walking down the corridor wearing a troubled look on his face, which only intensified when he saw us emerge from the carriage. Defeat is the one thing you never want to see on a physician who's caring for someone you love, but as much as he tried to hide it, I saw it there in Dr Vaughan's eyes as he walked towards us.

His gaze went from Mum to me, and suddenly it was really hard to swallow.

'Is she in any pain?' It was the only thing I could think to ask.

Dr Vaughan shook his head. 'No. Not now. We've given her medication and we can up the dose later when...'

He bit his lip as though the truth had slipped away from him. His use of 'when' rather than 'if' was not lost on me.

'She's in her old room,' he continued. That was all it took. Without saying a word, Mum hurried down the corridor at a speed someone half her age would have struggled to match.

'Is there *nothing* you can do?' I asked the doctor, not realising I was gripping the fabric of his sleeve until he gently pulled his arm free from my hold.

'We can keep her comfortable; we can assist her breathing; we can—'

I shook my head, cutting him off. This man *knew* me. He knew how diligently I would have read up about this moment over the last few months. I knew exactly what to expect *and* what was coming next.

'I'm so sorry, Lexi. I truly am.' I didn't need to hear the crack in his voice or see the tears in his eyes to know how true that was. He'd journeyed with us for a long time, but now after fifteen months together, our association was coming to an end.

'I have to go. I have to be with her,' I said, looking beyond him to the room my mother had just entered.

Dr Vaughan nodded and, with a look of helpless regret, stepped aside.

I would have thought we were in the wrong room had it not been for the fan of chestnut-coloured hair splayed on the pillow. Amelia's skin was chalky, but her hair was still as vibrant as the strands I'd brushed that morning in my own bedroom. Everything else about her, though, seemed paler, almost translucent, as though the mirror image I was used to seeing was slowly dissolving before my eyes.

I couldn't move. My feet felt glued to the vinyl of the hospital floor. I didn't know this colourless, fragile figure in the bed. She was a stranger, and she scared me. For a moment, all I wanted to do was run from the room. But then the stranger turned her head and when she saw who had entered the room, she shot me Amelia's smile and freed me.

Mum was already ensconced in her old position on one side of the bed, and my feet took me on the familiar route to mine on the opposite side. Amelia's cheek felt hot and dry when I bent to kiss it, and despite the nasal cannula delivering a steady supply of oxygen, her breathing sounded worryingly short.

'What day is it?' she asked.

I frowned. 'It's Wednesday.'

She nodded slowly as though she'd been expecting that answer and then shook her head in disappointment. 'It's such a boring day to go. What a typical accountant thing to do.'

'No one is going anywhere,' I disagreed hotly.

Amelia reached for me with a hand hooked up to a drip.

'Let's make a promise today that we only tell each other the truth, huh? Call it my last request.'

I was ready for lots of things, but not this gallows humour.

'I can do that,' Tom said gruffly as he took a hesitant step towards the end of Amelia's bed.

'Hello, Tom,' Amelia said, her voice hardly more than a whisper. 'I'm so glad you're here to be with Mum today.'

Tom shuffled his weight awkwardly from one foot to the other before replying, 'Actually, lass, I'm here to be with you. And you know that's the truth because no one's lying today. And I'll tell you this: for a lifelong bachelor who's never had kids, this sure feels like I'm losing a child.'

'No one is losing anyone,' I said. My voice had risen in volume and was now that of a frightened child.

Amelia turned in my direction, and there was such tenderness in her eyes when she looked at me. 'Can I have a minute alone with Lexi?' she asked, her gaze never once leaving my face.

I heard rather than saw Mum and Tom leave the room.

'You have to stop this,' Amelia insisted, her voice surprisingly strong, as though she'd been storing reserves for just this moment.

'I can't.'

She shook her head vigorously. 'You *have* to, Lexi, you just have to. Because I can't do this if I'm worrying about you too.'

'Then don't do it. Stay. Stay here with me.' The tears were flowing so quickly down my cheeks there was no point even attempting to wipe them away, but Amelia raised one hand and gave it her best shot.

'I know you, Lexi. I know you want to fix everything and

make it better. But there's no fixing this, and we've both known that for a long time now.'

'It's not fair,' I cried, sounding like the child version of me; the one who'd looked up to her older sister with unswerving love and admiration. Who still did.

'We're not promised fair, and I chose this path, remember.'

'I don't know how to be in a world that doesn't have you in it,' I said. 'I've never had it be "just me". Even before I was born, there were two of us.'

A single tear fell from Amelia's eye, making the torrent running down my own cheeks look excessive.

'It'll never be "just you",' she said, reaching for my hands and winding our fingers together so tightly it was impossible to tell which were hers and which were mine. 'As long as there's one of us, there'll always be two of us.'

Time is a cruel trickster; racing away when you want it to linger and dragging its feet when you want it to hurry. It felt like hours before Nick finally messaged to say he was on his way to the hospital.

'Is that Nick?' Mum whispered, anxious not to wake Amelia, who'd been drifting into pockets of sleep that seemed to grow increasingly longer. Each time she woke, she seemed a little less present.

I nodded and ran a shaky hand through my hair, realising how off kilter I felt without him; I needed him here with me.

It was hard not to count Amelia's breaths as she slept, especially as there were worryingly long periods when she seemed to stop taking them altogether. And yet, even though it was an effort, she doggedly refused to switch from the nasal cannula to a full face mask. 'I want to be able to talk to you and see you all properly, and I can't do that through a fucking mask.' She'd paused then and turned to Mum, waiting to see if she was going to pick up on the blasphemy. 'Going to let that one go, eh?' she asked.

'Fuck, yes,' Mum replied. I hadn't thought anything could possibly make us laugh on that day, but we did then.

We took it in turns to go on coffee runs, and when I got to my feet for the next cafeteria trip, Amelia's hand reached out to grab my wrist.

'I want...' She paused to trap the next breath before it escaped from her. 'I want you to do something for me.'

I ran my fingers gently down her cheek. 'Anything,' I said.

'Get me out of here. Take me home. I don't want to be here... at the end.'

The room echoed with dissenting comments.

'I don't think you can do that,' from Tom's corner.

'That won't be allowed, darling,' was Mum's response.

I ignored them, looking deep into my sister's eyes, and felt the longing in them as though it was my own.

'Okay. Leave it to me,' I said.

I met the resistance I knew I would. What I was asking to do was apparently 'unreasonable', 'foolish', and possibly even 'dangerous'. I stood firm under the steely gaze of a senior charge nurse who I'd never met before.

'It's my sister's wish to go home and I'm going to take her there. I'm not asking you to approve or condone her decision,

I just need you to sort out whatever discharge paperwork she has to sign to make it happen.'

'This is highly unorthodox and irregular,' the woman standing before me said. 'I shall have to get Dr Vaughan to come down and discuss this with you.'

'By all means, call him, but there really is nothing to discuss. I'm taking Amelia home.'

I saw the charge nurse draw breath to begin a new onslaught of objections but then her eyes flickered, and the words stilled in her throat. Warm fingers wound through mine.

'Whatever you can do to help my wife honour her sister's wishes would be really appreciated,' Nick said with quiet authority.

I didn't get emotional, not even when I saw the woman reluctantly back down in the face of the *don't-make-this-any-harder-than-it-already-is* look in Nick's eyes. It had been a long time since I'd thought of him as a superhero, but I did in that moment as the nurse reached for the phone to summon Dr Vaughan. The consultant joined us less than ten minutes later.

Nick didn't once let go of my hand, but he was silent in his support, never speaking for me. Even so, I felt his strength as though it was surging through both of us. It made my voice as steady as my resolve.

'You do realise she'll be discharging herself AMA – against medical advice?' Dr Vaughan questioned. 'I wouldn't be doing my job correctly if I didn't advise you against this course of action.' It sounded like he was reciting lines from a script. He was required to say those words, but I could tell his heart wasn't in them.

'I understand,' I said solemnly.

'I'll expedite the paperwork,' Dr Vaughan said, before breaking all sorts of protocols by stepping forward and laying a gentle hand on my shoulder.

'Take our girl wherever she wants to go.'

We left the hospital in two cars. There had been more pairs of hands than we needed to help transfer Amelia from the hospital wheelchair into the back seat of Nick's car. Quite a few members of staff from the ward had accompanied us down to the foyer to wave goodbye to the woman who'd once been called their miracle patient.

Mum drove my car back to the cottage, freeing me to travel with Nick and Amelia. Five minutes into the journey, it became clear that Mum and Tom were going to get there long before we did. Nick – who was never reckless behind the wheel – was driving as though transporting nitroglycerin. At our current speed, we'd be lucky to get back before dusk fell.

'We're under a bit of a time crunch here, Nick,' Amelia said, her voice breathless but amused. 'There's a good chance I could die of old age before we ever reach the cottage.'

I saw Nick's bittersweet smile in the rear-view mirror and the look he shot me in its glass. My arm was looped around Amelia's shoulders, and I drew her a little closer against me. *This* was how I wanted to remember her, finding something funny in even the worst of days.

I watched her during the drive as her eyes darted left and right, taking in everything that flashed past the car windows. I thought I knew why. She was storing everything: the bleak, the boring and the mundane, logging it all because she knew she was seeing them for the last time.

426

We're not meant to know when the sand is running out of the hourglass, but Amelia did. She had for a long time now. The thought jarred something within me, and I spoke without thinking, not giving myself a chance to change my mind.

'I have something important to tell you, Mimi.'

Amelia tore her eyes away from the shops, buildings and passing scenery.

I took a deep breath. 'The results of my genetic test came back earlier than we were expecting.' I felt her stiffen in my arms and forced a smile on to my face. 'It's good news, honey. I don't have it. I haven't inherited the faulty gene.'

Her eyes went to mine, presumably searching them for a lie, but she didn't find one there. Her face, as pale as a ghost's, broke into an enormous smile. People talk about 'feeling relief' as though it's simply an emotion, but I could feel it in the most physical and literal sense as her body relaxed against me.

'Thank God,' she breathed. 'Although I knew it already, I really did. I'm so happy for both of you,' she added, including Nick in her words.

My eyes went to his in the rear-view mirror. 'It really is wonderful news,' he said with sincerity.

As predicted, Mum and Tom got to the cottage first. By the time Nick scooped Amelia into his arms and carried her inside, Mum had already set up a makeshift bed on the couch beside the window, where Amelia could look out at the beach beyond.

My steps faltered for a moment as I watched my husband carry my sister over the threshold. I suddenly remembered

Amelia telling me how Sam had carried her through that same doorway after their wedding. Did that faulty memory still linger somewhere in the dusty corners of Amelia's mind?

The journey back from the hospital had exhausted her and while Mum fussed around, adjusting pillows and cocooning Amelia in blankets, I slipped from the room, murmuring something about making tea. I was staring at the kettle, watching it boil, when Nick's reflection appeared beside mine in the shiny aluminium. I wasn't surprised.

'You lied to her,' he said.

'I did. And I'm not sorry. I know we promised only to speak the truth today, but I don't regret breaking my word.'

I turned away from our blurred images to face him, needing to see if he was disappointed in me for lying. We both knew my results weren't going to be back for at least another week.

It felt like a very big moment in my sister's small kitchen and the relief I knew when he slowly smiled and opened his arms to me made my knees suddenly unsteady. The water boiled and then cooled, and still Nick held me against him.

'I'm glad you did it,' he whispered softly into my hair. 'It was what she needed to hear.'

Amelia drifted through the next few hours. Sometimes awake and alert enough to join in our conversations, at other times lying back with closed eyes and a small peaceful smile on her lips.

'Keep talking,' she said softly when Mum tried to hush us with a concerned whisper, worried we were disturbing her. 'I like hearing you all speak.'

We talked of the past, of Christmases and holidays we remembered, and of dogs we had loved and lost over the years.

'Maybe they'll all be there waiting for me,' Amelia said with a wistful sigh. 'It would be lovely to see them again.'

I nodded fiercely and – not for the first time – had to bite down hard on my lip to stop it from trembling. By the end of today it would probably be in shreds, but I was determined to stay strong for her.

The sun was beginning its slow descent towards the horizon, filling the lounge with its last burst of warmth, when Amelia's eyes flew open. There was an urgency in them that hadn't been there before.

'I want to go outside, on to the beach.'

I glanced through the window. 'I'm sure we could set up a chair for you on the sand—' I began, before her flailing hand silenced me.

'No. Not here. I want to go to the place where they found me that night.'

Every pair of eyes in the room telegraphed the same worried expression.

'I don't think that's such a good idea, sweetheart,' Mum said.

'I *need* to go there,' Amelia insisted. Her eyes went to mine and the distress in them felt like a laser slicing into me. 'Please, Lexi.'

I nodded, not bothering to check with anyone else.

'I'll get the car,' Nick said.

'I've some folding chairs I can throw in the back,' Tom said, following Nick from the room.

I knew Mum was torn, but even she could see how

important this was to Amelia. 'You'll need to wrap up warm,' she said, all the fight knocked out of her.

Amelia took her hand, saying with a wheezy laugh, 'Wouldn't want to catch a cold, would I?'

While Mum raced around, filling Thermos flasks and hunting down even more blankets, Amelia leant on my arm to sit up.

'She's going to bundle me up like an Egyptian mummy,' she said, slipping her hand into mine. It was cold. Almost icy. I knew what that meant.

'You'll need gloves.'

'And a hat,' Amelia added. 'In fact, there's one in my room that I bought ages ago and never found the courage to wear.'

I followed her instructions and found the hat where she'd said I would. I carried the canary-yellow felt beret with its enormous fluffy pompom down the stairs, unable to hide my amusement as I passed it to my usually conservatively dressed sister. She took it with a smile and placed it on her head. I adjusted it, setting it at a rakish angle.

'How do I look?' she asked, her hand going to the out-of-character headwear.

'Jaunty,' I declared.

She gave a small satisfied nod. 'Exactly the look I was hoping for.'

We piled into Nick's Range Rover and drove down the sandy lane towards our destination. For a group who had talked continually for the last few hours, we were all strangely silent. With a small thump of the tyres, Nick swung the car off the lane and on to the sand.

'I'll go as far as I can, but I don't want to get us stuck on the mudflats.'

Mum was staring determinedly out of the window and I only knew she was crying by the trembling of her shoulders. I went to reach for her hand, but Amelia beat me to it.

'Everything's going to be okay, Mum, it really is,' she reassured her.

Something strange had happened to my sister on the journey to the spot where she'd been found. Yes, she was growing weaker, noticeably so, but there was a new strength and an expression of calm on her face that hadn't been there before.

Nick drew the car to a stop with a regretful shake of his head. 'This is as far as I dare go.' I'd already felt the damp sand hungrily sucking on our tyres and trusted his knowledge of the local beaches.

Tom and Nick set up the motley collection of folding chairs, then we all stood back as Nick carried Amelia from the car and set her down in the sturdiest of them.

Mum took the seat to Amelia's right and I the one to her left. By unspoken agreement, we seemed to know that the time for talking had passed. The gulls swooped low overhead and their cries sounded mournful, as if they knew why we were there and were sorry.

Nick took up a position behind my chair with his hand resting lightly on my shoulder, a silent confirmation of his support.

'Do you think we should go back?' Mum asked after less than ten minutes. Her face was a mask of panic and despair.

Amelia shook her head.

'Why don't you and I go and stretch our legs for a minute?'

Tom suggested, holding out a wrinkled hand to Mum. I shot him a grateful look, glad he understood that she needed a few moments to pull herself together. I watched them walk slowly towards the water's edge, Mum's head resting on the old fisherman's shoulder. They paused and he pulled her into his arms and even from this distance I could tell they were both crying.

'Do you want to hear something strange?' Amelia asked, her voice now a painful-sounding rasp. 'I don't think I was ever meant to leave this beach. I don't think those doctors were meant to bring me back that night.'

'Don't say that,' I cried.

'I think it upset the way things were meant to play out. And that's why I came back so... *confused*.'

I said nothing, knowing her 'confusion' had been a symptom of the FAD, but perhaps Amelia had forgotten she had that. If so, I was glad. Not every memory deserves to be retained; sometimes it's better to set the bad ones free.

'But if my heart hadn't stopped for so long, then I don't think I'd have "seen" the future for you and Nick when they brought me back. And bringing the two of you together will always be the best thing I've ever done.'

My eyes travelled down the beach towards the spot near the water's edge where I'd first seen Nick. I didn't need to look up to know he was doing the same thing. If Amelia needed to believe she'd somehow 'foreseen' our future, I wasn't going to dispute it. Not today.

'I'm glad I got to see everything come true, although I'm sorry I'm going to miss the rest of it. I'd have loved to have met my nieces.'

I flashed Nick a worried glance. Was she growing delirious? He gave a small helpless shrug.

'Do you think I'll get to see Dad?' Her thoughts were becoming untethered, jumping from one topic to another.

'I hope so,' I said, leaning across to kiss her cheek gently. 'Be sure to say hi from me.'

She nodded slowly, as though taking down a message she might easily forget.

'I'm getting really tired now, Lexi. It's so hard to keep holding on.'

Something inside me felt like it was tearing, ripping the connection between us apart.

'It's okay to let go now, Mimi, if you want to. Don't worry about Mum, I'll make sure she's okay. You can trust me.'

'I always have,' she said on a sigh that seemed to go on and on. Her gaze went to Mum and Tom, who were still some distance away.

'Can you get my mum, Nick?' she asked, her voice starting to tremble.

A feeling of terror swept through me. This couldn't be it. It couldn't. Out of the millions of conversations we'd had, I wasn't ready for this to be our last.

Mum and I remained beside Amelia as her breathing grew shallower and shallower. And then she gasped, as though breaking through from an unfathomable depth of water.

'Sam!' she cried, her voice full of panic. 'Sam, where are you?'

Mum moaned softly in distress as Amelia's eyes flew open; they were glazed.

'Where have you gone, Sam? I can't see you.'

I felt the touch of Nick's hand on my shoulder and looked up into his eyes. There was a question in them, and I answered it with a small nod.

He stepped out from behind my chair. 'I'm here, Mimi. I'm right here.'

Amelia sighed and switched her unfocused gaze to his face. I slipped out of my chair to let him take my place beside her.

'Is it really you?' she whispered, bringing her trembling fingers to his cheek.

'It is.' His voice was gentle.

Very slowly, Amelia smiled. 'I've been waiting for you for so long.'

'I know. I'm sorry I wasn't here sooner, but I'm here now,' Nick said. 'I won't leave you again.'

My heart felt like it was breaking with the pain of loving and losing, but there was also a feeling of something being put to rights, of the world settling back on to its axis.

The wind whistled a mournful tune across the sand, and beneath the cries of the swooping gulls I watched as my sister took her last breath with a peaceful smile on her lips and Sam's hand in hers.

EPILOGUE

LATER

It happened for the first time at the dry cleaner's. I'd just dropped off a couple of Nick's shirts and was already planning the next stop on my round of errands.

'Can I take a telephone contact number?' asked the young girl behind the counter.

I was looking through the shop window, wondering if the uniformed figure walking slowly down the street was a traffic warden.

I was distracted.

'Phone number?' the assistant prompted.

I spun around, with an apology. 'Sorry. It's 079— No, its 0971— no, that's not right. It's 0779...' My voice trailed away, and I frowned in confusion.

'Don't worry,' the girl assured me with a carefree laugh. 'No one can ever remember their mobile number. Most customers need to get their phones out.'

It was an obvious prompt telling me what I was meant to do next, but I made no move to extract my phone from my bag.

'But I *know* my number. I give it out all the time.'

There wasn't much the girl could say to that, and I could tell she was anxious to move on to serve the customers waiting in line behind me.

Embarrassed and flustered, I retrieved the phone from my bag and read the number off the screen. I'd like to say it sounded instantly familiar. But it didn't.

Several weeks passed before it happened again. Just long enough for me to convince myself the incident in the dry cleaner's had been a random one-off occurrence.

Mornings in our house were always chaotic. They were filled with *Don't forget your...* and *Have you got your homework...* comments from me, and the usual dramatic teenage sighs and eye-rolling in reply.

They forgot things. They lost things and I found them. That's how it worked. But not that morning.

'You're both going to be late,' I warned, as one child snatched up a slice of toast from the table. The other was still upstairs. I picked up the car keys and then stopped and looked around the kitchen.

'Have you seen my phone, Cassie?'

My fifteen-year-old rapidly swallowed her mouthful of toast before grinning cheekily. 'You know, if you put your things away, you wouldn't forever be losing them.'

At any other time it would have been funny to hear my own words being quoted back to me, but not today.

'Seriously, Cassie, have you seen it?'

Perhaps she heard something in my voice, for she began a half-hearted search, moving a couple of items on the table, none of which were big enough to conceal my phone.

'I'll ring it for you,' she said, reaching into her school bag for her own mobile.

A thundering stampede of feet shook the staircase as Jessica, our younger daughter, hurtled into the kitchen the same way she moved everywhere, at speed.

'What's up? Why isn't everyone in the car already?'

'Mum's lost her phone.'

'It's not lost... it's just... misplaced,' I said, wondering why this all felt horribly familiar.

The three of us looked expectantly around the kitchen as we waited for the call to connect. When it did, the ring tone sounded oddly muffled and tinny. I followed the sound to the far side of the kitchen. Behind me, both girls were already giggling as they realised where the sound was coming from. Like a magician performing a big reveal, I pulled open the bread bin. Inside it was a sliced loaf of wholegrain, a packet of crumpets, and my mobile phone.

'Why exactly did you put it in there?' Jessica asked.

I shook my head. 'I didn't. I mean, I don't remember doing it. I've no idea how it got there.'

'Well, it's a great hiding place, Mum,' my younger daughter teased, dancing across the kitchen to give me a quick squeeze. 'And not weird. Not weird at all.'

I smiled weakly but couldn't shake the feeling of unease that had crept over me.

'We're going to be late,' Cassie predicted, pushing her sister towards the back door. She moved to follow her and then stopped and looked back at me over her shoulder. I was still standing by the worktop with my phone in my hand.

'You probably dropped it in there by mistake when you were making our lunches,' she suggested.

'Yes, that's probably it,' I said. I didn't sound convinced. It was a logical suggestion that anyone would agree with. Anyone, that is, who couldn't remember finding a missing mobile phone at the back of a freezer ten years earlier.

I didn't mention either incident to Nick. I swept them aside, as though by ignoring them I could somehow diminish their significance. But that wasn't the end of it.

I never did get the results of the genetic test for FAD. That's not strictly true: I *did* get them; I just chose never to open them. They came through a week after Amelia's funeral, and I wasn't in the right frame of mind to deal with them then. Instead, I arranged to collect the results in a sealed envelope.

'I *will* open it,' I told Nick, wondering if he was disappointed by my decision.

'It's up to you,' he said. 'It's always been up to you.'

'I think I wanted to know more for *Amelia's* sake than mine. It was always more important to her than it was to me.' Even then I was beginning to question again whether anyone should know what the future had in store for them.

'Just remember, we're here for you if or when you decide you're ready to open it,' the doctor told me when I collected the envelope.

But I never did. Ten years passed and although there were moments when I thought about retrieving the envelope from where I'd stored it, the closest I ever got to breaking the seal was when, two years after our wedding, Nick and I decided we wanted children.

We had two clear options: PGT, which would involve intensive IVF assistance, or adoption. Both choices were part of my family history, but it was my dad's adoption story that swayed me in the end. I'd never known that he'd spent his entire life feeling that being abandoned and unwanted was something to be ashamed of, and I was desperate to set right that wrong.

Cassie and Jessica were matched with us when they were seven and five years old. On the night they first came home, Nick and I stood at their bedroom door watching as the two young sisters slept. We'd pushed their beds close together and they'd fallen asleep holding hands, which had brought back memories of Amelia and me. It also reminded me of something I thought I'd long since forgotten.

'That last day on the beach with Amelia, do you remember what she said to us?' I whispered to Nick in the shadows of our hallway. 'She said she'd have loved to have met her nieces.'

It was too dark to see the scepticism in Nick's eyes, but I was pretty sure it was there. I knew he'd be unable or unwilling to believe that Amelia had predicted we'd one day become parents to two little girls.

'She made a lucky guess, that's all,' he said.

I smiled secretly in the darkness. Just because you love someone, it doesn't mean you always have to agree with them.

The girls no longer shared a room, and after saying goodnight to Cassie I paused for a long moment at Jessica's bedside. The memory of what had happened that afternoon was still horribly fresh in my mind.

'I really am sorry about today,' I said.

Jessica looked up from whatever video she was watching on her mobile.

'It's no biggie, Mum. You don't have to keep apologising.'

I leant down and pushed back a few strands of strawberry-blonde hair that had fallen into her eyes. She was letting me off the hook far more readily than I was prepared to.

'Well, I still feel bad about what happened.'

'Bad enough to buy me a new phone?' she asked hopefully.

I smiled. 'No. But nice try, sweetheart.'

It was late when Nick's car finally pulled into the driveway. I hadn't realised how dark the room had grown while I sat beside the fireplace with the old, unopened envelope in my hands.

Nick looked tired but jubilant as he bent to kiss me. 'One healthy foal, safely delivered,' he said, dropping on to the chair on the other side of the hearth.

Even in the dim light, my smile must have looked a little strained.

'Is everything alright?' he asked, his eyes narrowing in concern.

'I did something bad today.'

'Did it involve a credit card?' he teased, but then he saw the expression on my face and his whole demeanour changed. 'What happened?'

'I forgot to pick up Jessica from ballet.'

I could practically see the relief flow through him.

'Is that all? I thought you'd killed someone.' He was smiling, and I really wished I could join him, but I couldn't.

'Tell me what happened,' Nick urged.

Out loud, it didn't sound so terrible. I'd forgotten today was Jessica's ballet class. Forty-five minutes after I should have collected her, I received an anxious telephone call from her tutor.

'I *forgot*. I wasn't just late, Nick, I forgot. I pick her up from that class every single week. How on earth did I forget?'

'It's not like she was left standing on a street corner somewhere,' Nick said reasonably. 'She wasn't in any danger.'

'But I *forgot*.' I was like a broken record, unable to get past that vital groove.

'These things happen,' Nick said.

'They do. And they've been happening to me more and more recently. Which is the reason why...' My voice trailed off and my eyes dropped to the envelope on the chair beside me.

Nick's gaze followed mine and I knew he recognised the white oblong from the way he swallowed, hard.

'What else has happened?' he asked.

There was a catharsis in finally admitting to the string of incidents that had led me to pluck the envelope from its box at the top of the wardrobe that night. Nick listened carefully while I spoke, never once interrupting. When I finished, he leant back in his chair.

'None of this sounds like anything to panic about. It was just a couple of absent-minded moments when you were probably distracted or busy. I'm going to discount misplacing your car in the multistorey at the mall, because *everyone* does that.'

'It took me *half an hour* to find it,' I murmured, worried

that he wasn't taking this seriously enough. 'What if this is how it all starts?'

'Honestly, Lexi, nothing you've said sets off alarm bells.' He crossed the room and took my hands, pulling me out of the chair and into a hug. 'You've been so busy recently: with your job, running around after the girls and keeping an eye on your mum and Tom. You juggle a thousand balls and spin hundreds of plates, it's no wonder the odd one slips through your fingers. And it doesn't help that you've got a husband who clearly isn't pulling his weight.'

I shook my head. 'I won't hear a word said against him.'

Nick smiled. 'You can't do it all. No one expects you to be Wonder Woman.'

I reached up and gently touched his face. 'Actually, when you're married to Superman, they kind of do.' My fingers grazed along his cheekbone before dipping into the thick black hair at his temple, where a few silvery strands had started to appear.

'If you decide you want to open that envelope tonight, then I'm behind you, one hundred per cent. You know that.'

I looked down at the envelope that held the answers to questions I still wasn't sure anyone should ever ask or have answered. Amelia was always convinced if she had FAD, then it would have passed me by. But even she had wanted proof.

'People always say your future is written in the stars,' I said, my voice low and not quite steady, 'but mine's written on a sheet of paper inside that envelope.'

Nick brought up his hands to cup my face gently. 'That's not your future in there. That's just a set of blood test results that we'll deal with, whatever they reveal. We're stronger than whatever that piece of paper tells us. Nothing inside that envelope could ever come close to rocking us.' He held me close while our eyes conducted a wordless conversation. A conversation that slowly began to unravel the knots of panic I'd tangled myself up in.

Nick was right. My future *wasn't* in that envelope. It was standing right there in front of me; it was fast asleep in two pink-painted bedrooms upstairs; and it was in an old weather-worn fisherman's cottage on the edge of a beach. The people I loved – and those I'd lost – *they* were my story: they were my past and my present and they were the only future that I wanted or needed to know.

I felt strong as I stepped out of Nick's hold and picked up the envelope. Amelia had claimed she already knew what my results would be. Perhaps she did, but that didn't mean I needed to.

For all his reassurances, I could tell Nick was anxious as I turned the envelope over in my hands. He drew in a long breath and then held it as I walked to the fireplace.

'Are you sure about this, Lexi?'

Five minutes ago, I wouldn't have been able to answer that question. But I could now.

'Absolutely positive.' I smiled. 'We've got this.'

Then, with no regrets, I threw the envelope and its secrets into the flames.

Acknowledgements

Writing acknowledgements is always a little bittersweet, for it signals it's time to say goodbye to the book you've lived with for so long and move on to the next. But before I do, there are people I'd like to thank who have helped me reach this milestone moment once again.

The Memory of Us has been one of my favourite books to write, and I know in part that is due to the support and enthusiasm of the publishing team at Head of Zeus and Aria. Spearheading the team is the incredible Laura Palmer who has been my editor for each of my Head of Zeus books since Fractured. This time we worked in collaboration with the amazing Lucy Ridout, who somehow managed to make even a structural edit feel like a joy. And there's a sentence I never thought I'd write.

Huge thanks as always to my editor Kate Burke at Blake Friedmann, without whom I would still be writing books and sticking them away on memory sticks in a desk drawer – and be forever lost on my way to meetings. Thank you, Kate, for everything you do, and thanks too to everyone in the BF family.

This book is about sisters, and although I don't have one myself, I'm lucky to have an incredible sisterhood of friends who I've known for a very long time. I'm so grateful to Hazel and Debbie (who read the books when they're still 'raw') and to Sheila, Kim, Christine, Annette, Barb and Heidi, for all the years of friendship. Thank you for continuing to find space for me on your bookshelves.

I've made so many wonderful friends in the world of publishing, and their support means more than I can put into words – a dreadful admission for an author. Special thanks to Fiona Ford, Sasha Wagstaff, Faye Bleasdale, Paige Toon, Tamsyn Murray and Gill Paul for all the fun we've had so far and for what's still to come.

And a very special thank you to my author BFF, Kate Thompson. If I'd never written a book, we'd never have met, and for that reason alone I'm truly glad I never gave up on this dream.

To the readers, reviewers, and bloggers, thank you seems inadequate. Writing can be a lonely business; you are very much a one-man band. But having the opportunity to share the stories with you and hear how much you've enjoyed them, makes all the difference in the world. You are the ones who make all of this possible, and that is something none of us take for granted. Thank you from the bottom of my heart.

And now for the personal stuff. Thanks to my wonderful family. To my daughter Kimberley who helps me in a thousand different ways and who obligingly never complains when I send her emails that begin "Can you just read this..." Thanks to my son Luke, who reads nothing at all that I've written, but is quietly proud of every book. And to my husband Ralph, who listens to the books in daily instalments, tiptoes into the office with endless cups of tea, and makes us dinner every night. I truly couldn't do any of this without him.

Unusually I would like to end this by also thanking my twelve-year-old border collie, Dusty. He has been my constant writing companion for the last decade. He has heard the plot of every book and endured numerous trial dialogues on our morning walks. He's by my feet as I write this. Dusty feels more connected to *The Memory of Us* than any of my other books as sadly this will be the last book he will see. Diagnosed with a terminal illness, Dusty will not be with us for much longer. This book is dedicated to him. Thank you, my friend.

About the Author

DANI ATKINS is an award-winning novelist. Her 2013 debut *Fractured* (published as *Then and Always* in North America) has been translated into sixteen languages and has sold more than half a million copies since first publication in the UK. Dani is the author of several other bestselling novels, three of which, *This Love*, *A Sky Full of Stars* and *Six Days*, won the Romantic Novel of the Year Award in 2018, 2022 and 2023 respectively. Dani lives in a small village in Hertfordshire with her husband, one Siamese cat and a very lively puppy.